I0745856

By Len Ferraguzzi

*Valiant The Few*

*Eyes of Glass*

# EYES OF GLASS

Len Ferraguzzi

First Edition: December 2017

Printed in the United States of America

ISBN: 978-1-939237-56-9

Published by Suncoast Digital Press, Inc.
Sarasota, Florida, USA

# Dedication


to

OLGA, SUE, LEE

&

THE GRAND SLAM

# Acknowledgments

I am most grateful for the exceptional attention to detail and guidance from my editor and publishing partner Barbara Dee of Suncoast Digital Press. Her availability to my persistent queries has been terrific.

Additionally, a special salute to the very talented Allison Daigle for designing and creating the outstanding front cover and maps for Eyes Of Glass.

*...the womb of time favors Marz Kavoyy.*

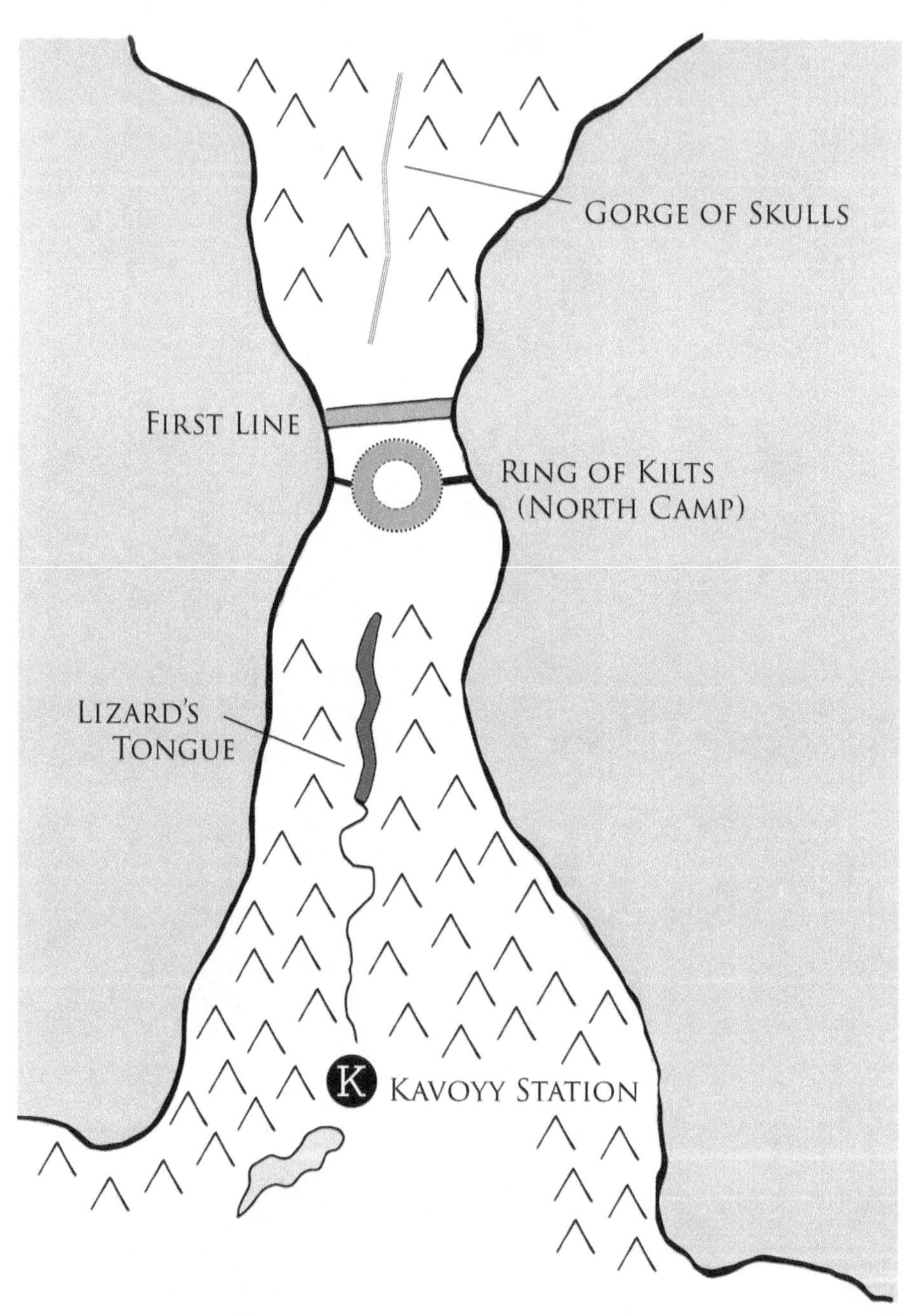


# THE ISTHMUS OF THE VAG

Isthmus
K
Ax
J
M
Capital
River Metarz (Big Lazy)
B
Orri Peninsula
Bread Basket
Wild Country
Ar
S
Gugububu Desert
Key
Ar  Arabella
Ax  Mount Aryxx
B  Barrier Camp
J  Jarra
K  Kavoyy Station
M  Muraverdus & Central Camp
S  South Camp
The Ring of Kilts & First Line/ The Chokepoint
Capital

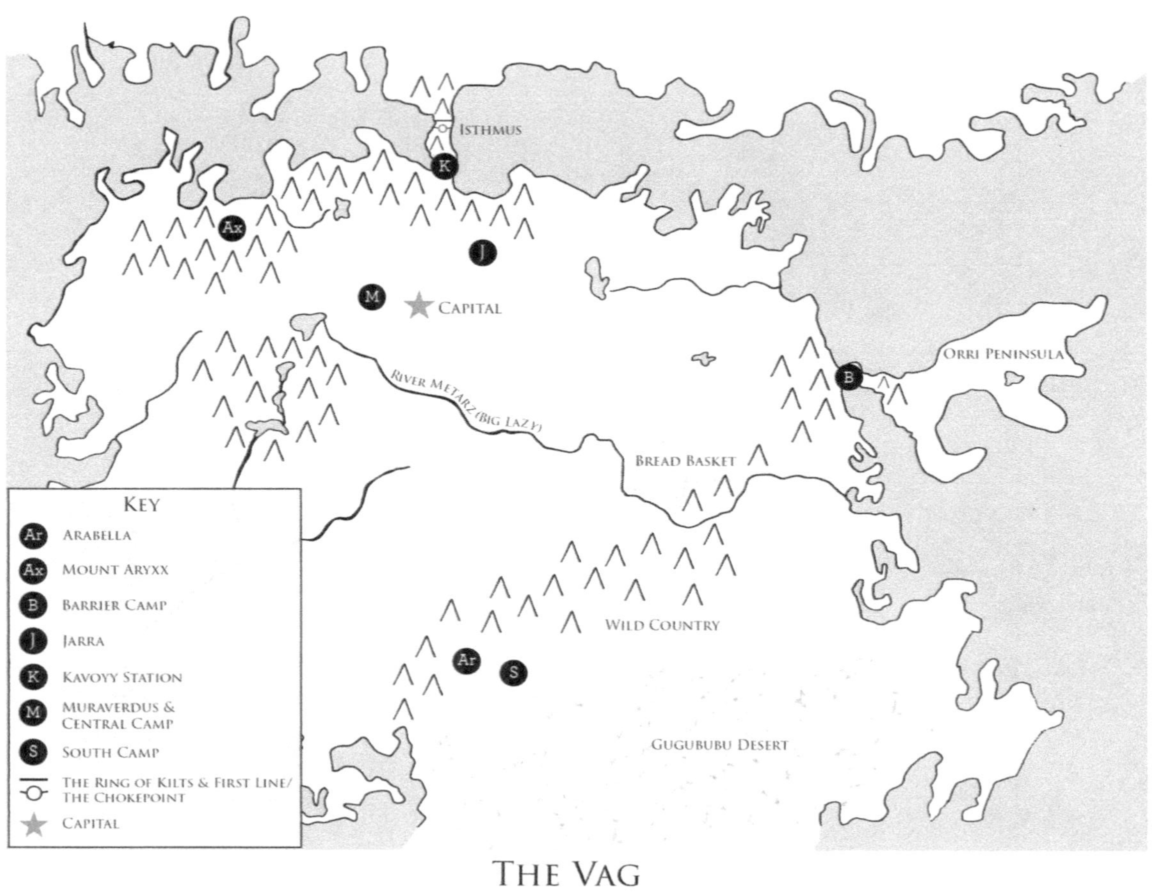

# THE VAG

# PROLOGUE I

Death came to me in a quiet way, painless and swift. Spirit separated mortal shell as the last pulse quieted, the final breath softly hissing through sleeping nostrils. Earth rapidly disappeared in a dizzy fade, like an untethered balloon caught in a draft eddy, lazily swirling to a distant pinpoint. I drifted seemingly aimless, floating along the periphery of fifty billion unchristened galaxies. Soul travelers such as I must have soared this celestial track, or one like it, from the first stirrings of soul-bearing life. If I had done it before I cannot say, for there is no recollection. And so I sailed, a buoyant ghost without propulsion yet possessing motion; lacking true sight but visually aware; void of temperature while sensing a cocoon-like warmth. No noise existed other than the nebulous sound of stillness.

Astro-physicists theorize that there is no time in deep space, that it stands in frozen suspension like a seized engine. There it awaits the lubricant of discovery. For someone must uncover the regularity of planetary orbit and axis rotation with their gift of seasonal change; of lunar revolution and it's precision of day and night and tidal flow. Once unlocked, time ticks for as long as civilization requires. My own experience, if you could call it that, will shed no light on the answer. Because for me my weightless drift was numb and uncertain, elapsing a timeless period. It could have taken micro-seconds or eons in duration. No clock accompanied the ride. However, regardless of tenure during that brief interlude in the grand cosmos, I felt all knowledge was mine had I wished revelation.

It had never occurred to me that my spirit would transmigrate to somewhere other than my native planet. That is to say, I assumed that if l were to be reborn, it would happen among those earthly continents familiar to me, amid species of which I had learning. Yet my spirit tumbled free of resistance on destiny's chosen path, swimming towards an orb three times the dimension of earth....on I spun to the great blue water planet Gala Rotaria. With its single land mass of countless peninsulas covering only about six percent of its vast expanse, Gala Rotaria welcomed me with a shimmering wink as if to call out, "Here traveler, here pilgrim of the universe is your new home!" Suddenly I was enveloped in a cozy darkness recognized from my past being. The miracle of rebirth commences with the spark of soul. And here was I secure in the womb of my mother, lolling in wet comfort, surrounded by my brood siblings. Indeed, now the clock truly ticks. The cycle of life moves forward.

As my new shell entered the corridor of living, tiny lungs breathed the first delicious measures of sweet, fresh air. I am born. I am born, again!

# PROLOGUE II

Nunale? I am born a nunale? Not female, not male, but nunale! Weak and sexless, neutered by genetic mystery, I am born of the gender nunale. In a universe where humanoids are identified by what lives between their thighs, I have been given a clefted button of a mushroom with no pro-creative or recreational function. It is solely a tool of urination that I have been permitted. Also be aware that we nunales are short of physique, our rotund bodies devoid of hair though a patch decorates the head. And our chests are absent of nipples. For the life of me I can't understand why the male gender has them in the first place. Most impractical.

In the land of The Vag, where dwell a fair-minded people known as the Vaghi, the families into which nunales are born are considered very lucky. We are children loved and nurtured as much as our sisters and brothers, and highly capable of returning affection I might add. Although without those hormonal juices which drive men and women to desire and passion, we have been counter blessed with brilliant minds enabling our kind to excel at mathematics, science, commerce, music and priestly pursuits. Perhaps as we nunales evolved over time, those organs and energies which could have been sexual were channeled into calculative brain power. Therefore, one could make the rational argument that to be a nunale is to be the preferred sex, or non-sex, because orgasmic ecstasy is enjoyed but for a few moments while superior intellect lasts a lifetime.

Among the Vaghi a brother/sister pair is always born together. Though twins they are referred to as brood brother and brood sister. Once in about every ninety pregnancies a third child is born, always a nunale. Though technically a triplet I suppose, the nunale is identified as a brood genther relative to the brood brother and brood sister. Children of the same brood enjoy a sibling bond unlike any other. My family is called Kavoyy, my given name Zoog. So I am the nunale Zoog Kavoyy brood genther to my brood sister Tyrra Kavoyy and to Marz, my brood brother. Yes, Marz Kavoyy is my brood brother. Possibly you've already heard of him. He is destined for greatness. My nunale instinct tells me so. I predict this not out of brood bias but from an innate, prophetic gift possessed by few Vaghi even among the nunales. You see, I too am special.

Before continuing, perhaps I should mention a few facts of Vag life and environment. All births occur during the Month of Mothers, the eighth and warmest month of the calendar year. It stands to reason then that all pregnancies are conceived nine months earlier during Olz, the eleventh month of the previous year. The month following the Month of Mothers is called the Month of the Yellow Sky due to an annual meteorological phenomenon. It is during the latter's final week that the newborn are taken high in the hills to the Ring of Muraverdus where the priests confirm each infant's identity as legitimate denizen of The Vag. Soil, grass and spring water are ritually rubbed on tender foot-soles accompanied by holy incantations passed down from millennia long past. Indeed the lyrics are almost cryptic for the language has long since graduated to its current, modern level. When chanted, the Vag speech imparts a heavenly aura to the ceremony, wailing babes notwithstanding. Tyrra, Marz and I were carried to the great slab altar by Gurz and Shaara, parents to our brood. Held aloft we were presented to the officiating priest, a middle-aged nunale called Daag Goraxx. As I was told later in life by mother Shaara, the priest was especially pleased when gee spied my naked truth. Daag Goraxx spent more time than is accustomed peering deeply into my yellow-brown eyes, searching for a glimmer of future worth or, perhaps, a past distinction. "The Kavoyy are blessed among others," gee smiled. "Your nuun will provide you with much joy and pride." And placing my unclothed bottom on the huge turquoise stone, saddled and worn smooth over the ages by innumerable confirmations, marriages and other sacred affairs, the plump priest raised a ladle of polished briar root and dipped it into an antique basin fed to the overflow by a streamlet of spring water. Gee trickled its clear fluid over my toes, allowing the coolness to spill down my little feet to the base of the heal and tendon. All this time gee chanted the prayers of passage harmoniously joined by three novitiate priests in rich baritone and bass voices. From a dull, red ceramic urn embossed with the black V and two headed wolf, ancient symbols of the Vag nation, the holy nunale removed a handful of smoky gray soil, the consistency of powdery talcum, intermingled with fine clippings of tuma grass. Both soil and grass had been retrieved earlier during the Month of Eyes from the part of Mount Aryx where the last signs of vegetation meet the freeze line. Anointing my feet with the mixture, the nunale priest announced to all that Zoog Kavoyy had been born a Vag, must live the true life of a responsible Vag, and die a Vag, ultimately to return to the ground represented by the caked paste drying about my feet. Mother was later to inform me that I never cried once, which was not the case for my two siblings. In good jest,

I sometimes remind them of their whining protestations whenever I feel a touch of pomposity overtaking their egos.

Like most who have the capacity for deep thinking, my brain often wrestles with thoughts of genesis, not for my personal beginning but for my kind. Who made the Vaghi? There had to have been a point in our pre-history when a primitive mind identified itself as 'me Vag' or 'we are the Vaghi.' Perhaps another group of people, like our neighbors the Orri, first called us such and we adopted the appellation for our own. Many seem to feel that several wandering tribes coalesced into a single people. Indeed our verb "to wander" is "avagar" and some scholars believe Vag is simply an abbreviated corruption of the verb. Or it has been suggested that possibly the land was first titled and our people took their name from it. If so, then why did they call it The Vag? The explanation awaits discovery. Confidence inspires this inquisitive nunale to unlock the puzzle, that it is mine to solve. But it will require a labor of investigation.

Of course there is yet the more profound question. From where came everything and anything? Even if there was nothing, from where came nothingness? This answer I leave for others to ponder and debate for I believe there will never by any real solution, only speculative theory. And if the force that is the great Creator chooses to reveal such truths only then will we know. In the meanwhile I will devote my scholarly hunt to determine the riddle of the Vaghi.

(The latter prologues are memory swipes plucked from the subconscious mind of Zoog Kavoyy, Vag nunale and denizen of the planet Gala Rotaria.)

# CHAPTER I

Streaks of morning dust flew from his pony's hooves as the kilted rider approached Kavoyy Station. Reining the lathered animal to a trot he allowed it to pick its way up the causeway and through the open gate. Snorting and shaking the wet from it's neck, the muscular little horse halted by a familiar water trough, there to lap its fill. Under normal circumstances the rider would immediately hand over the dispatch pouch to the station master for the final five medec trip up the steep climb and along the twisting spine which forms that section of the Vag Isthmus known as the Chokepoint. So difficult were portions of the terrain leading to North Camp that ponies found it impossible to negotiate. Only a runner, sure-footed and swift, could make the passage. The station master's oldest son usually made the run, covering the harsh ground in less than an hour. And following a brief respite he would return to the station bearing the camp officer's daily report which the rider and a fresh mount would carry south stopping periodically to switch ponies. At midpoint a second relay rider would complete the journey to the Capital. But something was amiss today. Oozing abrasions marred the horseman's face, itself twisted in a pained grimace. Traveling the length of the forearm from elbow to wrist an ugly slash, raw and throbbing, caused the stubby messenger to hold it aloft so as to avoid brushing it against his side. Graveled dirt caked the bloody laceration. Fresh crimson coated the knuckle points and palms.

"Take a spill," inquired the station master, grabbing the bridle?

"Aye, Gurz," he sighed clutching at his boot just below the calf. "Think I've busted my ankle and a thumb too. Happened about eight medecs back. That's why I'm late. Took me that long to come to my senses and locate my mount. Hurts like hell I'm not ashamed to say. My head too!" It had taken an extraordinary effort to haul himself back in the saddle.

The master eased the crooked foot from the stirrup trying his best not to twist the limb. Regardless his toughness, the messenger hissed a breath of discomfort through clenched teeth. "By the ten fingers," he cursed. "I'll not be able to sit a pony for a year!"

Having heard the commotion, a wiry young man came out of the harness shed and helped swing the rider's good leg over the saddle pommel and lower him to the ground. The maneuver proved agonizing. Both knees had also lost much skin. Unknotting the bootlaces, the station master examined the puffed ankle and issued a confirming nod. It was broken.

Though a stripling of sixteen years, he was already taller than his father but without the brawn. However, the son's physique was most athletic, slender and well-knit. His rugged features struck all and any who viewed him. Firm of jaw with tanned skin accentuating his clean white teeth, indeed he was the handsomest young male of the clan Kavoyy. Manly he stood, not pretty like some others his age whose pink cheeks had yet to feel the razor's drag. He wore his hair longer than most men of The Vag, not too long but just enough to offer a statement, the kind young people everywhere do to assert a modicum of independence. However, there wasn't any rebellion in his attitude, only the twinkling of youth. It really didn't matter a whole lot because in six months he would begin his citizen and warrior training, the first step of which involved a traditional head shaving. The sight of dark brown tresses heaped on the grounds inside the Ring of Muraverdus would signal his initiation to manhood. Similar to all people of The Vag, the eyes were yellow; however, his pair carried a particularly gold cast, like nugget flecks in a stream. Presently they met those of his father as the elder unslung the rider's dispatch pouch and passed it to the boy with parting instructions. "Marz, get this up to the camp on the double. They're probably getting nervous wondering why it hasn't arrived."

"How late am I, Gurz" groaned the courier now seated in the dirt?

"About two hours," answered Gurz.

"I must have been knocked senseless for longer than I suspected. It's a good thing the first bone to make contact with the road was my head," he laughed through the pain.

"By the ten fingers, it's a good thing!"

The two Kavoyy hefted their casualty to his good foot, supporting him as he limped towards the stone and stucco house, there to be tended by Gurz Kavoyy's wife and family.

Draping the pouch strap over his neck and across the shoulder, Marz Kavoyy paused to sip a few mouthfuls of water from a clay ewer before bolting out the door, and with long, graceful bounds ate up the distance. Off he loped up the inclined grade leading to the stepped trail and the high ground beyond.

Marz knew the route well. He recognized every twist, each configuration of rock and bush, one and every dip where ages of run-off had formed uneven pockets. Feet danced over the contour hardly ever breaking stride, never a moment lost. The higher the trail, the cooler the air. An autumn sun shone freely now, neither cloud nor haze scarred the morning sky. Racing along the ridge-line he could view the sea both east and west, the isthmus allowing such vistas from its loftiest points. This part of the trek the young Kavoyy enjoyed the most. He had been doing it almost daily for more than three years. Occasionally a younger brother or cousin would accompany him, learning the land, building endurance, absorbing self-reliance as he himself had done when another runner had been his mentor. No pony could ever manage this ground. Portions were steeped close to fifty degrees. Those segments were known as the Verticals. Many centuries, perhaps millenia, earlier, men of The Vag had terraced the trail's most precipitous inclines into gigantic stairways of broad steps allowing bodies of warriors to traverse the heights four or five abreast. Stretching his stride the youth ran along a green swath for about twelve hundred paces. An ancient runner had dubbed this expanse the Lizard's Tongue. Mostly grass and moss the Tongue represented the most effortless part, its line relatively flat, the forgiving soil cushioning heels and joints. Perspiration had gathered along Marz's brow. He muttered a grateful "thank you" to no one or no thing in particular when a breeze pushed across the Tongue. Fall days like this were especially pleasant for his runs. The temperate climate of the northern Vag witnessed few spells of harsh weather, excessive heat and cold seldom settling in. Although periods of chilling wind and rain could last for weeks at a time making it miserable for a runner's mission. Winter nights rarely reached the freeze-point. Nevertheless, traces of snow were known to sprinkle the higher ridges. Snow in itself hardly mattered to Marz. It was the unseen glaze of ice which caused for treacherous footing. He had learned to run flatfooted when such conditions were evident. There was more to making haste than simply placing one foot beyond the other. One had to read the rises and flats cataloging each nuance for future trips.

Though he had been pumping along at a quick clip, the young messenger barely seemed winded. Stamina thrived in the lungs and calves of Marz Kavoyy. A long sleeved tunic, the color of dry oatmeal, covered the breadth of his torso, beneath it a lightweight sweater newly woven by his mother.

The bleached yarn was cotton-like, soft and comforting where it touched his arms. And under the sweater clung a thin undergarment soaking up the light sweat surfacing on his back and chest. Banding the tunic tight to the waist was a leather belt hued like ripe chestnuts. It sported a dull bronze buckle inherited from his mother's father. Above the posterior, firmly fastened to the belt, a rolled slicker awaited the call to fend off passing showers. Seated next to the slicker a sheath containing a short bladed, flint knife rested upon his hip. Buttocks and loins were protected by tan drawstring pants, called bragghi, extending midpoint to the knee. Warrior boots laced with rawhide thongs completed the attire. As a runner of the station, Marz had been receiving free footwear from the army, a most appreciative entitlement that his mother often saluted inasmuch as her son's feet "grow in spurts like mushrooms on a log, buttons at dusk, stems and caps in the morn." Marz took a lot of good natured ribbing about his feet.

The wind picked up as he neared the Tongue's tip. Soon winter would be upon The Vag and he would don the traditional sheepskin vest and long legged bragghi. He began his descent onto the plateau below, the great earthen Ring of Kilts looming at the far end. Some day he would wear the kilt, he thought. Vaghi upon completion of training were awarded the kilt signifying acceptance into the warrior society. Composed of layered leather strips each roughly 1½ digits wide with tips cut to picket points, the kilt served as a second hide defending that part of the body from the elements in addition to blunting hostile blows. But most of all it was symbolic of a status, a status of mutual respect spanning the generations. Bedridden Vaghi who hadn't thrust a sword in decades, awaited death's knock wearing the kilt. To be buried in the leather skirt is to have died with pride. So revered is the kilt that in the army warriors are referred to as 'kilts' and addressed accordingly. There are few emblems in this life that are more precious than the breath of existence. The kilt among them stands alone. Aye, better to be a kilted Vag dead in hell than a living stranger swaddled in robes of golden thread.

Routinely, a lesser officer would accept the pouch and empty it's contents. He would then refill the very same with the daily report for the return trip to Kavoyy Station and ultimately the Capital. This particular morning, however, after Marz had surrendered the dispatch, he was escorted to the North Camp commander' s headquarters for what the subordinate officer termed "special instructions."

Within the huge circular embankment whose earthen walls reached a height of four men, warriors were lining up in ranks for the noon roll call prior to lunch. Outside the Ring of Kilts the precipice was yet more dramatic for a dry moat surrounded the entire perimeter. Almost two medecs in diameter, the fortress served as residence to four kords of Vaghi soldiers, over two thousand men in total. Crowning the ring for a full 360 degrees a stone lip protected the camp defenders from any raider unlucky enough to scale the wall. From behind it kilts could thrust their lethal short swords with minimal exposure. Extending from each side of the ring, two walls or wings, reached the sea, effectively plugging the bottleneck.

Non-commissioned officers barked out the names of their charges as rosters were checked, absentees accounted for, either on patrol or detail, or in the case of a handful, on the mend in sick bay. Barely a thousand strides north of the ring a full kord manned the other great bulwark, or First Line, which bisected the isthmus' narrowest stricture, referred to by all as the Chokepoint. Feeding the Chokepoint, from north to south, a slender canyon ran it's course perpendicular to the First Line. The canyon, or Gorge of Skulls, represented the sole invasion course for foreigners intent on penetrating The Vag. Should the alarm be raised, kilts within the ring would speedily reinforce the First Line for it represented the most defensible position. Like the ring it's height too was formidable but more difficult to assail for beyond it the plateau dropped off sharply to the Gorge of Skulls. Over the many centuries, hundreds of thousands, possibly millions of enemy skeletons had accumulated, bleaching the landscape with macabre evidence of futile incursions. Indeed Vaghi patrols venturing up the isthmus above First Line had to crunch through the brittle bone yard though echoes of the last great battle had silenced over nine years past.

Having been given the order to stand at ease, files of warriors shuffled in place stirring up puffs of Autumn dust. The season had been dry. Nostrils and lips bore parched proof of the powdery soil swirling about. Once the final count had been tallied, they would break ranks for a meal of coarse bread dunked in the communal olive oil basin, along with chick peas and garlic. A dried meat ration and an apple or two from the recent harvest would complete lunch. Marz and the officer cut through the formation toward the squat brick structure bearing the camp commander's pennant. Several soldiers, all of high rank, collected under the shade roof fronting the structure. Looks of concern strained their faces. Marz knew them to be officers from the red leather strip that ran down each thigh of their black kilts, the red stripe of command. Spotting the young officer and runner approaching, the senior man stepped forward. Marz recognized him at once. Kirz Morann, commander of North Camp. With a reputation for zero tolerance, the stern Morann was as much feared as respected by troops under his sway. Among the officer corps he was considered highly competent, and a man not to be challenged. Two rules dictated much of his military behavior. First, the only thing more important than caution is precaution. And secondly, there are no coincidences. No doubt it was precisely these principles which guided his summoning of the courier standing before him. "Are you the runner," he asked, searching the golden eyes for a clue of attitude? *Do I see confidence, intelligence, resourcefulness, perhaps a hint of tenacity? Or do I find the antitheses of all these traits? Give me a telltale blink, a droop of the lid. Stare at your boots. Do something, anything!* Marz returned the stare, not fazed by the inquiring orbs searching his own. Remembering his father's monition not to be cowed by a man's glare regardless of status or strength of arm, he kept a firm jaw and steely eye. *Oh, this one's cool. No quiver in his chin, nary a twitch on his lips,* thought the veteran commander. He believed in reading a man's pupils, for nothing betrayed a weakling's character more so than his eyes. Confident eyes supported the righteous, darting ones divulged guilt or something wished hidden.

"Yes, sir. I am Marz Kavoyy." No indication of nervousness passed his lips.

Eyeballing the youth from forelock to boots he nodded grudging approval of the composed figure. Stretching himself to his fullness, the camp commander stood half a head beneath that of Marz. "With a name like Kavoyy it stands to reason that you know the way to Kavoyy Station," he quipped. Kirz Morann raked his fingers through thinning hair and brushed an itch from the deep crags surrounding a seasoned nose. Sarcasm was not beyond his wit.

"Yes, sir," Marz confirmed. "I've been your runner for over three years."

"A three year veteran, lad," he bellowed. "By the sweet tears of Gala Rotaria soon you'll be petitioning the Lord for a pension." It was one of the few times any of his staff could recall the commander displaying any playfulness. Taking note, the attending knot of officers offered a collective guffaw. The higher the rank, the louder the chuckle.

To Marz, the observer, the scene was one of curiosity. He had never been in the company of so many senior officers before, but it didn't take a nunale sage to recognize boot licking when he saw it. "In six months time it will be my turn to swear the oath." The statement was matter of fact, the look impassive.

Realizing he could not shake the youth, Commander Morann was satisfied the young runner was not the frivolous sort. Holding forth a short canister coated with wax bearing the imprint of his personal seal, he pressed it into the palm of Marz Kavoyy. "Lock this in your pouch and deliver it to the station master with instructions for the rider to deliver it as swiftly as possible to General Povezz at the Capital. This is to take priority over all other deliveries. Allow nothing to impede your progress. Do not stop to drop a fart or pinch your dolly's sweet cheeks. And the same goes for the rider!" Grunting he pivoted a half turn away from Marz only to promptly return to his original stance, but this time the tone was more friendly. In the blink it had taken to complete the spin he had decided to temper his disposition. Placing a hand on Marz's shoulder, he gave a gentle squeeze while his eyes again met those of the young Kavoyy. "Now, son, I'm depending on you to do it right. This message concerns the Kala. So you know it's important." A paternal seriousness had entered his voice.

"Yes, sir." He almost hesitated, considering whether to inform the commander that the dispatch rider's fractured ankle, among other breaks and injuries, made it impossible to mount a saddle, and that most likely his father had poured enough painkilling brandy into the poor fellow to float a goat. But he thought the better and chose not to mention it. Just a detail. One way or another the mission would be completed as directed. *The Kala,* he thought to himself, *were they swarming again?*

'Where's the bundle," the commander snapped, breaking Marz's thoughts of Kala?

An officer stepped from the group offering a gray blanket knotted securely with thick, wiry twine. Wrapped inside something was long and stiff. Nodding to the officer, the commander gestured to him to sling the parcel across the messenger's shoulders which he did, slapping it twice to ensure it was tight at both ends. "This bundle is part of the message you grip in your fist. Make certain the rider is aware that it is to be delivered to the general with the canister. Dismissed!"

Shrugging to seat the blanketed package comfortably, Marz Kavoyy placed the message scroll into the pouch and fastened the horn buckle. "It will be done, sir," he assured, presenting a snappy cross armed salute across his chest as was the military custom of The Vag. Kirz Morann responded in kind. Executing an about face worthy of the Capital parade ground, he took off at a full gallop weaving through the troops breaking for lunch.

Slapping his worn kilt in soft cadence to Marz's pace, the commander of North Camp watched him until he disappeared from the Ring of Kilts. "I don't remember ever being able to run like that," he admired aloud.

*Kala, Kala, Kala!* The words would not be purged from his thoughts though he tried. Perhaps an all out sprint the full measure of the Lizard's Tongue would help. Like an untamed steed he charged across the verdant swath emitting a shrill scream over the final fifty strides as if to exorcise the troubling Kala from within. It had taken perhaps four minutes to cover the Tongue from tip to gullet. Pausing to recapture his wind the words re-surfaced in the ocean that was his mind, a buoyant cork not to be submerged. *Kala, Kala, Kala.* Children of The Vag who had misbehaved at one point in their lives had been menaced with threats of, *If you're not good, the Kala will eat you!* Dreaded more than monsters of the underworld, images of flesh eating Kala terrorized the dreams of juvenile minds. Though cruel in concept the warning served well. No better deterrent ensured an outpouring of exemplary decorum.

Today at age sixteen the Kala scourge danced fresh in the thoughts of Marz Kavoyy. Though a historical reality, the Kala had always been distant, almost mythical inside his head. This morning's brief meeting at North Camp had shaken whatever indifference dwelled behind the golden eyes. For on his back and within the leather bag swinging to his side were ominous news and evidence of the living, breathing, furious Kala. An eerie chill traveled his spine and it wasn't the mid-day breeze that slips across the Tongue. Nay, it was the vile prospect of a Kala deluge funneling down the isthmus which caused hackles and skin to tingle.

Sidestepping several potted holes, his mind floated back in recent time to a dissertation prepared by his brood sibling Zoog. Gee eventually delivered it to a panel of nunale scholars screening potential entrants for the science academy. Every evening for six weeks his sib practiced the speech in booming voice until Marz himself had committed it to memory. Like so many drips of water, it had left a permanent impression.

*The Kala display an extraordinary tolerance for suffering. Though physically weak by Vag standards, the undersized, naked bodies defy the elements. Harsh living is an everyday part of life. Somehow the springy Kala skin, of a waxy blue hue and virtually hairless save the raggy thatch atop their skulls, allows them to function without icy shivers or solar burn. Exposure, though punishing, seldom seems to be fatal. With calloused foot-soles tougher than saddle leather, they chirp and gnaw their migratory cycles over time worn patterns. To interpret their strident screeches as language, or even sub-language, would be a huge overstatement. There don't appear to be words. Simply inflections to express pleasure, distress or other basic emotions. Among Vaghi scholars the general conclusion is that the Kala tongue is a licking tool exclusively used for tasting, wiping and aiding in the swallow of a vulgar diet.*

*Birthing on the move Kala females litter five to eight offspring at a delivery. Culling the strongest, they scoop up the hardy and with nary a postpartum break they melt into the fluid herd, suckling on the go. The abandoned runts are for other females to carry if their instincts are so inclined Gestation lasts roughly sixty days. Boon or consequence, a matter of perspective, it is not uncommon for a female to 'enjoy' three pregnancies per year. The high mortality rate among the Kala no doubt demands frequent birth cycles. In four months time the newborn are afoot, moving freely without adult assistance. By three years Kala are full grown, aggressively crazed at the suggestion of a meal. Short life cycles and high birth rates represent the Kala formula for existence over the ages. Without strength of body or intellect, only a blind urge to spawn drives each generation. Survival of the species feeds off the laws of probability. The greater the number of hatchlings, the better the chance that some will reach adulthood.*

*Evening sees them in huddled masses. The colder the temperature, the tighter the compact. They know not the comfort of caves nor fabricated shelter, the concept too complex for their puny brains. Instead, clustered bodies provide a protective mass. Precipitation warrants a piling technique; however, the top and bottom-most would seem to suffer the worst discomfort. Ideally a position somewhere in the middle stratum is best, those on the surface obviously becoming wet or snowcapped, the lowest layer crushed into the mud During frozen extremes the outermost do not waken come morn, their sacrifice simply another rhythm of the great migration. And therein their clustered huddles the horde defecates, fornicates and rests for the next day's quest of roots, leaves, twigs, bark, insects and animals of any variety. Habitually they sniff the air for signs of the edible, though it's difficult to understand how Kala nostrils could detect anything through the malodorous stench of the herd Unwitting bowels fertilize the cycadian path, energizing the soil for future grazers.*

*Blessed with sharp, pointy teeth, they devour wild pigs and feral dogs in minutes with echoes of death squeals yet reverberating. Consumption is absolute. Everything is eaten. Bone, tendon, hide, everything with the exception of teeth perhaps. Unlucky Vaghi and Orri are a welcome menu fare including whatever clothing they might be wearing. It is said the Kala who trail the horde will feast on their own dead cousins who've succumbed along the trek. The ghoulish rear guard instinctively munching the morbid bounty scattered in the wake. More scavengers than cannibals, they simply cleanse the landscape of rotting corpses which otherwise would be absorbed into the ground. If nothing else, one could never accuse the Kala of being wasteful. It should be noted that the Kala never kill their own for the purpose of devouring the remains. Even so, an observer should not conclude from this that they've developed a moral code. Burial is never an option.*

*Weaponry consists primarily of jaws containing rows of viciously sharp teeth and claw-like fingernails thicker than those of the large rodents which inhabit the edges of the Gugububu. Many carry dull-ended sticks of varying lengths, the bark having been snacked upon earlier. The sticks are used to slap and prod, a technique used by the more hostile Kala while maneuvering within the pack, facilitating 'elbow room.' However the prodding sticks don't usually survive too long, the temptation irresistible. Eventually they also are chewed to nothing. If a pair of contestants happens to challenge each other, the sticks are wielded with little skill, martial dexterity neither art nor science among the Kala. In battle their strategy is to overwhelm their Vaghi opponents, smothering them with waves of naked blue bodies, disregarding any semblance of personal protection. Sinking fangs once engaged are difficult to dislodge. A sword point through the throat is the preferred technique to relax a locked jaw. Rarely a Kala will throw a stone using a weak pushing motion, clumsy and ineffective.*

*Leadership is unknown among the breed. Central authority exists at no level. So sub-primitive are their kind that even the family social unit is non-existent. Fathers are paternal only in the genetic sense, seminal donors unaware of their progeny. Mothers nurse infants and dump them when they sense it is time. No bond endures.*

*The Kala move in an unknown number of herds ranging from several thousand to possibly over a hundred thousand combing the northern climes of Gala Rotaria. How great is their population no one knows for certain. Instinctively they travel the patterns of past herds, occasionally colliding with another blue mass, perhaps merging for months. And then without any predetermined plan the enlarged group might sub-divide into three or more herds. Possibly a few Kala at the front randomly gravitate left or right and those behind follow for no explicable reason. In that sense those bodies in the vanguard might be termed 'leaders' but they have no control.*

*Captives have never shown any inclination to learn. Food is attacked, shelter ignored, tricks beyond learning. Reward and punishment training escapes them. Prisoners prefer dying to comfort, beating their leathery blue heads against the firm ground until the dull ring of concussion signals the first whisper of death. And then they lie down to die.*

*Because the Kala are both leaderless and speechless it would be impossible to negotiate a treaty or some sort of truce. Unquestionably the concept of honor would be beyond their grasp.*

*Kala are without organization, without reason, without culture, without law, without technology of any kind Even the most minuscule threads of civilization exist not. Perhaps it is best that way because it makes it easier to slay them without conscience.*

# CHAPTER II

It was no surprise to the young Kavoyy when Gurz told him he would have to replace the injured rider. For 54 medecs he would gallop along the route to Midpoint Station stopping twice for fresh mounts. And each time he'd have to explain to the local station manager why he was lugging dispatches, how the scheduled messenger had suffered an ugly tumble, that his pouch contained a message of the highest priority. Before departing Kavoyy Station, Marz took the hobbled man's red and black kerchief and knotted it about his own neck so all who might be traveling the road would recognize him as a courier. He had grown up with the speedy ponies of The Vag, feeding, watering, grooming and scraping their droppings from the stable floor. As a matter of course, he had learned to ride proficiently at an early age. But to sit this long in the saddle, jouncing over the choppy road, was a new experience. It gave him pause to appreciate the gritty dispatch riders who regularly made the trip. Usually, they were selected because of their size; short, slender men who wouldn't overly burden the critters racing beneath them. Called ponies they actually were lightweight horses; however, to distinguish them from the thick legged draft horses which lumbered in the fields, the sleek beasts which bore riders were termed "ponies". Plodding horses dragged plows and ripped stumps; ponies, sturdy and swift, transported passengers.

A dull ache moved along his shoulders and through the blades where the bundle rolled with the pony's motion. Sweat laden bragghi stuck to his buttocks, their wetness chafing the numb skin. "Soon," he thought, "in less than six medecs I'll reach Midpoint Station where the relay rider will relieve me. Let him bear the pouch and parcel. Let him carry on to the Capital. And while he bounces I'll be sleeping with sated belly, stretched out by a warm hearth." Such inviting thoughts caused him to urge his mount to gather more speed. The animal seemed to respond. A veteran of the route, it understood a cooling drink awaited their arrival to be followed by a full manger and soothing rubdown. Spurred by the prospect, he ran with renewed strength to the unmistakable cluster of tiny buildings perched on the horizon.

Midpoint Station sat equidistant to both Kavoyy Station and the Capital. Charging up the gravel ramp, he passed through the open gate and entered a rectangular corral opposite the feed barn. Pleased with what he had accomplished, Marz Kavoyy slipped from the saddle and surveyed the yard looking for an attendant to secure his mount. Stiff-legged the first few steps caused him to wobble slightly. Keeping a steadying hand on the stirrup, Marz squatted several times to shake the kinks from his knees and ankles. He tugged at the clammy cloth of his bragghi, which had bunched up in his crotch, and issued a muffled snort, inviting the cool air to circulate about his loins. The round trip dash through the isthmus, followed by hours ahorse, magnified the enjoyment of such simple pleasures.

With a leathery suntan and short cropped gray hair, the station boss' wrinkled face appeared from behind a three walled outbuilding. A brown spotted dog slithered from under the fence's lower rail to join his curious master. Examining Marz the man asked, "Where's the rider?"

"Tore himself to pieces in a spill," replied Marz, trying to sound as mature as the rider he had replaced. "Looks like a broken ankle. He's banged up pretty badly."

"And who, sir, might I ask are you?" A touch of sarcasm, the kind men of experience are permitted, touched his voice.

"Kavoyy, Marz Kavoyy. There was no one else to…"

The station master cut him off. "Gurz's son? You're Marz, Gurz's son?" Eyeballing the full presence of the young Kavoyy, the old man clucked in admiration, walking a half circle around him. "By the ten fingers, lad, you've been blessed with your daddy's strong likeness. But you must stand a fist taller."

"Yes sir. Gurz Kavoyy is my father. You know him?"

Continuing to marvel at the figure before him, the master of Midpoint Station reached out a hand. "They call me Varo. I worked at your family's station for three years."

"Really?" answered Marz. "Must have been before my time." Snatching Varo's hand, he shook it vigorously to the point where the gray-head had to pull free.

"I left when your brood was about a year old. Had a lucky nunale in your bunch as I recall." He grinned broadly exposing several toothless gaps.

"Yes, that's my genther Zoog. And my sister is Tyrra. We're sixteen and a half years now."

"You look older," he smiled. "Be sure to pass my good wishes on to your mom and dad. Tell them old Varo fondly remembers them as kind and fair-minded people."

"I will, Varo. I will…that is as soon as you can give me a bit to eat and a corner where I can catch a few hours of sleep. Of course I'll need a pony for the trip back home." Before Varo could respond, Marz, realizing no one else seemed be to about, inquired, "Where's the other rider? I have a priority dispatch for General Povezz."

"By the fingers! I knew it! I just bloody knew it," exclaimed Varo punching his fist into a flattened palm. Startled, the dog skittered a few steps.

"Is there a problem?" the puzzled youth asked.

"I'll say there is. A priority dispatch for General Povezz, the first one in half a year and my rider and both back-up riders are gone!" He kicked at an invisible pebble. "Everyone's gone, even my station hands!"

"Gone? How is it possible? Where are they?"

"Jail," he groaned. "The louts slipped out last night to a pub no more than two medecs from here. Snuck out against orders mind you." He kicked the dirt again emphasizing the disgust already written across his grizzled face. "The lot of them got pissy drunk and ripped up the place. Bad enough they broke every table and chair, but the pub keeper got himself stabbed in the melee. Nothing too serious, but enough to have the magistrate show up this morning and arrest everyone but me and the bloody dog." As if on cue, the mutt jumped up and began licking Varo's hand. He pushed it away gently, not letting his frustration punish it. "So there is no rider, no back-up rider, and no back-up back-up rider, if you catch my meaning, lad!"

A weariness filled the bones of Marz Kavoyy foreseeing the conclusion inside Varo's mind. Varo was too old and the dog couldn't ride, so it would be up to Marz to jockey the next string of ponies from Midpoint Station to the Capital. A disappointed breath blew heavily from his lungs.

"Aye, son, it's your ride to make. If the dispatch wasn't for General Povezz, I'd tell you to stay here overnight and haul your ass to the Capital at first light. But you've lived around a station long enough to know that 'Priority' means 'Ride like the bloody wind' with no delays…no excuses." He touched the young man's arm in a gesture of empathy.

"Aye, Varo. I understand." The words carried nary a whimper. Duty prevailed.

"Good lad. But first go inside and refresh yourself with some drink and food while l saddle a proper mount." As the station master ambled to the stable, he laughed out, "And remember to take a bloody leak. All that time in the stirrups can cause a man's bladder to scream."

By the time Marz had eaten his fill and relieved himself, an impatient mare stood waiting outside. Pawing the hard packed dirt, she signaled the long limbed rider that she was anxious to carry him to the next relay station 18 medecs south. Varo loaned him a sheepskin vest to fend off the evening chill. Resetting the blanket bundle he climbed astride and set himself for the journey. Varo stuffed a handful of jerky into the vest pocket and gave him a prideful wink. Varo had found a link with his past and relished the opportunity to enjoy the discovery.

"Beef or lamb?" the young rider inquired.

"Mutton, lad, mutton," he roared. "As tough as the tenth finger of Gala Rotaria!" And slapping the powerful rump he yelled, "Yahhh!"

"Yahhh!"Marz shouted in spontaneous response, digging his heels into the pony, and off they flew down the ramp. Sore as he was, the feeling exhilarated him. Fifty-four jarring medecs and two pony exchanges loomed down the road. He knew his body would ache from neck to backbone, from rib cage to derrière, from groin to toe, pleading for respite. But this moment was special, the sensation invigorating...at least in the short term. Aware of the bulge in his pocket, he pushed his free hand downward compacting the stiffened jerky so it wouldn't escape into the dusk. And solid it was, tougher than the boot heels seated in his stirrups. "Harder than the tenth finger of the Great Goddess herself." He giggled inside, recollecting Varo's metaphor. For every Vag knew that the tenth finger represented iron!

Truly, this was a medecstone moment for the sixteen year old. Over the next few hours the pain would come, the pain would numb and he would have a memory unlike anything he had experienced before. The glorious ride of Marz Kavoyy would live with him for the remainder of his life. "Yahhh!"

Even silhouetted against the night sky, the Capital city managed to project a majestic presence. Gabled roofs and pediments jutted upwards piercing the darkness. Traces of haphazard shadows complimented the irregular geometry, columns and archways contributing to the melange. Situated high on a broad hill, the walled metropolis silently awaited the exhausted rider. A few lights sparkled directing him up the cobbled road to the main gate. Two soldiers rested by the portal, there more to maintain a presence rather than guard the passage. Spotting the kerchief they waved him to their post.

"I have a message for General Povezz." The voice was deliberate, the tone heavy with fatigue.

"Take it to the guardhouse inside the gate. The officer of the guard will handle it," directed the nearest kilt, yawning in the drowsy night air.

The pony clopped to a halt outside the squat blockhouse. Marz was grateful that the officer stood in the doorway. He could talk to the man directly from the saddle, sparing his stiffened bones the discomfort of dismounting and remounting at conversation's end.

"Sir, I have an urgent dispatch and package to be delivered to General Povezz. Can you direct me to his quarters?"

"Urgent, how urgent? He's supping late with the Lord and doesn't wish to be disturbed for something trivial." The officer examined the blanket parcel straddling the courier's shoulders. Pointing, he inquired, "Is that it?"

"Aye, sir. From Commander Morann at North Camp. My instructions were to ensure its immediate delivery to the general."

"Do you know the way to the Lord's residence?"

"No, sir."

"Do you know how to get to the Lord's Quadrant?"

"No, sir."

"Ahhh, you country bumpkins," he laughed good naturedly, "couldn't find bread in a bakery. Come on, I'll ride along with you."

The metropolis, known simply as the Capital, contained four districts referred to as quadrants: Market, Military, People's and Lord's. Marz had accompanied his father and uncle to the city two years earlier, visiting each of the quarters and their wonders, especially attracted to the Hall of Protectors and it's statues of Vaghi heroes. Though he remembered it somewhat, at this late hour in the ink of night, very little was recognized. Riding in file, the two horsemen moved onto the principal thoroughfare and proceeded into the city proper.

First to come on their left stood Market Quadrant. Here the wheels of commerce turn. Banking, trade, real estate and their attendant contractual and various legal details are conducted in Market. Mostly it is an open bazaar of tented stalls and shops. Inasmuch as all trade is internal and primarily involves consumer goods and services, a system of barter credits prevails. Such credits represent The Vag's media of exchange. For instance, a farmer might trade a pig with a value of 100 barter credits, and in turn redeem the hundred for a bolt of wool cloth (75 credits), a haircut (5 credits), and a saddle repair (20 credits.) Banking is a fairly primitive business, it's most useful purpose in establishing values for various goods and services based on supply and demand. It is an economy controlled for the benefit of The Vag society and not to make rich Vaghi wealthier.

Grain, however, is the one commodity excluded from trade. Wheat grows in abundance on the expansive steppe which sweeps across the southeast Vag. Dutifully planted and harvested by males and females in their seventeenth year, it is stored in state granaries dispersed throughout the nation. Each citizen receives a generous ration, the amount contingent upon the annual yield and the judgment of the Lord.

Over ninety percent of the land is held in common, again controlled by the Lord, the remainder owned by citizen families.

Glancing to his right Marz peered into the orderly Military Quadrant housing the city's small guard plus a wing of cavalry. The barracks are also the point of departure and reception for the courier riders. Two full kords of troops are stationed outside of the city at a camp adjoining the earthen citadel known as the Ring of Muraverdus. Within the quadrant blazes a forge, along with the arsenal, which is the receptacle of its product. Here bronze is fashioned into weapons and tools from The Vag's plentiful resources of copper, tin and zinc. The scarcity of iron makes it the most precious of metals, more valuable than gold and silver; because from super-heated iron, pounded and hammered till the reluctant carbon is purged from its very nature, comes steel. And steel is transformed into penetrating points and honed blades, more punishing, more lethal in the grip of Vaghi warriors. Additionally, those tools which are designated as 'necessary' by the Great Lord are also fabricated from steel: chisels for the quarries, axe heads to the forests, saws delivered to the carpenters cooperative and scalpels to facilitate the surgeon's skill. For many decades, however, the few iron mines had been virtually depleted of their ore. Though new depths were plumbed, the yields remained puny, almost a non-existent trickle. Steel short-swords reaching back twenty or thirty generations are passed down to young warriors by family elders, so precious are their worth. Broken tools are melted and re-worked, old steel recycled into shiny hammers, blades, crucibles, whatsoever the need. Meteorites, rich in high grade iron, represent the one item eagerly sought in trade from the Orri. A shepherd can name his price for a lucky find. High density meteorites, the size of a man's head, command a worth beyond gold. Indeed, the Fingers of Gala Rotaria representing the ten elements from which everything flows include iron. So sparing, it could only be a gift of the great goddess herself; a blessing not to be squandered on things frivolous.

Riding through the quiet city, only the hollow echoes of their hooves stirred the urban air. Up the Capital concourse they traveled, past the intersection formed by the city's chief crossroad known as the Crossway. Beyond it, left and right respectively, lay the People' s Quadrant and the Lord's Quadrant. The former is nothing more than residential housing. Fewer than 11,000 live here, bureaucrats, servants, teachers, merchants and their families. A municipal dispensary catering to the community' s medical needs, as well as public baths and toilet facilities, also are centered in the quarter.

Unquestioned authority resides in that section which dwarfs the other three in the elevation of its rooftops; its brawny architecture proclaiming the omnipotence within. For here in the Lord's Quadrant dwells the seat of power. From this impressive patch the Lord directs all aspects of Vag life. Supreme in his governance, he is a tyrant, empowered by the vote of warriors for a twenty-four year term, an investiture enjoyed by four or five Vaghi leaders per century. In keeping with the absolute nature of his office, the Lord's Quadrant embraces the most dramatic stone structures in the land. Broad granite blocks of white and pink steps encompass the entire perimeter of Gala Rotaria's temple, ushering worshipers through a level of fluted marble columns, great pillars of purest white supporting enormous friezes bearing likeness of the Great Mother amid floral designs skillfully chiseled into the superstructure. Riding parallel to the temple front, the mouth of Marz Kavoyy fell open in awed response.

Next in line stood the Hall of Protectors, cold and stern, a building without exterior decor. The two ponies moved silently along the adjoining concourse, perhaps to avert disturbing the glass eyed ones who, frozen in motion, inhabit its cavernous vault. Among the people of The Vag there is a special expression which is used to predict that one is destined for greatness or has already, in fact, achieved greatness. "He has the look of glass eyes!" Indeed that is a metaphor of distinct meaning! For when a luminary of the nation has attained a status of heroic proportion, he or she or gee is memorialized with a life sized marble statue in the Hall of Protectors. The faces of such likenesses contain realistic glass eyes, yellow of course, which some believe provide a guardian vision for the ages.

Eight statues adorn the great hall, the last having been erected over two hundred years past. Those sixteen eyes are believed by many to protect The Vag from enemies both far and near. The hall itself is used by several nongoverning councils to oversee various needs of the country. It is difficult for council members to connive while under their watchful glare. Even those who claim not to be superstitious have been known to suffer a guilt-fed uneasiness when eye contact is made. The illusion of impassive stone lips transforming into disapproving scowls makes for sweating palms and queasy innards. Better to plot outside the hall where the sculpture is unseen, where the glass orbs are unseeing. For one never knows for sure where myth and reality overlap.

As with most metaphors, "He has the look of glass eyes" is often wasted on posturing lords and swaddled babes regardless of talent or bloodline. For only great deeds earn the eyes of glass. Truly it is the act of superior accomplishment, that which saves the nation or propels it to a higher level, which elevates the patriot to immortality.

It should be noted that the expression is also uttered sarcastically in reference to dolts who couldn't pour pee from a scabbard.

Lesser buildings followed, splendid in their own right but minimized by the edifices which surround them. *Here is where Zoog will seek his vocation,* thought Marz. *The Academy of Science.* Other structures of the bureaucracy followed and then the grand boulevard ended...appropriately. Here, radiating the eerie chill of power, stood the Lord's residence, broad chested, flexing its columnar muscles, announcing to all who dared approach that in this place every command, every desire, every capricious whim, is obeyed.

For the moment his weariness disappeared. Dismounting, a ripple of uncertainty moved through his legs, causing the knees to weaken a bit. Young Marz, who had refused to buckle under the stare of Kirz Morann, suddenly felt squeamish at the prospect of entering the Lord's domicile. Shifting the bundle to ease the twine where it had cut a groove into his shoulder, he followed the officer up the steps and past the guards. They moved through the outer reception area and approached a nunale secretary seated behind a small desk. Oil lamps illuminated the hallway beyond causing Marz's shadow to grow elongated against the far wall as if on stilts. The officer and secretary spoke for several moments in hushed voices. Nodding, the rotund one rose and departed. Several minutes later gee returned instructing the two visitors to proceed through the hall and the anterooms beyond. Sensing his appearance was unkempt, Marz attempted to offset the sweaty grime clinging to face and hair by standing as erect as his frame would permit, walking with confident paces...as though he belonged. Watching his confident shadow dance across the walls, a tinge of premonition entered his mind. It was as though someone or something had whispered to him, sowing seeds of future glimpse. 'Maybe you do belong,' it said. And just as suddenly as it had come to him, the idea disappeared, perhaps startled away by the enormous double doors which swung open before his wide eyes. "Enter," commanded the forceful voice of Taz Povezz, General of the Army, first kilt of The Vag! The young officer nudged the courier forward and departed.

It took a good degree of Marz's mental strength to contain his emotion. Here in this very room, no more than twenty strides to his front, were seated the two most powerful men in his universe. Breathing deeply, he advanced, taking care to control the gape threatening to betray his awe. For alongside the general, munching from a bowl of dark green olives, sat the tall and stately figure of Lanz Varaxx, almighty Lord of The Vag! Spitting a pit into a low brazier of coals warming his feet, he motioned the messenger to move closer. A pair of oversized glass goblets dominated the table, gaming tiles scattered across its surface. No doubt he had interrupted their post meal entertainment, a game of Spots. Marz had seen the great Lord from a distance the only time he had visited the Capital, but it was from a far greater distance than the table length which now separated them. Very tall with puffy, ruddy cheeks, he appeared to be in his mid to late forties. The hair hung long and fair, but there were signs of thinning, pink scalp showing through at the pate.

"I have an urgent dispatch from Commander Morann to General Povezz," he announced without first being directed to speak.

"Well, let's have it," Povezz ordered. And taking note the messenger was without the warrior's leather skirt, he observed aloud, "You're not wearing your kilt?"

"I don't enter my training cycle for another six months, sir."

The general barely heard him, concentrating instead on the sealed canister being passed across the table.

URGENT DISPATCH

TO: GENERAL T. POVEZZ

FROM: COMMANDER K. MORANN

ORIGIN: NORTH CAMP HEADQUARTERS

DATE: 24 SECCUS 23/18

EARLY THIS MORNING ONE OF OUR PATROLS RETURNED AFTER RECONNOITERING THE NORTH ISTHMUS BEYOND FIRST LINE. 7 MEDECS ABOVE THE CHOKEPOINT THE PATROL AMBUSHED A BAND OF 4 MALE KALA. ALL 4 WERE SLAIN. AS YOU ARE AWARE, ON OCCASION KALA CARRY STICKS, USUALLY CROOKED, WITH NO UNIFORMITY OF SIZE. 3 OF THE 4 POSSESSED STRAIGHT STICKS, EACH ABOUT 60 DIGITS LONG AND <u>SHARPENED TO A POINT</u>, APPARENTLY BY RUBBING AGAINST A STONE SURFACE. WHETHER THIS LITTLE BAND WAS AN ISOLATED UNIT OR THE LEAD ELEMENT OF MORE SIMILARLY ARMED KALA. ONLY TIME WILL TELL. AS A PRECAUTION, I HAVE DOUBLED PATROL ACTIVITY AND PLACED NORTH CAMP ON ALERT STATUS. RESPECTFULLY SUBMITTED,

K. MORANN

COMMANDER

The seriousness of the news moved the Lord's military chief to emit a raspy acknowledgment. The implication was clear to Povezz. Somehow the pea brained Kala had figured how to transform branches into spears. Clumsy prods had evolved to lethal weapons...an enormous leap in technology and obviously a breakthrough in communication, for three Kala carried the spears. Yes, this represented an extraordinary innovation in the relationship of Kala to one another. Because with intercourse comes organization and its' inherent impact on the Vag nation. The Lord, however, was either unimpressed or unable to assess the gravity.

"Though they are uncoordinated, the huge mass of numbers armed with spears represents a potential threat unlike any we have ever known," shared the general. Gulping his wine, the Lord rose to pace the floor, permitting Povezz to formulate his conclusions.

Marz unslung the blanket parcel and held it forward. "Sir, Commander Morann instructed me to deliver this as well."

"Open it," ordered the general.

"Yes, sir," the youth replied. Deftly he slit the rough twine using his flint knife to do so. He knelt and allowed the blanket to unfurl, surrendering its content. Clattering on the stone floor the spear stick wobbled to a halt digits from the Lord's sandaled foot.

Whether the Lord had consumed an excess of wine, or his was a brain lacking in deductive reasoning, the young Kavoyy was uncertain. Kicking the stick the leader of the Vag nation emitted a raucous guffaw, rivaled only by the rolling fart which escaped his bragghi. "This filthy stick, this piece of kindling is what that alarmist Morann bothers us with? By the sweet fingers of our beloved Goddess, I fart on the Kala and their sticks. You call this a spear? You call that a point?" he ridiculed. His bellowed laugh echoed through the chamber. "Come Povezz, let us enjoy another goblet and finish our game. I believe I was leading at the time of interruption."

Frustration at his leader's dismissal of the news was evident in the general's troubled eyes. He would have to diplomatically explain the significance of the sticks when the moment was opportune. For the Lord easily took offense to 'insubordination' especially in the presence of third parties. Povezz would let it rest a few days before broaching the matter. "Wait in the outer room," he ordered Marz, at the same time signaling him to leave. "Someone will come by to give you drink and rations. I understand you've had a long and difficult ride." The general, like all good officers worth their salt, took care of the troops.

"Yes, yes," approved the Lord, popping another olive into his mouth. "And remove that, that...deadly spear." His sarcastic laugh boomed through the room.

Povezz sat mute, offering but a weak smile to placate the ego of Lanz Varaxx.

The sun must have been up for a couple of hours. It's rays peeked over the windowsill warming the slumbering figure sprawled across the stone bench. Stirring, it took him a few lazy moments to orient his thoughts. Slowly came the realization that he was yet in the alcove adjacent to the Lord's anteroom. Obviously he had fallen asleep while awaiting the meal that had never arrived. Undisturbed, the exhausted messenger had dozed off unseen by servants and staff As he prepared to leave, muffled conversation drifted in from the main chamber.

Wishing not to be embarrassed by what might be perceived as a lapse in behavior, he decided to stay put until he could slip out undetected. And so eavesdropping became unavoidable. Easing off the bench, he crept toward a bulbous green urn and peered through the narrow space formed by the pottery and wall's edge. Inside a nunale clad in priestly garment approached the seated Lord, apparently alert and fresh after a night of tippling.

"Hail, Lanz Varaxx. You summoned me for consultation?"

"Not so much for consultation as for instruction, Daag." The visitor was Daag Goraxx, chief priest of the Vag and keeper of the temple. "Daag, how long have I been Lord?"

"How long? I suspect it has been close to eight years, my Lord." The priest looked quizzical. Why did the Lord need him to confirm his tenure?

"Eight and a half to be exact!" The Lord, a big man by any standard, rose to his full height, a most imposing figure considering the chunky nunale before him. "And who was my first appointee, my initial selection to guide the spiritual needs of our people?"

"I was, my Lord." Gee gulped, sensing something distasteful looming.

"Indeed it was you. A most gracious display of patronage if ever there was one. Wouldn't you agree? I elevated you over all the other priestly candidates. Some suggested it was only because you enjoyed the richest of singing voices." Arching eyebrows emphasized his sarcasm.

"Yes, sir. An appointment for which I am eternally grateful."

"Good, good." The Lord squeezed his hands together, interlocking the fingers, then pushed them inside-out toward Goraxx, allowing the knuckles to crack. "And even though you must be obedient to my every lordly command, I have never imposed my will on you with respect to religion. Is that not so?" he smiled. The Lord, despite not being a brilliant man, was at his best when conniving. "But I do need a favor, or will need a favor. Call it a future commitment to be honored by you..." The Lord's finger reached out to tap the nunale square on the forehead, then tapped his own... "for me." Again he allowed a narrow smile to form. "So l am delighted to learn you are eternally grateful. For I am going to provide you the opportunity to confirm your gratitude with action."

Sweat beads covered the nunale's upper lip though the morning was void of heat. A feeling of entrapment was evident. "What is it you wish, my Lord? I am eager to please."

The Lord returned to his throne-like chair behind the desk and gestured Daag to be seated before him. "My thoughts, Daag, are of succession. What will happen after my term of office expires? Or if the merciful Goddess decides to take me before my time? Who will lead the Vag? Who is capable of shouldering the awesome burden? I want to guarantee that my legacy carries on." He paused trying to read the blank expression looking back at him. "Are you following me?" he demanded.

"I, I believe so," stammered Daag Goraxx:. "But you are without offspring, therefore, I am puzzled as to the identity of your hand-picked successor, if that's what you're implying. Even so, at the time of the new Lord's selection, the process is one of election, a division of the kilts. Therefore, how could I possibly be of influence?" The high priest, palms turned upward, shrugged to emphasize his perplexment.

"You know my wife, Kaara, do you not?"

"Aye, my Lord. A lovely woman."

"Save your horseshit for your nunale underlings, Daag. She's as comely as a Kala bitch and you know it! But her family, the house of Javatt, is the most influential in the Vag, more influential than the Varaxx:. Who knows? They might even have been instrumental in my own ascendancy." He noisily sucked air up his nose, hawking the loose phlegm that had accumulated in his passages. Swallowing hard, Lanz Varaxx prepared to make a difficult admission. "Because she, or should I say we, didn't have children, as was our nuptial agreement, we are without direct heirs. You see, priest, the rumors are true. She prefers the company of other women to that of men. Being a sexless nunale you might find that difficult to comprehend, or at least confusing. So ours was a marriage of agreement, of convenience. For me it was power. For her...respectability and of course, prestige." As if to assuage his ego, he added, "Naturally she permitted me all the dalliances I wished, as long as they proved discreet!" Swallowing hard he switched his conversational demeanor to one of fearful threat. "I have taken you into my confidence, priest. If your tongue wags of this, I will have it ripped out and fed to the swine! And if I'm not around to do it, the Javatt surely will!" Lanz Varaxx savored the bully's mask.

Daag Goraxx trembled in his seat. Terrified drops of urine escaped his clefted mushroom dampening thighs and bragghi. "My lips are sealed," he croaked. The terror had also drained the mucous from his throat.

Shifting to a voice calm and friendly, the Lord continued, "Now my wife has a brood brother to whom she is devoted beyond rational belief..."

"You wish him to be your successor?" a nervous Goraxx interjected.

"No, you fool. His son. My wife's nephew...and mine too, I suppose. She has doted on him since the day of his birth, as though she had conceived him herself His name is Rooz, Rooz Javatt. Currently he serves as an officer here in the Capital. This was the covenant I made with the Javatt when they supported me eight and a half years past...that I, Lanz Varaxx, would honor the Javatt by, in turn, manipulating, yes, manipulating Rooz to the Lordship." The tone had changed, this time to one of exasperation.

Daag Goraxx sat stupefied. Two strides to his front sat the most powerful man in The Vag kowtowed by his wife's family. And through some twisted sense of honor, he was now attempting to engineer an act of dishonorable proportion. In his mind the priest knew he would obey the Lord. No doubt the Code of Laws forbade dealings such as these. But in act and deed he would ignore his oath and perform as directed. His soul was another issue, however, it would harbor contempt for the Lord, hidden from all save his creator. Despising his words, nevertheless, he allowed them to speak. "How shall we do this?" he gasped.

Lanz Varaxx grinned the smugness of conspiracy. He had effectively compromised the highest priest in all the Vag. "Aren't we despicable, Daag?" he laughed. "Laugh with me. Laugh away the guilt so we are rid of it now and forever. For once gone, it will make our task that much easier."

Effecting a half-hearted laugh, more like a snicker, the nunale nodded his compliance, signifying to the Lord that he was aboard for the ride.

"My wife and I have worked this out," cackled the Lord, his mood once again shifting, bordering this time on glee. "Rooz Javatt was born with a birthmark. I've never seen it but Kaara assures me it is formed like a sunburst, perfect in symmetry." Winking to Daag he added, "I don't doubt she's examined every pore on his body. So infatuated is she with him that doubtlessly he'd be the only male body she could become excited about. Eh?" The priest nodded without comment, taking guard not to overplay his interest. "A sunburst, Daag, a sunburst! Sitting permanently below his left armpit. Awaiting interpretation. Awaiting exploitation!"

"I don't understand the significance, I am sorry to say, my Lord."

"The high priest is the sole non-warrior allowed in the Ring of Kilts during the election for the Lordship. It is the priest who officiates the division. It is the impartial priest who calls upon Gala Rotaria to sanctify the result. And you, my dear nunale visionary, will be that priest! You will announce just prior to the division that after days of meditation and prayer in the holiest of temples, you have been given a message from above. And what do you think the content of that message will be?" The Lord licked his lips in anticipation of delivering the final piece of the puzzle.

"I know not," lied the nunale, though he had already figured it out. "Please continue."

"You, in your finest priestly robes, shall proclaim to every kilt present that the spirits have indicated that the new Lord will bear the sign of the sun!"

A beaming Lanz Varaxx elevated his arms, stretching hands and fingers to the vaulted ceiling. Jumping from his chair, he came around the table to Daag Goraxx and energetically pulled him to his feet. "Well, what do you think? Is it not divinely inspired?"

"Brilliant, my Lord, brilliant. But..."

"But what?" A scowl transformed his huge face.

"Well, it is foolproof I believe, however, we can't be too obvious, too definitive. When the supernatural speak, it is in more cryptic terms, my Lord. A *sign of the sun* is so precise that when Rooz steps forward to display his birthmarked sun, someone might smell something rotten, and I refer not to his armpit. Think of it, my Lord. Is it not too neatly packaged? So neat it might provoke a skeptic's response?"

"Well, priest, then what would you suggest'

"If I said, the spirits will only be pleased by a Lord who *Bears a mark of the sky,* then Rooz can come forward with bewildered face and say,"I believe I carry such a mark." Then he'll remove his tunic and I'll gasp. And every superstitious kilt will make the connection and divide in his favor." Daag Goraxx looked up into his approving Lord's eyes. "Of course, the idea was all yours, I've simply improved it by a tiny margin."

"It's wonderful. A mark of the sky! So be it!" The Lord slapped Daag's round shoulders with a loud thwack, the force of his palm causing the nunale to clutch the table for support. "And, Daag..."

"Yes, my Lord?"

"You can inform your College of Priests that you have persuaded the great Lord Varaxx to finance a splendid commission. A temple frieze celebrating our divine Goddess' propensity to anoint her favorites with..."

"With special signs," chimed the chief priest. Completing the sentence served to confirm to Lord Varaxx that gee followed his intent to lay the groundwork for future persuasions.

"Precisely."

Soft mist floated in the morning air greeting Marz Kavoyy's exit from the Lord's residence. Unfastening the rolled slicker, he pushed his arms through the sleeves and descended the stairs and on to the concourse. What had promised to be a sun filled day, had deteriorated to gray overcast perhaps matching the bleak scheme he had just witnessed. His knowledge of the plot, he realized, could put him in jeopardy should he carelessly share the details with others than the most trustworthy.

Blending in with pedestrian traffic traipsing the cobbled avenue, he would make his way to the dispatcher's stable and secure a pony for the return journey to Kavoyy Station; but not before he had emptied a breakfast bowl of sausages and grilled bread. And fruit too, he thought, to cleanse teeth and gums. Nothing like the crunchy pulp of an apple to scour a filmed mouth staled by sleep. Approaching the Hall of Protectors, he felt the tug of wind. However, there was no breeze evident this day, only mist. Seemingly it propelled him to the tiered platform surrounding the hall. And then it came, a numbing inside his head, driving out the street sounds so nothing remained but sensation, much like a tingle pushing out from deep within the scalp. Without being conscious of his action, he entered the wide granite apron and climbed the platformed steps. Slipping the slicker hood from his head he allowed it to drape upon his shoulders. All energy appeared to desert him, not that he attempted to resist the unseen force-encouraging him through the open portal and down the wide corridor. Inside pungent air hung thick, his nostrils inhaling the fumes of smoldering incense, expelling the musty pall which would otherwise pervade the great hall. The councils were not in chamber this week. Only a few oil lamps lit the cavernous space, their illumination scant, yet causing long shadows to stretch along the far wall, distorted shadows formed by eight stoic statues. He felt small, not only dwarfed by the dimension of the great vault, but by the glass eyed octet whom he couldn't help but sense was examining him. It was as though he were a specimen under observation, their probing gaze attempting to determine his worthiness. And always the eyes, the haunting eyes, dizzying his mind, preventing rational thought, stripping away whatever shred of will he might try to rally. The natural inclination is to oppose such forces, and at first that is what he did, as much reflexive as conscious. But why not allow this experience to continue? Why not yield to the process? What was the harm even if a crystal brain existed behind those eyes of glass? Blood and tissue, not the brittle climax of fired sand, control the senses. Superstition succeeds only because the believer is a willing partner, he thought. But perhaps this was all a dream and he slept yet on the stone bench outside the Lord's chamber. Oh damn it all, enjoy the dream! Let reason be suspended and fancy the voyage...and so he succumbed.

What followed is still somewhat cloudy. No bolt of truth infused his being. No fist of revelation gripped the soul of Marz Kavoyy. Instead his mind drifted to another plane where the mood was one of belonging. A feeling of "here you belong" crept over him. "Here I belong," he spoke aloud. But where was "here?" and then something yet more peculiar took hold of him. A realization, an affirmation of what he had always known, but never felt the desire to articulate, entered his being. *Every so often an ordinary man emerges from the faceless throng to lead his people, to correct the misdeeds and neglect of the past, to raise the future welfare of his people. Had this not been self evident*, he thought? And suddenly the fog which dulled his mind lifted, freeing him to act. "IT IS MINE TO SEEK," he announced as much to himself as the eight motionless Lords carved in purest marble. Frozen in motion, none confirmed his conclusion. He wheeled around, conscious that perhaps someone among the living had witnessed his proclamation, cryptic though it might have been. Flushed with embarrassment, he moved across the polished floor searching to detect if ears of skin and cartilage had listened with amusement to the ravings of a sixteen year old stable hand. Fortunately be was alone, his lunacy yet a secret, he mocked himself.

"It is mine to seek." This time he whispered it under his breath. "Am I to believe I am special, empowered, nay challenged by the Protectors to seek a destiny as lofty as their own? Or is this the inspiration of my own creation, convenienced by the presence of chiseled images decorated with eyes of glass?" Through the ages motivation has planted it's sperm in the souls of those who wish to dare, and in doing, every symbol, every spark is embraced to fulfill the calling.

# CHAPTER III

Mounting the public podium, the white robed priest half waved to the gathering crowd. Tradition had it that from that spot polished orators and bumbling novices could speak their mind without fear of retaliation. So in a way the podium pedestal represented a sanctuary closely guaranteeing free speech. Topics ranged the gamut of civil complaint from chilly water at the municipal bath to untethered dogs roaming back alleys. Very rarely was the subject matter profound. This noonday's audience included many strangers to the Capital, disciples of the nunale about to deliver a message that would buoy their beliefs, while shocking those curious citizens who paused to listen. Over the centuries various religious sects, all under the canopy of Gala Rotaria, surfaced to espouse a return to the *morality of our ancestors*. And after creating but a pimple on the public conscience they would disappear without distinction. As a general rule, the sects originated in the parched deep-south where the 'wild country' borders the great Gugububu Desert. Speculation had it that the blistering sun of that region addled the brains of locals, making them susceptible to radical overture.

Recognizing individual cultists with nods and finger pointing, the priest awaited the hum to subside. Gee was both tall and slim for the nunale gender, approaching the size of an adult woman. Even the facial appearance was non-nunine, with extended chin and aquiline nose. The eyes, deep-set and shadowed, projected a muted hue like that of yellow-brown mud. A brilliant tan surrounded the face, contrasting a jumbled row of crooked, white teeth seated behind full lips. Shaved tight to the skin, the bronze dome shone radiantly in the Capital sun, like a beacon summoning ger cultists to chant the name of Huug Taratt.

"Taratt, Taratt, Taratt." Rhythmic hand clapping accompanied the repetition, attracting a growing number of passers-by to the square. Among the followers were people of every gender, most middle-aged, all under the hypnotic sway of Huug Taratt. About forty had made the long trek to the city ostensibly to spread their doctrine, in hope of recruiting new members.

With arms lifted to the autumnal sky, the priest allowed a warm sun to flood the strange face, channeling a swath of golden light inward, inviting the rays to infuse ger spirit, absorbing their energy. Throughout the exercise, the chant carried on. "Taratt, Taratt, Taratt." Standing motionless Huug

Taratt squinted deeply, then shuddered as though a solar force had entered inside and was now co-mingling with the vitality already residing there. To the believers it was a signal that gee had received a divine strength to purify The Vag and its people, to steer them on a mission ordained by the Great Goddess. Reacting to the spasm, the chant grew louder, more frenzied. "Taratt, Taratt, Taratt." Savoring the drama, the gaunt priest gestured left and right emitting a feeling of both benevolence and superiority. Working a crowd came naturally.

Huug Taratt had always harbored a rebellious nature. Recognized at an early age to possess a brilliant mind, the young student was often seen arguing with scholars of the academy, always taking an extreme position. For Huug every issue had a hypothetical explanation contrary to conventional belief... which in itself is not necessarily bad for traditional wisdoms need to be re-examined periodically and, where warranted, challenged by new ideas. But for the unyielding Taratt issues and personal aggrandizement became intertwined. And having alienated fellow scientists to the point where ger presence became unwelcome, the priest abandoned the Capital in exchange for a more aesthetic life in the wild country. Where one could develop "personal philosophies." And now, twelve years following the self-imposed exile, Huug Taratt had returned on the wings of religious zeal. Today would be a test of Huug's ability to reach beyond the impressionable 'unwashed.' To extend ger influence beyond the primitive down country. Something bold would be advanced this day, a proposition so extreme as to shake the very foundation of the temple itself. Over the years Taratt had learned that controversy strikes fear in the hearts of the timid. And once fearful, the timid have two options, to resist or obey. The priest would skim the obedient into ger fold and lead them to what Huug called *spiritual compliance*. However, in order to set the scheme in motion, Taratt first required an enemy against whom the nunale could wield the most lethal of power...a scapegoat to destroy in the name of righteousness. An enemy void of strength, defenseless as sheep in a pen with no ability to lash back.

For thirty-five minutes Huug Taratt assailed the moral abyss into which the nation had fallen. Citing examples of pervasive misconduct, the priest preached the coming of a great catastrophe should the Vaghi not mend their ways. The message scrupulously avoided love. Instead gee wove parables dealing with extreme behavior and harsh punishment invoking the wrath of Gala Rotaria. She would "damn the families of those who had strayed from the religion of our early fathers," gee threatened. Taratt transformed what had been a giving, motherly goddess to one of vindictiveness, one who demanded the severest of penalties. "I am but a prophet," Taratt declared. "A humble messenger of the Goddess. No doubt some of you will curse me for the message I carry. But I am willing to suffer the scorn, to withstand the abuse. And you loyal people who follow my path to Gala Rotaria will evermore be known as her *Chosen.*" Huug Taratt removed a small drawstring bag from the folds within ger robe and held it aloft for all to view. "A return to the old ways of correctness, the basic values of our ancestors, that is what I preach, my children. And to symbolize our acceptance of all I have said, to proclaim one and all that we are The Chosen, let us anoint our faces with the most basic of Gala Rotaria's gifts." Unknotting the sack, gee poured a thin stream of white powder into ger free hand. "Flour," gee announced. "The most basic of foods which nourishes us all." And with that Huug Taratt wiped the hand across ger forehead, smearing it over the perspiration where it caked and clotted like some bizarre cosmetic. Taking cue The Chosen acted likewise, coating their faces with a paste of flour and sweat. Alertly, they had already identified those spellbound citizens who had reacted with avid interest to Huug's sermon, and now offered them what amounted to a baptism of flour. Once marked they would represent a most recruitable lot.

"Bless you all," the priest boomed. "Bless The Chosen."

This prompted the chalk faces to pick up a new chant. This time it came out like more of a cheer. "Blessed The Chosen. Blessed The Chosen," they boomed, the echoes vibrating throughout the square.

Huug Taratt extended a flat palm to the followers, hushing their enthusiasm. Now that they were whipped up, gee would advance a most drastic overture. Even Huug was unsure of how those in the audience who had not made the trip north would react. "Appeasement, my children. Appeasement. How to appease the great mother Gala Rotaria for the sins of our generation...and, yes, recent generations past? The Goddess herself has answered my query with a solution of absolute brilliance. It permits us to rip out a blight that stains our very existence while offering the most basic of sacrifice. For true contrition can be achieved only through the spilling of blood. The sacrifice of life!" Those not of The Chosen remained unmoved. There was nothing new here. Animals, especially sheep, had always been ritually slain on holy days, their blood offered to the spirit world in gratitude or atonement depending on the nature of the occasion. Another few carcasses on the slab wouldn't make the ceremony any more dramatic. Huug Taratt continued. "My studies of the ancient allow me, with the inspiration of our grand matriarch, to have visions of the past. Revealed to me are many aspects of the holy rituals practiced long ago. I know for certain it was the custom to take those born of deformity, with hideous features too grotesque to bear, and return them to the blackness from whence they came. Offspring mutilated of limb and brain, too malformed to grip a spoon or recognize a song, were silenced at once, sacrificed with a swift chop to the neck, a slit to the tender throat. And the blood would enter a soil that is the womb of Gala Rotaria. The very same soil from which wheat and fruit and all life springs. Indeed the vast green garden which is The Vag grew rich and prospered...unlike the present. Have not we noticed these last two harvests that the yield has shrunk, the grape lacking in juice?" It was true. The output had been small by comparison. But it had been attributed to less than normal rainfalls which were cyclical, or so it was assumed. Regardless, it gave the average Vag in the street pause to consider. But what was Taratt getting at with all this talk of the ancients and their deformed offspring? Could gee be suggesting the unthinkable? "No longer do we return these miscreants to the soil, back to the Goddess. And so little by little the land grows arid, abandoned by its protectoress. The Goddess and land are one in the same, yearning to drink the sacrificial libation of purest kind. That is why mutants are created. That is their role! Why else would they exist? Why so their purpose? I'll tell you why. They exist for sacrifice!" Many in the throng were dumbstruck, unable to voice disgust. In some instances, though, the seeds of agreement were taking hold.

To the rear of the crowd, two men in long, hooded robes listened intently. The shorter of the two commented to his companion, "I smell the stench of evil in this one."

"Let ger stink continue," voiced the other. "Repulsed as I might be, the more gee babbles, the greater my amusement. In a way this makes for entertaining theater...and perhaps an opportunity to make hay."

Huug Taratt's eyes traversed the multitude. They burned with the zealot's fervor, staring wildly at any who might resist the passion of ger logic. "And there at Arabella they await their purpose, my people. We are taught that they are the Children of Misfortune. Hah, I think not! Creatures of the Underworld would be more apt. Condemned by goddess before drawing a first breath, denounced by our kind at first sight, sentenced to an existence without purpose, they are coddled at Arabella, rewarded for their deviant form, their incoherent idiocy! Left on their own they would perish of self-neglect. Unable to cope with the most primitive of requirements they would wither into the dust trickling down to the depths of the netherworld. But instead of allowing them to expire, a misdirected few defy the grand design of Gala Rotaria by nurturing the infantile beasts. Accordingly they grow, swollen in their ugliness, to adult monsters, blinking, drooling, stumbling unaware of their own existence. Dispatch them now, the Goddess beseeches us, and quickly so, in order that she will be placated! In order that she may deliver them to the bowels of limbo! Aye, slay them all at once. Gush their blood like a crimson cascade, and I promise you that with so bountiful a vintage the sweetness of Gala Rotaria will rain her pleasure upon the fields and orchards, among the flocks and herds. Permit them to endure and her wrath will bring desolation to us all!" Huug Taratt had worked genself into a lathery sweat. Floured rivulets ran down the bronze cheeks, hanging in driplets along the jawbone.

The Chosen heeded the call for sacrifice with shouts of, "Slay them! Death to the beasts!" and "On to Arabella." However, the great majority, those not of The Chosen, screamed their disgust, booing and hissing. Shoving matches ensued. A few fists found their targets, sending adherents from both sides sprawling onto the stone pavement. At this point a small contingent of the city guard swept in, using their shields to push apart the hostile factions. Order restored, the priest prepared to renew the attack.

"Huug Taratt," a voice boomed , resonating above the quieting bedlam. The tall, robed onlooker stepped forward, pushing the hood back revealing the face familiar to all. Silence prevailed. "Huug Taratt. You are an abomination to every Vag proud to be identified by that magnificent title. You and your putrid mouth have dared encourage Vag to slay Vag!! That in itself is heresy not only for the dastardly act it incites but in usurping the Lord of The Vag. For only I have such power. It is not yours to wield or even insinuate, you sunbaked, flour stained rodent!" Lanz Varaxx exuded his most scornful scowl and in doing, searched the mute audience for a glimmer of defiance. Every eye cast its look downward, not wishing to inadvertently infuriate the Lord. Even the anti-Taratt citizens glanced away in fear of being misinterpreted. "Leave these walls. Take your pack of fleas with you, and let me never hear word of your obscene solution again! Have you understood me?" he challenged.

A shaken Huug Taratt sought to save face...at least among the watchful followers. Gee bowed slightly in deference to the Lord who now worked his way through the gathering, closer to the venomous priest. In Lanz Varaxx's wake his smallish companion trailed, electing to leave the hood intact. Playing to the crowd, Taratt spoke, feigning a wrongful hurt, confused by the Lord's harangue. "But my Lord, here on the public podium am I not permitted to speak my mind with impunity? Is this not my right as a citizen of The Vag?"

The Lord recognized Taratt's game playing and decided for the moment to humor the posturing nunale. "True, priest, you make a valid point."

Gaining confidence, Huug Taratt attempted to recapture a semblance of respect. "And so I stand before you, a free Vag, expounding a position which the goddess herself delivered to my soul. I stand without fear knowing that on this hallowed spot I will not be punished for asserting my ancient privilege. Is this not my right, my Lord?" The priest knew gee was leaning perilously close to antagonizing the absolute master of their world, yet gee continued to flirt with the dire penalties such actions invite. "Is it not my right?" Taratt again baited the patience of the Lord. Perhaps, Huug reasoned, gee had overestimated the forcefulness of the Lord. Maybe rumors of a wine sodden brain were valid. Possibly the whispers of a man unable to think on his feet were well-grounded.

Lanz Varaxx did possess a reputation for avoiding matters of governance, preferring involvement in things of less consequence. Nevertheless, he harbored a fierce ownership of the Lordship and the preservation of its power. Irrespective of the issue at hand, that is the liquidation of the Children of Misfortune, the Lord of The Vag would never tolerate insolence. Especially among so many witnesses. The majesty of both man and office had to be re-confirmed from time to time. Today's episode presented a splendid opportunity to do just that. "True, Taratt. It is your right," he conceded. "But eventually you must vacate your perch. And if your impudence pushes me but one micro digit more, I shall plunge you into a dungeon so deep the brightest spot in all that darkness will be the ring that is your rectum. Is this not my right as your Lord? And as for your misguided band of scum, if they go near the Children of Misfortune, I shall deliver them to the Ravenhood of Jarra for archery practice. Targets to leak the blood you so eagerly wish to suck from the innocent. Is this not also my right as your Lord?" The easy smile of Lanz Varaxx belied the seething hostility inside. The unmistakable brutality of his response left no margin for misinterpretation. "Now I suggest you and your dough-faced friends slink from the Capital within the hour.

And from this instant hence, know that you are banished to that region we call the wild country. Am I understood, Huug Taratt? I command an answer!"

The return came out weakly, a squeak. "Yes."

"What?" roared the Lord.

"Yes, my Lord Varaxx."

Riding the powerful rebuke administered by Varaxx, his companion lowered ger own hood exposing the moon-faced presence of Daag Goraxx. Steeled by the supreme glow of the Lord, the keeper of the temple jabbed a pudgy finger at the cowering Taratt. "You are also stripped of your priestly sacrament," gee informed. "With no authority to conduct holy services or any administrative function. Furthermore, I declare you a false prophet. You have shamed those of us who worship the benevolence of Gala Rotaria by blaspheming her very nature. And as fitting result, you have been vilified and proscribed by our good Lord. Now leave this place understanding you have earned the contempt of me and every priest in the land."

Pleased with his handling of the situation, Lanz Varaxx walked slowly from the square, the cheers of his fellow citizens filling his ears. Moments like these thrilled the very fabric of his being. Word would spread rapidly of his actions. Object lesson such as Huug Taratt's banishment would weaken the resolve of those who might consider future resistance of the Lord's will. Lost in most of this was the awareness that he had preempted a tragedy in the bud, trampled a small fire before it could mature to a holocaust. Basking in the afterglow, the two Vaghi made their way through the quadrant acknowledging the smiling nods of approving countrymen.

It was Daag Goraxx who spoke first. "Well done, my Lord. At the risk of blowing the sycophant's horn, I must say you were magnificent in your rebuke."

"Yes, I did crush that pimple of an upstart, didn't I?"

"Beyond question. There now remains but a quivering puddle of ashes where once stood the fieriest of nunales."

Without acknowledging the bouquet Goraxx had tossed his way, the Lord loosened the commoner's robe which had provided a spectator's anonymity minutes earlier. As he shucked it, he contemplated the specter of Huug Taratt, mulling in his mind whether to have gen watched. "The priest...er ex-priest, is gee predictable?

"About half the time, I would think."

"About half the time? What do you mean? Is that not in itself a contradiction?"

"I mean Taratt is about as predictable as unpredictable."

"So then, that means that Taratt is not predictable."

"I guess so, my Lord."

"Hmmmmm."

So a day of minor triumph closed on a note of peculiar exchange. For the Lord was inconsistent in things of depth.

# CHAPTER IV

A shepherd boy's pan flute played an eerie tune, sometimes melodic but more often a series of random notes drifting through the emerald vale. Soothing sound assured the flock that a secure force watched close by. It also served warning to feral wolf dogs of a human presence. High pitched and haunting the echoes survived over long distance, all the way to a rock strewn hillock upon which the rider enjoyed a late morning breakfast, as did his pony. The rugged little horse grazed on juicy tufts of weeds and grass. The horseman gnawed hungrily upon a chunk of blue-veined cheese and dark bread, the kind laced with chunks of cured brown olives. Listening to the strains he paused to gaze at the woolly mass wobbling along a narrow swale. The herd boy slowly stepped behind, the instrument never leaving his lips. A small dog, much like Varo's, guided his bleating charge across the valley floor, allowing the boy to work the flute without concern.

The unending refrain encouraged the diner to develop his thoughts, to extract allegory from the scene below. "One beast's comfort is another's alarm," he mused. "But ironically the shepherd will one day slaughter the trusting lambs so others could eat the roasted flesh." Marz's head bobbed slowly confirming his own reflection. "A lesson to remember," he told himself Indeed, yesterday's exposure to the reality of politics had left an impression deep and stimulating. The long ride home had given him time to dwell on the Lord's intimidation of Daag Goraxx. To contemplate their conspiracy and how it would impact The Vag. It had been an education in raw power. Marz Kavoyy had looked into the bowels of corruption...and it had stunk! Webs of doubt spun within his young head. Respect for a system gone awry would have to be rethought. Equally troubling had been the Lord's refusal to take seriously the issue of Kala spear-sticks. Had his breakneck ride been for naught, a futile message fallen on pompous ears? Truly he had learned something about the motivation of men in their quest for supremacy, about ego and its drug-like control. Disdaining the most obvious call for common sense, the Lord had chosen the trail of contempt, opting for a show of invincibility in lieu of careful measure.

And then there were the rustlings in his own head pushing him to seek the uppermost of goals. In some ways the trip home had been more exciting than the ride to the Capital. Marz Kavoyy had examined the future and the part he wished to play.

Washing down the final crusts with a swig from his canteen, he remounted. Slapping his stirruped heels into the pony's hide he pushed on to the next relay station with troubled meditations yet rumbling inside.

Meandering along an indirect route, at a pace counter to the hell-for-leather ride several days earlier, he permitted the pony to pick its way along the gravel road. Sensing no urgency to his master's journey the pony paused at random to munch on sprigs of sweet grass sprouting along the shoulders and embankments. It gave him time to think again the same thoughts which had buzzed within all day. He reviewed the whirlwind events experienced at the Capital, mulling those leaders who controlled the nation's fate. Dissecting their personalities he projected himself into their roles, testing his own attitudes, analyzing and planning appropriate action, formulating little speeches. Occasionally he'd have to reel in his more extreme ideas, tempering them with a wisdom he had yet to learn, encouraging a more evenhanded response. He convinced himself that his playacting was not an idle dream but a discipline. Training, he reasoned, preparation for the unknown, for eventualities yet to be unwound...if ever.

As the course began its uphill slant the youth eased out of the sweaty saddle and slid into a walk, sparing his mount during the tedious climb to the high ground. Reins in hand he led the way with fleeting images of the Hall of Protectors dancing behind his golden eyes. Periodically he'd nod approval or grunt dissatisfaction with a particular deliberation, but otherwise he remained expressionless, his face revealing no emotion. It was to remain that way for the rest of the day as the two figures plodded upward to the green hills.

Half way to trek's end he arrived at Midpoint Station. A spirited station master peppered him with questions of the Capital and General Povezz. Like a proud uncle Varo slapped his thigh at every highlight. Of course Marz said nothing of those things which were 'dangerous'. But he did inform him that he had met the great Lord himself, and watched with delight as the old man howled with glee. Begging his guest to spend the remainder of the day and night at Midpoint, Varo pretended a pained disappointment when Marz told him he would have to push on. The old timer mentioned he had sent word to Gurz that his son had lugged the courier pouch to the Capital and would be days late in his return, an act for which Marz thanked him repeatedly. In all the excitement he had not thought about how his absence would worry his family. Before departing Marz promised to keep

Varo apprised of how he was progressing by using the courier system freely available to them. After much back slapping and embraces of friendship Marz Kavoyy hauled his frame into the saddle and trotted north, an ample wad of mutton jerky bulging under his tunic.

As he watched horse and rider melt into the horizon, the smile of an idea grew across the tanned face. Moving quickly into his cabin he walked to his bunk and slid out the wooden locker box beneath the bed frame. Lifting the lid he removed the most prized possession of his sixty-eight years. Unwrapping the faded orange cloth he held the object aloft, stretching it to the ceiling. Testing its heft he slipped the sheath from blade and yipped a playful little sound. The master of Midpoint Station stabbed the air repeatedly, the unmistakable glint of steel catching the windowed light. "By the ten fingers," he roared. "By the bloody ten fingers!" He twisted the sword, jiggling the shank so it dazzled in the sun's glow like a hundred mirrors. The pleasured satisfaction of knowing a torch of sorts would be passed on to a fitting bearer rippled through the eyes of Varo Rokazz. Aye, the old man had found an heir.

"Marz, Marz," she whooped. Tyrra had been the first to see him and she announced his arrival with particular enthusiasm.

"Good evening, brood sister," he smiled through dusty lips.

"Why do you walk your pony when he is perfectly capable of bearing even a rider as clumsy as you?" she teased through flashing white teeth. The excitement in her gold flecked eyes matched his in every respect.

"Because my arse is as rough as the Gugububu. Too many hard hours in the service of the great Lord himself will do that even to the halest of warriors." He feigned importance, encouraging her jibes. They hugged with the special caring that comes from the brood sibling bond.

"Warrior? I see no kilt hugging that roughworn arse, my brood sib." Breaking their embrace Tyrra Kavoyy threw an arm about his wide shoulders and escorted him to the corral. "But you must tell me every detail of your great mission." The thrill of sharing his adventure could not be contained by Tyrra. Genther Zoog would be equally enthralled, for when one of the brood experienced something unique they all felt the glory...or the shame if that be so.

Together they unsaddled the pony and turned him loose to water at the huge trough hollowed by their father years earlier from a single tree trunk. "I'll tell everyone about it at dinner so I won't have to repeat it over and over. You know how much I detest talking about myself, Tyrra?" Rolling back his handsome head he cupped his palms about his mouth and hooted at the sky, mocking his words. She joined in, cawing until the station echoed like a rookery gone mad. Skipping to the stone house they rejoiced in their own silliness. Inside the door Zoog greeted them with a happy grin. The brood complete, gee reached out for the brother high-stepping through the entrance. Though gee hadn't the foggiest notion as to why they were laughing, Zoog immediately became swept up in the mirth. Within seconds the three were giggling noisily as they danced about the clay tile floor.

Catching sight of his mother's loving face, he lifted her with a great hug and reeled her about the kitchen table, her feet never touching the tiles. The protests escaping her lips were halfhearted at best and Marz knew it. Shaara Kavoyy, enjoying the affection of the moment, signaled her happiness with a high pitched bird sound of her own, shrill and long, to the delight of her prime brood. "All-right, all-right, enough" she calmly said attempting to recapture adult reserve. Eyes yet sparkling she pushed gently, prevailing upon the strapping son to release her. Within minutes Gurz arrived with the younger brood. Siblings Zaara and Borz, spying their big brother, immediately rushed to shower him with embraces and kisses. They had been gathering mushrooms in the small forest west of the station. The young twins, following the others' example, howled amid a fresh round of raucous prancing. Amused, Gurz Kavoyy mouthed a noiseless chuckle and slowly shook his head at a family gone daffy.

The delicious aroma of lamb stew had eluded Marz during the clamor but once the fun had subsided his nostrils filled with the hearty essence of sweet meat, onions, celery and the tangy carrots for which the northern Vag is noted. As the thick gruel simmered, Shaara rinsed the fresh picked mushrooms and sliced a generous quantity into the cooking pot. By the time Marz had scrubbed the last stubborn traces of road dirt from face and hands, supper awaited. Wooden spoons fed the stew into hungry mouths along with a kind of polenta made from wheat and oats. Bread, baked that very afternoon, sopped up the remnant gravy, scouring bowls to the glaze. A dessert of plump grapes found its way to the table, the seeds dropped into the empty dinner bowls, a politeness insisted by Shaara. And through it all Marz fascinated them with his tale of adventure. Commencing with instructions from the North Camp commander, he told of the reckless ride, "more like a charge," he related, and of his new found camaraderie with Varo, pausing to pass along the station master's fond salutations. And his presence with the mighty Lord as well as General Povezz. He spoke of every detail, of each compliment thrown his way...cocky in the telling. He informed them of how the two powerful Vaghi differed in their analysis of the Kala spear sticks, and how the general had recognized Marz's difficult ride remembering to have him fed. Laughingly he added the Lord's habit of spitting olive pits into the hot brazier. To the delight of the avid Kavoyy listeners, he demonstrated using grape seeds which he spat the distance to a bowl placed on the floor. A description of their stature, clothing, hair, wrinkles, jewelry, everything followed. Everything that is except the discussion overheard between Lord and high priest. That information he would hold for more private discussion. Nevertheless the evening had been a splendid family gathering. As they broke from the table to while away an hour or so before bedtime, Shaara indicated with her eyes a desire to have words with Tyrra and Marz. Moving to her side the two awaited, unaware of what was to follow.

"I want to make it clear that I don't approve of your coarse language. You set a poor example for the little ones as well as offending the ears of your mother." The voice was firm.

"What coarse language is that?" the oldest daughter inquired, having no idea of her mother's rebuke.

"Arse!" she stated, wagging a chastising finger. "I heard you two all the way in the kitchen. When one has to resort to profanity for expression, it displays a mind too weak to draw on a proper vocabulary. Civility is a virtue which I wish you would hold dear, not only as a sign of courtesy for me, but your personal respect for each other."

"Yes, mother," Tyrra responded, her eyes lowered.

"Yes, mother," Marz answered in like style.

As they departed, an impish Zoog pointed a teasing finger, no doubt relieved ger own rough words had escaped detection.

Purple streaks yet clung to the western horizon as Gurz made his final livestock check and secured the stable gates. Seeing his opportunity, Marz trailed his father outside and offered to accompany him on his rounds. The elder Kavoyy, aware of his son's need to talk, made it easy by pausing to admire the painted sky, his elbows propped upon a fence rail. Together they enjoyed the final translucent whispers piercing the skyline. "Speak, my son. Is something troubling you?" The invitation was soft and comforting. The kind one wouldn't expect from a man rugged as the land which gave him breath.

It came out quickly. How Lord and priest had plotted to control the next election, distant as that might be. He related the shock he felt that great men trusted by the faithful mass of Vaghi citizens would manipulate and deceive to achieve a dishonorable end.

Gurz acted neither outraged nor indifferent. His was not a life of naive experience. Before settling down to run the family station he had worn the kilt, wielded the stout sword during the Kala wars with a ferocity equal to any warrior of The Vag. And wishing to seek a star beyond Kavoyy Station, he visited Mount Aryxx and the sages who dwell upon its flanks. Two years he spent among the wise, learning the psychology of people and why they act the way they do. He listened and asked questions. And listened some more. The star he had sought never came clear to him. Gurz had hoped to find it written in the heavens above Aryxx. Instead he became soured on the shallowness of mankind. And so he abandoned his quest, opting instead for a hardy life filled with simple pleasures. "I had not the will to entangle myself in the slime of Capital muck," he had declared. Now he found himself educating his son, sharing a brief knowledge of what drives the driven. "Once a man drinks the sweet wine of power it is difficult to resist its intoxication. Having tasted it, all that matters is its preservation. For some it is preserved via a so called link with immortality, the passing of power to a next generation : offspring, cousin, clansman or however one wishes to interpret 'link.' Ethics, if they were there in the beginning, usually give way to expedience. Dynasties and controlled legacies fly on the unworthiest of wings. Our nation has suffered the haughty behavior of a handful of elite families. We despise the system, yet each time the division is effected, the baton passes to a name connected to the last. Dynasties are conceived, nay perpetrated by parties self convinced that only their family can pilot The Vag. And so the system is subverted by bribes and other corruptions. Necessary evils are justified on the pretext that the nation 'benefits' from their superior leadership. Marz, be assured of this. Theirs is an attitude born of arrogance! And it is as true in the cities and villages as the national seat." All this Gurz Kavoyy told his son.

Lips pushed tightly together, Marz absorbed the lesson well. It would be a lecture to be revisited when circumstances demanded a need to weigh the motives of kin and stranger alike.

The next discussion was an extension of the last, making it easier for the young man to segue into it without a stumble. Hours in the saddle had given him time to rehearse. "Father, I believe that I, Marz Kavoyy, am destined to occupy the Lord's seat. That I one day will rule The Vag. Voices deep inside compel me to seek the leadership when that rare moment is presented. Spirits float within my head encouraging me to prepare for the marble throne." His golden eyes sparkled brilliantly in the departing light as if to project his thoughts onto Gurz's mind. With an economy of words Marz continued, telling of the mystical force he had experienced in the Hall of Protectors, and how the ride home had been a journey of contemplation feeding his soul all the more. "And now, father, I need your counsel."

Without surprise Gurz Kavoyy extended his arms and gripped the youth's shoulders. Looking deeply into his pupils, his own squinted causing wrinkles to collect at the corners. The younger Kavoyy returned the look, searching for a sign of whatever was to come...ridicule or support? Gurz had always understood the personal compulsions which drove his son because he had experienced some of the same, though not so lofty. But Marz also possessed an unshakable confidence along with his striking physical appearance and athletic skills. And this set him apart from the pack. Had not Marz been blessed with these traits, Gurz might have bolted at Marz's revelation.

"Marz, ours is not a family of wealth or influence. Nor of conspiracy and secrets. The humble blood of the Kavoyy has never known a regal moment though it is of noble character. The bond of the Kavoyy is one of duty...and soul. That alone, I am afraid, will qualify you for little in the politics of the Capital. If you are to successfully capture an ambitious destiny, one of the highest order, you must commence laying the foundation now." Their noses were no more than a hand's length apart. Already taller than his father the young man inhaled deeply as if to breathe in Gurz's words. What his father obviously meant was that the name of Kavoyy did not represent a political asset, though not, by any stretch, a liability

Marz had never regarded his father to be particularly eloquent or especially wise for that matter. This evening would change all that. Henceforth, he would view his sire in a new and revered light. Marz could sense the energy of deliberate thought being transmitted along the arm bridge connecting them. It surged into the stripling's body and flowed to his memory vault like night wind through a camp fire causing ashen embers to flame, encouraging glowing tongues to lick and rekindle. And so his mind was stimulated to a new awareness. Indeed the next morsel of advice would brand itself for a lifetime, to be plucked again and again in future moments. From this day forward the genesis of every plan would begin with this inspiration. Inflecting a steady tone, the elder Kavoyy enunciated each word, ensuring they would not be forgotten. "Be cunning in preparation without exposing purpose. Be passionate in your pursuit. And always remember that victory is gifted to the bold!" He squeezed the shoulders tightly emphasizing support for his son's venture, knowing full well chances for success were remote, its consequence potentially disastrous.

What son of The Vag had not dreamed of the Lord's marble throne? The children of herdsmen and masons and, yes, station masters, spent many an idle moment staring at summer clouds until the wisps rearranged themselves into warriors and Lords. But Marz Kavoyy was more than a cloud drifter. His was a mature dream driven by a spirit of belief. Vision, not illusion, helped fuel the thoughts of Marz Kavoyy. To believe is to expect, and expectation often is the mother of reality. "And know this, my son. I believe in you just as you believe in yourself. I have always sensed you and your brood siblings own a specialness. And I also am certain that your destinies are interlocked. Of this there is not an arrow of doubt in my quiver! Go forward with my blessing and strive for your future." Each gazed deeply into the other's watery eyes. Emotion contains a power beyond physical resistance. Neither avoided the flow. They hugged tightly, chest to chest, cheek to cheek.

"Thank you, father," Marz whispered. "Your wisdom is something freshly discovered by your son. I know it has always been there. Unfortunately it has taken me some sixteen years to recognize it. Forgive me for ever feeling otherwise."

The words came out tenderly. "Nothing to forgive, my son."

With this single conversation Marz Kavoyy had entered a new compartment of a life yet to be fulfilled. But now his soul felt enriched with a philosophy for action...and the approval of his sire. Already a distant plan was formulating, one that relied upon experience, timing, and of course opportunity. As for now though, he would be content to dig the foundation. Aye, Marz, be cunning in preparation without exposing purpose.

# CHAPTER V

"Poona! Poona will determine if the brood has a calling. She has a gift of palmistry like no other!" Shaara Kavoyy, upon learning her prime brood had grandiose ambitions gathered them and Gurz around the smoothworn table. "But first I want to know if this is of their mind or of yours, Gurz?"

He deliberated a few moments, choosing his words with precision. "I believe I am accurate in saying that for Marz it is his instinct alone, which I support with *my* own. As for Zoog and Tyrra, l must confess we've had little discussion. But you and I have always sensed a unique future for them...in which they now concur. Regardless, I have always been of the opinion that all brood sibs of the triplet kind are blessed above the ordinary. That the genther by virtue of the nunale intellect, whether by accident or divine design, affects that of the other two. The benefits are obvious from early on. Brother and sister speak and think more maturely, more logically, than their counterparts born of a two child brood, Having that advantage serves to convince me all the more to hearten their goals. I speak with conviction, Shaara. I am not a man of convenience." Gurz's and Shaara's union was one of parity, of give and take. Her question was not one of challenge. The intent of her probe was to be certain of everyone's position.

Zoog, from a young age recognized he had the intellectual upper hand on all. Nevertheless, gee treated them with high respect. For gee also realized that they possessed other skills in which gee was deficient. The intangibility of experience represented Zoog's greatest shortfall, notwithstanding the evident physical deficits. Tactfully, gee always avoided a show of superiority. "Mother, I speak for all of us when I say we think ours is a specialness. But in all candor to myself, I must confess a doubt of 'how special?' So perhaps we need Poona to confirm these things." Ever the diplomat, Zoog benignly played to ger mother' s lead.

"And what if Poona snuffs Marz's and Tyrra's dreams like a wickless candle? Will they be content to chase a humble life? If their four palms are maps to nowhere, will they accept the vision? Will they remain close to Kavoyy Station to follow paths as modest as their parents?" Shaara looked about for an answer.

"Why do you speak of them and not of me?"Zoog inquired.

"Because you are a nunale and, therefore, already special. Every nunale is! Your future, your success is already foreshadowed by gender alone. This is not false flattery, my nuun. It is a fact of life."

"But perhaps I wish to be special among nunales. Special among the special!" A cherubic smile lit up the smooth, round face.

"You always have the right answer," she smirked affectionately.

Pushing out from the table, Tyrra's chair squealed along the terra cotta tile as if to trumpet her wish to speak. Tall and athletic, she wore her hair at the same length as her brother. Like Marz, she too enjoyed the long legs of her mother's family. Striking, but not gushingly beautiful, Tyrra claimed a strong mindedness equal to the two sibs seated at her right hand. Small of breast and narrow of hip, her womanhood was just now blossoming. Because she often spoke freely without care to temper her point of view, it was easy to regard her as cheeky. "Mother and father. I don't require the murmurings of a dizzy witch to predict my fortune. But if Zoog and Marz feel it is appropriate to visit her then I will bow to my brood sibs. Regardless of Poona's 'magic' though, I will decide my own course. And the self-determination of Tyrra Kavoyy will prevail...of this I am confident. My aspirations will thrive or die as a result of my perseverance or lack thereof...which I share with you now." She looked from mother to father, and back to mother again to measure the impact of her impending disclosure. For her brood sibs already knew her intent. "I plan to apply to the Ravenhood of Jarra. I will wear the archer's cowl and feather the long bow before any man takes my hand."

Shaara groaned the sigh of lost cause. "As I am painfully aware, Tyrra, the Ravenhood is nothing to be wished for. It is a distinction to be earned. Very few aspire to the 'hood' and less are successful. Two thirds the way through training, my ankle cracked from the persistent stress, a victim of weeks of pounding. It left me expelled! A casualty dismissed without sentiment. On days of dampness it yet limps to remind me, perhaps taunt me, of my non-achievement. There is no margin for failure, daughter. No sympathy. No kindness. Only the command to go home." Shaara slid out her chair with similar squeal and stood to Tyrra's height. "I tell you these things not to dissuade you, for the 'hood' is an honorable calling. It is the single way a female can earn the kilt. The only way womankind is enfranchised with the vote of division." Shaara, it was visible, had not cared to revisit thoughts of her greatest disappointment. Decades later the pain was yet evident. "But I do wish to impress upon you that to be invited to the Ravenhood, to stand in the ranks as a naked recruit in itself is difficult. However, to survive the training cycle, to pass the trial and earn your leather skirt is brutal at best. I'll not agonize you with the details. Some things are best not spoken." Composing herself with a smoothing of the graying hair, Shaara Kavoyy sat again. "I apologize, Tyrra, if I seem to discourage you, but the reality of the 'hood' is by its very nature, one of discouragement. At Jarra they wish only the swiftest of limb, the strongest of heart, the sharpest of eye... and sometimes that is not good enough. Because you still must survive the attrition of ordeal." Reaching across the tabletop, she took Tyrra's hand in her own. "And knowing this, do you wish to proceed?"

"Yes, I do," she whispered hoarsely. The conversation had diluted the strength of her passion.

"Of course. I knew it before I asked," she smiled. "And the three of you, be aware. Poona, if she yet lives, is not a witch, dizzy or otherwise, my dears. She is a hermitess, admittedly an odd one at that. She is kin to my grandmother on my mother's side. And if you approach her with respect, she will honor you. All of you!" Shaara's finger waved a lazy arc lest someone be confused as to the identity of 'all of you.'

"Yes, mother."

"Yes, mother."

"Yes, mother."

⯈━━━━⯈

The little band had ridden the good part of the day, arriving at Midpoint Station before sunset. A delighted Varo eagerly agreed to stable their ponies while they backpacked on foot to Mount Aryxx. But tonight they would be his guests, sleeping around the open hearth like a trio of dogs, or more accurately four inasmuch as Varo's mutt curled up next to their blanket rolls to entreat Tyrra's comforting strokes. For Zoog it had been the most welcome of respites for the bulbous nunale did not sit the saddle well. In deference to ger limitations Marz and Tyrra trotted at a pace slower than normal. The bond that was theirs prohibited any serious complaints though Zoog's bouncing technique did provoke some good natured banter.

Presenting their host with several gifts including salami-like sausage and Shaara's double apple pie, the latter cradled in a basket atop Marz's lap during the trip, the male Kavoyy offered remembrances and greetings from his parents. Following sibling introductions, within the hour Tyrra and Zoog soon shared their brother's fondness for the station master. Delighting in his story-telling, they reciprocated with tales of their own experiences about Kavoyy Station. Talking shop, so to speak, they ate and chatted to near midnight.

The next morning, as the rim of first light glowed the eastern skyline, the prime brood of the family Kavoyy hiked south towards the Pilgrim Trail. Zoog estimated another one hundred sixty medecs to Mount Aryxx, probably seven to nine days depending on the weather. And so they pushed on to the lair of Poona and a glimpse at the future they hoped would have promise. Nights were spent huddled in bedrolls, sheltered behind roofless stone enclosures thrown together by travelers from another age. Evenings when the mist hung wet, Marz would tent the shallow walls with a canvas-like cloth he had brought for just that purpose. Breakfast, comprised of bread staled from the journey and chick peas, was eaten cold. Dinner of an identical fare, improved by brined olives, saw its bounty consumed before the friendliness of a fire. Tyrra carried her mother's tinder box, the ancient steel having been gleaned from a broken steel chisel many years earlier. Though the container included chips of flint, they rarely used them, preferring to summon the spark within using their flint knives. As they progressed Tyrra and Marz would observe landmarks, marrying them to distances. Apparently Zoog did the same in a subconscious way. Seemingly gee always understood them when later they spoke of salient guideposts. Zoog's interests though, were more involved with examining plant life and outcroppings of stratified stone, making comparisons, cataloging data in a memory of boundless capacity.

After several days the path swung west near the sea. A frequency of fords and footbridges indicated their closeness. The wind also picked up confirming the proximity of the goddess' great wetness, the accumulation of countless weepings over the eons. Ascending a hilltop a soft growl greeted them as they looked upon the fury of the great ocean. The waters which flanked the isthmus closer to home, though violent, were less furious than what they beheld this day. Marveling at the mighty spectacle Zoog raised ger arms so the wind filled the sleeves of ger tunic, measuring its force from different angles. Unstopping ger canteen the young nunale allowed the rushing air to engage the orifice, listening to the whistles, testing their pitches. Always curious, ever anxious to learn, Zoog thrilled at discovery.

The shorelines of Gala Rotaria are void of beaches. Tall cliffs, steep and stony, fall off into the frantic surf like the walls of a well. Relentlessly the ocean spanks the unyielding land in a ferocious clash of wills. The sea, always turbulent and loud even beyond the crashing breakers, prevents navigation of any type. It boils without heat, seething and spitting its constant spray. What little there is of a tide-fall is so minimal it goes unnoticed. Many fresh water streams assemble at points close to the sea. There they congregate into magnificent, truncated rivers which blast into the waves without estuaries to ease their force. Stone canyons funnel the voluminous rush directly into the ocean, the process being one more of injection than flow. And the wind huffs so powerfully that very few choose to dwell close-by. Nature's raw energy roars loudest where the thumbs of Gala Rotaria meet. This Zoog Kavoyy witnessed in awe, and with a view towards invention.

"If only we could find a way to harness all this strength," gee mused aloud, "like the power of horses to pull wagons and plows."

"Sometimes, genther," Tyrra teased, "you speak more like a child of misfortune than the next great nunale sage." And wrapping a sisterly arm about Zoog's convex shoulders, she hastened gen to a speedier step where the trail twisted inland.

Before them Mount Aryxx stretched its majestic bulk across the blue autumnal sky. Erupting from the attendant hills it proclaimed to any who cared to observe that as long as Aryxx stood, the great Vag nation would survive. Symbolically the mountain was said to be the breast of Gala Rotaria, its mammary twin elsewhere on the land mass sheltering a mysterious people yet unknown. To the mystics and aesthetes who inhabited Aryxx's slopes it provided spiritual nourishment, suckling them with the milk of inspiration. For two days it loomed ahead of the brood seemingly never getting closer. Earlier that morning, having heard the rush of water they ventured off the path to refill their canteens at its source. A stand of cadnut trees grew within eye shot of the small waterfall from which they drank and washed the dust of a week's travel. Timing being the cousin of opportunity, the strong breeze of the previous night had rattled the branches delivering a windfall of cadnuts. Having munched through their fill of the sweet nut meat, they filled pockets and pouches till they bulged to the seams. Marz spread the tent cloth and swept eight dozen or so upon it, the largest half the size of a fist. Fastening the corners, he slung the makeshift sack over his shoulder and headed the way to Aryxx.

Seven hours later they could finally declare that their boots trod the first incline of the great mountain; however, it would require another five to locate the cave of 'Poona the palmist.' Some of those they asked for directions acted with irritation, their meditations interrupted. But upon realizing the presence of Zoog, they became more considerate, pacified to kindness. Two nunales reached out and reverently touched the brood genther, as if to acknowledge the existence of an invisible halo surrounding gen. They communicated to Zoog a special respect, sensing that this was someone to be honored. Gracious in response, Zoog remained without self-importance.

Her cave was somewhat of an open cabin extending from a cave front. One had to step around the protective stone ring fireplace in order to enter the domicile. By the time the three arrived, the light had dimmed to a soft gray. The cave faced north, the last rays disappearing lazily beyond the inclined horizon. Sitting cross-legged before the ring Poona sipped a tea of bark and dried roots. She fanned the lazy embers causing them to flare, illuminating her intruders. Though she tried, the old woman couldn't make out the faces. "Who are you?" she screeched. "What do you want?"

Taken aback by her visage, their tongues were momentarily unable to respond.

Tyrra spoke. "We are kin, Poona. Here to ask your help in guiding our destinies."

"Kin? I have no kin. Leave me alone." The voice was harsh, her appearance of the kind sorceresses are described. A ragged cape covered her stooped frame, corkscrews of yellowed grey hair dangling from under the hood which shadowed her wrinkled cheeks down to the dented chin. Over the decades Poona's eyes had faded to a weak tint, like old straw. Snagged and worn, the few teeth she still possessed hid behind lips cracked by the mountain winds which prevail Aryxx' s girth.

"Our great grandmother was cousin to you. We are told so by our own mother. The cousin to be remembered claims the family name of Savann. Do you recollect it?"

"Of course I do, deary. It is the same as mine. But I haven't heard it spoken in many years," she croaked. "As to which cousin you refer, I am unclear." Poona's voice cracked, causing her to gulp from the tea bowl.

"Mother said her name was Laara. Laara Savann."

"I don't remember her. And what is your name?"

"Tyrra Kavoyy. And these are my brood sibs, Zoog and Marz." They half bowed as she repeated the names. "We've brought you several gifts."

"Gifts! Oh goody, I love gifts," she cackled.

The three knelt before Poona, Marz dropping the sack on the mat to her side. Zoog appeared not to participate, opting instead to observe the hag's odd behavior. For all her strangeness he felt her to own an uncommon ability. Marz unfastened the knot exposing the cadnuts.

"Cadnuts? What shall I chew them with, sonny? I am almost toothless. These nuts mock me," she complained. Poona eyed the young man, befitting her failing vision. Her scrutiny was purposeful, a test of his patience. Zoog realized it, but before gee could interject a diplomatic offering ger brother swallowed the hook.

"Am I to be chastised for an act of good intent!" he barked. "If you are unhappy, I will gladly gather them up and give them to someone on this mountain who is more grateful." As soon as the last syllable escaped his throat, he knew he had misspoke. Marz had hardly heeded his father's advice.

"Pahhh!" she spit into the fire, and hissed her displeasure.

Immediately Tyrra attempted to placate her with the suggestion that Poona grind the rich nuts into a meal to be added to bread dough or used to thicken soup.

This suggestion she accepted with an unattractive grimace. Shifting her position, Poona ignored Marz and directed her comments to Tyrra's genther. "She has a rare feel that one. I know her kind. If there's a rat about, she'll hear the heartbeat before it stirs a toe. Hee, bee," she giggled. "Like me, only...prettier. Hee, hee." The old hag offered a crooked eye to punctuate her little joke and jabbed the dusty coals until an orange flame lifted. With her free hand she tossed a bundle of broken sticks into the stone ring and pushed them with her cane. At once their dryness was consumed by the hungry fire. The cane served a host of functions. Besides supporting her weakened state, it acted as poker, pointer, weapon and impaler of things to be skewered, a source of security over the many years.

Zoog smiled warmly at the shriveled bone of a woman clinging to the worn cane. Her' s was a wretched existence, but of her own choosing, gee supposed. "Yes, Poona, our sister is one who recognizes only the extremes in life. For her it is always midnight or noon. Dawn and dusk exist only to usher the hours of twelve. And so she is the same about people." Gee laughed calmly, indicating to Tyrra the observation was one of analysis and not uttered in criticism.

Tyrra emitted a tempered smile signaling a reserved approval of the open discussion concerning her personality. From a hard leather case fixed to her tunic belt she removed a piece of soft cloth much like muslin. She unrolled its folds, allowing it to lay flat, exposing four gleaming slices of volcanic glass. "Obsidian blades," she informed. "Sharp as any you'll ever hold. They'll cut or shave like razored steel. We thought you could use them." A flickering from Poona's fire reflected upon the liquid black blades reinforcing their keen image.

"A gift of the ninth finger!" Poona exclaimed with delight. "For these I am truly pleased. And now what can I do for you?"

Marz, feeling excluded from the exchange, saw an opportunity to assert his role. "Poona, beyond the fact that we are brood siblings of the Kavoyy, we believe we are siblings of a special destiny. And so we have trod these many miles from the northernmost reach of The Vag, from the isthmus itself, to Mount Aryxx and you. We wish our palms read with a look to our future."

"Your genther is already special," she said.

"Of that our mother reminded us just two weeks past. But even gee desires a deeper confirmation of how special. For in six months we will begin our training cycle. It is important to us that we approach that day with a better understanding in hand."

Poona pushed the blackened sticks provoking a flurry of sparks. A few crackled to interrupt the silence while she thought. "I don't read palms, anymore," she announced, electing to avoid their eyes.

"Why not, Poona?" Tyrra whispered.

"Because my eyes are good only to search the skies." Again she stabbed the coals. "I am farsighted! Things close are fuzzed like muddied ice. Is it not ironic that the stars are as sharp as the obsidian blades you gifted me yet I cannot see the dirt under my own nails? The lines which streak your palms are invisible. No longer am I able to view those conduits which render one's fate."

"So you cannot help us?" asked Marz, his face a source of anguish.

"What do you think?" She cackled a bizarre little giggle.

"I think we have come many medecs to be thwarted," responded Marz. "Though the fault is not yours." This time diplomacy did not suffer in his frustration.

Looks of despair marked the faces of brother and sister; however, Zoog emitted a perceptive smile, and leaning forward on ger knees gee said, "You toy with us, Poona. You still have the power...but not with your eyes."

"Hee, hee. When the Goddess made the nunale gender she knew exactly what she was doing. Yes, Zoog, I have the power." Poona was enjoying her odd charade, disappointing them, then offering hope. "I really shouldn't be so insensitive. My apologies to all of you. But profit from my lesson. The nunale saw through my little subterfuge. That's why they're ideal for the priesthood. The holiest ones twist emotions just as I did; except they do it on a more cosmic scale, promising damnation in one hand, then offering salvation with the other. Am I not a nasty old girl? Hee hee."

The brood offered a collective laugh, relieved that their palms would be interpreted though not sure how. So they inquired, "How?"

Poona enjoyed their interest. Tonight had been important to her. No one other than her own kind had been permitted to share her fire for more years than she could recollect. "My young guests, be aware that when one sense declines, the others heighten. So it has been with my sight and the palm. Through sensation I am able to feel motion rippling silently through one's lifeline. Through touch I hear the quiet voice of tomorrow as it swims along the stream of duration." She spat into the coals. "Now leave me for an hour to meditate."

Squatting on a flat ledge perhaps seventy strides below Poona's fire, the three awaited her call. It was Zoog who detected Marz's discomfort. "Brother, are you having second doubts?"

"Yes," he answered. "But my doubts do not concern Poona's predictions."

"Then what?"

"Genther and sister, I am distressed about my reluctance to share knowledge of a different sort. I have deceived my siblings, ignored my blood."

"You talk in riddles," Tyrra said. "We are, the three of us, of the same brood, bonded for life."

Marz shifted from squat to sitting position and looked to the starry heavens. From their vantage point on the great mountain, the stars were more multitudinous, more brilliant than he could ever remember seeing. "That is the point. By my silence I have violated the very bond of which you speak. That night I spent in the Capital I witnessed something...uh." Groping for the proper words, he gathered his knees under his chin. "Something so dishonorable that it bothers me to this day, and will continue to do so for the decades to come. The secret I am holding will be shared with you if you insist because our brood bond demands it. But know this, I have avoided disclosure for your own protection. For if you are unaware you cannot divulge. And once divulged your lives could be in peril, siblings, for this reason I would rather you be ignorant of what I have beheld."

Zoog spoke first. "If it is your judgment to carry this burden alone, I believe Tyrra and I should respect it, for as you have indicated, our protection lies in our ignorance. But if at any point the burden becomes too cumbersome to shoulder, enlighten us and each shall carry one-third of its weight. And," gee laughed, "you are hereby granted absolution for your silence." Zoog always had a way of taking the edge off things before they got too maudlin.

"Well put, genther. I have nothing to add other than beyond respect there is also love in this brood, Marz. And it is yours to draw on." Tyrra touched her brother's cheek, letting the warmth of her hand carry the words.

The spell was broken by a shriek from above. "Kavoyy. Come quickly! I haven't the rest of my years to await your presence. Hee, hee."

"Dizzy witch or not," Tyrra snickered. "By the fingers, she sure sounds like one!"

"I will take you in the order of your birth. Which one popped out first?" she shrilled, stifling a giggle. So Tyrra took her place, cross-legged on the ragged mat before Poona. Closing her eyes the wrinkled seeress inhaled deeply and sat motionless, summoning the force within. A full minute or so passed before she released her breath, the air escaping in a low hiss. Lids yet shut Poona groped for Tyrra's hands and locating them she ran the tips of her fingers along the girl's palms. Barely touching the skin she absorbed the energy channeling along the life courses. For several minutes she held herself in trance-like fashion before breaking the spell. Then quickly Poona seized Tyrra by the wrists and clasped the palms to her wizened ears, listening for the hums of prediction. Completing this stage of the ritual, she allowed the fingers to slide slowly along the eyelids, cheeks and finally over the lips before releasing them. Without opening her eyes Poona murmured, "You will be the huntress of the eye. Twice! You will be the huntress of the eye." With that she snapped awake and reached for the bowl of bark tea and slurped a long draught.

"Is that it?" inquired Tyrra, unsure of what it meant.

"Yes," answered Poona, a look of whimsy crossing her face.

Acting a bit flustered, the female Kavoyy asked the obvious. "Huntress of the eye. What does it mean?"

"Twice," corrected Poona.

"Once, twice, what is the meaning? I mean to say, it is too cryptic for me to understand."

"I don't know everything. In time it will make sense to you."

"Will I succeed in my quest to join the Ravenhood of Jarra? Will I..."

"I DON'T KNOW!" Enunciating her reply, she spat a tea-stained wad of phlegm into the fire. The action was meant to signal closure. "Next."

In like manner, Zoog the second born, presented ger palms for examination. The rite was much the same except, in this instance, she smiled as though enjoying the vision, pleased by the augury. "Young nunale," she called. "You are the harbinger of discovery, your soul gifted to The Vag from across the universe. She held onto Zoog's hands, reluctant to surrender the trance, her shriveled head lolling in the reverie. Zoog said nothing, a pleasantness upon ger lips as though gee had been aware of Poona's revelation from the beginning. Once awakened her eyes fixated on the rotund face. "Thank you, Zoog of the Kavoyy, for all you will do."

Gee barely nodded, just enough to acknowledge her recognition.

An anxious Marz knee-walked into position as his genther eased off the mat. Poona drained the bowl, wiping the dregs from her chin with a grubby sleeve. "So now it is your turn, my chesty rooster," she snapped. The chemistry wasn't right between them and Marz feared it would affect the divination. Perhaps she had prejudged him. So far the inferences, the looks, the reactions had been negative. What chance did he have under the weight of her pessimism? She took his wrists, her hands feeling clammy upon his skin. "Perhaps it is the wetness of the tea I feel," he thought. He pushed the idea from his head, concentrating instead on opening his mind to the probes of Poona the prophetess. The fingertips which caressed his palms were rough, rougher than his own. Slowly she began stroking the flats along the grain.

The convulsion which surged her skinny frame was apparent to all three. A series of spasms in fast succession quivered Poona's head, forcing her to release Marz' s wrists. It was as though they had transformed to glowing coals. Laboring to her feet, she looked even more frazzled than that which was her natural appearance. Seizing her cane she hobbled into the hovel. "You I cannot help!" she called back, and shuddered in the act.

Miffed, the young man pursued her into the depths of her cave-hut. "What is it, old woman? What did you see?" he demanded.

"Yours is a prophecy beyond me, Marz Kavoyy. I have not the capacity nor am I empowered to delve the likes of you."

The frustration caused him to cry out, "But what is my fate? Am I to be blind to my calling?"

She turned quickly and touching his tunic she whispered hoarsely, "You already know it! Of this I am certain. Here in the darkness, away from your sibs, I am able to tell you only that. However, you must journey alone to the far side of Aryxx at once, and there seek out the nunale Genu Zig, a sage and oracle above all others."

# CHAPTER VI

Rounding a bend in the spiral trail the tall hiker was startled by the presence of a dumpy nunale setting upon a weather scrubbed boulder. Gray, but without the wrinkles affecting most ger age, the nunale's skin enjoyed a radiant quality like an apple buffed to its hidden luster. Wearing elfin ears and pugged nose, the turnip shaped figure casually sipped from a clay mug. How many years gee had graced the landed expanse of Gala Rotaria it was impossible to determine for gee owned a timeless quality. The traveler sensed this one had to be 'substantial' in age, the latter being as non-committal as he chose to speculate.

"I've been waiting for you," gee greeted.

"For me? How could you know I was coming?"

"Yes, for you, young Kavoyy."

"You know my name? But how? Poona suggested I visit Genu Zig. Are you he?" The questions came rapidly.

"Yes, I am Genu Zig. And to answer your query, much of my time is spent in meditation. And from meditation comes vision. Not the vision of the eye, but of the mind and soul. For lack of a more definitive word, I am what many call a 'mystic', blessed with the gift of charisma. Do you know what that is?"

"No," he admitted, puzzlement stirring his handsome face.

Genu Zig scanned the skyline and beyond. "Charisma is an ability to communicate with the powers of the universe. I wish not to overstate my worth for I am but a humble creature of Gala Rotaria. She and I do not have a dialogue. But I am permitted to summon the past, to see some things that are written in the future, and occasionally to ascertain the vocation in people...especially people like you, Marz Kavoyy!"

"Like me? You know why I've come?" Marz shrugged his shoulders, a skeptic's hope flirting within.

"You feel you are destined for more than the ordinary. Am I correct?" Genu Zig displayed the confidence of knowledge. No doubt etched the placid face.

"True."

"And you desire to know if your instincts are merely the wishful thoughts experienced by most common beings or of a true calling?" The aging sage slid off the perch, the stubby legs stretching for solid ground. Locating firm footing, Genu Zig let the full weight of ger corpulent, little body rest on its heels.

"Exactly, Genu Zig. But it goes beyond the voice inside. For I have been exposed to certain situations which I feel are guideposts toward a life beyond the average, a life which will be…" Marz's mind searched for the proper word, one which would not sound too conceited.

"Heroic?" the nunale offered. "Is that what you want?" Genu's sandals scuffed closer to the young visitor. Resting an elbow on the same boulder upon which gee bad been a fixture, the sage's squinty eyes asked for an answer.

"Yes, I guess so." His response was a halfhearted concession. "Heroic" sounded a bit overbearing, even to Marz.

"I think not," the old nunale chuckled.

Marz felt somewhat trapped. Was Genu Zig testing him? Proffering a word as bait, then yanking it out of reach when the youth snatched for it? "Why do you tease me like a crippled bird in the paws of a cat?" His voice was firm without being offensive.

However, the return came out forceful, almost scolding. "Because you are aware of what stirs in your belly. You already understand what is driving you. Leadership, Marz Kavoyy! Leadership! Yours is the stuff of lords!" Zig's eyes bore into the youth like ribbons of flashing sparks conveying a power to meld with Marz's innermost essence.

Within his skull he felt a vibration, a numb tingle like that which captured him at the Hall of Protectors. It imparted a feeling that he was not alone. Someone else, someone almost supernatural , shared his vision, saw what he saw. In effect it confirmed to him a plane of mutual understanding. "Yes, Genu, yes. That is precisely what I feel. Though I have accomplished little in my stable boy' s life, the essence that is me says, *Stalk the prize which offers itself but once every twenty four years. Plan for that day!*" There was a passion in Marz' s voice that glowed the core of Genu Zig.

"So you know what you want. Good. But do you know why?"

"Well, because I feel compelled by forces which are not totally clear to me."

"Not good enough, my stalker. If you aspire to the Lord's throne only to bag the golden fleece of vanity, to drink the giddying wine of power for the sake of power alone, then you will be no better than that dolt of a Lord who currently rules The Vag."

"You think he is a dolt?" The tone was indignant. For Marz who had been raised to respect the law in all its forms, such thoughts bordered on treason... though he had heard them before. It was one thing to criticize the Lord, he believed, but a far different thing to ridicule him.

Unperturbed the nunale spoke again. "If I might borrow an expression from those salty warriors who defend our fair land. "The fool couldn't drain pee from a scabbard!" Pleased with ger words, a smile crept across the learned one's lips. "Marz Kavoyy, you stand before me inexperienced and unproven, with only the barest inkling of a mission. From this point on you are reborn. Henceforth, all your energy will be focused on capturing the seat of power. But you must have purpose beyond the obvious. Think about what you wish to accomplish for the Vag nation, for its citizens presently and generations still to enjoy the largess of our country's fields and orchards. Think not of how to rule your people but how best to serve them. Such are the deeds which warrant eyes of glass!" Genu Zig's cheeks flushed with fervor. Eyes the cast of pale ocher shone a capacity not only to read the past but to orchestrate events yet blurry on the rim of expectation.

"Tell me, have I been anointed by Gala Rotaria?" Marz eagerly inquired.

"I wouldn't hasten to such an absolute conclusion. Let us say the womb of time favors Marz Kavoyy."

A sense of exhilaration gushed through the visitor, his face unable to contain the surety coursing inside. Genu Zig, visionary of Aryxx, fountain of charisma, had indicated a future of extraordinary proportion. "My family will be pleased," Marz beamed, which was a roundabout way of inferring his personal glee. Swept up in the pronouncement, all modesty departed his young mind. "Perhaps I will be known as Marz the Great, or maybe Kavoyy the Magnificent," he bubbled. "Which do you prefer?"

Though he had said these things in jest, the undercurrent of self-admiration prickled the old nunale. The frown souring Genu Zig's chubby mouth dampened Marz's enthusiasm, drowning the flames of narcissism as swiftly as they had ignited. "Rein in your vanity, young Vag," gee chastised. "Tear it into splinters and drop the kindling lot into a fiery furnace until all vanishes." A scolding finger pointed to a spot between Marz's embarrassed orbs. "The crown of stewardship rests cockeyed on a swelled head! Heed what I say."

A remorseful Marz, cheeks stinging, offered a weak, "Yes, Genu. I meant it only in fun. I apologize to both of us. It is not my true nature to behave juvenile."

Genu Zig rolled ger pudgy shoulders beneath the loose fitting frock. No longer rankled, the huff left ger voice. "Well, you sound contrite," gee conceded. "Perhaps it is better you tooted your arrogance to me now and here before it could damage whatever rationality exists between those stable boy's ears." Shuffling a pair of horsehide sandals on the pebbled trail Genu touched the arm of Marz with a comforting hand. The old wizard thought silently for several moments, calling on the wisdom of the mentor who had schooled gen in the workings of mortal minds. Together the two Vaghi walked to the stone cottage set back from the path. Genu gestured Marz to enter and trailed him inside. The interior was a jumble of unraveled scrolls and instruments of the scientific kind. Peering at the rafters, purposely avoiding Marz' s pupils, the nunale spoke softly in deliberate tones. "He who has a lofty opinion of himself often feels compelled to tell his neighbor how very special he is. However, when one is truly special, the neighbor will tell him. For talent is goddess given. Conceit is self given. And fame is peer given."

Silence prevailed for two or three minutes as a humbled Marz sponged in the impact of a lesson well phrased. "These things I will remember till my mind turns to dust."

"Good. You're making progress already," Genu Zig allowed, and raised ger eyes to meet Marz. "With my help you will acquire a sign of the sky, a symbol which will supply you with proper credentials, my young hunter. For though the Lord's tenure is twenty four years, the cycle can be broken prematurely with an unexpected suddenness. My sense tells me such a possibility is imminent."

A wide eyed Marz gasped. "You know about the mark of the sky?"

"It is more an intuition than knowledge," admitted Genu Zig. "You must speak to me of the details."

For the next few hours Marz told the nunale priest all he could about his birth, his family, everything that he felt would explain himself. Especially vivid was his description of the scheme between the Lord and Daag Goraxx to engineer the ascension Rooz Javatt.

"Yes, now it all makes sense to me," an enlightened Genu Zig smirked. "Lanz Varaxx wishes to guarantee that his extended family will hold the lordship beyond his own term. Having no children he can call his, he now maneuvers his brother-in-law's son onto the seat of succession, enlisting the high priest of Gala Rotaria to falsely anoint the candidate at the most critical of moments. Nepotism gone to the extreme! And he uses the pressures of his wife's corrupt family as a convenient excuse to compromise Daag. No, I don't believe it is the Javatt who steer Lanz Varaxx. It is the Lord himself who wishes to dictate beyond his term, to control the succession. This way the new Lord can never speak ill of him, can never shatter his accomplishments, wretched as they may be!" Genu Zig slapped a palm against an innocent scroll causing it to spin off the makeshift desk. "And though it is not his to give, Lanz Varaxx and past lords of similar ilk often prevail because Vaghi of lesser mettle seldom challenge such intimidating circumstances, seldom contend with foes whose victory could mean retribution of the most vindictive sort. Because to lose invites reprisal." Genu Zig scratched the thinning patch of silver hair above ger pixied ear.

A ravenous Marz gobbled every word. "You've taken apart the pieces, Genu, and reassembled them into a clearer picture," he admired. "A complex mechanism made simpler!"

The nunale nodded in agreement before continuing. "The oath taken by the Lord of The Vag, upon assuming the title, is a concise assertion of his potency, Marz. You should learn it if for no other reason than to fathom what defines the Lord. After the election is affirmed, the division of warriors as we call it, the confident new Lord stands upon the great slab within the Ring of Kilts and declares the following: *Know this. I,* and he states his name, *am the Lord of The Vag. In me all power rests henceforth for twenty-four years. I am the head of state in the absolute, holding all executive, administrative, military, judicial and spiritual power. I do acknowledge the Code of Laws and vow to obey it. I also remind all citizens that to be Lord of The Vag is to be undefied.*

Undefied, Marz, undefied! That is the summary of our political system. One undefied Lord. So it is important that the kilts elect a good one, and if possible an outstanding one. Not a lineaged puff who treats the office as some sort of ceremonial inheritance!" Gee drank from the mug, giving gen pause to advance the next point. "And within the Code of Laws those few commandments which restrict the Lord's actions are meaningless. Why? Because he is accountable to no one save the goddess herself So it is but an easy thing to circumvent the Code. Why again? Because the dictatorial nature of the office invests the Lord with unchallenged authority. Indeed his power is absolute!» A heavy breath escaped the wise one's lungs. This particular subject was one gee had pondered many star filled nights on the great mountain.

"I learn from your every word, Genu Zig." His was not a fawning reflex. For sure the young Vag absorbed it all, sopping up every inflection, each nuance his teacher spouted.

"So, Marz Kavoyy of the isthmus, let me instill in you one more thought." Gee cleared a stale mouth with a sip of minted water from the clay mug. "Ahhh, the libation is especially refreshing. Would you care for a cupful? Some fruit, perhaps? I'm so caught up in my lecture that I'm afraid I've been remiss in my host's duties."

"No thank you, Genu. I'm too engrossed to be thirsty." He smiled, showing the neat, white teeth of his brood. Fascination had truly captured him for Marz was a son who devoured mixed fruit by the dozens, often emptying his mother's larder.

"'Good, good. A diplomatic answer. Perhaps we're getting somewhere." The pedantic sage bowed in acknowledgment, a curious little smile etched on ger lips. "Now, as I was saying. Before you can pursue a life of the highest duty, you must first make a covenant with your inner self and the sacred spirit which dwells within us all. And having been true to this contract you will be at peace with your decisions. But that is only part of the equation, Marz. You must also discipline yourself in preparation, in the pursuit of experience, and in the maddening virtue of patience. Preparation, experience and patience! Commit them to memory."

Marz silently lipped the three words. "I will remember what you have said and honor them in my everyday life." He spoke with an awed reverence. "Will you help me form the covenant? Will you be my mentor, Genu Zig?"

"Of course," beamed the nunale. "This is for what I have been preparing, patiently, my entire life. But come," gee exclaimed, "first we must shave your pubic hairs."

"My pubic hairs?" blurted an astonished Marz. *Was this part of the mysterious covenant?*

"You do have them, don't you?" The question was playful, asked with a wink.

"Yes, yes. Certainly." A glint of confusion ringed his eyes.

"Then let us do it!" Genu Zig reaffirmed while stifling a gremlin grin. Ah, gee was savoring the moment. A life's fulfillment, though still many years away, was finally within grasp.

Five months elapsed since that initial session with Genu Zig. After escorting his siblings back to the isthmus, Marz returned to live in the stone cottage the sage called the most tranquil spot on Gala Rotaria. And here began his rebirth. Most days were spent under the tutelage of his mentor, learning things he had never contemplated. Zoog had taught ger brother the rudiments of geometry and a smattering of science. Genu expanded on them, giving Marz an understanding of how to apply both the absolute and abstract to everyday problem solving. Laws of nature were explored; the transfer of heat and why various materials conduct differently; the properties of water, buoyancy and displacement; leverage, pulleys, gears and a host of things mechanical. All these things were explained and demonstrated to him. And ever-present, threaded through this knowledge, were lessons of a metaphysical kind, pushing his mind to new perspectives. The student was encouraged to visit other intellectuals occupying Mount Aryxx in order that he might gain alternative points of view, to ask questions, to examine, to ponder. The final day he climbed the summit and spent a cold night drinking in the brilliant constellations, talking mutely to himself. Inhaling the rarefied air Marz held it within his chest and with lids closed confirmed the covenant he had composed with Genu Zig's guidance. Aye, Marz Kavoyy would pursue the lordship with zeal and patience, his life-quest nothing short of the throne itself. Neither temptation nor intimidation would untrack him. And once successfully attained, the seat of power would uplift The Vag and its citizenry in every conceivable manner. "I will be the patriot of my people," he vowed. "By the ten fingers, I will."

When it came time to bid good bye to his mentor, Marz was focused beyond his years, prepared to engage the twisted corridor of life. Prior to reporting to Muraverdus for his training cycle he would hike back to Kavoyy Station to spend a week or so with his family. He looked forward to seeing them all. Especially though, he wished to reunite with his brood sibs. Together they would take flight on a voyage of promised adventure.

Proud of the transformation gee had nurtured, Genu Zig beheld ger confident young eagle. Genu couldn't help but be misty eyed at Marz's departure. The old nunale stretched to embrace the stooping youth, squeezing him tightly. After several quiet moments the little body pushed away. "I shall miss you very much, dear Marz. Very much."

"And I, you. You have given me something which no jewel could ever surpass in value."

Zig reached up to stroke the strong chin. "You are in my thoughts and prayers, young Vag. When things become difficult, think of me with great concentration, and perhaps I shall be able to provide inspiration."

"That is good to know," he smiled softly.

"One final idea I would like to pour into your already crowded brain...if you don't mind?" Conscientious as the first day they met, the teacher proposed a last monition.

"There is always room, my Genu." Again the warmth of emotion rose, pleasing his lips.

Gee clutched the strong hand of Marz Kavoyy, prospecting the golden eyes for a vein of reception. As always, it was there, responsive, ready to receive. He began slowly. "Often truly great men are figures of controversy, chided by those who claim to act for the public good yet speak out of self-interest, ridiculed by demagogues who justify the selling of personal morality by hiding behind legalisms." Genu paused, choosing his words with an orator's deftness. "Equally repulsive are those who place expedience before ethics. Generally they view themselves with an eliteness stemming from a perceived superior intellect. And somehow this superiority rationalizes their exclusion from those sacrifices suffered by their countrymen. Communal labor is waived, military service shunned by minimal participation or none at all, duty avoided. In doing so legal manipulations replace justice…to the consternation of the great dutiful mass. Marz, I ask that you remember these thoughts as you weave your course. Know your adversaries and mark them well!"

Marz nodded vigorously. "Aye, Genu. To be double sure I will. For this was the same conclusion voiced by my father but with different words."

"Young Vag," Genu Zig beamed, "evidently your sire learned well during his time on Aryxx…as have you."

# CHAPTER VII

Fyum, the Month of Rivers, ushered in the tepid rains which bathe The Vag every Spring. The final day of the month also welcomed each male and female who would celebrate a seventeenth birthday that year. Consequently the roads and trails were heavy with damp, young pilgrims streaming to the great Ring of Muraverdus. Almost exclusively in brother-sister pairs they plodded through the wetness, although there were exceptions where sickness, pregnancy or the premature death of one sib made it impossible. Accordingly, Marz and Tyrra joined the human flow, backpacks and canteens light upon their sturdy frames. Posted along the roads at key junctions, warrior patrols kept watch, protecting and directing the youths who would register at Muraverdus. In a way the muster represented a census of sorts. From registration forward they would be considered adults, controlled in their behavior, responsible for individual actions. Here they would receive a 'training assignment' as required by law. Usually the great margin of trainees were sent to the southeast steppe to toil for six months cultivating and harvesting the vast wheat fields, not surprisingly called the Breadbasket of The Vag. All the young women worked the wheat as did most of the males. However, some of the men would see themselves placed in the quarries, brickworks or tanneries performing labors more demanding than those in the agricultural sector. Certainly a rite of passage, the work represented civic duty as stipulated in the Code of Laws. Nunales were excused from the training cycle. Small in number, roughly one in every one hundred eighty-one children born were nunine, the gifted gender attended several academies at the Capital. Advanced courses prepared them for vocations in the priesthood, science and medicine, business and government administration. Scholarhood pointed the way to teaching careers for many as well. Schooling was also available to their brood siblings toiling for the public good. Specifically, at the conclusion of each workday and the 'rest' day, classroom study was mandatory for two months. After that, those wishing to enhance their education farther could continue.

And so it was that Tyrra Kavoyy, having been registered, found herself assembled into a march unit for the trek southward. Everything had happened so quickly she barely bid her sib farewell, waving to him as he entered a formation of marchers. She and her contemporaries moved out about a half hour after dawn, expected to average twenty medecs daily for three days until reaching the River Metarz. From there they would embark on transport barges and poled a casual three hundred medecs to their destination, the Breadbasket. This Spring season had been drier than the average, even more so in the south. Yet plenty enough water coursed the wide river permitting a pace both steady and smooth. Referred to by all as the Big Lazy, the Metarz proved kind to its riders. Shallow of depth, slow of current, the voyage took on the mood of a leisure cruise. With but a few drizzly mornings to interrupt their comfort, new friendships were easily formed among the young women. A tented deck protected them from the river mist's slippery dew, and thankfully from hovering water fowl. Though she enjoyed the experience, by the time the Big Lazy delivered them to the unloading wharves, Tyrra had tasted enough of barge life to predict a sailor's endeavor would never be her calling. Confinement had stiffened bones and muscles alike to where she welcomed the two day march on to the agricultural camp.

Along the route the young Kavoyy couldn't avoid noticing the pairs of archer warriors trotting aside their flanks. Predators of both the four and two legged kinds were wise to keep hidden from their presence. Compared to the chattering, immature herds of lasses treading the dusty road, the sisters of the Ravenhood were lock-jawed stoics, often choosing to signal by hand or body movement. Laconic of mouth, they rarely spoke more than a phrase or sentence even when pressed. Determined of eye and mood, little distracted them from their mission. Each wore the kilt of leather straps tapered to picket points. Underneath, the short bragghi were standard uniform, although some dismissed them on sweltering days, preferring the freedom of a bare bottom. Black cowls, the signature garment of the Ravenhood, sheltered head and shoulders, providing a mysterious image, one that forbade intrusion. A quiver hung across each back cradling two dozen bronze pointed arrows. The broad waist belt pinching their gray tunics carried a military pouch and slender dagger, also of bronze. A single water skin was shared by the pair, though it seemed they never sipped from it. Laced boots identical to those worn by Tyrra's brother, climbed to just below the calf muscle. And the fundamental weapon of their fury, the longbow of Jarra, was carried at the balance. Polished to brilliance, all who gazed its sleekness knew the bow's reputation to propel a deadly rain over 300 strides. Toted unstrung, Tyrra was aware from her mother's description, that in a matter of seconds a competent archer could step inside the bow, bending its flexible shaft with just enough force to slip on the unyielding bowstring. Immediately steady fingers would retrieve an arrow from the shouldered nest, feather it, pull, aim and release with a velocity powerful enough to penetrate, perhaps exit, a rib cage, whether Kala raider or Vag outlaw. A company of such archers patrolled the female trainees' area, ensuring protection in addition to maintaining peace among battling 'ladies' of differing persuasions. As the pair effortlessly dog-trotted past her group, the fascination became apparent in all their eyes. This day the warriors would cover double the ground of Tyrra's unit. Where her marching compatriots were rapt in their observation, Tyrra was inspired. Glimpses of warrior women jogging silently in the open sun reinforced a glory to be sought. There was no swagger in their stride, but she knew they ran with the knowledge that all surveyed them with a revered respect. For Tyrra Kavoyy, stable girl of the isthmus, such recognition would be reward aplenty. Shaara had schooled her in the basics of archery these last five months, and to instructor's and daughter's mutual delight, she had taken to it with great ease. Or as her mother phrased it, "as natural as mouth to breast your first day of life." With encouragement so positive, Tyrra fired thirty arrows every morning, honing her skill in anticipation of a calling to the 'hood.'

By the time the planting season drew to a close the ground had been broken, the great steppe seeded. Long and strenuous, the work had toughened all. One only had to look upon the tanned cheeks exuding their healthy shine to know The Vag had been diligently served by its youth. Toiling side by side with their male counterparts, it was a predictable conclusion that flirtations would ripen as would the wheat sprouts themselves. Summer proved a less difficult period for the laborers. Field and tool maintenance along with classwork represented the bulk of activity. Inevitably many a flirtation blossomed into romance, filling free time with eager couples sneaking into sheds and groves. During periods of 'fraternization' males were permitted to visit the girls' compounds, though not allowed to actually enter the fenced perimeter. Outdoor tables and benches were arranged on the day of rest, prompting a festive mood. Songs and storytelling followed. In some cases siblings were rejoined making for greater merriment. For Tyrra no such meeting was possible inasmuch as Marz had drawn his training duty at the Lord's brickworks some fifty medecs away. Still she enjoyed the camaraderie. Her table sat nine girls from her dormitory and five visiting boys. Arms interlocked they rocked happily through a medley of farmers' songs where the singers had to mimic bird songs. It took her back to that time when she and her sibs had hooted and cawed with Shaara in the station kitchen. Her face glowed with the recollection, but alas the smile did her in for the striking lad across the table thought it was aimed at him. Directing a coltish wink at Tyrra, he gestured her to sit beside him. She mouthed the word "No," her flashing smile signaling him not to be too disheartened. His name was Monz Kelozz, everyone called him Monty, the brood sib of Luura, the girl clucking like a chicken to his left. She was having a grand time swaying ever so tightly to the beau on her left side.

Shouting above the raucous din, Monty called, "Perhaps another time?" And he toasted her with a mug of the weak beer they were allowed to drink on such occasions. His voice was cheery, making it clear he was not offended, still maintaining an interest.

Working an arm free from a swaying partner, she raised her own mug. "Another time," she laughed. Her smile dazzled him, matched only by the glittering gold of her Kavoyy eyes.

At that instant Monty Kelozz was swept away like the great rush of water that plunges into the sea of Gala Rotaria. What a captivating smile! Come harvest season he would find a way to sharpen her sickle, glean her field, load her wagon or whatever it took to get close, to breathe the same air surrounding her lips. And hopefully Tyrra Kavoyy would be waiting for him at the completion of his service.

The ninth month of the year, the Month of the Yellow Sky, was almost upon the steppe. Four weeks had rolled by since that initial, heart skipping introduction to Tyrra, but Monty had yet to spot her again in the fields or barn clusters. Much to his despair the girl of his dreams always seemed to work a different shift. And come rest days she no longer participated in the songfests, choosing instead to study lessons or run exercise laps within the compound. Wherever he went his attention directed itself to groups of young women, yearning that she might be among them. But, alas, it was not to be, triggering a great frustration inside. He had promised himself he would be patient in his pursuit, not wishing to come on like an overeager boor. However, in Tyrra's total absence, it had become impossible to behave in any manner, boorish or not. Finally in an act of surrender, he asked his brood sib, Luura, to intercede on his behalf, inviting Tyrra to sit with him at the next fraternization. When word came back that she would indeed sit with him, his joy knew no end. In his mind he had placed her upon a pedestal so exalted that he had to reel in his bubbling emotions, reminding himself that she was unaware of her elevated status. Regardless, soon the lofty Tyrra would be sipping warm beer with someone named Monty, perhaps doing so out of kindness. Their expectations would be polarized, no doubt. Who knew what his twin had spoken to entice Tyrra to sit with him? Perhaps she had portrayed her sib as a lovesick juvenile filled with moonstruck infatuations. Sister Luura was capable of such representations. Was this to be a sympathy date, hollow of mutual fascination? Disconcerting thoughts plagued his mind, mostly irrational, yet he considered them all. Ah, love is an agonizing business. "By the fingers, it is!"

Oiling his stubbled face, the young swain proceeded to shave away a week's growth. Using an obsidian blade to scrape away the last stubborn remnants, Monty ran a finger across the chin to confirm a job complete. He had already bathed in Sand Creek, a nearby tributary of the Big Lazy. And his soft, brown hair, lightened by many exposures to summer rays, had been shorn of its shagginess earlier that morning. Tunic and bragghi retrieved from the communal clothesline smelled fresh as the wind. Slipping into the clean garments, he wondered if Tyrra was doing even half as much in her preparation. "Probably not," Monty concluded. His irises sparkled a soft, lemony hue in the reflecting glass. "Unlike hers," me mused. "For Tyrra's eyes glitter like sun on gold!"

Whistling a farmer's song they hopefully would be harmonizing in a few hours, he buckled his polished waist belt and exited the dorm. Strolling across the yard to the combination kitchen/mess hall, he went inside and begged an apple from the cook's assistant. He would bite into it just before arriving at the women' s compound, leaving teeth and breath cleansed and sweet. Yes, Monty Kelozz had thought of everything. "Nothing to chance," he twinkled, and climbed an oxen wagon en-route to the women's quarters and Tyrra!

"Ravenhood of Jarra? That's why you've been avoiding the company of males?"

"Yes," she said, smiling. "I wished not to develop any relationships which would have to be terminated so soon. Do you think that selfish, or considerate?"

"Well, well," he stuttered a bit off guard. But Monty quickly gathered his wit. "Considerate, perhaps, for the great mass of insincere oafs who might flutter their eyes in your direction, Tyrra, but selfish for poor me, deprived of your presence." He laughed aloud while feigning a wounded heart.

"You sound much like my brood brother," she teased. "Only he would have rolled in the dirt to dramatize his hurt."

"Do you wish me to do the same?" he challenged in jest.

"Of course not, Monty."

She had spoken his name. Nay, she had sung it. Like music it had lilted sweetly from her tongue. "Is your brother here? I'd like to meet him."

"Better yet, I think it is I who wishes to meet him," interrupted Luura, seated across the rough hewn table.

"I suspect the prime brood of the family Kelozz has but one thing on its mind," Tyrra playfully observed. They all laughed. "My brother labors in the Lord's brickworks, hauling clay, constructing forms, chopping wood, loading barges for the ride North." She hesitated, for she wished not to appear weak. When one aspires to the hood, syrupy emotion is something best contained. But she gave in. "I do miss him greatly," she sighed. "And my genther also. Gee studies the sciences at the Capital. They are very special in my heart."

"If they are from the same brood as you, they must be exceptional," Monty boomed, never failing to overstate a compliment.

"The horse dung deepens at this table," Tyrra winked at Luura. "Perhaps we should raise our sandals before it overcomes us." Again they laughed.

The great phenomenon of the yellow sky was making its first impression on the horizon. In another few days the entire canopy would be filled with a dim yellowness.

Born of a meteorological marvel no one could explain, it had been mythicized as the glow of the Goddess which ripened grain and prepared women for Seccus and Olz, the months of conception. Monty pointed to the skyline, tracing his finger along its linear path above the mature wheat stalks. "Is it not beautiful?" he observed aloud.

"Aye," Tyrra and Luura agreed in unison.

"And it reminds me that I have to pee like an ox," announced Luura as she excused herself and made haste to the compound privy.

Shaking his head in amusement, Monty half explained to Tyrra, "Though we are surely of the same brood, my sister and I are not of the same character or temperament." His intent was to signal that he was not a crude fellow. Nor was he courting her for a quick roll in the hay...though it had entered his mind. For nothing would have provided greater ecstasy than to slide between the thighs of Tyrra Kavoyy. At an age where glands were groaning to assert their vitality, Monty Kelozz heroically pushed aside thoughts of lust and swigged a mouthful of warm brew. Noble of soul, he shifted the conversation back to Jarra, childhood, and things of social interest. Luura never returned, having found a young buck to captivate. And so Tyrra and Monty chatted with such intensity so as to be unaware, or indifferent, to the rollicking chorus of unending medleys.

Whereas the Kavoyy were of the extreme northwest portion of the country, Monty's family, for as long as anyone could recall, lived on the fringe of the Orri peninsula about as far to the east as is possible in the northern Vag. "Sometimes we trade with the Orri," he informed.

"Really, I've never seen one! What do they look like close up?" She had never spoken to anyone with firsthand information about another world. The idea of Orri fascinated her.

"They're just like us. Well, almost," he kidded. "For none could be as beautiful as you."

She blushed. "Stop it, Monty." No one, save her family had ever called her beautiful before. Though somewhat flushed by his flattery, she enjoyed the attention. Regardless she glanced from side to side in an attempt to determine if anyone had overheard.

"I meant it," he whispered. "But if it makes you uncomfortable I won't mention it again, least not in public surroundings." He grinned, showing teeth almost as neat as hers. "Now, getting back to the Orri, what would you like to know about them?"

"Everything."

"What little I know I'll share with you. Now I'm the embarrassed one for my knowledge is limited."

Now she became the flatterer. "Oh, I'm sure you know more about them than most Vaghi. After all you've actually seen them, you living on the frontier.

His cheeks pinked slightly. *Why is it she makes me feel so unsure of my own impressions?* he thought.

"If it makes you uncomfortable, I won't mention it again," she parroted. A brief moment held still, then they giggled together.

"Without trying too much to sound like a schoolmaster, I shall continue," he nodded. "For the most part, the Orri are just like we. Similar of face, yellow eyed. They brood-birth like we do, but as far as I know they are not blessed with the nunine gender. The men, though, don't have the capacity to grow facial hair. Peculiar! If anything they are of smoother skin than our kind. On the average I'd say they're a few digits shorter than Vaghi. Maybe a bit slighter of frame, less robust. And their hair color is uniformly dark, whereas ours varies. However, the thing that separates them from us most assuredly is their docile nature. Theirs is a profound shyness, so deep that when trading with us they often drop their heads, avoiding eye contact. Confrontation is beyond the Orri, preferring to break off a negotiation rather than haggle! None are allowed to set foot in The Vag, so the trading occurs in a valley within the great Barrier Mountains which divide our land from the peninsula. Shepherds and farmers, theirs is a pastoral life void of government, without laws. Only an instinct of fairness controls their actions. To their great benefit is The Vag nation, for if we did not exist the Kala would have gobbled the last Orri before the first Lord swore the oath. There is an expression, *The meek shall be devoured by the Kala.* If not for the warriors of The Vag, this proverb would be the epitaph of the Orri people."

"So you know your neighbors well, Kelozz of the Barrier Mountains," Tyrra marveled with a wink.

"Aye, lassie," he countered, happy in her jestful praise. "Remember it well Tomorrow you'll be tested, and a failing grade will get you an empty bowl come supper time."

"Hah," she shot back. "You covered all but their language. How is it they speak?"

"The tongue is mostly foreign from ours, yet it is surprising how many words are similar or appear to have a similar root. Perhaps they learned them from us or we from the Orri, as remote or inconceivable as that might be. Unfortunately they are also without literature." He smiled. "Any other questions?"

"Just one, great sage. What of their women? How do they appear?"

"Hmmm," he thought. "I've never seen one. I doubt they ever venture beyond the mountains. But my father said they compliment the males in every way just as Vaghi women do their men. The Orri of both genders wear long robes. Tunics, bragghi and, of course, kilts are not to their fashion."

"And religion?" she queried.

"None, save a meditation of sorts. Gala Rotaria stirs not in their souls."

"How primitive!" she remarked. "Lives as uncultured and empty as theirs deserve to be pitied."

"Or envied," Monty suggested. "They know not war or turmoil. Their's is a society unaware of pressure. They survive without hunger or privation. It is the simplest of existences. What they suffer from is a lack of technology with its resultant benefits. Certainly there is a childish innocence about them."

"Innocent or naive?" Tyrra asked. "It seems they are limited in their emotions. Without glory. Lacking spiritual fervor. And the total absence of aggression robs them of the competitiveness which drives our kind to excel. Would you agree?"

"Perhaps you're right, Tyrra. You make some good points." He turned to look with admiration at the lovely face. "I've never had a conversation like this with a woman before...I mean other than my sister. We have a good rapport, we do. We stimulate each other's thoughts."

"Aye, Monty. I feel much the same."

Placing his hand upon Tyrra's shoulder, he eased her off the bench. Together they strolled across the hard packed road to a shade tree. Under the coolness of its branches he took her hand in his. "Tyrra," he began, "I have a very warm feeling for you and would like to continue seeing you. Would that be to your liking?"

"Yes, Monty, but with conditions." She searched for words which wouldn't hurt him, for she cared for Monty. Physically he was all she had ever dreamed for in a companion: tall, athletic, handsome. And his intellect and bearing were ideal for her. Smart and thoughtful, Monty Kelozz was without the self-importance consistent with so many of the cocky young men aspiring to the kilt. Also he possessed a playful kind of humor, which she enjoyed. "Monty, whatever our relationship shall be over the next two months, it will be on my terms. This probably sounds selfish to you but I am committed to earning my kilt at Jarra. Nothing must be permitted to cool my ardor. For I am driven in pursuit of what was denied my mother. I seek the hood for both of us." Clouded mists welled within her eyes so strong was her passion. "Therefore, think me not disinterested if I wish not to get involved. Think me not frigid if I choose to defer love. Because the kilt and what it represents is of the uppermost priority." She squeezed his palm to emphasize her conviction.

Monty's eyes too were teary. "I accept you on your terms, Tyrra. Willingly I do."

Blotting away the wetness with her tunic sleeve, she emitted a nervous laugh and pressed a finger to his sternum. "Ever since you raised your mug to me four weeks past, I've purposely been avoiding you, because I was afraid my heart would betray my mission to Jarra. Aye, Monty, know that I am strongly attracted to you and have been since that day."

He wrapped an arm around Tyrra's shoulders and tugged her close, the strength of his chest comforting her. "By the fingers," he sighed, "I am filled with respect for you, and the honesty you have shown me. Aye, it is on your terms that we shall continue."

What followed were weeks of a gentle relationship. Together they would walk the fields, hand in hand among the mellowing harvest, talking softly, rapt in the sweet glow of youth. Conversations ranged a spectrum of topics from the starry heavens to horse-care and philosophy. It didn't really matter. Awareness of their mutual preferences and idiosyncrasies were explored with reciprocal interest. And even though the glands were aching to satisfy their hormonal needs, having come close in several instances, they remained true to her terms, compulsion shelved...at least temporarily.

Near the conclusion of Tyrra's service, just before the ripened wheat was to be reaped, those interested in pursuing the hood were instructed to gather in the mess hall.

Of the nearly one thousand young women working in the agricultural camp, slightly over a hundred attended. Almost all had been pointing at Jarra long before the trip down the Big Lazy. Several, though, showed up yet unconvinced...or simply curious. In no way, however, was this a frivolous group. With quiet confidence they awaited whatever announcement was forthcoming.

They didn't have to wait long, for among the warriors of the Ravenhood punctuality is more than a virtue. It is a ruling zeal. Of less than average height, the presence of Skyyra Jakivv entering the hall stilled what little motion might have prevailed. With a soldier's gait she strode to a makeshift stage and mounted the wooden steps. Spread-legged, her bragghi-less thighs flashed through the kilt's shiny leather strips. Fists on hips the seasoned warrior peered out at her audience, tacitly surveying the band of prospective recruits. Skyyra Jakivv, Senior Capitana of the Ravenhood, Commandant of Jarra, answerable but to General Povezz and the great Lord himself, stood with the poise that springs from self-reliance. The cowl hood hung down her back exposing the handsomely hawkish face used to issuing orders... and having them obeyed. From her wrist dangled a short ceremonial quirt, symbol of her rank. Among the warriors of Jarra, she was called First Arrow in deference to her primacy. "Yellowed steel' someone had once described her eyes, and this evening they were true to the term. Effortlessly they observed all within their periphery, head motionless, lips sullen. Quiet reigned the best part of a minute. Finally she spoke, deliberately enunciating each word. "We don't want all of you!" The frost of her greeting was exceeded only by the ice of her stare. To be sure even the most stouthearted of candidates trembled a bit. "Those of you who are here for a look-see can now depart. Your moment is over. I am not here to recruit new warriors, but to glean those who have a chance—but not from ladies of false interest." Jakivv's tone was matter-of-fact. No emotion surged her delivery. A few shocks of silver threaded the pixied hair, her rugged skin weathered to a rich tan. "If anything, I am here to dissuade rather than to enlist. For you shall be subjected to the most demanding of disciplines, the harshest of physical strain. At Jarra it is test by ordeal! Nothing but a granite will can see you through. If your loins flutter for the warmth of a village beau then return home in the knowledge that there is nothing to satisfy you at Jarra other than imagination and the lump in your sleep mat." This evoked the only smiles of Skyyra Jakivv's address. "Tomorrow, a half hour before dawn, be here at this spot for a physical inspection and interview. That is, if you still are intent on applying for the hood." She lowered an arm, fingertips resting against the red strip designating Jakivv's officership. Pointing the stubby quirt towards the noiseless crowd, she announced with a half grin, "One last thing. If your ass is wider than your shoulders, don't bother showing up. Dismissed!" It was the sole time they laughed.

A scalp shorn of its tresses awaited the razored edge which would skim the last vestiges of hair. Around her, other young women completed the process, one that identified them as raw enlistees. Though she was without regret, Tyrra felt a bony nakedness as she finished shaving the remnant bristle. Piles collecting on the wide-board floor were soon swept into larger heaps by a broom wielding recruit, her initial duty at Jarra. Deplumed of their glory, ninety six white skulls reflected the dim light of their new home. Following a quiet trip up the Big Lazy they had trekked for four days before arriving at the hilled fortress perched high amid the plain of Jarra. From its heights lookouts could observe expansive vistas a full 360 degrees. Issued regulation bragghi, tunic, belt, sandals and boots, Tyrra marched to the dorm with the other selectees where sleeping spaces were assigned them. All were aware of the shearing ritual before volunteering, yet it still came as a shock when called to actually do it, to ultimately run one's palm over a surface no longer thick with the ringlets and bangs, void of the shag which had been teased and braided since early memory.

"On your feet!" the husky voice echoed across the barracks. "Girls! And I do mean girls! For until you are acclaimed 'warriors' you will be known as girls." Striding through the arched portal and across the center aisle, a lanky woman in her late twenties, accompanied by two sergeants, swatted the rump of a recruit slow in rising. "Whenever anyone wearing the kilt enters this area the first to see her will yell, Attention! And everyone will spring to her feet, straight as an arrow. Eyes straight ahead, chin in, tits out, shoulders back, hands at your sides, heels together." She spun a tight circle, observing as the 'girls' shuffled to the designated position. I am Capitana Ryya Ferann, Mistress of Recruits. When permitted to speak you will address me as Capitana, my rank. Is that understood?"

A weak murmur rippled through the barracks, the new trainees unsure how to respond.

"When I demand an answer, I expect to hear Yes. Capitana loudly and in unison. Now, is that understood?"

"Yes, Capitana," they barked.

"Good. Remember that for the future...if you're still with us. Commencing from this moment forward you will not be permitted to speak unless calling cadence in ranks or instructed to respond. Anyone caught even whispering a prayer will be dealt with severely. The only two words you are allowed to utter are <u>I quit</u>. And after that you can chatter all you want !" Ferann wove through the clusters of young women daring them to follow her with their eyes. . Fortunately not one wiggled an orb. Showing her teeth, the dark haired Capitana hooked her thumbs within her tunic belt, left palm resting upon the sheathed dagger carried by all warriors of Jarra. "You are a lucky lot this fine morning, girls, Today is bath day! And you stink from many medecs on the march. So let us cleanse ourselves, shall we?" She moved to the middle of the large dormitory. "Form three ranks on me. Now!" she ordered. They scurried about, the sergeants pushing them into three rows each containing thirty two bodies, similar to the marching formation which saw them hike from the banks of the Big Lazy to Jarra. "All right, girls. Strip to the skin! Everything off, boots included!" Very few had expected this. Most obediently removed their clothing, Tyrra among them. Several, however, were reluctant, modesty a virtue difficult to cleave. "I said, strip!" commanded the Mistress. "If you are shamed by your own nakedness. If you don't have the guts to let your sisters gaze upon your pimpled buttocks, if that revulses you, then how can you be expected, without conscience, to slit a Kala throat? To deliver an arrowhead into an enemy heart?" The recalcitrant few complied. Still two or three stood cross-handed, protecting their pubic ground. The sergeants roughly yanked their arms apart. Tears escaped one closest to Ferann. "Girly, conserve your tears. Over the next six months you're going to need them for things more threatening than an unclothed ass!" Slapping the leather kilt with a loud thwack, Ferann shouted, "Company, left face! At a column trot, forward march!"

Ninety six baldies jogged into the morning light, the first time their hairless domes had seen the sun since infancy. The column ran along the sand road down the hill, maintaining an easy pace for half a medec. At the bottom of the slope the ground flattened. Nudity forgotten, legs stretched out eating up the distance. Layers of cushioning sand permitted them to run without discomfort. Soon they were all shouting cadence, responding to the sergeants' call-outs. Tyrra ran effortlessly near the lead of the center column, yelling to the beat of the run. Maintaining a proper interval they raced onward paralleling the River Jarra. Up ahead by the narrows she could glimpse a wooden bridge spanning the flow. "Column left, march!" Column left? But they weren't close enough to the bridge. Immediately it became apparent. The ninety six would run through the river, not over it. Splashing into the hip high water, churned higher by their action, the young warriors-to-be braved the chilly shock. Intent on sustaining their balance, shivered screams constrained, they exited the far bank yet calling cadence. Standing on the bridge, Capitana and cadre shouted encouragement. Minutes later they ran a tight hairpin tum causing the recruits to reverse direction and the inevitable re-crossing of the River Jarra. This time the jolt wasn't quite as raw, taut skin having been conditioned, or numbed, by the earlier introduction. Plowing through the swirling water, Tyrra could feel the spray lapping breasts and shoulders. Nipples perked, erectile tissue dilated to the maximum, the bathers of Jarra trotted the long grade back to the barracks to begin the first day.

The weeks that followed toughened bodies and resolves of the survivors to a new hardness. In the process there were casualties of limb, broken bones dashing the hopes of prospective warriors. Still others suffered failed perseverance, betrayed by an unwilling psyche. And so, "I quit," passed fourteen pairs of lips, dwindling the group to 82. All this happened before any had so much as drawn a bowstring.

Finally, an accomplishment of sorts came to pass. One morning after their wake up run and breakfast, the sharp faced Mistress marched into the barracks and announced, "For three weeks you have been silent. During that time I hope you have learned that speech, especially the idle kind, is unnecessary. A disciplined tongue, if nothing else, has kept you out of trouble. It has also prevented you from getting to know those around you too amicably. There has been purpose to this. For when a friend with whom you have shared close comradeship fails the ordeal, a piece of you despairs. The ban is lifted... but remember its lesson! The remainder of the day is duty free. No duty!"

Bracing at attention, Tyrra Kavoyy wondered if she would feel like talking right off. After having communicated via hand signals, body language and a rare word scratched in the mud, she had learned the peace of muteness. Even more importantly, in a training community of sparse reward, there would be no duty today, the first time to herself in twenty three days. The Mistress having departed, Tyrra rubbed the furry patch sprouting atop her head. She was about to announce to no one in particular that she was going to leisurely soak her ankles in the river, relieving the inflammation of relentless pounding. But why declare her intention aloud? If the lesson of silence had made any lasting impression, it was the unnecessariness of whimsical conversation Moving to her sleeping space, she unlaced the warrior boots and slid into sandals. Mother had advised a most important safeguard, foot care! Tyrra would spend an hour massaging and soaking her heels, chilling away the persistent soreness and swelling.

Dangling her legs in the cool current she savored the ripples coursing between her toes. The soles were rugged as hide. During the first week, each night a bucket and brush were passed among the recruits. Vile in odor, the mixture concocted of tree saps, various herbs and brine was painted on the bottoms of feet, callusing the skin. The sergeants referred to the smelly liquid as Kala Juice, that breed possessing the toughest of soles. Eyes closed, Tyrra's thoughts skipped back to Monty, and were about to be transported to the isthmus when a stirring caught her ear. Pivoting on her rump she beheld the cowled presence of Skyyra Jakivv. The young recruit's attempt to rise was cut off by the First Arrow's command. "Stay as you are!" Relaxing, Tyrra allowed her body to settle back. Jakivv sat next to her, elbow supported by a bent knee. "How goes the initiation?" she asked in a tone warmer than any heard in almost a month.

"Senior Capitana, it has been a true test of the spirit."

She smiled. "You are wise to take care of your feet. Most of those who break down physically, do so between the knees and toes."

Having been without conversation for some time, Tyrra felt she had earned a verbal exchange. Besides, how could she ignore the Commandant who obviously wished to chat. "Yes, Commandant, my mother was an ankle casualty while training here at Jarra."

"Your name?" she inquired.

"Kavoyy. Tyrra Kavoyy, Commandant."

"From which region?"

"The isthmus, Commandant."

"No doubt of Kavoyy Station?"

"Aye, Commandant. The very same."

"Some of our finest warriors are of your region." The First Arrow shifted her position, shaking the stiffness from her shoulders. "And your mother. What was her name before taking a mate of the Kavoyy?"

"Savann. Shaara Savann, Commandant."

Pushing the hood from her graying locks, she tossed her head backwards and laughed aloud, showing the absence of several molars. "Ah, girly, now I see the bloodline!"

"You know my mother?" Her jaw dropped open before remembering to title her superior, "uhhh, Commandant."

"Girly, there was a time when your mama could out-leg and out-shoot any recruit in her class. And that included me!" She slapped the short quirt against the kilt making her point the more.

"Really? But my mother is so, so...."

"Maternal?" She tucked the quirt under her belt.

"Aye, Commandant. Maternal."

"Like I said, girly, there was a time! Had Shaara Savann not shattered an ankle near the end of our training cycle the cowl and kilt would have been deserved by her before any of her barracks sisters. So good was she that the Mistress at that time bent the rules in an effort to retain her. But, alas, the injury would not respond."

"To this day she bears a slight limp when dampness hangs in the air, Commandant."

Rising to her boots, the First Arrow dusted the dirt from her calves. "Tyrra Kavoyy of the isthmus, if you are but a fraction of what I knew Shaara Savann to be, then you shall persevere to win the kilt." As an afterthought she added, "And take care of those feet." Removing the quirt from her belt, Skyyra Jakivv looped the thong about her wrist and sauntered towards the walls of Jarra.

For the major part of a month the recruits underwent another bout of rigorous training. When they weren't engaged in crawling or 'stalking' exercises, hikes and climbs, they scrubbed floors, dug post holes, unloaded wagon-loads of supplies destined for the true warriors from whom they had been segregated all this while. The strength in their upper bodies increased dramatically, a necessary development if they were to draw a bowstring to its maximum force. In the field they ran everywhere. When in garrison they ran everywhere. It was all the same. Continuing the tradition of their initial bath, once a week 'whether we need it or not,' the entire group, now down to seventy six candidates, braved the River Jarra's late season coolness. Their number smaller, hair longer, confidence higher, a strong bond grew among the hardy class. One particular aspect of their training which affected a squeamish few involved the taking of life. Each warrior in training was required to kill a chicken and in a handful of cases, goats;the theory being if you "couldn't kill the damn chicken, how could one propel an arrow into a Kala throat?" All passed the test satisfactorily, an easier task for the experienced farm girls. Of course the butchered livestock found their way to the Jarra menu.

Ultimately it came to pass. "Girlies, this is a bow and arrow. The one with the point is the arrow." So began their indoctrination to the weapon of their purpose, the longbow of Jarra. At 1.75 strides long (63 digits) it stood about identical in height to the average female archer. Of unusual springiness its missile could strike a target in excess of 300 strides. Each recruit was issued her own bow, spare strings and an arm-guard to protect the forearm from the bowstring's sting. And with their archery tackle came a new lexicon: shaft, nock, fletching, crest, vane, pile, etc. Intense instruction interspersed with repetitive drills conditioned their reflexes to a fine precision. From the moment they loaded their quivers from the armory's arrow racks, the bow-women never deviated from a fixed routine. Within four months virtually all had mastered the individual skills and positioning techniques: standing, kneeling, behind trees and barricades. They also absorbed the value of cluster firing in formation, saturating designated target areas in rapid bursts. Importantly all was synchronized on command. The discipline of the hood, to react as one, gave them a collective strength beyond their numbers.

Particularly adroit in her bowmanship was Tyrra Kavoyy. Advantaged by her mother's tutelage, the young archer never failed to impress with her uncanny knack to puncture the targets' innermost ring. Of the now seventy four remaining recruits, she stood among the three or four best. Sharp eyed with an accurate sense of wind, the aiming point always perfectly judged , Tyrra rated high on the Mistress' evaluation slate.

Without the trumpeting of horns or thump of drums, the finale came upon them one mid-day after a lunch of lentil gruel and black bread. The third month of the year, Ventus, had drawn to a close. Capitana Ferann instructed the mess tables cleared before her announcement. The first word to depart her lips informed that indeed their day had arrived, the ordeal a thing of history. "Ladies, give me your attention." Ladies! Not girls or girlies or recruits, but LADIES! "You heard me correctly, ladies." The first real smile any had ever witnessed on the Mistress' usually taciturn face lit up the hall. "You are as of this noon...warriors of the Ravenhood. Your training is complete. Know that the Commandant has approved the lot of you to receive your kilts ten days hence within the Ring of Kilts. As of now you can don the cowl. They await you at the supply shed." Commencing at the rear of the room a cheer erupted. Like a wave it rolled forward picking up momentum as every new kilt joined in. Ferann awaited its end before continuing. "You're an outstanding bunch," she went on. "I know I've been an ugly bitch to most, if not all of you. But you're better for the experience. Please form up and approach the head table. I'd like to shake hands with each of you."

Again a few at the rear initiated a clamor, this time with a rhythmic pounding on the tabletops. Chanting "Jar-ra, Jar-ra", the relief from six months in hell bounced off the unflinching walls. Within seconds all were hollering, the throaty cheer reverberating out the windows and across the plain. "Jar-ra, Jar-ra." They formed a line, each new warrior paying respect to her Mistress with a cross-armed salute before grasping the Capitana's hand. She responded in kind and with kind words of welcome addressed every one by name. In the background it endured. "Jar-ra, Jar-ra." When it came Tyrra's turn, the emotion caught her tongue. This day belonged to her mother too, she thought. If only she could freeze this moment and rush it home to Shaara's eyes. Unable to speak, Tyrra issued a snappy salute and shook the waiting hand, mouthing the words, "Thank you," in so doing. Re-seating herself she picked up the chant slapping the table in strong beat. "Jar-ra, Jar-ra."

The last warrior having completed the ritual salute, the Capitana rose to close the festivity. "Ladies, once every five years, the Ravenhood hosts the Commandant's tournament, a competition to determine the finest archer in The Vag. All women who have earned the kilt, whether they be on active duty or retired for fifty years are eligible to vie for the title. And that includes you! A golden arrowhead pendant will be awarded to the victor." Removing the ebon cowl, she reached inside the tunic collar to retrieve the chain about her neck.

Withdrawing it she held it high so all could view the shiny piece suspended from the largest link. "This is what it looks like, ladies. Well, almost," she corrected. "This one is copper. Fourth place," the Capitana explained. "Gold, silver, bronze, copper. That's the pecking order." Returning the pendant to its cleavaged nest, the officer next announced, "Well we've delayed the next piece of tradition too long. Does anyone need a bath?" she shouted. Cheers and hoots greeted the offer. "Then let's do it. Strip!" With that Capitana and both sergeants peeled to the skin, the new warriors cheerfully following suit. "Let's do it right. Fall in. Three ranks facing me." Enthusiastically they took their places. "Right face! Sergeants, take your positions at the front of the column. 1 will join you there." The two naked warriors ran to the assigned position eager to lead the formation. The double doors were opened and Ferann headed the company. "Company, at a trot. Forward march!" Out they slithered like a great skinless snake down the sand road. Cheering at a decibel beyond anything Tyrra had ever heard greeted their jaunt. Aye, over five hundred kilts, the entire kord of the Ravenhood screamed their approval as the column went at a full gallop through the river and beyond. Within minutes they reversed course and plunged in once more. "Wash and rinse," the veteran troops confirmed, their way of welcoming the rookie group into the most exclusive of sororities. Morale of an exhilarating strain surged the ranks of Tyrra's mates. Prideful in her accomplished group, Capitana Ferann spearheaded the charge. Mistresses for countless centuries past had followed the custom of the 'last bath,' and she wasn't about to snap the chain. Up the final grade they double-timed between a gauntlet of good natured shouts. They were bonded this lot. The supreme camaraderie which affixes itself to such rituals thrived at Jarra.

Standing at the mess hall doorway a beaming Skyyra Jakivv issued her new archers a long salute, holding it until the last proud warrior trotted by. She would give them a few moments to dress and wind down before entering to congratulate and lead them in thanksgiving prayer to Gala Rotaria.

Under a moon-bright sky rich in stars, the kilting ceremony at the Ring took on a mystical aura. Torches staked into the Spring grass flickered in a soft wind, causing shadows to streak their faces. Primitive in its origins, the rite leaped back to a time when the earliest warriors of The Vag received their hallowed kilts. When it came her moment, Tyrra thrilled in the vibration which traveled her spine. She, like her warrior sisters, wore the short bragghi this evening. Upon donning the stiff skirt, she removed the bragghi wishing to feel leather on her muscled thighs. Long nights lying on a coarse sleeping mat, exhausted of body and mind, she visioned herself in full kilt, the distant goal of ordeal. Tonight dream and substance fused in factuality. Allowing her fingers to ripple along the strips, her thoughts were of Shaara and the disappointment that tormented her yet. *This is for you too, mother*, Tyrra whispered inside. *By the ten fingers, it is ours together!* Squinting hard she dissipated the hint of a tear lest someone spy its wetness sparkling in the torchlight.

Early next morning the silvery mist that frequents the isthmus hung upon a solitary figure. The dampness settling below her shin prompted a faint limp. Though not pronounced, it was enough to remind her of why she had been waiting these past few hours. Resting upon one of the neat cairns marking the station's westernmost pasture, her heart swelled to the distant bodies descending the escarpment. Among them she knew her daughter moved with the rugged grace reserved for warriors of the hood. She wished to intercept them, to glimpse up close the young woman who had earned the cowl and kilt. But she held her location, better to hold fast than risk embarrassing Tyrra. They would draw within two hundred strides. Perhaps she could pick her out. They marched swiftly in a column of twos. Hopefully the daughter had positioned herself in the file nearest the station, figuring a family member might be watching for her. At this distance it was difficult to distinguish much. As the quick stepping band approached the closest point, the fourteenth warrior dropped her cowl hood and raised the longbow, jiggling it as if to signal, 'Over here, Mama!'

"Aye, that is she," an excited Shaara spoke aloud. "Tall and straight. Slim of hip even with the kilt swaddling her buttock." Lifting her arm, a tearful Shaara Kavoyy gave a lazy wave. A moment like this is to be remembered till the final breath. Last night she had risen from her bed touched by the unseen glow of emancipation. She didn't comprehend the why, only the mood it imparted. Now she understood. Shaara had been purged of the demons of failure, rid of the unfulfillment which had tormented her these many years. Tyrra, the extension of her being, had freed her.

The great tournament was but a day forward. Archers retired from the kord returned to rekindle old friendships, to celebrate the sisterhood and to compete. They congregated on the Plain of Jarra where tents and privies had been erected. From the far reaches of The Vag they came, journeying long days to participate in an event held but once every five years. Among her contemporaries of the recent recruit class, Tyrra was considered among the finest sharpshooters, although she'd never been pressure tested. Practice field and a contest were very different indeed. Certainly all the current warriors would be competing, almost six hundred women. Additionally, of the thousand or so who had re-donned the kilt, perhaps one third would toe the line. Besides the two hours of practice, sending many dozens of sleek missiles down range, Tyrra had walked the fixed distances noting the unevenness of target positions resulting from dips in the terrain. The morrow would bring strong sunshine, a day without dampness, void of the moisture which affects the tautness of bowstrings.

Striding from the barracks area she made her way across the parade yard to the arsenal. The sweep of leather yet felt rewarding against her thighs, the ring of accomplishment still fresh. Entering the arrow smithy she sought out a senior fletcher. Here craftswomen adroitly fashioned the longbows and arrows of Jarra. Racks of their finished produce lined the armory's stone walls. Farther inside the workshops, wooden shafts in various stages of completion hung about, still to achieve their final shape. Forms, vises, clamps, knives, saws, all the tools of the arrow maker's art were neatly stacked by the workbenches. Warriors too old or crippled, unable or wishing not to take a spouse, after mustering out could earn their keep as semi-civilians fabricating the Ravenhood's weapons. Spotting a grey head, Tyrra approached an artisan breaking for a cup of herb tea. "Can you help me, sister?" the young woman asked.

"Aye, sister. How can I be of service?" The old gal put down the cup. Pleasant in her manner, who knew how many Kala she had dispatched long decades past.

"Rosin, sister. I fear tomorrow's sun and the jitters sure to come will sweat my palm. I thought perhaps you could spare me a cloth packet to keep me dry."

"Ah, you compete on the plain, eh young warrior?"

"That is my plan," Tyrra smiled.

The arrow-smith ambled slowly to a shallow bin and lifted a canister. She removed the lid and withdrew a cloth packet. Handling it to the archer, she advised, "Blot this on the palm which grips the bow and you shall have no problem."

"Thank you."

"May I offer some advice?"

"I would be grateful."

"If the sun is of concern to your palm then surely it must also concern your eye. Glare whether direct or bouncing off the sheen of your bow can distort what you see. If you darken the area beneath your eye, where the skin rests tight against the socket bone, it will diminish the glare. The blackness of burnt cork is ideal for such a purpose." She looked up at the taller warrior to determine her receptivity. "I have some."

"Anything which helps, gives me an edge, regardless how marginal, is accepted with thanks. If the sun is bright, I will heed your counsel."

"Aye, that's the sister." Placing a chunk of charred cork inside a roll of ragged cloth she passed it to Tyrra. And one last reminder, sister," she winked.

"What's that?"

"Keep your elbow up!" The gray head laughed.

"Aye, sister. I know no other way."

Indeed the sun shone splendid and hot as the initial line of archers toed the mark. For a full day the buzz of arrows streaking downrange filled the Jarra air. By mid-day three quarters had been eliminated, and three hours after that the remaining group had been halved. The following bright morning 104 contestants reported for competition, among them Tyrra Kavoyy, smudges of black underscoring the gold eyes. With targets repositioned thirty strides more distant than yesterday's finale, accuracy suffered for the majority, quickly shrinking the group to two dozen. And yet the stable hand of the isthmus held her own among the finest The Vag had to offer. Through the most demanding of measurements the rules dictated that only four archers survive the day. She had learned her lessons well this markswoman, applying every instruction, recalling each helpful hint offered by coaches during her apprenticeship. Whether the charred cork helped is difficult to confirm. But as the sun dropped below its zenith, its angle dancing upon the polished longbow, the confidence of the corksmear removed but one more potential nerve jangler. She wasn't the only one to darken herself. Several seasoned archers had spat in the dirt and with their thumbs stroked a dull mud on the same reflection points. Irrespective of rosin or cork, the arrowheads of Tyrra Kavoyy consistently punctured the innermost concentric circles. When the whistle blew signaling completion, her score announced she would shoot again at tomorrow's shoot-off. With many hands clapping her tired shoulders, a joyful Tyrra walked off the field with the knowledge that at worst, she had won the copper arrow pendant with its attendant recognition.

That evening as others reveled and swapped stories of superior shots and excruciatingly near misses, Tyrra remained in the barracks sitting on her cot. Discipline is the mother of consistency, she reminded herself. In less than eighteen hours the last arrow will have blurred its path downrange and a champion declared. Her chances would not be diminished by a night of partying and the loss of focus it would surely bring.

"Tyrra Kavoyy!" The familiar voice calling her name stood straddle-legged in the doorway, silhouetted against a dusky sky.

"Yes, I am here," answered the new kilt.

"How are the nerves?" Capitana Ferran' s husky voice inquired.

"I am trying to concentrate on tomorrow."

"Tyrra Kavoyy you were outstanding today! As natural an archer as I have witnessed. To your credit you've worked diligently to maximize that goddess given ability. You deserve to stand among the final four. By the fingers, you do!"

"Thank you, Capitana. I am honored by your praise."

"Eight years ago it was Ryya Ferann seated in silence thinking of the perfect shot. So hard did I concentrate that the next day I performed as poorly as a rookie girly's first practice shot. And so I had to be satisfied for an arrowhead pendant of dull copper. I shouldn't belittle it for there are thousands of sisters who would yearn for its glory And if you are to march off the field with such an honor then so be it. For your comrades will hold you in renewed esteem whenever it peeks from about your throat."

"Your words are somewhat comforting, Capitana, but I suspect there is more to your message."

Ferann sat on the cot across from Tyrra. Very little light illuminated the room. Shadows dappled both their faces. "Am I so transparent?" Her lips forced a thoughtful smile. "Don't think so much, Tyrra. Go out for a few hours and circulate amidst your approving comrades. Absorb their good wishes with a warrior's humility. Savor the inspiration they no doubt will provide. Return to a night of sound rest. Then tomorrow for an hour or so before the match, think about why you want to win. For your mother! Yes, the Commandant told me of her situation. For your sibs, classmates, instructors. For Gala Rotaria. But most of all win it all for Tyrra Kavoyy! Be selfish in your pursuit, my lady!" In a barracks of obscured vision the fire in Ferann's words blazed a path to her subordinate's soul. "Perhaps twenty minutes prior to your name being called, check your bow, study the ground, the wind, your aiming points...and do whatever has proven to buoy your confidence."

"Shall we go outside together?" laughed an energized Tyrra.

"Aye, lady. But this time we'll defer rank to celebrity. You go first."

"Archers, draw your lots!" So commanded Skyyra Jakivv. The field flowed with a crowd of over one thousand kilted women. Black and red banners ringed the grounds. The crimson V and two headed wolf, ancient symbols of The Vag adorned the various tents and outbuildings. Grasping the leather bottle which held the lots, Tyrra shook out a yellowed die. Every facet bore the number two. She would be second in shooting sequence. The Commandant introduced the archers by name and number; the crowd cheering each. All four shook hands and strung their bows. "Secure your arrows. Eleven in a quiver. One in hand." Of the quartet, three were of the kord, the fourth a woman a few years removed but one who obviously had maintained an archer's regimen. Choosing their arrows from the racks to their rear, they checked them for depth of nock, feathering and balance. The shafts had already been pre-selected, those with the slightest warp having been discarded. "Twelve arrows in two minutes at a distance of eighty strides," called Jakivv. "First archer, nock your arrow and toe the mark!" Number one took her place, settling feet, butt and shoulders till she felt comfortable. "You may commence firing when ready!" Downrange a thick straw target, its one stride diameter covered with heavy canvas, awaited, its concentric rings shriveling in the archer's eye. Her first arrow overflew the target by a hand span.. The second fell short. In total it proved to be a poor showing for a finalist.

A spotter called the score before withdrawing the shafts. "Eighteen," she shouted. The disappointed archer kicked the dust and spat, certain she had squandered her opportunity. Copper it would be.

Blotting rosin on palms and fingertips, Tyrra moved to position. "Second archer, nock your arrow and toe the mark!" Nestling into a shooter's stance, she took a couple of deep breaths never taking her gaze off the center ring. Standing erect, her left arm horizontal to the ground and gripping the handle, head turned 90 degrees right of target as were hips and shoulders, Tyrra stood prepared to deliver her first arrow. Fingering the arrowed bowstring with three fingers she drew the arrow back, allowing string and fingers to anchor comfortably against nose and chin.

"No wind. Good," she thought. "Elbow up, elbow up." Sighting along the tiny notch grooved above the handle, Tyrra picked out the center circle and let if fly. It struck home tearing the edge of the innermost ring. In ninety seconds the quiver had emptied, every arrow striking the target, the last barely ripping the perimeter. "Sixty four points," yelled the spotter. "Including three centers!" A great cheer went up from the onlookers. Restraining her emotions, Tyrra's impassive features belied the excitement churning inside.

Number three followed with a score of fifty one, meaning Tyrra had locked up the silver prize at worst. The final archer stood rock solid in her stance. "No nerves in this cat," mused Tyrra. Archer number four, "Gaara" her fans shouted, had left the hood three years earlier to oversee the family farm. Last night those kilts who gambled on the outcome, had installed Gaara as the favorite, her reputation spanning a half dozen years. Powerfully built, she dispatched her arrows with fluid precision.

With so many hits in the center, the young woman stood certain Gaara had bested her. Tyrra swallowed hard, trying not to wear her disappointment. "Sixty four points with three centers," came the cry. A tie! The air of resignation went out of Tyrra. A tie! Quickly she moved to Gaara, shaking her hand as well as the other two finalists. "A good match," Gaara roughly called out to Tyrra.

"A good match indeed," confirmed the young archer. "Will there be two gold pendants?"

"Small target," grumbled Gaara.

"Small target?" Tyrra echoed. What's...."

"Small target." interrupted Jakivv. "One arrow each. Best shot earns the gold.

Gaara will shoot first inasmuch as she shot last earlier.

"Fine," roared Gaara staring hostilely at her adversary. "Let's get on with it, girly!" Purposely demeaning, she hissed 'girly' with a throaty emphasis.

Dispelling Gaara's attempted intimidation, Tyrra stretched to her fullest height, taller by four digits than the squatter opponent. "Aye, Commandant," she bellowed to Jakivv. "Let the truest woman carry the day!" Grimacing with confidence she turned a frigid eye to Gaara. Six months of conditioning in the crucible of Jarra had steeled her beyond coercion. By the fingers, Tyrra Kavoyy would not be bullied on this the greatest challenge of her young life. "It is only fair that an aging warrior be given first chance," she mocked. Two could play the game of nerves.

Fuming, Gaara took a half step to Tyrra. "Aging warrior, my ass!" she fumed.

The Commandant was quick to step between them. "Gaara, select an arrow and move to your position!" It was the First Arrow's duty to remain neutral, but she couldn't help but admire the spunk of Shaara Kavoyy's daughter.

Down range a small disk had been fixed to the target easel. Fashioned from compacted straw its diameter spanned roughly ten digits, about the size of a head. Painted on the canvas overwrap a large eye stared out at the archers as if to dare them to pierce its surface. The crowd immediately took sides, the current warriors of the hood robustly heartening Tyrra, their own. As to be expected, Gaara' support came from the retirees who bellowed loudly for their champion to best the upstart. After much commotion, the crowd hushed to the raised arms of Skyyra Jakivv. "Fire at your pleasure," she signaled the husky archer. With little exertion, Gaara in one fluid motion selected her aiming point, drew and let loose. Cutting through the warm morning air it struck the target flush, perhaps two digits within the perimeter. A great roar went up from an appreciative throng for in fact it was an outstanding shot. Passing Tyrra on her way to the mark, the confident Gaara crowed, "Beat that one, girly, and even I'll dip my bow to you."

Tyrra said nothing, electing instead to choose the optimum aiming point. Erect and graceful, she ran through her mental checklist, ensuring every detail had been addressed. As she released her arrow, the timeliest of thoughts flashed into her mind. *Poona! Poona predicted me Huntress of the Eye. I am the child of destiny and prophecy!* As it zipped along its swift trajectory, Tyrra watched the feathered tail shrink into the center-most ring. It had struck the pupil head on, as superlative a shot as Jarra had ever witnessed. Screams of joy erupted from the gathering. Regardless of which archer one favored, all wildly cheered the astonishing shot. They had beheld history this day. Her comrades rushed to lift Tyrra upon their shoulders, noisily parading her around the field. Happiness of an indescribable nature blazed the face of Tyrra Kavoyy. The champion's pendant would match the color of her eyes. Gold of the richest hue. Trying to control her balance atop the many hands, she caught sight of Gaara alone but for a handful of consoling friends. Tipping the point of her bow first to her head then towards Tyrra, she shouted, "The best shot won! The best woman won!" Generous in defeat, she again saluted Tyrra.

"Thank you, sister," yelled the bouncing victor. And she was whisked away before being able to congratulate Gaara for a fine effort. At the awards ceremony she would find opportunity to say something personal.

"Tyr-ra, Tyr-ra." The boisterous cheering deafened every ear, conversation impossible. Riding the crest of human tide, a triumphant Tyrra Kavoyy, Huntress of the Eye, basked in the shine of unbridled praise. Suddenly the notion came to her. Poona, predictor of her glory, had indicated "Twice!" *Didn't that mean five years hence history would repeat itself. Aye huntress, what else?*

# CHAPTER VIII

The Capital, core of Vag religion, culture and science, embraced a large nunine community. Several hundred dwelled in the metropolis proper and its suburbs, debating, learning, experimenting, plying one trade or another and minding the wheels of government. It was into this cerebral nave that Zoog and eighty two nunales of ger class were introduced. Competition beyond anything experienced at the isthmus energized Zoog to heightened levels of scholarship. Quickly gee ascended to the top of the student group, excelling in all that gee studied. Attesting to the young Kavoyy's brilliance, ideas developed in the brain of Zoog's childhood surfaced anew to strike the minds of even the most conservative scholars. Soon masters of the Academy of Science recognized that among them the precocious young thinker, who instinctively grasped all they taught, was now expanding on their knowledge, offering provocative solutions and hypotheses. Without conceit, void of affectation, Zoog dazzled them repeatedly. The more they talked with gen the greater they understood that Zoog Kavoyy stood special amid the special. For when a nunale gazes into the orbs of another nunale, there is an ability to read the divine breath of intellect stirring inside. And when they delved Zoog, they saw a force of superior faculty. Several instructors of high repute half jested that the young Kavoyy must have been conceived in a stratum apart from Gala Rotaria and magically gifted to the Vaghi. So exceptional Kavoyy's mind that the high priest, Daag Goraxx, came to know of Zoog's reputation and sent for gen.

As primate of The Vag, Daag enjoyed the use of an opulent villa a few medecs east of the city walls. Tilling the estate's sunny fields a few workers gave pause to observe the cheerful nunale treading along the cart path. Gee waved and they waved back leaning upon their hoes for a moment's rest. Moving up the incline toward the stucco building freshly capped with reddish barrel tile, Zoog wondered if Marz's sweat three years past at the brickworks had helped mold Daag's new roof. Entering through the peristyle, gee immediately noticed the drop in temperature, grateful its coolness was now drying the perspiration beading ger forehead. Physically Zoog hadn't matured much over ger time at the academy. If anything, the waistline had lost a few digits. Food was fairly basic at the Capital. Without Shaara's cooking to tempt the hardy nunale's palate, meals were often skipped in quest of education. Whereas most of the nunine gender possessed a natural dumpiness, Zoog

Kavoyy owned a less bulbous figure, though hardly svelte. Perhaps because gee preferred tunic and bragghi to the billowy robes worn by most students, the overall appearance was decreasingly nunine.

The salon, comfortable with furniture of the upholstered kind, small tables and several rich carpets plush with floral patterns in soft blues and yellows, featured sweeping murals of rustic life. On closer inspection the visitor determined the wall art to be mosaics of the finest order. So fluid were the colors, so gradual the tones, that one had to stand very close to discern the individual tiles. Images of fish from The Vag's plentiful lakes and rivers decorated the borders emphasizing the motif of a bountiful land. A pair of facing alcoves sheltered sculpted busts of ancient Vaghi long forgotten in name but appreciated for their handsomeness.

Seated upon a tufted armchair, the high priest of Gala Rotaria snacked from a fruit basket, depositing pits and stems in a small alabaster bowl. "So tell me, Zoog Kavoyy, now that you've examined my humble surroundings, what is your verdict?" Looking more to break the ice than angling for compliments, the primate flashed a broad smile.

"My origin is of the isthmus, my high priest. There was never fanciness in life there. Though I've been at the Capital for three years, I yet marvel at the creations of our minds and hands. And your domicile is among the most spectacular, rivaling that of the Lord. Or so I am informed by architects at the academy, for I've never stepped inside the Lord's residence." Cautious in response, Zoog was sure not to provoke controversy.

"Ah, take my holy word for it that this is the more splendid of the two. The house of the Lord, though magnificent in outward appearance, is cold in its appointments. There is nothing warm there, nothing welcoming. The objects within are more trophy in conception than artistic." Goraxx gave the younger nunale a knowing wink as if to convey that this was 'our little secret.' "And please call me Daag here in the privacy of my home. Naturally in public more formal appellations will be necessary. Such is protocol!"

"And rightly so, Daag," responded Zoog not wasting any time addressing Daag in the familiar. "Respect without adoration is the sign of a healthy society."

Unable to ascertain if Zoog's comment was a simple statement of conviction or a prickling, Daag chose to agree. "Yes, by all means. And without self-respect comes social decadence and its immoral consequences, I might add." Offering a plump fig to the declining guest, the priest cleared a throat which necessitated no clearing for it was moist with juice. So it is with people planning tactics in mid conversation. Sizing up ger caller, Daag decided on a course of flattery before getting into the true purpose of the discussion. "Zoog, they tell me you have exceptional talents, with a future as rosy as the sweet cheeks of the great goddess herself And now that your formal education ends you will be selecting a vocation commensurate with your excellence. For most this is a relatively simple task, the ultimate vocation being the field in which one best excels. But for you who excels in every endeavor, it has to be an agonizing choice."

"Daag," the young Kavoyy interrupted, "I have already selected science as my calling."

"Yes. So I am informed. So I am informed," gee repeated, a troubled rasp gripping the repetition. "My reports are that you possess a memory which recalls images in their precise nature whether they be texts or columns of numbers. Is this all true?"

"Aye, Daag. And it has always been so with me. A veritable blessing of the goddess." Zoog pushed both palms together in prayerful pose.

Seeing the opportunity to play on Zoog's words, Daag advanced the conversation. "Perhaps the goddess blessed you to follow her path, to shine in the priestly vocation?" Pleased with the turn, Daag nodded while pointing a thick finger at the relaxed visitor now seated before gen.

"You make a logical argument, Daag. One which I have considered with great deliberation. However, my spirit tells me I can accomplish more for our people in the realm of scientific discovery and invention."

"And I think you should deliberate some more!"

Indifferent to Daag's pushy persuasiveness, an unperturbed Zoog answered, "I think not!"

Backing off, the high priest fumbled for the last few grapes rolling in the basket bottom. "Perhaps there is compromise," gee offered. "What is it you wish to accomplish?"

Zoog thought for a few moments, considering whether to confide the aspirations within. "To solve the riddle of The Vag!" gee finally announced in a voice much louder than they had been speaking.

"My dear Zoog," the priest chided. "The girth of Mount Aryxx is littered with thinkers pondering that very same puzzle."

"And that is the problem. They ponder!! Without scientific research, without stone-hard proof they attempt to determine the origins of the Vaghi!"

"And what would be your mode of discovery, young Kavoyy?"

"Digging and searching our earliest existence. Cataloging, sifting, comparing, drawing conclusions from systematic evidence. And in doing, I will develop my own sound manner of investigation." This time it was Zoog who directed a finger across the table.

"And where will you commence this, this investigation?"Daag inquired. "Will you probe the hub of our beginnings at Muraverdus?"

"Nay, Daag. I believe footprints of the earliest settlements exist a long way from the green wall of Muraverdus. The wild country and farther south... that's where!" Zoog smiled knowing ger statement had startled the round nunale biting down on the last purple grape.

"The Gugububu?" gasped Daag, juicy spittle dribbling from the glistening lips.

"Aye, genther of my gender. The Gugububu!"

"But as you know, it is forbidden. No one is permitted but with the Lord's permission."

"As you said before, perhaps there is compromise." Again Zoog showed the perfect teeth of the Kavoyy. Already two steps ahead of the priest, Zoog had baited the hook. The student's purpose from the start was to elicit a concession of dual vocations.

"One for the other?" Daag's response was both question and confirmation.

"One for the other," affirmed the confident scholar. "But please tell me why in all truth are you so driven to enlisting me in the priesthood?"

An exasperated Goraxx threw both arms skyward, astounded that this upstart genius had backed Daag's derrière into a narrow corner. "Here I, Daag Goraxx, highest cleric of The Vag, sit sticky faced with juice driveling my cheeks, bargaining with a pup but three years off an isthmus beet field! And I'm being bested at my own game. By the fingers, the eyes of glass will never fill the sockets of Daag Goraxx's likeness," gee self scoffed and guffawed, the moon face shaking from side to side. "Young Kavoyy, I sense you have played me like the fat fish which swim the Big Lazy. But if you have learned nothing else this day, be assured I don't take my ego all that seriously." Again, Daag chuckled aloud.

Zoog joined the laughter and, in good humor, spoke. "Know this, Daag Goraxx. Twenty years ago at my confirmation it was you, yet junior in your priesthood, who presided my confirmation. And it was you who gazed my eyes to predict a specialness. So it is your own fault."

"Aha," exclaimed Daag, enjoying the repartee. "So I am victim of my own ability!" Gee collected ger composure before continuing. "Zoog, my motive is honorable. Over recent years many of the more gifted nunales have elected to pursue careers in science and medicine outside of the religious sphere, fearful the clergy would stifle their freedom. Consequently the priesthood finds itself competing for the best talent. It would be a matter of great prestige if the tug of Gala Rotaria could attract you to her altar. Selfishly it would also enhance my reputation as one of influence. And there is no doubt that if you come to us, your example will attract others who are particularly gifted."

"Yes, yes, Daag. I understand your dilemma. Perhaps I realized it all along. But I need not the chains of clergy to squelch my calling. To flourish on my chosen path, I require freedom. Freedom to follow my Star. So let us compromise in the best of faith."

So they worked it out. Zoog Kavoyy would be enlisted in the priesthood with Daag's directive to uncover the roots of what they termed 'Vaghism,' supported by the resources of Daag Goraxx and the temple of the goddess. In a sense they both won. And though the disparity in age was a full generation, the pair would enjoy a friendship beyond mentor and protégé.

"I will obtain a document of passport permitting you entrance to the Gugububu." Daag exhaled strongly, the huff loud. "I break out in blistered sweat just saying the word Gugububu. How deep do you plan to penetrate that horrid place?"

"I'm not sure. But I suspect that the perimeter of what is now desert sand was once lush. And therein sleep the answers to our origin. How many square medecs that entails is something yet to be determined." The young scientist crossed a leg, pulling the ankle over the opposite knee. Zoog's calf muscle bulged causing Daag to take notice. "I'm robust for our gender," explained Zoog. "My father, bless his gritty soul, made no exceptions when it came to stable work and plowing. For which I am especially grateful. The point is that the roughness of the wild country and the Gugububu do not dishearten me even though there is a strong respect for what lies ahead. My upbringing has prepared me for such things."

"Ah, Zoog, I suppose it is true that without first experiencing discomfort it is difficult for one to totally appreciate pleasure."

Gee nodded agreeably. "As my daddy is fond of repeating, one must shovel a barnful of horse shit to fully enjoy a hot bath!"

"Truly your father is a golden tongued fellow. Now I comprehend where his nuun derives such eloquence." With that they both roared. Then quickly shifting back to Zoog's mission, Daag Goraxx's mood became one of serious thought. "Young Kavoyy, in your quest for the beginnings of The Vag, I offer a piece of information which could be helpful...but dangerous. There lives in the wild country a lunatic nunale, stripped of priestly powers by me some three and a half years ago. The lunacy of which I refer is an evilness which shivers my spine. Gee and ger followers believe sacrifice of the Children of Misfortune will appease the goddess, and so reward The Vag with an end to the dryness prevalent these past years. The Lord proscribed gen to the wild country where gee slithers to this day, no doubt fomenting an ugly anger."

'Huug Taratt?"

"You know the name?" Daag's eyes bulged.

"Aye, it is spoken at the academy...with disdain."

"Regardless the iniquity within Huug Taratt's soul, gee is an exceptional scientist. And Taratt has knowledge of the past...supposedly supported by evidence of a physical nature. I am not telling you to seek out Taratt, for that is your decision only. But it is there for you to consider. In any event, beware the malevolent powers of Huug Taratt!"

"I will heed your advice, Daag. And I will report my progress from time to time." Zoog uncrossed the leg and leaned forward.

"Good," the primate returned. "For if I am unaware of what you do, then I cannot provide assistance should you need it."

"From what I've read of the wild country it is highly possible my needs could become desperate,"Zoog laughed.

Picking up on Zoog's half serious comment, Daag cajoled, "And try to avoid the poor habits of those wild country Vaghi who gamble incessantly when not imbibing that vinegary wine they favor. Perhaps the harshness of the environment encourages such temptations."

"Have you ever succumbed to temptation, Daag?"Zoog asked the question in the rhetorical sense, never expecting the introspective answer Daag returned.

A somberness overcame the priest causing the jaw to hang, eyes to droop. "Yes, in truth I have," gee confessed. "But even worse I have bowed to intimidation. And in doing I have corrupted myself...to my everlasting dismay." It was the weakest of moments. After a soundless pause gee snapped out of the funk with, "But enough of that!"

Unbeknown to Zoog, ger brother knew the source of Daag's pain. "Everyone's past bears some regret. You are no different than any of us in that respect," consoled the younger nunale.

"I suppose," sighed Daag, yet troubled by the secret within. "But unfortunately my regret is one which profoundly affects our future."

By law no Vag is ever permitted to travel into the depth of that enormous expanse of desert called the Gugububu. How it was named no one is quite certain. Most popular of myths is that the lone survivor of an early expedition could only mumble an unintelligible "goo-goo-boo-boo" after crawling from the scorched wasteland. They were to be the final sounds uttered through his blistered lips. Within hours dehydration, coupled with a brain addled by the cruelest of temperatures, stole short his deliverance.

At the beginning, or northernmost perimeter of the Gugububu, sits a vast depression known as the Cauldron. The lower rim of the Cauldron represents the limit of penetration for explorers lucky enough to have returned. Fools and daredevils, usually one and the same, oft times must be protected from themselves. Only the Lord of The Vag himself could approve a foray beyond the upper rim.

How expansive stretch the lands of the Gugububu is an unanswered riddle. Even if water were plentiful, why would one care to travel its merciless flatlands, its treacherous creases? The known topography of Gala Rotaria, that portion which the Vaghi and Orri inhabit, comprises itself of peninsula upon peninsula. Sometimes hundreds of free-form land fingers swell into bulbous feet and they in turn sprout many toes...appendage squiggling from appendage, offshoot from offshoot. So why should the Gugububu be any different? Logically the farther south into the desert hell one roams, the greater the heat. Unending horizons ripple in distorted waves. Nights are cool and windy, confusing those mechanisms which regulate the body and its ability to cope. For every sand blasted step in there must be an equally exhausting step out...if a body is to return. Land navigators need to accurately recall exiting passages twisted in memory by the fiendish desertscape. Orienteering is a difficult task in any strange land; however, heat baked reasoning will misdirect even the most brilliant trailblazer into absurd conclusions. And the peninsula labyrinth only compounds the probability of error.

The prospects get worse. Folklore speaks of a punishing horror beyond the Gugububu, if that is possible. It is said sulfurous skies and volcanic spew await souls unfortunate enough to tread its ashen floor. Ground hot enough to singe the toughest boot sole. Air so toxic it claws throat and lungs with equal fervor. For the great goddess Gala Rotaria has balanced her land mass in three tiers: the extreme north where ravenous hordes of Kala forage through wind lashed forests and frosted tundra; the verdant mountains and plains of the Vaghi and Orri which make up the central belt; and below that the Gugububu and beyond Yet everywhere, irrespective of region, spurt thousands of peninsulas. It is as though the great mother, in forming the land, splattered gigantic buckets of cosmic mud on the surface forming misshapen tentacles and water courses with broad gulfs chinking land from land. So is the ground of Gala Rotaria.

Having been expedited along the path of priestly consecration, Zoog Kavoyy packed may sheets of reed paper, writing instruments, candles, various articles of apparel and blankets into a single small trunk and pointed to the wild country. Off-loading at the Big Lazy's southernmost terminal, gee joined a trade caravan plodding to Arabella. While Zoog's baggage rode atop a creaking wagon, the young priest walked its flank, inspecting the soil, examining stones and rock formations. By the time they reached their destination, gee had observed the subtle changes in landscape from day to day, noticing how particular plants had adapted to the shifts in environment. Outside of Arabella, in a farming village barely larger than Kavoyy Station, Zoog presented Daag's letter of introduction to the local priest who provided a small cabin. Once used to store agricultural equipment, the stone building tucked into a hillside had the delightful ability to remain reasonably cool even on the warmest of days. Scavenging an old door which gee converted into a desk and an equally senior chair borrowed from the elderly host, Zoog had the makings of a headquarters from which to commence 'operations.' In obedience to Daag Goraxx's directive, meals and other cooperations also would be afforded the young priest for the duration.

It had been four months since Zoog's arrival, most of it spent traveling among surrounding hamlets, chatting with old timers, soaking up the folklore, listening to stories of the ancients. For in legend and myth there is often a root of truth. Passed down mouth to ear spanning the ages, stories unwittingly become corrupted over the retelling. In ger journal a recurring reference was noted. Repeatedly it was said the Vaghi sprang full grown and clothed from a 'great seed' along with the domesticated animals of their need. And it had all happened on but a single morning.

On one occasion after having been on the road for almost a week, Zoog broke bread near the ruins of a crumbled site. Scrub brush and scrawny gray trees had overgrown the dilapidated piles of stones still arranged in geometric pattern. Limping from the opposite direction an emaciated relic of a Vag, ravaged by the winds of time, approached the priest. Coarse white hair wrinkled as the parched land on which he tread, grew in ragged clusters atop the cadaverous head, like tail feathers on an aroused chicken. Wobbling to an unsteady halt, he peered from his one functioning eye at the nunale rising to greet him. "Will you share my loaf with me, old man?" Zoog politely asked.

"Aye," he answered in a voice barely above a whisper. "I drank from a muddied creek a few medecs back as the sun was lifting. But no real food has passed these lips in two days other than a few mashed roots." Virtually toothless, the black hole of a mouth forced out words with difficulty.

Zoog assisted him to a sitting position and also sat. "I am Zoog Kavoyy, priest of Gala Rotaria. How are you called?"

The man stared without blinking. Perhaps the effort would sap what little energy remained within his frail bones. Better to conserve what eggeth of survival yet coursed his veins. "I don't know," he finally responded. An existence harsh and squalid had taken its toll. The brain baked by dementia had stolen his identity.

Zoog ripped out the bread's soft center, tearing it into edible bits which he slipped between the old one's gums. "Where do you go?" gee inquired.

"Arabella. To the Children of Misfortune. Maybe they will pity me with food and shelter." He spoke in a mumble while allowing the bread to dissolve in what little spit wetted his mouth. Seeing his throat bob, Zoog determined he had swallowed enough to insert a few more crumbs. "Thank you genther," he nodded. "I've been called many ugly things lately for I am a beggar cursed by fate. But my own name I have not heard spoken in so long that I have forgotten it, blurred like wax on glass. My mind is numbed by senility, some days worse than others. It makes no difference. I am at the end of my journey. I am confident that the great goddess will recognize me at the gathering of souls."

"You have my blessing for a peaceful afterlife, old man." And with that Zoog compassionately pressed an open palm against the shriveled brow while invoking the name of Gala Rotaria.

"Thank you, genther," the toothless one rasped.

"And what is this rubble heap upon which we squat? Has it a name?"

"I do not know," he coughed dryly.

"Alas, too bad," sighed the nunale seeking clues of any sort to feed the journal. "Is there anyone who would know?"

"I don't think so. But the people who lived here long, long ago, before there were Lords, were called Kwinarvy." He coughed once more.

"Say it again," encouraged Zoog.

"Kwinarvy." Incredibly, this leathery scrap of life, unable to recall his' own appellation, yet retained a spark of memory, recollecting a name infinitely more remote than his own.

"Who were they?" gee pressed.

The man looked puzzled. "Why, Vaghi," his voice almost chided. Who else? "Vaghi of the great seed!"

Gee never saw the old man again. And though Zoog probed 'Kwinarvy' among the area's citizens, all were ignorant. Not one claimed to have heard it uttered before. The Kwinarvy were a people lost to the sweep of time. The young scientist returned to the site often to sift through its debris. But it never yielded any secrets, although gee did determine that it encompassed a much larger area than the rowed stones. Only charred hollows remained, the residue of cooking fires lit many ages gone. Yet Zoog measured the perimeters and sketched a diagram. Perhaps it would have future value. And if gee continued to scratch and probe, hopefully a telltale trace would surface.

One very bright day, a day when the sun shone with a whiteness that bleached the pigment from all that one viewed, Zoog stumbled upon a chance encounter that would provide much to ponder. Traveling about the lowest reaches of the wild country where it touches the outer apron of the Gugububu, Zoog was beginning to wonder if gee had underestimated the region's severity. For Zoog was already wilting without yet having encroached upon the forbidden desert lands. Sweat had seeped through the backpack, salty stains forming irregular patterns on the rough fabric. Directly overhead the solar disk radiated with an intensity unlike any other gee'd experienced before. The straw hat gee bought earlier didn't seem to help much. Since the contact with the emaciated fellow a month ago, no lead had turned up, nothing to stimulate an eager curiosity. Constantly mindful that patience must override frustration, gee doggedly pushed genself to distant towns and villages. Derisive responses, occasionally greeted the priest's presence, a discourteous riff raff mocking Zoog's polite questions. Reluctant to share information, in part because they possessed none, they responded to honest inquiry with a nasty sass. Hostile and unkempt, their taunting attitude was borne of ignorance and a sub-culture which exalted such behavior. Nevertheless, the young Kavoyy persisted. Most disconcerting to overcome were those who purposely misled. Not only did they waste time but they dashed the newfound hopes of the young scientist...testing Zoog's resilience in the doing. Basically

Zoog lumped the local population into three categories: the good, the bad and the dissenting. The great majority were good, hardworking citizens scrimping a meager livelihood from a hard pan further fatigued by too much sun and a paucity of water. Alongside lived a lawless breed of cheats, brawlers, petty rustlers, and outright bandits surrounded by women of equal character... the bad. Periodically, when things got too far out of control, the army would sweep through, rounding up the worst offenders and, with the Lord's prerogative, punish them! Penalties ranged from forced labor to execution by hanging for the most offensive. One would think the object lessons of such punitive measures would virtually eliminate criminal behavior. But apparently where there are but two forks in the road, there is an ornery kind that always chooses the evil path. The third variety, the dissenters, often are non-conformists escaping the restrictions of family, society and government. From all points of The Vag they trudge to the wild country, some solitary in their refuge, others in groups or sects. Unhappy and impressionable, irresponsible but never wrong, they claim to seek everything from spiritual truth to freedom of expression. It is among this last compartment of citizens that Zoog found genself this blistering afternoon.

The hollow clunk of wood chimes swaying gently in the late morning heat caught the ear of Zoog Kavoyy. Climbing the crest of a low hillock gee spotted the source, a makeshift stockade constructed of twisted posts. Irregular in form, the compound was more of a sloppy corral, unlike that which would hold a military encampment. Chinks, some the span of a child, permitted the nunale to view flashes of activity inside. Crosspieces had been inserted into the bottom, giving the woven fence an appearance akin to nests built by large, predatory birds. The tall gate stood ajar, and so Zoog slipped through the opening. Within the compound ramshackle sheds and open shack-tents served as housing for the one hundred twenty or so inhabitants. The chime sounds were louder here, constantly ringing in noisy harmony. No one seemed to pay much attention to Zoog. To be accurate a few gandered in the nunale's direction, aware but not concerned Zoog was a stranger. Their awareness came not from the unfamiliar face, or floppy straw hat, or even the backpack, but from the absence of chalk on Zoog's forehead. For all milling about the central walkway wore a white streak upon their brow. The visitor stopped a young man robed in rusty brown, not much older than gee, to make inquiries. "Water from blood," greeted the local. Curious. After but two minutes of conversation Zoog determined that the people were of a sect called the Chosen; that the chalky paste, a substitute for the 'basic-ness of flour,' represented a symbolic marking of their commitment; and in this compound they prayed and meditated, living under the goddess' command apart from the tyranny of formal government. The answers were catechismic, spoken like one under the control of an invisible ventriloquist. At once Zoog realized gee must be in the domain of Huug Taratt for these 'dissenters' of the Chosen were as described by academy gossip and touched upon in conversation by Daag Goraxx: "And who guides the Chosen?" asked Zoog, already certain of the answer.

"A nunale of the highest vision. One who speaks with the great mother herself. The Prophet, Huug Taratt." Again the delivery was as if by rote.

"How would I speak with Huug, the Prophet?" Zoog inquired, humoring the man with a reverent tone.

"To the rear of the compound the ground is elevated. Atop the mound sits the Prophet's retreat. It is the only solid building. It will be difficult to miss."

"Thank you."

"Water from blood," the man murmured as he departed.

*Water from blood?* thought Zoog. *Again. Was this the all-purpose salutation of the Chosen, a benediction to be repeated in lieu of hello or farewell?*

Surprisingly Huug Taratt's building was more substantial than Zoog had expected. Built mostly of stone with a faded wooden roof, it commanded a wide view of the sprawling community jumbled below.

"Enter, genther of my gender," the voice called out. "I've been watching you since you passed through the gate." Inside the open door stood a gaunt nunale with shaved head. "It is rare that I get to speak to our kind, genther. What brings you to my doorstep?" The chalk smear and sun darkened skin contrasted a bizarre image.

Zoog crossed the threshold, the auric eyes slow to adjust from bright light to dimmed interior. "Hail, Huug Taratt. I am Zoog Kavoyy, priest and scientist, on a mission of the latter vocation." The shadowy features soon took form, defining the deeply tanned host clad in but loin cloth and sandals. Zoog removed the hat, a tunic sleeve mopping ger forehead in the same sweep. As usual a friendly pleasantness exuded the round face.

"A scientist, eh! You look awfully young to be so called." Tall with sharp features, it would have been easy to mistake Huug for a male However, the chest void of nipples confirmed ger nunine being.

Not wishing to provoke a debate of ger qualifications, Zoog ignored the comment. Instead the young Kavoyy glanced about the tables strewn with what obviously were the gadgets and concoctions of Huug's experiments. "Your laboratory fascinates me, Huug Taratt. Your reputation as an able scientist is yet spoken at the academy." Zoog slipped the pack from perspired shoulders and draped it over a stool.

"They still remember me, do they?" Huug was definitely pleased with the flattery, especially from a nunale of the scientific gentherhood. Zoog moved among the tables quickly identifying the nature of the various projects. An impressed Taratt rapidly realized the exceptional perception of the nunine visitor and soon they chatted without pause, exchanging thoughts and theories relating to the work lying before them. Engrossed for over an hour, Huug was amazed that Zoog Kavoyy was able to predict the sequential next steps for all of the experiments, even speculating on the outcome. In an effort to outdo, the older nunale led ger precocious colleague to a tiny chamber containing shelves piled with writings and scrolls of varying lengths, no doubt the notations of Huug's labor. A desk and rough chair crowded the room as the two nunales stood before an odd instrument. Comprised primarily of a glass bulb and stem, Huug explained that unseen 'pressures' in the surrounding air caused the special liquid gee had developed to rise and fall. Gee concluded that these 'pressures' were influenced by impending weather patterns, and though the elder scientist admitted an ignorance as to exactly why it happened, a lowering of the liquid signaled the coming of storms. Conversely a rise predicted fair skies and dryness. Huug's invention, though still primitive, was undergoing a "calibration," gee elucidated, and when complete would be able to accurately foretell the weather.

Zoog was truly raptured by Huug's weather machine and was in the act of saluting the slender nunale when a knock shook them from their discussion. "Water from blood," a voice boomed.

"Water from blood," responded Taratt suddenly transformed from scientist to Prophet. Intense of eye, gee strode to the doorway to confer with a messenger.

Zoog didn't require an explanation to unlock a deeper meaning from Huug's bizarre salutation. Pretending to be unaware of what the young priest recognized to be the essence of the Chosen, Zoog turned a wondering glimpse to the glass bulb, musing how unseen air particles could swell and shrink in response to 'pressures.' Very logical, gee thought. After all, doors swell on humid days and shrink to normal thickness when it's dry. Why not a sensitive liquid prepared to exaggerate the action?

Pushing aside the insanity Zoog knew lurked within Huug, gee asked the returning Taratt, "How is it you are addressed, genther of my gender?"

"As you no doubt are aware, I am stripped of my priestly orders, prohibiting my officiation at official services. So I praise Gala Rotaria in a more secular manner. My followers address me as 'Prophet.' For if you gaze my eyes, young priest, you will see a power that reaches beyond this land, that communicates on a plane outside our kind." The Prophet scowled dramatically as if to invoke the very spirits gee alluded to reach. "Of course, the special bond we share permits the more familiar 'Huug'...in our privacy. I notice you have already presumed to call me such. However, among the Chosen you should address me as 'Prophet' or not at all." For the first time in their brief encounter, Taratt smiled broadly.

"So much for protocol," spoke Zoog, recalling a similar conversation with Daag Goraxx at the high priest's villa. "But if I gaze your orbs, Huug, remember the vision works in both directions. Therefore, you will view my stirrings as well."

"Shall we?" Taratt challenged, the lips pressed into a tight grimace.

And so they performed the ritual of the gaze, sort of an intellectual wrist wrestling. After a full two minutes they broke it off, the concentration incredibly intense. Zoog, having witnessed the swirl of genius and evil, ascertained that a megalomaniacal sickness consumed the Prophet. On the other end of the gaze Huug saw a distant well, a depth beyond the deep with a knowledge exceeding even the nunine kind. "I bow to your potential," acknowledged Huug. "But I own a superiority in matters of the spiritual."

"Perhaps," Zoog half conceded. "Let us agree that at worst we are equals."

"Agreed," nodded Taratt, somewhat unsure of the awesome young priest. "Zoog, your purpose in coming here is yet unclear. Unless you wish to join the Chosen, to wear the chalk?"

"No, I'll defer to true believers." Zoog and Huug left the confinement of the chamber and returned to the principal room cluttered with the host's scientific paraphernalia.

"Think of it, Zoog. A nunale of your ability could do well among the Chosen. Every day we recruit more novitiates. What you see in this compound is not the whole of our numbers. You and I, we nunales, are the superior few. Unlike our stone-brained brothers and sisters we possess the power of creativity, to conceptualize, to invent. It only follows that the nunine gender should make those decisions which control The Vag ! Though you may not wish to admit it, you surely must sense these things. We are the ones who should rule with inspiration flowing from the great goddess."

"We nunales...or you nunale?" The look, though impish, struck a truthful chord.

"Yes, Zoog of the golden eye. Me! A theocracy of one!" A feverish pitch accompanied the declaration. "'With the support of nunales who someday will exclusively own the vote, I would be Lord. The warriors are but muscled idiots who divide without thought. If only the nunale possessed the vote, the election would be one of intelligence and, therefore, best for The Vag. Is this not logical?"

"You make a tempting overture," lied Zoog, realizing Huug's disclosure could jeopardize the Kavoyy's life. "I need time to deliberate such a radical move."

"I gazed your eyes, Zoog. You could be a fitting successor to my lordship. Deliberate well!"

"Aye, something to think about, Huug."

"Is it not fortuitous that you came here today? Is it not fate, part of a great scheme, that you and I are of a similar scientific mind? And at this moment both contemplating technology beyond the brain of Lanz Varaxx and his dense minions? Pah, they are as fit to rule as pumpkins!" Huug spit in the tradition of Pah.

Zoog Kavoyy, seeking to turn Huug's zeal to an advantage, asked, "Would not your cause be more noble if you could reach back to the past for an endorsement of your worthiness?"

"How so?" an avid Taratt jumped at the idea.

"My passion is the origin of The Vag. If we could discover its secret, maybe you could use the information to assert your leadership."

"An interesting prospect, Zoog Kavoyy. Go on."

Zoog poured a mug of water from a glazed ewer, gesturing a similar offer to the Prophet who declined. Greedily gee drank, draining the tankard in one thirsty gulp. "By discovering the legitimate nature of The Vag, perhaps you could manipulate it to your own benefit. Truly only one anointed by the goddess herself would be blessed with the greatest of her secrets. She in her miracle of discovery could be said to have endorsed you and your new political order."

"It's a stretch, Zoog. Devious...but a stretch. I don't believe it's worth the energy. Although I have often felt that if l exerted all my efforts, I could solve the puzzle, for I already possess more evidence than any nunale in The Vag." Gee puffed a bit, emphasizing self-importance of a high regard.

The gamble had paid off. Zoog had smoked out an admission of evidence. Now, how best to gain the specifics of Huug's knowledge? "While I am deliberating my next step with respect to the Chosen, why not let me devote my time to solving the riddle? With your guidance, of course." The cheese was in the trap.

Seeing the prospect of an authoritative candidate, a junior partner more cunning than gee could have wished for, Huug Taratt reached out to grip the young nunale's wrist. "It's a deal," gee chirped. "And when the moment is perfect, I am confident you will be with me. But only when the moment is absolutely precise. For once before I became impatient and challenged the Lord. A gross miscalculation. And so I have been forced to be overly patient. Now I know how to proceed. By the fingers, I must create the optimum opportunity. Through technology, Zoog, I will win!"

"Hmmm, interesting," hummed Zoog, becoming a bit bored with Taratt's ravings. "Let me ask you. Does the name Kwinarvy mean anything to you?"

"Kwinarvy? No. What is it?"

"Probably nothing. I just thought I'd ask.

The next morning Zoog was stirred awake by the pressure of a sandal against ger thigh. Looking up gee spied the form of Huug's courier, the same man who had delivered the message to the Prophet yesterday. "Water from blood," he hailed the nunale slowly rising off the mat.

Stretching a kinked leg joint, Zoog bid the man a halfhearted "Good morning," and proceeded to massage the laziness from a sleepy scalp.

"The Prophet commands your presence," the chalk face sternly informed. Chin up and cross-armed the messenger showed little sign of friendliness.

*"Commands,"* thought the priest. *"My, we are bossy this morning, aren't we!"* Wearing only bragghi, the night air having been warm and breezeless, Zoog fumbled for tunic and footwear. "I'll be with you as soon as I wash."

"The Prophet says Now! Besides there isn't enough water to squander on the unnecessary. There is but one well for the entire camp."

"Alright then, let us not keep the Prophet waiting," gee huffed. No sense in antagonizing the best prospect Zoog had developed since arriving in the wild country.

Buckling the broad tunic belt as gee entered the stone quarters, Zoog was surprised to see Taratt similarly dressed and in the act of shaving. Dragging an obsidian blade across the oiled dome, Huug patted the taut skin with the free hand, checking for reluctant stubble. Content the surface was smooth, Huug rubbed the remaining lubricant into the sun dried pores. "Prevents it from wrinkling," gee felt obligated to explain.

"You commanded my presence?" Zoog asked dryly.

"Yes, Zoog, I did." Gee worked the unctuous fluid yet lustering ger fingers under the tunic along the clavicle. "I find my responsibilities are none today. Nothing is pressing. So I am going to take you on a little stroll...back in time. Do you feel up to it?"

"What did you have in mind?"

"A hike in the Gugububu. You see, I'm going to hold up my end of the bargain and take you to where it all started." The voice was almost teasing in inflection.

"You mean where The Vag all started?" the wide eyed priest gasped unable to contain the thrill.

"Aye, to our ancestral womb," Huug vouched. "Last night I decided to reveal a place destined to be revered more than Muraverdus. For within its ancient keep lies the answer. You see, Zoog Kavoyy, even though I wish to reorganize the ruling order of The Vag, to assert nunine supremacy, to shed blood in postulating my personal mystique, I am also a scientist who believes the nation must know the pollen of its very existence. However, for me to divulge the location of this place would seal my death, because those forces which wish to see me destroyed will have me executed for having violated the Gugububu." Huug breathed heavily in apparent frustration, a nunale caught on the horns of a dilemma. "Besides, I no longer have enough hours to properly apply against this task. But I have you! And I have the Translator!"

"The Translator?" responded Zoog, interested by this latest wrinkle.

Huug Taratt strode briskly to the chamber, quickly returning with a stack of reed paper pressed between polished boards of identical dimension, a makeshift binder. "The Translator," Huug announced. "The language of the ancients!"

"Please explain," encouraged the young Kavoyy.

"In time, in time. You see," boasted the elder nunale, "I have more answers than you have questions. Those closed-minded academicians at the Capital wouldn't trust their smell of excrement without first licking the chamber pot. Never do they rely on their instincts, never follow a hunch. They resist ideas like frightened sheep avoiding shears, fearful they'll be stripped of the puffy fleece which swells their illusory size." Taratt threw his arms to the sky in exasperation. "By the fingers," gee exclaimed with a special disgust aimed at the scholared class which gee felt had abandoned gen, "the whole gregarious lot is afraid to force issues! You and I break with tradition, Zoog. Though we are born without scrotums, without the wands of life, we have balls!"

"In the figurative sense, of course," laughed Zoog. "You have a way with words, Huug. But tell me of the sheaves you clutch, the Translator?"

Huug rapped a clenched knuckle on the wooden binder. "I understood long past that preliminary to uncovering our origins, I must first comprehend the importance of language as it was uttered and written by the first literate Vaghi. How better for the past to communicate with the present? The Translator, though still primitive, is a rudimentary compendium of words and phonetic nuances in the language of our forebears."

"Huug, you are so right. Phonetic change will be a key ingredient. For I too believe there is an evolution of words and meanings which reach to our current dictionary. For all we know our word *dog* might have been *dook* in its earliest form. And with your compendium, you have taken the first great step," enthused the younger nunale sincere in ger salute.

Basking in Zoog's praise, Taratt smiled in that broad, wolfish grin which the young priest bad come to recognize. "Taratt knows! Gee knows!" Bellowing self-praise in the third person, Huug held the Translator high above ger gleaming pate, rotating it from side to side. It was as if the audience of one was a host of thousands crowding the Capital plaza.

Playing to the Prophet's ego, Zoog bowed generously and echoed, "Taratt knows! Gee knows!" A playful grin danced ger lips. And though Huug realized gee was being patronized, gee enjoyed it nevertheless.

"Today we will descend into the Cauldron, young scientist who in twenty-four hours I have adopted as my protégé. And with this rough compendium as our guide, Taratt will demonstrate the first scratches of the beginning."

The heart of Zoog Kavoyy raced with a quicker rhythm than gee could ever recall.

⊱──❯❯──⊰

"You know we are breaking the law, don't you?" the wolf howled, a gleeful spark catching ger eye. "When we traversed that wide gully you officially entered the Gugububu. So now, you dastardly felon, your very life could be forfeited to the Lord. At this moment you tread where few living Vaghi have ever set their feet."

"Aye, Prophet of the Chosen," answered Zoog. "But more importantly, I pray to Gala Rotaria you also know your way out of this desolate frying pan." Though the blazing heat staggered ger very bones, the priest tried to concentrate on memorizing the unmarked trail, picking out land points and assigning names to them, then twisting ger head to view the very same from the reverse angle. There wasn't much on which to orient oneself, to count strides between. But Zoog persevered, focusing on the mental picture taking hold in the great mind, never letting Huug know ger ability to accurately recall images. Taratt had insisted they didn't need water skins, claiming there would be water enough once they arrived. A wary Zoog didn't trust the Prophet. All the more reason gee should meticulously memorize the landscape. Upon returning to the stone cabin Zoog would have to prepare a detailed map with distances marked for those who might follow. The young nunale kept silent about the passport tucked within the tunic pouch. No need to flaunt ger relationship with those powers estranged to Huug. At this juncture there was no telling how a venomous Taratt would react.

"I'm sure I'm the only one who knows the way, so you had better remain close on my tail. It took me many wanderings, each time venturing out a bit farther on an invisible tether. And so it is I am able to recognize but this small portion of the Cauldron. To read the subtle markings is no simple task. It would be dangerous if even I became distracted for a minute. I doubt you could come close to finding your bearings, my young friend." In this instance not only is knowledge power, it is the difference between life and death. So communicated Huug Taratt.

"Aye," grunted the sweat soaked Zoog. "I am lost already." Playing the fool's role, gee continued counting the strides to the next remote point. They had been hiking the rough ground for over an hour, about four medecs gee estimated, when the undulating terrain abruptly transformed from hardpacked grit to countless dips containing boulders of every dimension. Great fractured slabs littered the desert floor, some seeming to erupt from deep inside the Gugububu. Huge jagged piles weathered by wind and sand over the centuries created a specter unseen before by the likes of Zoog Kavoyy. Even an imagination as far reaching as Zoog's never conceived so horrid a place. Only the absence of flame separated this blistering wasteland from the furnace of hell itself. For another hour the nunine pair wove through the maze. They traveled many twisted land waves, blind to the scope of the land ahead due to the immediacy of the soaring rocks which prevented any appreciable ranges of sight. Zoog thought that ultimately it would be simple enough to mark a permanent trail over this portion by blazing the most prominent boulders.

Ascending a particularly large scattering of stone, cleavaged sharply in pyramid fashion, Huug announced, "Behold the end of the rock farm." Beyond lay another belt of flatlands leading to a hillier country littered with yet more igneous shatterings of an age before beings. If anything, the heaps were taller than before. Zoog captured the panorama within the mind's eye and continued to count as once again they trudged to the horizon. Finally on a sweltering rise seemingly like all others, the Prophet removed the cotton wrap protecting ger glistening head and stamped a boot. "This is the place!"

The opening was barely discernible. A vertical slab concealed a descending staircase to a depth of eight strides. At the bottom another slab, half the size of the other, lay horizontal in a grooved track hewn out of the stone base. Carved into the face, three letters, VAG, provided with certainty that indeed this was the place. Huug rubbed a candle stub on the track thus lubricating its surface. Grunting with energetic effort gee worked ger fingers into the holds and yanked. The rock slid smoothly, revealing a passage about shoulder high for Zoog. The wolf grinned and gestured the young companion to follow. In file the two stoopwalked down a steep ramp, sun from the open doorway flooding their immediate path. When the corridor took an abrupt right angle turn, the light dimmed dramatically. Taratt dropped to one knee and removed a tinder box from the tunic pouch. Within moments gee coaxed a flame from the tangle of dry grass and wood shavings brought for that purpose. A stash of candles and oil lamps neatly stacked by the Prophet during an earlier visit, sat on the uneven floor. Huug lit a pair of candles, handing one to Zoog. Down they proceeded into a great orifice, treading eighteen stone stairs in the descent. Chiseled by dedicated artisans long ago, it must have taken many strong backs to muscle the huge blocks through the passage, and then lever each into place for future footprints. Now as Zoog pressed ger boots into the dust of time, a feeling of oneness touched ger soul, a coming together of then and now. Here perhaps the progenitor of the clan Kavoyy also set his feet. Ogling the enormous cavern, a tremor of anticipation rolled up the nunale' s spine.

Taratt moved with quick ease, obviously familiar with the layout. Soon gee had lit many candles already positioned to provide optimum illumination. Macabre in their glow, the candles rested in rather small, yellowed skulls, expertly lobotomized to catch the wax melt. The cavern's significant drop in temperature, coupled with the eerie shine of grinning skulls, chilled the priest's skin. Zoog shrugged hard, hoping to shake away the involuntary shudder gee was certain would convulse ger joints and bones. That, gee felt, would be an admission of weakness for Huug to exploit. And it would be folly to show any vulnerability to the Prophet, to display signs of a fragile side. "Children?" asked Zoog, pointing to the bizarre candlesticks.

"Kala," informed Taratt, "again performing valuable service after centuries of retirement." The leer seemed to convey a particular delight in the gruesome scene. Within the great cavern two smooth, stone slabs supported by granite-like blocks formed a broad table or possibly an altar. Upon it lay parchments weighted at the comers by small rocks. "They were curled by the ages. So I've been straightening them ever so slowly in order that they might not crack. The parchments will require delicate cleaning before they can be read. The same is true for that stack of scrolls piled over there. They must be treated with equal patience. I think a special carrier should be designed so we might remove them to study their revelations." Huug looked directly into Zoog's excited face. "By the fingers! What do you think now, young scientist? Has not Huug Taratt discovered the great link? Is this mysterious place not the library of our existence, a shrine to be hallowed? Can you feel it?" gee boomed, the hollow echoes filling the chamber. "Who else but Taratt could have uncovered this dormant cocoon? And to find it in so remote, so hostile an environment? Here it sat for unknown centuries, nay millenia, napping in the silence of time. Opened finally by someone anointed, someone deemed worthy by the great genetrix Gala Rotaria. The slumbering womb of The Vag has been unsealed by your favorite, mother! Yes, it is I, Huug Taratt. Your prophet is home!" Huug's frenzied oration caused gen to gesture wildly in its delivery. "And now I drink the reward of my journey, sweet mother. From the pool of your treasured tears, I rush to drink!" With that gee dropped the candle and swept past Zoog to a ring of stones sheltering a large cistern. A slow trickle of water constantly kept it full, the excess spilling out the far end, running off between a narrow fissure. In this way the liquid in the cistern was always fresh. Kneeling on the lip, the Prophet scooped out the clear water, drinking from hands cupped together. A quiet Zoog stunned mute by Huug's crazed ego explosion followed Taratt's example, filling the straw hat and slopping its comfort on face and arms.

*Maybe the old wolf had an excess of sun prompting the outburst,* mused Zoog. So gee shifted the conversation while splashing more water on ger face, replenishing the moisture baked away by the desert hike. Zoog offered a hat full of cool water to Huug, encouraging the Prophet to bathe the dome. Logically that was the area that housed the rabidness. *Aye, these many trips in the Gugububu broiler must have jellied the brain.* The younger nunale dripped what remained directly on Taratt's head. "What a magnificent discovery!" gee marveled. And to think you did it alone. Why it astounds me to think of it. The odds of a single person stumbling on this are stupendous!"

"Stumbling?" challenged Huug, taking the compliment wrongly. "You think I wandered into this by chance? I was summoned here by the light of Gala Rotaria, glowing like an invisible beacon for only Huug Taratt to see. And don't you forget it!" gee hissed.

"A poor choice of words," Zoog soothed. "How else could it have happened? My profound apologies, genther of my gender." Zoog took a long breath and said no more, hoping the water would take effect, dampening the impaired ardor surging Taratt's veins.

After a few minutes the erratic Huug had regained ger composure, returning from prophetic zealot to scientist. Taking Zoog's elbow gee ushered the priest to an area behind the altar. "Now my young colleague, drink this time with your eyes and tell me what they taste!" Taratt lit two oil lamps extending the larger to Zoog.

Holding the lamp aloft, Zoog was stunned by the image painted on the recessed wall. A text. Rows of run-on sentences stroked by hands from another age now attempted to speak their message. Most of the words were strange to Zoog as gee tried to sound them out phonetically. But a goodly few made sense. Scanning the text, the young scientist was immediately able to determine that several were cut words or abbreviations. The excitement coursing inside caused the breath to come in short gasps. "We must copy this quickly," gee rushed.

"It is already in the Translator," Huug proudly answered.

And then it was there. "WE PEOPLE OF," Zoog translated from old Vag to the current. The next word, "ARVUMQUIN" could be broken down gee reasoned. "Our word 'Arbim' is a 'Field,' one that is plowed or cultivated. But I've heard it pronounced in parts of the wild country as 'Arvim.' And 'Quin' is possibly the ancient word or an abbreviation of 'Quint,' our word for 'Fifth.' Therefore, a logical interpretation could be, WE ARE THE PEOPLE OF THE FIFTH FIELD. Isn't that a curious appellation?" Oh this was great fun. The Kavoyy's face swelled with the glee of discovery.

"You are a shrewd scholar, young Vag." Even Huug had to admire the quick study Zoog had performed, as so many at the academy had learned to esteem.

But a charged Zoog wasn't listening, for lightning had crashed the galloping mind. If one placed the adjective in front of the noun, reversing the sequence, the rearranged ARVUMQUIN became QUINARVUM. And a month earlier gee had squatted with a feather of a man who identified the archaic people whose stones yet traced the ground, calling them KWINARVY! *"Aye, old man, you were right. They were Vaghi, People of the Fifth Field."*

# CHAPTER IX

Six months of toil at the Lord's brickworks had left him eager to depart its dismal collection of kilns and warehouses. Most days had been spent loading wagons and barges for the trip north. In some respects it had been time lost for he gained no new knowledge that half year. Even the schoolwork provided little enlightenment, Zoog and Genu Zig earlier having filled his mind with things more advanced. There were two benefits, however. The brickworks were located in a remote stretch of The Vag, adjacent to the fine grain clay deposits. A red dust clung to man and land alike discouraging any productive activity other than the manufacture of tile and bricks. Few diversions existed, certainly nothing recreational. Said another way, there were no women about. Unlike the Breadbasket, courtship here was impossible, half the equation absent. Only nocturnal wolf-dogs yipping their sexual song enjoyed such liaisons in the place of clay. But it did provide time to contemplate all he had absorbed at Mount Aryxx, to rehearse situations looming out there where some day he would make his mark. It also strengthened a physique already athletic to a hardness rivaling that of the bricks he hoisted. On 'rest days' he would run along the nearby ridges recalling duties of his courier days on the green carpet of the Lizard's Tongue. An escape of sorts, the jaunts carried him back to the sweet air of Kavoyy Station where everything seemed clean and fresh.

After finishing the last shift, his nostrils and eyes were ringed with a parched redness, the lips similarly caked. Sweat and powdered clay swirled to form a sticky paste streaking his throat, the boots puffing out floury clouds with each step. Every laborer wore the pale red hue. A uniform without exception, it coated all with impartiality. And the hair filled by a grittiness down to the root resisted all attempts to tame its wild dryness. Like henna smoke, tiny particles seeped into the very food they ate. Loaves of bread tinted with the residue of yesterday's output were eaten with casual apathy. Today it made little difference, Marz supposed, because in twelve hours, his obligation complete, he and his mates would travel to the verdant wall of Muraverdus. Finally their warrior training would commence. With it the dusty locks would be shorn, gritty scalps opened to a climate more forgiving.

Muraverdus, a great circle over one medec in diameter, stood on a high plateau. Crudely constructed, its earthen walls climbed to a height of sixteen strides held fast by deep rooted grass. Goats were allowed to roam its steep sides preventing the growth from becoming overly ragged. Within its embrace several rows of brick buildings of various size and a tented campground at the west end composed the training site for Vaghi males of proper age. The remaining area included the military headquarters of General Povezz and his logistical staff. Located at the extreme east portion, the military HQ took up roughly a sixth of the ring. The abiding interior fields were used for drilling and maneuvers, and surely, parades. A half medec outside the ring a permanent barracks held two kords of warriors charged with protecting the Capital while positioned about four days quick-march to the isthmus chokepoint. Central Camp, as the entire complex was called, represented the best duty in all The Vag due to the optimal weather and proximity to the joys of the Capital. Of course for the non-kilted newcomers cloistered inside the green cage, no such joys were available. Yet the ancient tradition of Muraverdus, first bastion of The Vag, held a special meaning for its fresh denizens. Almost one thousand mustered that first day, excited at the prospect of earning the leather skirt, of being accepted as men. Rapidly they were formed into two training kords, sorted alphabetically into smaller units of companies and bolts. For Marz Kavoyy it was a moment to be relished. This, he told himself, would be the initial stride toward destiny's goal. Muraverdus, where it was believed The Vag drew its national breath, where the early Lords learned to hurl the javelin, would be his step-stone to a life of noble service.

From the moment Marz saw the commander of his training kord he sensed there would be discord between them. Not that he would purposely seek to cause trouble, for that would be both non-productive and foolhardy. But oft times a negative chemistry is unavoidable. When water and hot oil collide, the sizzle is predictably noisy, the splatter violent. The man had been recently promoted to the rank of Capitanus, well on the road to loftier sights. Whispers had it he was nephew to the great Lord Varaxx. Whether fact or latrine rumor, the relationship deserved consideration of a forewarned nature. Regardless, he did belong to one of the most influential families in all the land which warranted this officer a special respect. Aye, Rooz Javatt, dripping with conceit born of the elite, strutted like a challenging rooster, confident the hen house domain would one day be his alone. As tall as Marz, with similar sleek build but without the hardness, Rooz Javatt's curly blonde hair shone like a halo in the morning sun. Smugly handsome, the face seemed most pleased with its appearance. But it was the large eyes which marked him different, would set him apart in an orchard of blonde heads. They weren't really yellow, nor orange. But a fusion of the two. Like 'fried egg yolks' a recruit laughingly mocked. And so it struck! Among the trainees of his kord, Capitanus Rooz Javatt became known as 'Yolks.' Naturally insubordination of this kind was uttered only behind Javatt's back. Punishment for disrespect could be quite severe in the army. But 'Yolks' survived throughout their training cycle. An apt epithet they agreed, for the egg eyed rooster of Muraverdus.

Eight days into their training, Marz's company had drawn the messy task of clearing a clogged portion of the moat circling the great wall. Knee deep in slime, the energetic Vaghi scooped out buckets of mud which they passed hand to hand out of the trench. Rich in decayed vegetation and run-off soil, the composition was enhanced by goat droppings giving it a distinctively sweet odor. Farmers from the surrounding patchwork would ultimately retrieve the sun-dried yield to be scattered upon their fields. Clad only in bragghi, the company was in the act of climbing from the moat to enjoy ten minutes of rest. It was at this point that Capitanus Rooz Javatt came by to confer with his subordinate officer and sergeants overseeing the detail. After a cursory inspection of their progress, he strode with that cocky walk of his to the men strewn along the grassy bank. There they lay passing about pails of drinking water. The young soldiers were instructed not to stand at attention, but to continue their break while the Capitanus addressed them.

Now it seems that Javatt prided himself on his exceptional foot speed. At 26 years of age he could still sprint as speedily as he did as a recruit, if not quicker. Indeed he occasionally raced fellow officers for bragging rights. But not only did the Capitanus savor the thrill of victory, he always angled for an advantage to ensure the win. So it was this day, as he surveyed the weary huddle of shaved heads who had been dredging muck for four hours. "Men," he shouted, sun rays prancing on the gorgeous golden hair. "I feel in a generous frame of mind today. So I'm going to make you all a sporting proposition. I, your Capitanus, challenge the swiftest of you to a foot race. If your representative wins, which is doubtful, I will allow the entire company to nap in the shade for the rest of the day. So tell me, which of you feels bold enough to test my shanks?" The question was more taunt than dare. No one stood to accept, though all were amused by the invitation. "Come, come, my weaklings. You choose the distance and we'll make a go of it." A grinning Javatt, pleased by their reluctance, postured a bit, knowing full well all eyes were riveted to his presence. Removing a hand from his hip, he pointed in the general direction of a number of red posts delineating fixed distances of 100, 200 and 400 strides. "Don't tell me you're so cowardly as to ignore the opportunity for a half day in the shade!" he teased. Rooz knew they were aware that each morning he sped between the posts, maintaining the quickness of his earlier youth. Admirable though his daily conditioning was, still it was wrong for an officer to ridicule his troops in such manner. For leadership is not born of intimidation, but of respect...and he'd earn none this hot noon. Javatt's idea of heading soldiers was to impose his manly superiority over them, to constantly remind them of his personal strengths. Certainly a leader had to be brave and strong to motivate troops in the most trying of instances. But Javatt's attitude was to build his own aggrandizement at the expense of his underlings. "Are you so shallow of guts not to seize my offer?" he chided. The sergeants looked away as did the young battle officer commanding the company. They had no alternative but to remain silent. Veteran kilts, they disapproved their Capitanus' conduct.

Javatt sneered at the lot, a scowl of contempt curling his mouth. He was about to turn away when a voice broke the stillness. "Sir," the voice spoke, "do I get to call the distance?"

"Aha! Do I detect the stirrings of a challenge?" Javatt responded, a hand cupped to his ear. "Call the distance as you desire. It is yours to lose!"

Jumping to his feet, an imposing recruit moved aggressively toward Javatt. When he got to the officer's side, he raised a well muscled arm and pointed toward the farthest pole. "I pick that length and back, sir," he said calmly, the squint of distance upon his confident eyes.

"The farthest pole?" questioned Javatt.

"No, sir. I point beyond it to the great tree atop that hill. A run to that tree and back here. That is the distance I name, sir!"

"But that tree must be three medecs distant," gasped Javatt, his face flushed with surprise. "Six medecs in total with the return here? Is that what you're proposing?" asked Javatt, hoping it wasn't true.

"Aye, sir. Six medecs with an uphill jaunt to test our endurance," confirmed the composed trainee. He turned his head from the far off tree to meet Rooz's look. "Shall I fetch my boots, sir?"

Sprinters are born with speed, it is said. But long distance runners are born with a heart. And from this inner nature, over time, they gain resolve, a tenacity which propels them to overcome obstacles, regardless of the issue. Running with a deliberate pace they are controlled by an internal drumbeat, driven by a discipline. Rooz's vanity had prohibited him from designating a sprinter's distance. He had assumed the challenger, already fatigued from the moat, would select the shortest measure. Not so! Betrayed by an ego void of preparation, Rooz Javatt had allowed himself to be ambushed.

Sensing Javatt's predicament, the company's full complement rose to applaud their mate. A few whistled, then more split the air. Hell, it would be worth it, even if their man lost, just to watch that arrogant, yolk eyed bastard sweat! As one they roared their approval of the gutsy, young comrade they hardly knew.

"Shall I fetch my boots, sir?"

"What's your name?" Javatt snapped. A watery anger fired his eyes.

"Kavoyy, sir. Marz Kavoyy!"

"Yes, Kavoyy. Get your damned boots!"

To save face, Javatt would have to make a go of it. In jeopardy of being made a laughingstock, he must find a way to salvage a degree of respect. And so a plan developed. The Capitanus, using his sprinter's legs, would race to an early lead. And when he sensed the wind going out of him, the calves losing their push, his competitor gaining ground, Javatt would feign injury, complaining later that victory would have been his had he not suffered the cruelty of misfortune. And everyone would raise an eyebrow, skeptical for sure. But it would be his word against their suspicion. And so the benefit of doubt would be his. Nevertheless, that insolent Kavoyy would pay for his spark of glory. By the fingers, he promised himself, Kavoyy' s future discomfort was a certainty.

Blazing ahead, Rooz was surprised to see Kavoyy not all that far behind. Perhaps forty strides separated them. Maybe he could burn out the inexperienced kid and cruise to victory. Revising his strategy, Javatt encouraged Marz to remain on his heels, slowing his own dash accordingly. Whereas the officer pumped with a vigorous motion, the younger racer glided smoothly, his legs reaching out to pull in the flat terrain. So Rooz picked up the tempo again, intent on overextending his adversary.

What Javatt didn't know was that Marz was saving himself, comfortable in his gait, pupils fixed on the faraway tree. He ran within himself trying to shut Javatt from his vision, concentrating instead on his own assets. Endurance would prevail this day, not spurts of velocity. There would be no steep 'Verticals', no isthmus holes to sidestep. In his mind he was the courier of Kavoyy Station running the spine, carrying dispatches along the Lizard's Tongue...on to the Ring of Kilts. He had done it more than a thousand times. Just maintain the powerfully easy stride, he reasoned, and the day would belong to him.

Once upon the uphill stretch, Marz planned to adjust his stride, taking shorter, choppier steps. "Preparation" he heard Genu Zig whisper, "is the mother of victory. Boldness, the father!"

It was no accident that the young Kavoyy found himself pitted against Rooz Javatt. For Genu Zig had predicted their paths would intersect repeatedly on the road to supremacy. And Marz, armed with information of the plot to seat Rooz on the Lord's throne, could pick his spots to test his adversary, to learn his patterns of behavior, to measure how Javatt reacted when pressed. Marz's thoughts drifted to the Hall of Protectors, and the eyes of glass focusing their hypnotic gaze, instilling a fire within him to seek the great prize. Whether destiny or coincidence prevailed this hot day, Marz was not certain. Nevertheless, Rooz had been delivered to him and he must take advantage of this opportunity for it could be years before another chance surfaced. As a lowly trainee he realized that Javatt's power of rank allowed the Capitanus to trump Marz in matters where might makes right. But Javatt's vindictiveness would probably be petty, of the backbiting variety, inasmuch as he had no idea that the sturdy Kavoyy was more than an ignorant country boy, no thought that Marz sought to preempt his lordly quest. The tiny stings of pettiness could be dealt with, he thought. His will would ensure that. *Aye, Marz, it will be a battle of wills with the Javatt unaware of your true mission. Remember not to overplay your hand too early into the game.*

Up ahead Rooz began laboring, the breath coming in rapid pants. Peeking over his shoulder he caught sight of the smooth running machine narrowing the gap. He cursed aloud in the realization that he had blown his energy, the stalker soon to overtake him. With but a medec and a half into the race Rooz

Javatt allowed himself to tumble. Rolling in the autumn dust he clutched at his thigh, teeth clenched in a tight grimace. To the casual spectator the poor fellow had pulled a hamstring. Sprawled on the ground, dirt dappling the bare chest, Javatt shook a scornful fist at the long striding pursuer rushing by. "I would have beat you," he cried.

Without so much as a sideways glance, Marz continued his gait. But he did utter something in response to Rooz's futile, if not disingenuous claim. "Pah!"

As Marz cruised past the finish line, his mates mobbed him with shouts of congratulations. As much as they were looking forward to a half day's relaxation, the notion that one of their own had literally run Yolks into the turf filled them with a spirited pride. An hour ago they barely knew this man of the isthmus. Now they lustily called his name. "Kavoyy, Kavoyy!" Every man, the company commander and sergeants more restrained, shook his hand or slapped the broad back. One recruit, though, having clapped Marz's shoulders, wiped the perspiration on his bragghi and stepped back to admire the triumph of Marz Kavoyy. With a smile upon his lips, he thought, *Aye, Tyrra, he is all you said and then some, this future brother-in-law of mine.* At that moment Monty Kelozz knew a bond of friendship would be formed to outlast any he had ever known.

And in the distance, Rooz Javatt limped unattended into the gates of Muraverdus. No one cared to inquire his condition, no one to console his injury. For none believed there to be any. Besides, they'd be too busy napping in the shade to give a hoot.

"Maintain your line! Keep a proper interval! Now, thrust and rip. Thrust and rip," the brawny cadre hollered. Wielding their bronze short swords the young troops stabbed the air from behind hide shields. Vag military doctrine emphasized minimal exposure of the legs and torso while thrusting sword point into a foe's belly, then upper cutting on impact. And all the time their tight formation moved forward maintaining momentum, pushing shields into an imaginary enemy. For Marz and most of his mates it was a technique practiced since childhood using sticks and barrel lids. Now they honed their skills in disciplined files, wondering how mechanical it would be once called to perform in earnest. Until troops are blooded, there is no guarantee how they'll behave. Practice with the short javelin was also long and tedious. Many hours on the practice field were spent heaving hundreds of the lethal shafts at straw targets. At close range the javelins were hurled on a straight line directly into Kala effigies. When distance became an issue, they were lofted in high arcs, a blizzard of death raining down at sharp angles, shredding the mute targets with near equal effectiveness, but without the impact.

Two months into training Marz had emerged as the top soldier in his company, probably in the entire two kords. Long marches never seemed to bother him. Loaded with pack and shield, toting javelin and sword, he often assisted those comrades fatigued by the intense training. So it was on one such hike that he was paired with Monty Kelozz, and there Monty told the Kavoyy of his strong feeling for Tyrra. Marz accepted the man from the barrier at his word, Monty owning a sincerity beyond challenge. Together they managed to stand in ranks. Together they retrieved tossed javelins , reconstructed targets, patched tents. Though they became close, occasionally Marz would suggest that Monty keep his distance lest Rooz Javatt learn of their friendship and find some twisted way to punish his comrade.

Periodically reports of Marz's military prowess were reported up the line as they were for all soldiers either excelling or deficient, the average mass receiving no notice. Unfortunately for Marz his exemplary soldiering caused an acid to curdle Rooz Javatt's guts. Instead of being rewarded, Javatt saw to it that Marz was given every filthy detail. Though others were rotated through the 'extra duty' roster, the Kavoyy name always headed the list. While others slept, he scrubbed the officers' quarters, scoured pots, or walked sentry duty on some worthless pile of stones. Yet he complained not, never gave Rooz's minions anything to report back to the Capitanus other than, "He's a damn fine soldier." For Marz this was a test of mettle, of his unyielding will. Because for men of determination, regardless how a situation worsens, there is little compromise. It is a stubbornness born of righteous belief. The greater the trouble, the harder their steel. So it was with the man of the isthmus. In the eyes of his mates, Marz's stature grew with every additional indignity. All those traits which men admire in each other clung to Marz Kavoyy, an aura inviting the esteem of his fellows. For they recognized him as a cut above their own. Handling weapons, on the march, in his knowledge of things scholastic and in his modest demeanor, Marz held the respect of his peers. Aye, the lessons of Genu Zig served him well, especially the virtue of patience. And so his self control inspired his mates. Whenever they observed his 'special details' they would express support with a nod to Marz's golden eyes accompanied by words of manhood. "You are one bloody tough Vag, Kavoyy. Don't let that yolk eyed son-of-a-Kala-bitch wear you down." Usually Marz said nothing, but signaled his appreciation by winking an eye, balling a fist. Such encouragement served to fuel a will already resolute.

The harassment of Marz Kavoyy continued throughout the training cycle. It's not as though he were flogged or deprived of sustenance. His was a series of unending irritants. As soon as one task was complete another arose, and then another, and another. For Rooz it was a casual thing, never thinking that perhaps his vindictiveness had run its course. By all measures he was a bully, constant in his piddling retribution, sadistic in pleasure. It was a mental game with him, the imposition of physical hardship an extension of his mood. That Marz enjoyed no rest days, no evening hours to himself, had to weigh heavily on the mind of the impertinent Kavoyy. Like those who delight in tearing a moth's wing, the Capitanus took pleasure watching men struggle only to dash their efforts by ripping the other wing.

If only Rooz Javatt knew that Marz half-welcomed the adversity with a mystic's logic. For Genu Zig had impressed upon him the need to perform penance to those spirits which guided his destiny. *Before one can stand closest to the sun, he must first climb the highest mountain.* A mountain of jagged precipices and dangerous footholds. In a way Marz sensed he needed Javatt to help purify a soul pointed to the Lord's throne. He viewed Rooz not as a torment but as a necessary obstacle, a hurdle to overcome. Willingly he accepted all that came his way, gaining for himself the high regard of his mates and cadre.

At the conclusion of their six months, the recruits were declared 'warriors' and hiked a joyful trek to the isthmus. There at the Ring of Kilts in a ceremony akin to the Ravenhood, they were awarded their kilts. Stiff and shiny the new leather felt good to the thigh, even better to the impatient egos striving for identity in a world where achievement is measured in honors won. And to win the kilt, the very same worn by father and uncle, and in some cases relatives of the female gender, meant fulfillment of boyhood dreams. The kilt, all would agree, was the most luxurious of garments. More valuable than a belt of golden links, than a necklace of precious stones. Aye, the leather skirt proclaimed to all their equality in a society of warriors. For Monty and Marz, standing in the flickering torchlight, the shared exhilaration prompted them to salute each other with crossed arms, prideful grins decorating their faces. "I hope we are posted together, Marz. I sense that to be close to you will guarantee years of excitement."

Finishing the rite, General Povezz mounted the speaker's stone and led them in the warrior's oath. Following congratulations and a robust singing of the Vag anthem, he announced the names of twenty candidates to be trained as battle officers. Predictably Kavoyy was not among them.. Though his immediate commanders had advocated him, knowing full well it would not endear them to Javatt, the Capitanus squashed the recommendation. Perhaps the final revenge in a half year of venom. Several young officers and sergeants approached Marz, expressing their disappointment. If he was discontented, he didn't wear it, preferring to be gracious in reaction.

Where the march to North Camp had been one of quiet anticipation, the return trip took on an air of celebration. Proud of the leather girding their loins, much of the cajoling centered on the attraction the kilt offered to women in search of romance. But most of the talk speculated on their eventual postings. In keeping with military policy they would be fed piecemeal to one of the three principal camps: North, Central and South, or the lesser post at the Orri Barrier. Without exception they all agreed that South Camp, deep in the wild country, offered little appeal.

Marz had hoped that somehow his company would break close enough to Kavoyy Station where he might see Shaara, Gurz and the young twins. But it was not to be, their march plan taking them twenty medecs beyond its location. However, the following evening they prepared to bed down at a regular campsite overlooking Midpoint Station. Having not seen Varo in quite some time, he requested permission to leave the bivouac for a few hours to visit his old friend.

"No one is allowed to leave camp," the bolt sergeant informed. He liked Marz, thought he'd been given a raw deal by Javatt. But he wasn't about to provoke the Capitanus' wrath by granting Kavoyy a special favor. Instead he ordered Marz to, "Get down there to Midpoint Station and tell the master we're camping here tonight, so he doesn't get skittish at the sight of so many men. Do you think you can handle that?" he deadpanned.

"Aye, sergeant," the grateful kilt confirmed.

"You've got two hours to accomplish this crucial mission Kavoyy. Now don't disappoint me." This time a smile burst his face. If Ol' Yolks learned of it, it would be just another bit of 'extra duty.'

Loping through the open gate he spied Varo, arms folded, leaning against the cottage door frame. His dog lay a few paces away soaking the late day sun. A few hands worked about the outbuildings, tidying gear, securing stables and barns. Beaming like a proud parent, the leathery face alive with joy, Varo limped to greet the strapping Marz. "Look at you! By the fingers, just look at you! I watched you coming from far off and I said to myself, this bloody kilt runs like somebody I've seen before. Ha ha. And so I was bloody right. Come here, lad!" They embraced, thumping each other's back with claps of warm friendship. Separating, Varo eyed the length of his visitor and nodded approvingly. "You've grown into a bloody brute. And kilted to boot!"

"Aye, Varo. It is good to see you too. We are camped just above here. On our way back to Muraverdus from North Camp where we received our leather."

"One more reason for me to be proud, Marz. Oh, you don't know how happy I am. You must stay for supper."

"Unfortunately I have less than two hours. So perhaps a snack would be the better choice."

Varo winked. "I've got plenty of mutton jerky. Tougher than that shiny, new kilt. And harsher in flavor." He laughed, slapping his thigh with a whack. "No, lad. I'll not force any of that steel down your gullet." Varo caught himself before continuing. "Steel! That reminds me. Come inside. I've got a little surprise for you."

"Surprise?" asked Marz, draping an arm across the station master's shoulders. "I pray to the goddess it isn't that horse jerky they call steak in the wild country." They laughed aloud and walked into the cottage.

"Sit here, lad, while I fetch something." Varo acted a tad nervous as he sucked in a deep breath and left the room.

Marz sat upon a bench, the kilt buckling stiffly into his crotch. It would take some getting used to. Only years of sweat and wear would soften it, impart a veteran's patina. He was about to stretch his legs when the old man returned from the back room bearing a clothbound bundle. Expecting it contained something for him to view, the new warrior stood to receive his host.

Varo was searching for appropriate words. It was an honorable moment for him and he wished not to cheapen it with a vocabulary short on eloquence, though he was hardly a silver tongued fellow. "Lad," he began. "I'm a man without proper education so I hope the sentiments I now express are fitting for this occasion." His eyes dropped to the outstretched parcel as he gathered the thoughts of a lifetime, seeking to encapsulate the emotion of so many years. "My brood sib died at birth. Both parents before my fifth birthday. Neighbors took me in. But it wasn't easy for them or me." Varo cleared the dryness from his throat. Moist eyed he looked up to drink in the presence of the ruggedly handsome man before him. "I soldiered for over nine years, having my share of thrills, before meeting a wonderful woman, a little bit of a gal. We had plans as I guess all couples do. But the great goddess had other designs." He shrugged a shoulder, allowing it to blot the tear welling within his eye. "My dear wife died in childbirth, and with her the twins we longed for. So today, lad, I am an old geezer without family, with few happy memories. But I do have your friendship! And though I am not kin, I feel a wee like an uncle to you."

"And I think of you as such," the young man spoke softly.

"It is good to hear you say that, Marz. You are the only light to enter my bloody life in decades. That is why I would be honored if you would accept this. Yours...from your Uncle Varo." A hint of a smile traced his craggy lips.

Marz, unaware of the content, handled it gingerly, as though a tray of eggs.

"Go on. Open it!" hurried the station master.

Unwrapping the cloth, the young warrior knew immediately from its heft what lay inside. Looping off the last fold, he held the scabbard to his chest, a hand gripping the gleaming handle. He hesitated to admire the powerful workmanship.

"Pull it out, lad. You're making me crazy!" implored Varo.

As the first few digits cleared the scabbard, Marz couldn't believe what he was seeing. "Varo," he gasped. "Steel! Fine steel burnished like glass!"

"Aye, lad. Steel it is, delivered from the stars in one flaming ball. This is not the stuff of ordinary iron. Not of the ore scratched from the Lord's mines."

"Meteorite steel! But where did you gain such a weapon?" No run through the isthmus had left Marz so breathless.

"I acquired it honestly. It is mine to give. And you have been chosen to receive it. But aye, there is a story if you care to hear it."

"I wish to hear every detail, Varo. Tell me. Please."

Varo ran his bony fingers through the gray-white hair and sat heavily upon the bench. Propping his elbows atop the table, he gestured Marz to sit opposite him. He did, placing the sheathed sword between them. "Son, as you know, when you were but a tyke, I groomed ponies and shoveled manure at the station which carries your name. One warm summer night I took my sleep mat outside near the old stone well. And as I lie there watching the sky lit up like a million jewels, a fiery streak blazed straight down from overhead. For a frightening moment I thought myself the target. But it crashed into that meadow about a half medec due east of your daddy's house. You know the one that I mean?"

"Aye, Varo, the one where my grandparents and others of Kavoyy are buried." Marz's mouth hung open as if to inhale Varo's next words.

"That's the spot, lad. As peaceful a meadow as any in the whole bloody Vag. But that night it trembled with the impact of Gala Rotaria's gift."

"Go on," the young warrior spurred his avuncular comrade.

Nodding the furrowed brow, Varo continued. "Well, you can imagine my trepidation. My chin was gaping like yours is now, eyes wider than a nunale's ass. Oops. Sorry I forgot your brood sib was nunine." The tanned face took on a sheepish cast.

"I am not offended," Marz laughed. "I've heard the expression many times before...as has Zoog I am sure."

"My intent, naturally, was to search for the meteorite, its value apparent. But if I found it, who would it belong to? The land was that of the Kavoyy. At first light I searched the meadow and soon located the shaft, smoke yet seeping out of the crater. I told no one. And working by starlight over the next two nights, I uncovered a pocked ball three times larger than your handsome head, but with the great weight that comes from density. When your folks were off visiting family, I hitched up an old plow horse and yanked it from the muddy hole, hiding it under a pile of field stones a ways distant. Being the schemer that I am, I filled the pit to prevent suspicion. I figured I could sell the bloody thing for a fortune. After all, wouldn't you?"

Marz shrugged in the affirmative. "I guess so."

Varo threw his hands up at the ceiling. "But the great goddess had other plans." Dropping off the bench to his knees, he retrieved a clay bottle from a weathered box neath the table. Yanking the cork with his teeth, he let it fall into an open palm. He started to take a swig, but then thought better to offer first gulp to his friend. Marz declined, eager to get on with the tale. The smell of wine distilled to strong alcohol filled the warrior' s nostrils though he drank naught. Varo gulped greedily, several driplets coursing his grizzled chin. He shuddered, the bitter brandy swimming his insides.

"And then what?" pushed Marz.

"And then I fell asleep. That's what! And dream I did, like never before. The most splendid dream a man could have." He sucked a mouthful and re-corked the neck. "Ahhh," and proceeded to wipe the wet puss with a sleeve frayed from an excess of wipes. "Was it a vision or a dream? I don't honestly know. But as I lay under the goddess' starry realm she came to me. And these are her words, as closely as I can recollect. *From this mass of perfect iron you shall forge the finest sword of keenest edge and sharpest point. And of this sword you will be its custodian. Protect it from any who would have it. It is not yours to wield but to save. For one day a warrior deserving of its worth will arrive. You will know him, for the sky has already pointed to him. The sword will be your legacy. He is your heir.* I remember the glow as though yesterday, Marz. Finally after years of despair, my life had but a singular purpose. Varo, guardian of the sword, entrusted by the great mother herself."

"But who fashioned the blade, Varo? Surely not you." Marz eased to the bench edge, both hands resting upon the sword.

"That was my problem, lad. Who but the most skilled of craftsmen could create a work of lethal beauty from a pock marked ball of metal? By the ten sweet fingers, that person wasn't Varo Rokazz. But I heard tell of an old armorer, retired from the Lord's arsenal. He worked a small smithy in the village of Angona along with a spinster daughter. Mostly made farm tools and items for the kitchen. You know the kind. Every village has one. Except this fellow was a master artisan having served an entire career at the

Capital." Disgorging the cork once more, the bottle entered his mouth for a final sip, the remaining lazy drops finding his tongue after much urging. "So a deal was struck! He would craft the most superb weapon of his life. With no word about it to anyone. And in return he would retain the extra steel. Enough to make him a very fancy profit."

Lifting the sword, Marz allowed it to rest on the flats of his palms. "And all these years you preserved it, protected it like a mother wolf her pups."

"Aye, and tempted about twice every year to exchange it for a Lord's barter. For there were skeptical times when I questioned my vision. Dueled myself with thoughts less honorable than I feel this moment. But today at last my wait is over. Because I know in my soul that you are the warrior to whom the goddess' dream pointed. You who were born in earshot of the hole gouged by her meteorite. Of your worthiness I am certain."

Sliding the sleek blade out of the scabbard, Marz tested the balance to his great satisfaction. Turning it in his hand, the young soldier admired the light reflecting off the polished shaft. He touched his thumb to the edge, pursed lips acknowledging its keenness. "If I live for one hundred years, I shall never be able to thank you enough for this, this treasure. You have sacrificed a life of comfort to safe-keep its secret. And yes, Varo, I believe I am the true warrior of your legacy, destined for things of which I cannot speak even to you."

"Your eyes are thanks enough, lad. And if you will permit this old kilt to extend a bit of advice, then listen well." He touched a fingertip to the hilt resting against Marz's fist. "Never forget that it's the man behind the sword who counts most. For no soul dwells within a cold shaft of steel. Use it with prudence."

"I am in your debt, dear uncle, and understand you well. Also hear this. I shall always know this magnificent gift as the Sword of Varo!"

"Pah!" Such was the response of each new warrior eyeing the South Camp assignment roster. "Pah!" Repeated many times over, the expletive took many forms. The carefree simply exhaled it. The angry spat it out like foul cheese. "Pah!" For Marz it came as no surprise, figuring all along that Rooz would engineer a parting slap. But Monty, who hung in suspense for days leading up to the posting, expressed his dissatisfaction by yammering "Double Pah!" Over two hundred fifty would be heading south to the wild country, there to be distributed among the two kords sweltering in the oppressive heat. "At least we are posted together, Marz. And with Kavoyy and Kelozz close alphabetically there is a good chance we'll be in the same unit. Alas, miserable together," he chuckled.

"Aye," answered Marz, a pensive mind yet on Varo unswerving in his loyalty to a distant vision. *There is a lesson in dedication there,* he thought.

"At least we are rid of Yolks," Monty went on. "If I never see another fried egg for the rest of my duty, I'll be happy enough. Every time I try to eat a couple of eggs, all I can see is that bastard looking up at me. Makes me want to mash my spoon straight through the whole gooey mess."

"You're forgetting the most rudimentary of rules, Monty,"Marz teased:

"And what could that possibly be, my isthmus friend?" grinned Monty, willfully accepting the bait.

"Thrust and rip. Thrust and rip, my man. That's the deadliest way to dispatch a pair of hypnotic yolks!" Slapping his comrade's back, Marz guffawed, showing the brilliant teeth of his brood. "And as for the wild country, think of it as four winters without chill."

Monty shook his well tanned head. "I still prefer the mashing spoon technique. It's more painful than a merciful thrust. About South Camp, though, you probably make a good argument. Not only is the camp without winter chill, but I understand there is also an absence of parades...unlike our present location."

"You mean you don't enjoy spit and polish marching to the stirring roll of drums? Your kilt flailing in the mid-day sun! Monty, Monty,"Marz toyed, "what in The Vag does my brood sis possibly see in such a crass oaf?"

"Probably the brilliance of my conversation coupled with dashing good looks. Simple enough," Monty shot back, a crooked grin breaking his lips.

"Well, you're probably half right!" conceded Marz, sarcasm implicit in his voice.

"Which half?" queried the young man of the Barrier, challenging his mate.

"My friend, you're half brilliant and half dashing. Without question I'm sure Tyrra would wholeheartedly agree!" With that Marz grabbed Monty's shoulder and pounded his free palm on the solid back.

"Ooh, how those words sting, Kavoyy. I owe you one," he promised.

Dust and heat greeted the new soldiers on their arrival at South Camp. Though accepted as warriors, they were still rookies among the veteran troops, hence, they drew more than a fair share of the less desirable duties. But that's the way it is in the military. Until there are shared experiences with the regulars, the new people hang on the periphery, unsure of when they'll fit in. Regardless, Kavoyy and Kelozz meshed well with their more established comrades, their personalities overcoming the status of 'last men in.' But that did not exclude their assignment from the foulest of details, namely hauling garbage. The pair took it in stride, emphasizing how critical it was to don one's kilt during such duty. No doubt, villains capable of hijacking the tasty cargo were omnipresent, necessitating a ready sword. At the dump site swineherds drove their ravenous beasts into the putrid slop. As Monty succinctly expressed it, "Everything has to eat something."

"Except the Kala," grinned Marz. "In their case, something has to eat everything!"

"Sometimes your childish puns surprise me, Kavoyy. Once you commented, oh so cleverly, that I was but half brilliant and half dashing. So I now observe that you possess half a wit. Need I explain further?" They roared together. Theirs was a friendship of oneupmanship, constantly alert to the other's jibe, each primed to humble his friend. Irreverent though they acted, the bond between them grew even stronger, cemented by the specialness they felt for Tyrra. By now they had learned of her victory at Jarra. Of the shot that vaulted her above every archer in The Vag, of the golden trophy adorning her neck. If she achieved no other notoriety in her life, a reputation for excellence would be hers to the grave.

"Not only has she eclipsed us with her beauty, but now her warrior status has blotted out whatever light dared shine upon us," commented Marz in good nature. "I'll not be able to speak as her equal, especially with that golden arrowhead winking its superiority at me...and superbly earned at that. But it's you I fear will suffer the most, Monty. Should you marry, she'll use you for target practice the first time you disagree."

Monty rolled his eyes, dramatically clutching his chest in the act. "Aye, mate, but they'll be arrows of love piercing my heart. By the goddess' lovely fifth finger, they'll be welcomed by this soldier."

Marz placed both hands on his lovesick friend's chest and shoved with just enough force to cause him to stumble off balance. "Enough!" he yelled. "You're making me nauseous with your romantic hogwash. Feed it to the swine with the rest of the slop!"

Months accumulated into years, the arid wild country seemingly without seasons, the landscape absent of change. Recognition of Marz's exceptional soldiering finally came to pass in the form of a promotion. Sergeant Minor Marz Kavoyy's duties included overseeing a bolt of fifty men, reporting directly to a young battle officer. The latter had come to rely on Marz, pretty much allowing him free rein to manage the bolt as he saw fit.

About three years into his tour at South Camp, Sergeant Kavoyy was instructed to proceed to the nearby town of Arabella. Disturbances of a sinister nature had been reported by the asylum's director, circumventing the town's indifferent administrator. The director thought a show of force might quell the activity. Apparently members of a religious sect had been harassing the Children of Misfortune. Taunts and threats showered the grotesque faces whenever they ventured outside the compound walls. These were not the thoughtless barbs of crude wild country rubes, but a twisted response to years of dry spells, now a bona fide drought. 'Chalk faces,' as the sect's followers were known, insisted that only prosecution of sacrificial kind would bring rain, that only blood flowing freely from the retarded and malformed would loosen the clouds. Deliberately the white faced bullies, incited by a renegade priest whose whereabouts remained a mystery, terrorized the innocents by dragging fingers across their own throats, the unmistakable sign of death.

Upon entering the beige-washed compound, Sergeant Kavoyy reported to the Director's Building. A number of residents watched him, curious of the long striding warrior who smiled warmly in their direction. Usually outsiders gawked at their differentness, but this one moved easily, without reservation. As he passed by they raised their hands about shoulder high, feeble gestures welcoming him among their midst. Some of the welcomers were perfectly formed. These, he assumed, owned minds so stunted the simplest tasks confused them to tears. Mature of body, only the puzzled expressions permanently etched across their faces suggested the idiot flaw. Fate had cursed yet others with the most hideous of features. Herky-jerky in mobility, they often suffered unintelligible speech impediments as well, though the brain enjoyed a maturity equal to most Vaghi. All, however, wore the look of peace. Attentive to their needs was the asylum's staff. Roughly half nunine, many proficient in medicine, they were of a disposition which moved them to do good. Earnest in compassion, they gave fully of their time, patiently minding those abandoned by the hand of fortune. Marz touched the shoulder of one particularly ugly woman, returning her pathetic greeting with a pleasant, "Good morning." Unaware of the eyes following him through the shuttered window overhead, the sergeant slowed his walk so as not to alarm the little groups of unfortunates. *I must appear fierce to these poor souls,* he thought. *'Mustn't startle them.* He wished a few more his hope for a good morning, taking effort to speak softly. Through the shutter slats the observer continued watching until Marz disappeared into the smaller courtyard leading to the director' s office.

Once inside Sergeant Kavoyy sought out the head man, Shaz Bezitt, making inquiries to a pair of officious nunales. One ushered him up the staircase to a second floor door. Gee rapped twice before opening it a few digits. "Someone from South Camp to see you, sir."

"Have him come in, Riig," a voice responded.

Marz nodded his thanks to Riig and entered. Slender of physique, the director rose to greet him. Threads of gray coursed his thick hair. Except for the nose, the face appeared sharp like a great bird. In a way the slightly hooked nose reinforced his fowl visage, the suggestion of a beak entering Marz's mind. The bleached tunic hung loosely over Bezitt's gaunt frame, sleeves swallowing his lanky arms. "You're earlier than I expected." His arm swung across the desk to shake the soldier's hand.

"Yes, sir," answered Marz, gripping the older man with an easy strength. "The commander thought it best we respond quickly to the disturbances, but not with quite the numbers you anticipated. I have less than half a bolt with me. The town administrator was fearful we'd upset the citizenry by overplaying our force."

"Nevertheless, I'm grateful. This sect is composed mostly of drifters, malcontents and a misdirected collection of impressionable nobodies seeking some sort of life-purpose. But I suspect they've much bark with few teeth. You know the sort. A ragtag bunch, vocal in numbers but individual cowards in the main. Yet they are capable of being ignited to evil." Concern scrawled Shaz Bezitt's face. "Therefore, I felt it prudent to inform the post commander, thinking a show of force would nip their aggressiveness." He paused before continuing. "That sorry excuse for a town administrator refused to take action, afraid it would reflect poorly on his ability. Can you imagine the negligence?" Bezitt threw his arms up as if appealing to the ceiling.

"How many troublemakers are there?"

"Never more than two dozen men as far as I can estimate. Occasionally a handful of women swell their numbers. But they do have the capability to rile up the townspeople. On the whole they have been harmless or should I say non-physical. I don't know. Perhaps I've overreacted in contacting the commander. I'm not certain of anything anymore," he confessed, skinny hands pushing his hair back at the temples. "It's just that their vile spew so terrifies the Children of Misfortune."

Marz said nothing, choosing to let the director get it all out.

"But I understand that this sect, the Chosen, as they call themselves, have many more followers living out in the wild, tucked away in a camp or two. The greater potential for danger, of course, lies in the teetering sympathizers who could join their ranks." Again, the director raked the graying hair.

Politely Marz informed Bezitt that he headed a twenty man detachment charged with "maintaining a presence," aimed at intimidating those who would foment trouble. "We will bivouac outside your walls for a week and accompany your Children during trips to Arabella. But tomorrow we will march in alone to give them something to think about."

"Good. I think that should dissuade the more cantankerous ones." Shaz Bezitt shook Marz's hand, indicating the meeting had run its course. "And your name?"

"Sergeant Kavoyy, sir, of the Eighth Kord." Marz snapped to a rigid posture, more of a reflex signaling his martial readiness.

"You have a pleasant manner, Sergeant. What little contact I've had with sergeants has indicated a gruffer nature. My sense is that your superiors have sent the right man." Bezitt smiled, exposing teeth yellowed by the combination of age and neglect.

Bowing slightly, the soldier smiled. "Your words are kind." Preparing to depart, Marz gripped the door handle. As he pulled, someone on the opposite side pushed, causing the sergeant to stumble backwards. At that very moment an off balance body fell through the doorway. Instinctively he caught her in his arms, her own pressing against his chest. "Ooooh," she let out, the voice high pitched with surprise.

Their faces no more than six digits apart, Marz Kavoyy looked upon the most beautiful woman ever to enter his gaze. With the golden tan which favors people of fair skin, her smooth cheeks showed little sign of blush. Soft, pink lips, the oooh yet formed upon them, framed her sparkling white teeth. And the exquisite nose, straight and narrow, gave gorgeous reference to an image alive with beauty. Wrapped in sunny brown hair, tinting toward the blonde, the woman seemed content to rest in his hold. Though it lasted but a split second, his thoughts turned to the self-conscious, secure he had shaved closely but several hours earlier. It was the eyes though, that set her apart from any Marz had ever known. Superb in color, like liquid amber, they reflected the light flooding through the open windows. Her body firm against his caused a shiver to ripple his loins, the sensation both welcome and disturbing.

Finally an amused Shaz Bezitt interrupted the pleasantly awkward encounter. "Sergeant Kavoyy, this is my daughter Mylla. And vice versa. Now that you two have met, I think it would be all right to release her."

"Mylla," Marz repeated aloud. Unintentional though it might have been, it embarrassed him. Easing her from his hold, his face slightly flushed, he stammered, "I, I'm sorry. I should have been more careful."

"Nonsense," she laughed, smoothing the ruffled blouse. "The fault was mine." Mylla's eyes never left his, fascinated by the golden hue glimpsing her amber. "Now I'm certain that Sergeant isn't your first name. How do your friends call you?"

Regaining his composure, the soldier softly shook her outstretched hand, its warmth reaching deep inside. "Marz," he answered.

"Marz," she exclaimed in a whisper, the sound pleasing to his ears. "You are gracious to accept the blame. Father, I think Sergeant Kavoyy is both diplomat and soldier," she smiled, the lips invitingly luscious. "Why don't we simply agree we were mutually responsible?" His eyes remained fixed on hers, a slow nod confirming his acceptance.

Interrupting their wordplay, Shaz suggested, "Mylla, why don't you show Sergeant Kavoyy...uhh Marz, about the asylum so he can become familiar with the property...militarily speaking of course." He winked his approval of their obvious flirtation.

"Yes, father."

More promenade than inspection, they walked slowly about the main courtyard. Children of Misfortune lovingly ogled the young woman, gurgling hellos to her ever present smile. In keeping with her father's request, she pointed out the various architectural features to the captivated sergeant. "They seem to be enthralled with you," Marz said.

"Most are very sweet. I've lived here almost all my life. I guess they view me something like a sister." A young boy fumbled clumsily with the toggle serving as a vest button. Mylla set it right and brushed the lambs wool nap. He grinned his thanks, spittle leaking from the tilted mouth.

Marz marveled that such an exceptionally beautiful woman could be so filled with kindness for beings her physical antithesis. "You have a way with them," he complimented.

"As do you," she responded softly. "I watched you from my window when you arrived. You were unspooked, without revulsion. I saw you treat them with gentleness. Soldiers are generally callous to their misfortune, or so that is my impression. But you have the gift of patience about you." She bit her lip, unsure whether to reveal her heart. In the end she decided to be honest. "I like that about you, Marz."

A wisp of breath escaped him, emotion dizzying his thoughts. *Am I being swept away?* he asked himself *I've known her for less than an hour and I find myself caught in her eddy...and enjoying it. Mylla, Mylla. Her name is like music, like a songbird's melody. Oh, Monty, is this what you were babbling about? I feel light headed, like the effect of too much wine.* Marz coughed a false dryness from deep down, more of a Hrrumph. He used the time to clear his mind, not his throat. She had committed herself. Should he react in kind? "You hardly know me, Mylla," he laughed. "Is my character so easy to read?"

She knelt to readjust a sandal strap. Attentively he bent to assist her. Feeding the leather tongue through the buckle, he tugged gently making sure it was fastened without being overly tight. He rubbed the skin as if to massage away any discomfort he might have caused. Catching his eye, Mylla grinned coyly. "I have the feeling you are no ordinary kilt, Marz Kavoyy."

They strolled outside the gate and around the perimeter wall embracing the asylum. On the off chance that peeking eyes were about, Marz pretended to examine the wall, feigning a military curiosity. But in reality his attention was all hers.

Volunteering to go first, she told of her family background, playing a stalk of dry grass between her teeth, chewing the tip as she spoke. Her brood brother had been born with a horrible disfigurement. Resisting social pressure, her parents kept the boy baby with them at the Capital. Most would have committed him to Arabella, but they persisted, moral in their insistence. Unfortunately the child's problems were also of an internal kind. At age two he succumbed, dying in his mother's loving arms. His tiny heart had ruptured, the merciful goddess calling him to her celestial realm. The experience caused her parents to question their purpose, to re-evaluate the mission that is life. Six months later they trekked to Arabella carrying their beautiful girl child, there to live an existence of devotion to the Children of Misfortune. And so Mylla had been raised among the unlucky, gaining a tolerance achieved by few. The last year and a half had been troubling, she admitted. While serving her six month stint at the Breadbasket, her mother had passed away. Shaz especially took it badly. Even this morning Mylla found him weeping. However, for the most part, he had plunged into his work at the asylum as if to make up for his wife's absence.

Mylla pointed out the large tract of farmland which supplied vegetables to the asylum. "The Children of Misfortune cultivate it with little outside assistance," she said proudly. Like a big sister bragging about her sibs, she identified the rows, calling out, "Squash, beans, peas, onions, carrots, melons, and over there on that separate field is where they raise our lentils. "See how neatly they line their crops," she beamed. "Productivity is their way of answering those who would not have given them a Kala's chance to succeed.

I wish the drought were over though," she sighed. "This season's yield will be meager, at best."

"Aye," he responded softly. "And it gives crazed logic to those fools who would do the Children harm." After a brief silence Marz talked of the isthmus and his family, telling her just about everything there was to tell. Properly though, he never mentioned his quest for the Lord's throne. Even if he had, it would only sound like a pompous boast, he figured. But he did speak of his 'studies' at Mount Aryxx, of his courier duties culminating in the ride to the Capital and subsequent meeting with Lanz Varaxx. Marz tried to speak matter-of-factly, without conceit. Purposely excluding superlatives, he avoided embellishing the "tales of my youth." Mylla's attention was genuine, devoid of gushing praise, yet offering thrilling eyes. Eyes that exuded a richness ardently treasured by the enthralled recipient.

Morning saw Sergeant Kavoyy leading his detachment into the Arabella marketplace. Bearing shield and javelin, the message was clear to any who would incite trouble. The square jawed sergeant in charge surveyed several groups of louts hanging about the stalls. Steely eyed he met their glare until they either looked off or slunk away. His men stood spread-legged, resting upon their shields. Prior to their arrival, he had instructed them to be polite to the citizenry. However, if they encountered any sassiness they should be firm, even challenging should they feel hostility being directed their way. Forming a single wide rank, the stern soldiers stood silently at ease for a full hour. Meanwhile merchants bartered from their stalls and carts, hawking pots, cloth, live fowl, footwear, but very little in the manner of fruit and vegetables. And what tiny amount was available seemed undersized, lacking plumpness. After a while the town's chubby administrator appeared, closely followed by an equally rotund secretary. Despite his protests, he had been prepared for the military presence by a letter from the South Camp commander two days earlier. Each week a fresh detachment would be rotated to Arabella, he'd been informed. *A deterrent force, the sergeants will be instructed to detain any chalk faces lurking about the area.* Today there were none, the most likely candidates having been forewarned. Marz assumed they had retreated to the outlying hamlets or simply scrubbed their brows clean of the pasty chalk...temporarily.

"As you can see, Sergeant," the administrator prattled, "this is a peaceful community. The so-called threat of the Chosen is overstated. As far as I know, a few may pass through here from time to time, but there are no evil plotters harbored among us. No no." He wagged a pink finger for emphasis.

The sergeant couldn't avoid noticing that each pretentious finger owned a silver ring, no two the same. "I'm not quite sure who you are, sir. Please identify yourself," an unimpressed Marz requested.

The fat man cackled nervously to his secretary. "He doesn't know me. Ha." Then turning to the sergeant, he puffed up an already puffy paunch. "I am the town administrator of Arabella, appointed directly by Lord Varaxx. My name is Pez Javatt!" He purposely accentuated the last name. "Do you make the connection, Sergeant?"

"Aye." *Another Javatt,* thought Marz. *Probably a distant cousin of the Lord's wife and Rooz.* The sergeant decided it best to play along with Pez. "It pleases me to learn there is no danger about, sir. I think we're finished here for today, but my instructions are to return tomorrow."

"A waste of time. Don't you soldiers have anything better to do?" Pez Javatt postured a bit. Fists upon his hips, he raised his smug chin, petulant in the question he proffered.

Sergeant Kavoyy glowered at Pez, causing the administrator to reconsider his attitude. "My orders are to arrest anyone interfering with our activity. Anyone! Do you make the connection?"

The remainder of the week passed without incident or interference. Each evening Marz and Mylla managed to spend several hours together. Seated on her father's veranda, a starry canopy overhead, the two chatted for as long as he dared. The young sergeant knew his unofficial visits to the director's home stretched his legitimate requirements. For someone as conscientious as he, dereliction of one's duty could weigh heavily. But for the amorously inclined, some risks are necessary if success is to be had. On the final night he rose to say goodbye, promising to return whenever he had sufficient time to make the trip. As Mylla approached him, his arms reached out to take her hand, but she slid between them into his embrace.

"This is the first time you've held me since that day when I fell into your arms. Do you remember?" she purred, the smile warm and inviting.

"Aye, Mylla. Was a moment I've thought of often." Her body felt snug against his, as if the two had been molded with closeness in mind. Marz's hands slipped to her waist, gently pulling her tightly against the kilt and the excitement behind. She offered no resistance, her supple arms encircling his neck. He felt the brush of her caressing lips on his. And then the kiss, tender as a delicate flower, the breath sweet. Brief as it was, it thrilled him beyond expectation. Greedily he returned for a second, the touch of her tongue upon his. Both could feel the heat building within, the breathing panted. Rapture united their young bodies like the confluence of two streams surging to form one.

"Mylla! Mylla!" The strident call suspended their enchantment, ardor doused by Shaz's beckon. "It's getting late, dear. Time to call it a night."

"Yes, father," she answered, the soldier showering quiet kisses upon her neck. Pressing his head to her throat, she added, "Marz was just on his way out." Mylla gently broke the embrace while snuggling several busses to his chin and cheeks, ending passionately on his mouth.

"Good night, sir," Marz called out, attempting to dispel all desire from his voice.

"Good night, Sergeant."

South Camp bustled with the usual morning activity, supply wagons rolling in line to the quartermaster depot, details of men marching to and from duty assignments, patrols exiting the massive gates. Dust kicked up at the slightest disturbance. The absence of rain had turned the dry soil into crumbly particles. Like powdery mist it invaded every nook and fold. Even the ever-plentiful wells had become less giving, taking longer to recover after surrendering their yield. Crossing the parade ground en route to the headquarters building, the sergeant looked down at the caked grit packed between his toes. When in garrison, troops wore sandals, preserving their boots for rougher fare. He would have to scrub doubly before departing for Arabella. Shrewdly he had volunteered to escort the outgoing camp commander, planning to linger with Mylla during the respite. The new commander was expected to arrive momentarily, following which a turnover ceremony, including parade, would see the retiree sent off with a flourish and the new one invested. Lovestruck, and delighted with the feeling, Marz's humor these days was upbeat in the least. Monty and he had discussed the phenomenon, the former amused beyond words at his friend's total infatuation with Mylla. "A heart surrendered is a heart lost," he winked. And Marz had agreed without protest.

Earlier that week Marz had been reunited with his brood genther, adding to an already ebullient mood. Zoog, now residing in the wild country, had stopped by to register the passport permitting passage into the Gugububu. Anticipating periodic visits by Zoog, and a firm relationship with Mylla, Marz felt more gleeful than at any point in his military life. South Camp wasn't so bleak after all! Mylla and Zoog occupied his thoughts, replacing what had been a soldier's regimen of hum drum repetition. Yet he realized his experiences here at South Camp would help sculpt his future readiness, preparation for a destiny awaiting fulfillment. Never must he lose focus. Quiet nights, lying upon a coarse mat, he heard the lectures of Genu Zig repeated anew, reinforcing those virtues pointing the way.

Taking three stairs in a single bound, he entered the building intent on securing orders for the trip to Arabella. As the duty officer read him his instructions, he couldn't help but work up a half smile. Ponies! The ex-commander would ride to Arabella with mounted escort. Marz was to pick a detail of five and draw an appropriate number of ponies for the ride... and return the following morning! Surely the kindness of Gala Rotaria embraced his fortune. With glowing heart he exclaimed inside, *It is a good moment to be alive!*

Tucking the orders into a leather pouch, he was about to leave the office when a knot of senior officers noisily filled the doorway. The new camp commander had arrived fresh from the Capital. As he entered the room, Marz and the other soldiers present snapped to attention. The voice sounded vaguely familiar, but Marz couldn't place it at first.

"The number one priority is to arrest all of those chalk faced scum, including the renegade Taratt! Hang the whole bloody lot and be done with them. And the Lord Varaxx wishes it be done swiftly!" The surrounding officers sounded their agreement. Realizing he stood in the new commander's path, Sergeant Kavoyy took a step backwards allowing the man room to pass by. At the same moment the commander's head lifted, causing an uneasy tremor to climb Marz's spine, though he showed no outward emotion. The yolks he had become so familiar with at Muraverdus, stared at him with cutting malice. "Well, well, isn't this an interesting turn of events," Rooz Javatt gloated. The words came out with a hiss, the old venom evident.

# CHAPTER X

"Kala!" the alarm swept through The Vag like a windstorm among stalks of wheat. "Kala!" Massing above the isthmus in swarms so staggering the scouts were fearful to estimate the number. Two hundred thousand? Two hundred fifty thousand? Commander Morann advised the Capital, recommending that every kilt be rushed north. Town officials dispatched riders to inform the outlying villages, the latter alerting the countryside. Each man capable of wielding a blade was expected to report to the local administrator, there to be banded into reserve units. Meanwhile the standing army would move out of South, Central and the Barrier Camps to the Chokepoint, soon to join their comrades manning the wall.

First on the march, at a trot, came the kord of the Ravenhood. Not waiting for sunrise, the archers departed Jarra at the midnight hour intent on establishing their firing positions before the initial blue skinned wave charged First Line. Traveling light as usual, only the burden of packs and tightly packed twin quivers riding their shoulders, the hooded warriors jogged absent of chatter, the rustling of kilts accompanying the cadenced boot steps. No wasted energy sped with them. The strictness of the march dictated a discipline of quiet. Heading the column, Skyyra Jakivv, First Arrow of Jarra, clutched the sleek bow that had carried her fortune for so many years. As she ran, the Senior Capitana's mind visualized the bastion heights, determining which of her companies would hold specific positions. Mindful of the huge arrow inventory at North Camp, she had instructed the auxiliaries to pack Jarra's arsenal into several wagons to plod in their wake. If the Kala numbers were as vast as reported, there could never be such a thing as too many arrows.

Getting on in years, she knew her running days were limited. Skyyra could still maintain a good clip, good enough to lead her warriors. But the ankles swelled over long distances, knees hummed a low grade ache, one hip nagging at the onset of each long run. With constant motion, however, the hip behaved without complaint. Like rusting axles, with continuous action comes a smoother ride. Stoic in demeanor, Skyyra Jakivv ran through the pain, pushing it from a mind conditioned by her stony will. Still, the moment would come when she could no longer stride with the others. Hopefully she would recognize it when it came. And at that time, it would be incumbent on her to step down, her decision alone. If she couldn't run with her warriors, she'd be damned to sit astride a pony! Sotto voce jeers in the ranks, likening her to the beast she rode, would not live well inside her proud ego. No, she would do as her predecessors had...step aside, make room for one more able. Such is the way of tradition, the way of the Hood. Thinking ahead to those days following retirement, a tiny smile eased above Jakivv's firm jaw. *Maybe I'll find myself a man! After these many mateless years, perhaps a husband? Something to be considered. Hmmm. Someone of property but not necessarily wealthy. A widower would be best,* she mused. *The kind who could make me laugh after decades virtually devoid of mirth. Someone with a hard ass!* Pah, she breathed in full stride. *You're a wicked girl, Skyyra. End this foolishness! The Kala await, girly. Assign your mind to more bellicose matters.*

At the Capital, General Povezz pondered the logistical necessities of five thousand Vaghi warriors swelling the Ring of Kilts. The prospect of Kala spear sticks also occupied his thoughts. Years ago, three Kala had been known to carry such weapons. Although primitive, heaved by the sheer volume of hundreds of thousands of enemy, they would rain havoc among rankers defending First Line. Patrols had been unable to creep close enough to the dust lifting mass to determine the presence of spears. *But so many Kala! Oozing down to The Vag like a river of blue slime. Why so many?* Speculation had it that the drought had touched even the northernmost reaches of Gala Rotaria, shrinking the vegetation on which they fed. Hungered to frenzy, the many hordes were gravitating south, collecting above the isthmus, inevitably to be funneled into the Chokepoint. There to squash themselves against the formidable ramparts and the Vag army. Accordingly the Lord had concurred with Povezz's and Morann's urgent recommendation to expedite the movement of the entire force to that narrow stricture of land. All recruits in training would be held in reserve.

Lucid of mind, the heavy drinking Lanz Varaxx had initiated the proper decisions. Fortunately the Kala incursion came during a period of lordly sobriety. As the days passed, however, the Lord became more reliant on the brandy flask to ease his insecurity. *So many Kala. Morann must be deluded by his own scouts!* The bitter liquid fuzzed his thoughts, causing flashes of suspicion to surge within. One moment it was an alarmist, Morann, the next Kaara, his wife, overstepping her authority, plotting the future of her nephew. The brandy sloshing his innards served to internalize an acid of discontent, issues of no importance often sparking his anger: a button missing, olives too bland, water heated to a disagreeable temperature. So, always there was blame. Servants and bureaucrats suffered his humiliating sneers, occasionally bombarded by makeshift missiles: inkwells, apples, sandals, whatever handy.

The truth was that Lanz was a lonely man despite the attention of his office. Both friendless and paranoid, the brandy fueled a growing negativity regarding Varaxx's tenure. Fearful history would judge his a vacuous stewardship, he withdrew, abdicating his power to initiate social justice, to reform a system yearning for fresh thinking. Uninspired to excel, the Lord languished in depression. Perhaps fatherhood would have extracted a more human side. But no children sprang from his marriage, no progeny to lighten middle age. Kaara and he led separate existences except for those dinners and ceremonial functions requiring her attendance by his side. Even they had diminished as time wore on. *I despise her,* he grimaced. *Her haughty insensitivity has robbed me of a brood to carry the Varaxx legacy. Though I agreed to a childless union as a condition to gain her, to enlist her family's support, she has stolen the flower of my loins to cavort with playmates of her own ilk. She has neutered my greatness, my masculinity, my link with immortality.* Draining the goblet, he heaved it to the floor, its metallic clank harsh as his mood.

Kaara and he had never really shared the same bed, not in the conjugal sense. Their few sexual encounters had been more an appeasement of his primal urges than expressions of mutual passion. Her interests leaned more toward her female escorts, their chambers conveniently lying adjacent to her private bedroom. Lanz's own sleeping quarters occupied a portion of the residence as far from Kaara as possible yet under the same roof. Dispassionate though her feelings for Varaxx, she burned with an avocation championing her brood brother's son, Rooz. She had been a marital pawn, a willing one...but on her own terms. In exchange for accepting her hand, and not the furrowed duct of her identity, Lanz Varaxx had received the support of his in-laws, propelling him without challenge to the lordship. As in most 'quid pro quo' arrangements, there was one extra 'quid.' The Javatt considered Varaxx but a friendly ass, one which would warm the throne until a warrior of their blood was ready to possess the power. Accordingly, Lanz, pledged to manipulate his own succession, had in fact rigged Rooz Javatt's ascendancy. Varaxx, although never enamored of the proposition, felt better about it recently, comforted in the assumption that Rooz would exaggerate his mentor's contribution to The Great Vag. Only this month Kaara had nagged her husband into promoting Rooz to command South Camp, a premature move in Varaxx's mind. *Maybe the impatient bitch is conspiring to poison me,* he fumed. *And see that pushy Rooz nesting upon my throne!*

Momentarily putting his thoughts behind him, Lanz Varaxx crawled on all fours retrieving the abused goblet. With a slight teeter he rose to refill its emptiness, allowing the rim to overflow. The huge man burped loudly while licking the sour wetness from his fingers. A generous mouthful soon followed. Returning his thoughts to the Kala, he seethed a promised reprisal. *If that bloody alarmist, Morann, embarrasses me with his babble of two hundred thousand, I'll yank his leash all the way to the Capital!*

Rooz Javatt couldn't believe his good luck. Commanding South Camp but six days, he was now to lead the wild country's two kords, the Seventh and Eighth, on a forced march five hundred medecs up the peninsula to North Camp. Javatt estimated the journey to take twenty days. *Three weeks to glory!* he grinned. Instead of rousting chalk faced hooligans, his command would be blooded against the fury of the Kala. *Aye, three weeks to glory and fame!* For warriors of The Vag are measured in blood. Until one spills the crimson juice of life, until combat is engaged, the warrior remains untested. Although the Kala threat represented the potential to over run the great nation, to gobble The Vag to extinction, each soldier welcomed the confrontation with glee. Blooded troops achieve singular respect in a society of warriors. And though it was not spoken, every kilt knew it to be the truth. Blood on the kilt elevated veteran and rookie alike to an elite prestige.

At various points along the route, supply points were being set up by Povezz's quartermaster, meaning Javatt's command could move without the anchor of food wagons dragging in its wake. With any luck they'd be able to shave forty eight hours off his estimate. Rooz Javatt was a pleased man this day. Things were coalescing in a way to facilitate his ascendancy. Since early on he had felt the goddess' touch, certain he was among her favored. That promise was now moving towards a special destiny, he thought.

One hour before sunrise the Seventh and Eighth would break camp, each kilt toting bedroll and pack, canteen, shield, sword, two javelins and rations for three days. And Rooz would whip them along a pace unlike any they had ever trod.

When word came to Marz Kavoyy, it was as though the darkest of clouds had set upon his orbs, shading gold to pitch black. Disbelief painted his face, the astonishment reaching knife-like to the gut. "Are we being deprived of the opportunity to be blooded, to validate our warrior's worth? When the entire army will be massed for the first time in a generation, we are ordered to remain here on guard duty? To protect this sand blown stable of a camp?"

"Aye, Sergeant. Those are our orders. Selected by the camp commander himself, I am told. Our bolt alone will remain behind." The disappointed officer stroked a chin bearing the shadow of overnight stubble. "Within the combined two kords are forty bolts. One must stay here...and we're it! I don't like it as much as you, Kavoyy. For whatever his reason, Senior Capitanus Javatt personally chose us. Perhaps he drew our unit from a hat!" So spoke the battle officer charged with commanding Marz's bolt.

When the other kilts learned of their ill fortune, they howled aloud, the profanity flowing in torrents beyond the stale 'pah.' Unknown to them, the denial of their blooding reached beyond 'the luck of the draw.' The obsessive snarl of Rooz Javatt had found a way to bite the aspiration of Marz Kavoyy. In Rooz's implacable mind it was preoccupation of a needling kind, a little reminder to Sergeant Kavoyy that he could control both events and the man. Fun!

As he watched the last soldier pass out of the portal, Monty Kelozz spat forcefully into the dirt before joining a mate in cranking the gate closed. Effectively the action sealed his bolt inside for the duration. Headquarters had ordered them to remain within the great earthen wall until the troops returned, and that could take many months depending on the inclination of the Kala swarm. Only their battle officer would be permitted to venture outside in the event of an extreme situation. *At least there won't be any damned parades!* thought Monty. For Kelozz the prospect of a march to the Ring of Kilts had offered an opportunity to seek out Tyrra, to glimpse her lovely face, to touch the smooth skin along her neck, to say something comic coaxing the perfect teeth to flash their brilliance. Oh, to gaze her golden eyes, the irises shimmering their auric glow. But thanks to Yolks, whatever chance there had been was now dashed. *What did you do during the Kala War, grandpa? I kept tidy the South Camp parade ground...five hundred bloody medecs from the closest blue nose!* Dropping the huge beam which served as a crossbar into the locking slots, the soldiers wore the empty look of the forlorn. Their duty from here on was to sit and wait.

Dutifully, Sergeant Kavoyy examined the gate. Pushing against the crossbar, he tested its heft. Satisfied it held secure, Marz signaled his approval to the kilts standing about. *No Kala blood to drip my sword No visits to Arabella and Mylla. I am isolated, frozen in motion. Suspended in growth. Genu Zig, if you can hear my thoughts, tell me if I have been forsaken. Has the great goddess soured on her choice? Help me, Genu, for my soul weakens. Perhaps I need a sign. Something to reinforce a will turning soft.* He searched the southern sky, half expecting a miracle, like silver birds of legend flying out of the sun to alight upon his head. But nothing happened, only hot wind blowing grit across the parade ground. Slamming fist to palm, Marz self-mocked his thoughts, chastising himself for whining like a spoiled child. *This is a test and nothing else,* he persuaded his wavering mind. *One more small ordeal to patiently overcome. For all I know, opportunity will spring from this dismal situation. Be prepared!*

Both devices behaved identically, confirming the other's action. The calibrations were the same, the liquid dropping at precise increments. Dramatic in their performance, the tandem instruments conveyed a meteorological coming of prodigious proportion. The nunale shuddered in anticipation, for gee understood the power of absolute prediction belonged to gen alone. Aye, rain would soon arrive in quantity unknown for many, many years. Unquestionably the goddess had arranged for the Kala threat, maneuvering the South Camp kords to vacate the wild country. And with their departure she eliminated the last obstacle, the final vestige of interference. Now she would command the heavens to wash the land in blessed rain. But not until Huug Taratt had made ger move, had instructed the most fanatical of the Chosen to open the veins of the Arabellan freaks. Then, after the bloodletting, the obedient first finger would send forth the deluge of her appeasement. Everything was in place. A most propitious moment, indeed. Finally, following an adulthood suffering the scorn of ger peers, the indignity of a desert hovel, Huug Taratt would be the prophet of action. Gee would make the most audacious decision of ger existence. And come the bountiful water, gee would be acclaimed an angel of Gala Rotaria. Henceforth, Huug Taratt's words would revolutionize the governance of The Vag. And leap Taratt from prophet to messiah!

Gasping deeply, the priest staggered up the South Camp ramp. Though yet dark, the sentinel had spotted the stranger's approach and called out to the battle officer making his rounds. Together they admitted the exhausted nunale through a small opening within the huge gate. Sweat saturated the tunic causing it to cling in bunches, the face scarlet with heat, locks dank. "You must send troops to the asylum at Arabella," gee wailed. "Hurry, please hurry!" Zoog Kavoyy had traveled the night on a desperate mission to warn of Taratt's impending treachery. The pony had gone lame about seven medecs back, forcing gee to cover the remaining ground on foot. "You must move swiftly," gee implored. "Please."

The officer summoned Sergeant Kavoyy, who having heard the commotion was already striding to the group. "Zoog," Marz called out, "what's the matter?"

"You know this priest?" the officer inquired, noticing the badge of Zoog's vocation.

"Aye, sir. Gee is my genther," answered Marz, "my brood genther."

"Oh, Marz. Thank goddess it is you," responded the nunale, relieved to recognize ger brother. Quickly they embraced, their sibling bond too strong to resist. "It is Huug Taratt. Gee is wild of mind, convinced the Children of Misfortune must be sacrificed this day. Huug and the rabid Chosen are at this moment preparing to attack the asylum."

"Where are they?" barked the concerned officer.

"On the East Road, about seventy of them armed with swords, marching to Arabella. It's possible they have already arrived." Zoog continued to pant, the strain still evident, the golden eyes wide with despair.

"I'm not authorized to dispatch troops," the officer informed. "Come now, do you really believe they'll harm the poor souls?"

"Beyond harm, they plan to slay everyone who appears even remotely deformed or slow of mind. It is imperative that you rush your warriors to Arabella. You must act at once!"

"I told you, I can not. My orders are firm!"

"Oh, no," lamented the sergeant. "Mylla is…" Marz restrained his outburst. "Sir, we must interdict them. The bolt must speed at once to Arabella. Surely it is the gravest of emergencies. Surely it is justified."

"Justified or not, Javatt will have me skinned alive if I send the bolt racing off to Arabella. No, sergeant, I'll not break my orders." Strong of jaw, he presented them with the only compromise he could. "But I'll mount a pony and ride there myself When those hooligans see a battle officer of The Vag awaiting them, they'll turn tail. By default I am interim commander of South Camp. I doubt they'll defy my authority."

A horse was immediately saddled, and off the officer sped at full gallop, waving a confident hand at Monty Kelozz guarding the gate. "He is a brave man," observed Zoog. "Brave but naive, I fear. I pray for his success though I believe his effort to be futile. Huug is too determined to back off at this late point. Only force will prevent disaster."

Barely nodding, Marz said nothing. Perhaps selfishly, his mind concerned only Mylla. Vulnerable as any in her charge, Mylla's safety dominated his thoughts. Ironically, her goodness had put her life in jeopardy. At this moment, others of the asylum were of no priority, their protection never entering his head.

A first hint of gray light filtered across the eastern horizon, the air uncomfortably heavy. The atmosphere felt buoyant in a sluggish way, an ominous tingle conveyed by the invisible current. There came a throaty rumble in the distance, a sound unheard in these parts for quite some time. Entering the compound walls, the silent figures fanned across the courtyard. No sun sparkled the metal shafts each carried. Silhouetted against the dim sky, however, the unmistakable form of the short sword became apparent. The raucous squawk of a startled cockerel caught the ear, strident against the rolling thunder.

As they positioned themselves near the dormitory entrances, each turned to face the central sun dial, uniform in their pasty whiteness, ghostly in the murky light. Standing by the dial where all could view ger signal, a breathless Huug Taratt raised a black dagger to the sky, the eerie chalk upon ger wrinkled brow. Grinning with a zealot's fervor, the bald nunale eyed the

Chosen poised for the dastardly act. "Now," gee screamed, and struck the blade downward, stabbing the unfeeling air. The command caused every door to be thrown open with a great bang. Shouting "Water from blood," the Chosen crashed into the barracks-like quarters, tossing bunks upside down, the confused sleepers roused to a frightened awakening. Pummeled and kicked, the Children of Misfortune were herded to the sun dial, several having suffered slash wounds to their limbs. There, at the feet of the posturing Huug Taratt, they were slammed to the ground. Yelling ugly obscenities, the chalk faces stomped any who dared protest. Pleading for mercy, those medics and attendants who had been tossed into the group, were subdued by cruel punches. "Prepare them for sacrifice," ordered Taratt. "Peel the cloth from their foul bodies!" And so they were stripped, sleeping garments ripped viciously from the cowed mass. Genitalia exposed, Huug's followers took particular pleasure in prodding loins with the toes of their boots.

Looking toward the Director's Building, a few of the Children screamed, "Mylla, Mylla," as the young woman was dragged by the wrist. Across the yard her captor roughly pulled her to their midst, there to brutally yank her tresses until she fell to her knees. A retarded woman whimpering in fear, crawled to Mylla's arms, to be hugged by her beautiful protectoress. "Leave this place,"Mylla shouted in vain. "Leave this place and let us be or you will suffer the harshest of consequences!" The emptiness of her threat amused Huug's thugs. They laughed at her impudent admonition, motivating a scrawny follower with red hair to step forward. A smile on his rotted teeth, he kicked her ribs repeatedly before tearing the gown from her writhing body. Leering with sadistic intent, he stooped to cup her breast, his purpose obvious.

"None of that," hollered Taratt. "We are here to do the goddess' bidding, not to trifle in carnal rubbish!" Rebuffed, the man squeezed Mylla's nipple with sadistic force, giddied by her scream. After a few seconds she pushed herself to her knees, tears flowing her cheeks. She cried, "Where's my father?"

"Where is Bezitt?" asked a calm Taratt of the henchman who had captured Mylla.

The man stepped forward to answer his prophet. "The old dog resisted my, uh, uh encouragement. So I killed him...I mean I sacrificed him. Right in his bed." Brandishing his sword, he displayed the blood yet fresh on the blade. This caused a round of snickers to rise from his fellows. "Should I haul his ass out here?" he asked, enjoying the attention of his fellow cutthroats.

"No, never mind," an annoyed Huug replied.

A gush of vomit burst from Mylla's mouth, the news of her father's violent demise driving her to nausea. Ignoring the pain from her crushed ribs, she struggled to stand. Defiant in her nakedness, she aimed her fury at the insane Taratt. "You filthy monster. My father was the most decent of men. In this world there are good and evil, as evidenced by all that is here this very morning. Shaz Bezitt was the finest of Vaghi, a good and honorable man to his final breath. But you are evil of soul, ugly of spirit, depraved of mind, infinitely more mutated than these innocents whose only problem is one of appearance. Aye, you are the most wicked of the evil. The blood you spill here today will drown your soul. May the goddess curse you for eternity!"

"So be it," retorted an impassive Huug Taratt. "Sacrifice them all!"

The moment they had impatiently waited for, now at hand, Huug's followers eagerly waded into the screaming cluster, each selecting a victim to his particular liking. The redheaded villain who had stomped Mylla's ribs carried a fiendish glint in his eye. Seizing her hair, he jerked the woman's head back and jabbed his sword point into her throat. So forcefully did he thrust that the tip exited the nape exploding a carmine shower upon the other unfortunates, themselves to be executed within seconds. The blood which left Mylla's lips gurgled an indistinguishable, "Marz," as she fell among the heap. The only love of her short life had been the final thought her mind would ever recall.

As the frenzied Chosen hacked the sacrificial herd to pieces, the asylum ground transformed to a coppery mud. Attempting to ward off the killing blows, wrists were chopped away before more vital targets were exploited. Those who tried to escape saw themselves cut down, their efforts futile against the murderous Chosen. Terrified shrieks silenced abruptly by Taratt's crazed minions, echoed the walled enclave. Eventually the last life succumbed, the massacre complete. When they were sure no moans responded to their prods, there followed a bizarre ritual. The throats were slit, the bodies held up by the ankles to blanch what little fluid remained. As they did so their unholy lyrics rose to the thundering sky. "Water from blood. Water from blood." The monotone chant filled the courtyard. And in the center, Huug Taratt, the buff robe sprayed with crimson, lifted both hands in macabre triumph. "Great mother, we have obeyed your call. Give us the tears of your largesse. Water, mother, water from blood!"

Hardly noticeable, the first few drops pattered upon Taratt's shaved skull with less impact than the shower of blood staining ger robe. "Rain," an awed follower shouted. "Rain! The goddess is pleased." Even the ex-priest didn't think the precipitation would come so quickly, although the instruments of Huug's creation had predicted it.

"My Chosen, the goddess is appeased! Let us set fire to this den of grotesque beasts. Torch the buildings, the fields, everything, before the tears of Gala Rotaria wet all beyond combustion. And slay the animals, for having been touched by the deformed, they too are unclean." A great cheer went up, the killer zealots making ready to finish their hideous labor.

Riding through the open gate, the horseman came upon the grisly scene so swiftly he was unable to absorb its meaning. His first instinct told him it was some sort of prostrate prayer ritual, the bodies strewn face down. Unfortunately he reined his pony to a halt at the very instant he recognized the slaughter for what it was. Horror bulged his eyes, the specter of so many butchered corpses momentarily numbing his action. Wheeling the confused pony, he attempted to charge through the raiders blocking his path. But the animal's momentum was spent. Amid much shouting, clawing fingers reached for him, ripping at the kilt. They yanked him from the saddle, the rearing beast causing his spine to be whipped backwards. Mercifully the neck snapped on impact with the hard gravel. Regardless, the men of chalk punctured him with at lest twenty thrusts. In the end his corpse was also blanched, the jugular slit to quicken the flow.

The mingling of so much blood took on a symbolic note, unrealized by Taratt's thugs. The malformed had perished with the beautiful. Young and old together. Male, female, nunale. Intelligent and retarded. Doctor, nurse, soldier. One could go on and on with yet more detailed contrasts. Perhaps the most unfair of all observations, though, was that only the evil survived.

For two weeks the skies never cleared. Rain fell with a blinding fury, inundating the valleys and lowlands, collapsing stands of timber, flooding farmland, undermining structures. Rivers overflowed banks, lakes encroached their shorelines, pushing inhabitants to higher ground. Abandoning their waterlogged homes, the hills were thick with refugees waiting for the great swell to subside. The entire Vag saw itself blanketed by a wetness more destructive than any in history. And with it came a pervasive cold reaching the borders of the Gugububu. Crops, stunted and struggling through the drought days earlier, were washed away before harvest. Unless fields could be reworked soon, a lean year, possibly famine, would follow. Most spent their time trying to stay dry, patching roofs, caulking chinks. Unsheltered animals disappeared, either buried in mud or swept into the swollen rivers and out to sea. The chill brought on by the storm touched all, firewood so dampened it was difficult to maintain a proper hearth. The moisture and cold coupled to afflict many with respiratory illness and fever. Marching to the isthmus, the army of The Vag became bogged down on syrupy roads churned deep by the many boots. Even the impassive Kala, layered in their communal piles, sensed an extraordinary happening. The Ring of Kilts wasn't spared either, the great drench collecting within the walls like a mammoth tank. Details of soldiers attempted to reinforce First Line and the Ring, using stone to buttress the weakened sections, digging drainage canals to tap the continually replenished excess. Never knowing the whimsical inclination of the Kala, the soaked kilts did their best to remain vigilant.

Huug Taratt, having delivered on ger promise of rain, had expected the people of the wild country to rally about gen, declaring the ex-priest an angel of the goddess. Overwhelmed by the enormous flow, most were too busy trying to survive. At the Chosen's campsite, Huug's disciples huddled under windblown tenting, their feet upon platforms of tree branches ineffective against the puddled rain. Their mission had been to spread the word of Taratt's miracle among the wild country's scattered communities. And ultimately to the upper peninsula. But the uninspired messengers refused to leave the relative 'comfort' of the sodden camp. Besides, they reasoned the town squares were empty, the deluge forcing residents inside. Surely with so much water borne devastation, the people would curse the name of Taratt, accusing the Prophet of offending the goodness of Gala Rotaria. The very rain which was to have delivered Taratt's legitimacy, now served to condemn Huug's being. Unable to rally a scornful populace, Taratt had retreated to the rim of the Gugububu to sit out the gale, to figure out how to turn this thing around.

On a frigid morning while icy vapor yet clung to the Capital's rooftops, the Lord of The Vag was roused from an angry sleep. Chilled and grimy, an exhausted messenger waited in the outer chamber. His leather kilt stiffened by the cold still bore the depression of a grueling night in the saddle. Accompanying him stood Taz Povezz, General of the army, his scowl foreboding for he had already learned the news.

Half-dressed, the Lord rushed his arms into the sleeves of a full length sheepskin robe and approached the two figures. The bulky garment swelled his image, a huge man made larger. Three gluttonous years had visibly plumped the once proud body.

Never before had the messenger been this close to the most powerful man on Gala Rotaria. The impression was one he'd soon not forget, something to relate to family around a holiday fire. Tousled from an uneasy sleep, Varaxx's locks had worked themselves into a mane of leonine likeness. Backlit by a single ray of gray light sifting through the shafted window, the hair radiated a misty quality, almost a halo. Unshaven grizzle added to his majesty, thought the awed rider caught up in the drama.

"Well, what is it?" Varaxx snapped. Reading the General's tawny eyes, he realized immediately the information would be ill. *Don't tell me there's been a disaster at the isthmus,* he thought, *I knew all this damn rain would weaken the earthen walls!* The messenger, shaken from a moment's fascination, straightened his posture. Short and wiry, his size rendered him ideal for a horseman. Pushing the rain soaked hood off his dank curls, he glanced to the general to confirm which of them would actually speak the news, though a formal dispatch canister remained clutched in his fist. Taz Povezz nodded his approval to proceed. Believing full well his message would be greeted by an explosion of rage, the courier hesitated. "Go on, lad, spit it out," urged the officer.

Stepping forward, the dispatch rider executed a snappy cross-armed salute and barked the grisly news. "Lord Varaxx, a communication from Minor Sergeant Kavoyy, temporarily commanding South Camp."

"Go on!" the impatient Lord demanded.

"Eight days past the renegade ex-priest Huug Taratt and his followers slaughtered the Children of Misfortune at Arabella. All were put to the sword, their bodies blanched in a barbaric blood ritual. Some one hundred seventeen including the Director, doctors, nurses and attendants who attempted to protect the children similarly perished. Males, females, nunales...all slain. Farm animals were butchered and burned. Buildings, crops and orchards torched as well. Huug Taratt proclaimed that only by sacrificing..." He swallowed hard. The words repulsed him. "..only by sacrificing they of the grotesque and addled brain would the goddess believe The Vag nation to be cleansed of its human blight, its chosen status restored to the favor of the heavens. This will be recognized by the gift of rain ending the drought." Heaving a deep breath, he continued. "Huug Taratt and about seventy followers appear to have retired into the Gugububu or nearby, there to fast and await the promised rain. So Huug Taratt informed in a document affixed to the only surviving tree. A copy of Taratt's statement is enclosed with this dispatch. Also I am instructed to inform you that Sergeant Kavoyy and a full bolt are fully prepared to take whatever action you and the general deem appropriate." Having delivered the message he had rehearsed over a hundred times astride a string of mud spattered ponies, the courier stepped backwards to General Povezz and handed him the canister.

With each phrase spoken by the diminutive warrior, Lanz Varaxx's bloodshot eyes appeared to grow wider, threatening to pop from their sockets. When the last word had been uttered, his lids closed tightly. No outburst came forth. No shout of outrage interrupted the morning drizzle. Instead a long silence followed, shattered by four words, each with distinct enunciation. "BRING ME GER HEAD!"

It is written in the Code of Laws, that the Lord of The Vag can, without formal hearing, execute by decapitation any Vag who commits nunicide, the murder of a nunale, or any fugitive who while fleeing from a crime, enters the Gugububu, thereby jeopardizing the lives of his, her or ger pursuers. Huug Taratt had violated both!

Over four thousand troops assembled within the great earthen fortress, another one thousand manning the forward-most position, First Line. Soggy and miserable they gamely endured the adverse weather. Many suffered the ague which arrives with such circumstances. Diarrhea played havoc too, compounded by latrines overflowing their pungent effluent. Fast forming channels carried the waste to other portions of the camp contaminating drinking water. Soon it seemed everyone had the trots. If their deteriorating health wasn't enough to concern the leadership, low temperatures and windblown rain were also combining to upset the organization necessary for military alertness. The ground had become so saturated that tent pegs refused to hold taut the canvas shelters, forcing kilts to seek refuge elsewhere. Consequently units became intermingled, breaking down control. Whimsically the Kala never moved down the Gorge of Skulls, electing to pile just above the isthmus. The longer they remained north of the slot, the greater the chance the Vaghi would become more run down, sickness and deprivation slowly sapping their strength. Naturally, the Kala weren't capable of understanding the strategic advantage afforded by their procrastination.

Finally one morning after twenty-nine sunless days, a huge orange ball lifted above the eastern skyline, the rain having ceased during the dark hours. And with it came the compassionate warmth of its rays. Many warriors stripped to their bragghi or less, inviting the glorious shine to reach inside their very pores. Quickly engineers oversaw the construction of drainage canals, emptying new formed basins which had collected a month's runoff. The higher ground continued to leach into the basins, however, the new drains managed to tap off the excess before levels again became problematic. Still water tends to stagnate and attract insect critters of the uncomfortable sort, so details cut additional swales into the mushy earth maneuvering the flow out through the south wall.

Up north the pulsing piles also responded to the break in weather. Unpeeling from their fleshy mounds like so many artichoke leaves, the aquamarine bodies shook the wetness from heads and limbs and began sniffing the air for signs of nourishment. The Vaghi scouts had been correct in their original assessment, the herd numbering in the hundreds of thousand. Unsure in which direction to move, they ambled in small circles waiting for the horde to develop the momentum which would carry them off in quest of breakfast. Roughly one in nine toted sticks, most of which had been gnawed to a dull point. These they used to poke others of their breed who got in the way.

A commotion stirred the outer perimeter among those Kala milling closest to the isthmus funnel. Something or someone was culling them into a separate herd, causing them to move apart from the rest. Skittering away from whatever the irritant, they collided with one another, chirping and squealing their displeasure. Within moments the figure of their irritation burst along the upper fringe swinging his stick at any not agile enough to avoid being hit. Perhaps the most imposing blue skinned creature ever to roam the Kala track, he stood over a full head above the tallest of his kind. Surely he stood equal in height to the average Vag male, but without the body definition. Yet he was stout of frame. Ruthless in his aggression, he jabbed his spear-stick at a slow moving buck, inflicting a raw gouge to his victim's shoulder. And all the time he grinned, his mouth permanently fixed in a smiling grimace. Cocking the bushy head to catch sight or sound, the big Kala showed his pleasure or dissatisfaction by snapping through the ever present grin. But it was the sheer size that set him apart, that established his superiority, escalating him to a position of dominance in a horde absent of customary social structure. One sensed that this particular Kala also owned a brain capable of thinking beyond food. His intelligence, albeit primitive, combined with the obvious physical dimension, rendered him the most remarkable of Kala. It begs the question, how did he come to be? Was he the first of an evolving strain of Kala or a unique genetic accident, singular among his race, a one time freak? Regardless of the genesis, the initial rumbling of Kala leadership was his. A king without regal concept. Disaster loomed for the Vaghi should his seminal bounty create a lineage of super Kala. The potential was there. For like a stud bull he roved the herd, coupling at will, displaying a boundless sexual energy. Females sensing an unusual being, approached him eager to grind his loins.

Having driven a group of roughly twelve thousand away from the main contingent, he guided them like a sheep dog, growling at the delinquent. As the sun rose higher he steered them into the funnel, pushing them through the narrows, stopping twice to lap water. Up front those in the lead sniffed with anticipation, the unmistakable aroma of warm blooded delicacies catching hold. Before the big Kala could swing his way to their front, the prospect of hot food stampeded the herd into the gorge and beyond. Frenzied they raced at full tilt through puddles of muddy slop. Less than three hundred strides ahead lay a huge dirt hill, the broad moat impossible to view from their depressed angle. Instinct told them that once over its heights a feast of delights awaited their jaws. Blind in their rush, they charged another eighty strides, indifferent to the shadows streaking overhead. Like a flock of angry birds the whirring shadows plunged into their midst penetrating the blue hued flesh. Hundreds fell unaware of what was happening. Behind them others tumbled over the writhing bodies, only to be caught in the next shower of death. Females, males, young children clutched at the wooden rods protruding from their tormented bodies. Confused in reaction, the simple minds failed to comprehend the nature of their plight. Too dumb to scatter, they froze in place, motionless targets. Volley after volley rained upon the helpless creatures until virtually none were left standing. The Ravenhood of Jarra, blooded to the last warrior, had wiped out the entire charge. Perhaps three or four reached within fifty strides of the moat, only to be picked off by clusters of archers. Methodical in their lethal work, the entire battle had lasted little more than an hour. Five hundred thirty bow-women, to the cheers of their male kilts, had annihilated the Kala threat. A kill rate of 200 per minute.

Standing out of bow range, the big Kala, his grin yet evident, tried to analyze exactly what had happened. He stared at the wall teeming with beings unknown to him, then looked at his own breed riddled with sticks. Pressing his tiny brain, he tried to make sense of exactly what had happened. As a detachment of warriors descended the First Line to dispatch the shrieking wounded and retrieve arrows, he moved far enough away not to be run down. Soldiers on the ramparts had been watching him, marveling at his physique. Was he a chief? Probably not. Everyone knew the Kala were leaderless. But to all he appeared to be the head Kala, supported in appearance by a head in fact larger than any of the others. Well founded, someone on the forward wall called him "Kalahead." And so it stuck. Perhaps the first of the Kala ever to have a name, the unwitting big Kala could lay claim to this distinction. Kalahead!

*So this was it?* more than one kilt exclaimed in his disappointment. The great Kala invasion, supposedly embracing hundreds of thousands, had fizzled to a mere twelve thousand. Evidently the scouts had panicked in their excitement, had badly exaggerated the estimate. An entire army, poised to resist the fiercest of onslaughts, had survived flood and dysentery, only to watch their warrior sisters efficiently destroy a relative handful. In effect, they had been nothing more than a cheering gallery.

Two days later Commander Morann sent out patrols to reconnoiter north of the funnel. To be sure they ventured an additional six medecs. No sighting of Kala was detected, only muddy footprints and feces. Probably from the group that had died en-mass. Unknown to them, leaching rainwater had destroyed whatever evidence of the huge herd might have existed. As a precaution, Morann would hold the extra troops at North Camp a few more days before releasing them back to their base camps. No doubt the Lord would be furious at Morann's feeble intelligence system. In Lanz Varaxx's brandy-soaked eyes, the commander would be guilty of overreaction, an "alarmist!"

Among the warriors of Jarra there is an expression, *An arrow regained is just as deadly as one from the fletcher's hand* Arrows salvaged from the killing ground were brought to the North Camp armory, there to be sorted. Those deemed suitable for re-use were cleaned of mud, and in some cases, fragments of Kala flesh, and returned to the arrow racks. The remainder were placed in baskets like clustered asparagus. Dissimilar to the vegetable, the tips were pointed down, nock up. Carts would transport the unserviceable projectiles back to Jarra where the arrow-smiths would scavenge the intact pieces, a shaft from one, the head from another, and construct rebuilt arrows, perhaps to be fitted with new fletching. Naturally all broken and twisted bronze would be deposited at the forge for recycling.

The last warrior in the armory, Sergeant Tyrra Kavoyy had remained behind to tally the racks and baskets. Many of the splintered shafts were the result of slapdash handling. Non-archer kilts assigned to drag Kala carcasses to the Gorge of Skulls, where the putrid stink would be less offensive, often were indifferent to the spent arrows. Some were snapped off in the dragging, others trampled. Tyrra shook her head at the piles of shattered shafts, certain most were the result of unthinking kilts. The day had been uncomfortably warm, the armory air baked to a stifling dryness. It would be good to get back outside where the heat was less confined. Like the warrior detail she had dismissed minutes earlier, Tyrra had shed the drawstring bragghi. While in garrison at Jarra, it was customary to strip the garment. Here at North Camp, though, with a multitude of horny males, it could create problems or welcome attention, depending on one's inclination...especially when one considers the men also went bragghi-less. Absorbed in her tally, Tyrra climbed about the racks, straddled work benches, bent over baskets, all in the efficiency of her task. With each action the leather strips of her kilt separated, exposing flashes of thigh and buttock. Her indifference was in stark contrast to the shadowy figure observing her every motion, enravished by the muscular roundness of the archer's derrière. Sucking in air through his teeth, he watched the tightness of her thighs straining to gain more height. As a senior officer he knew better, but the opportunity was too perfect to resist. No witnesses to contradict his version of whatever would transpire. There wasn't much light in the armory, the oil lamps having been extinguished by the departed detail. As she turned to leave, he stepped out from behind a stack of wooden cases. Startled, she exclaimed, "Ohh, I didn't realize you were here, sir." Tyrra, though blasé on the surface, knew immediately he had been peeping. *Probably put on a fine show for him,* she thought.

"Did I frighten you?" he asked, a hint of mischief in his tone. He moved closer, crowding her until very little distance separated them.

If she was uncomfortable, she didn't show it. So perhaps her casual air encouraged his boldness. "No, sir. You didn't frighten me. It's just that I didn't expect anyone else to be in here."

"Maybe it's to our mutual good fortune that we find ourselves alone together." He leaned yet nearer. "I was captivated by your beauty. Indeed, you are a jewel in a kord of stones." His eyes hunted hers, seeking a glimmer of interest. "Yes, a jewel set in eyes of richest gold."

"Commander, I'm flattered by your compliment, but I must be off and about my duty. With your permission, I'll withdraw to...to." Her sentence never reached completion, the sensation of his hand gripping her naked thigh. Still she showed no outward distress. Instead the woman stared at the eyes opposite hers, his irises wide and curiously orange. *Like egg yolks!* she reckoned.

Because she hadn't recoiled, it motivated him to creep his fingers higher, promising to touch the region of her woman-ness. *She likes it,* he surmised. *Why shouldn't she. She's probably never lain with one so high born as I.* He sensed she was coming on to him, the wetness between her legs ample indication of her heat. *Aye, this would be a dalliance to remember. Screwing like dogs, right here on the armory floor!* Her wetness grew more pronounced, the thrill of her heat becoming uncontrollable. And all the time she coldly stared into him, insensitive to her own excitement. Suddenly it became evident there was more to her reaction than common foreplay. The warm stream flooding his hand was urine, the drip now noisy on the wide beam floor. "You've pissed on my hand!" The outrage contorted his face, the yolks dilated to their maximum. "How dare you...you, you insolent bitch!" he stormed. Shucking the wet palm, he raised it as if to strike her.

Unflinching, Tyrra batted her lashes in feigned innocence. "But Commander, I was so startled by your touch that I lost control of my bladder." The puckish smile that lit her face yet added more insult to his seething.

"That's enough of that!" a voice barked out. From behind stands of javelins the silhouetted head of Skyyra Jakivv, Commandant of Jara, interjected her irate presence.

"Jakivv! How much did you see?" the flustered commander inquired.

"Enough to know you've overstepped your trust," she chastised. "Enough to see you've scared the pee out of one of my warriors!" Skyyra came around the javelins to confront him head on. "Rooz Javatt, I think it best you leave this place now. Though I hold you a dishonorable man, I'll speak none of this incident as long as you do the same. As for Sergeant Kavoyy, I'm sure she'll be equally closemouthed."

"Ka-Ka-Kavoyy!" he sputtered, and turned on his heel. Angrily Javatt strode to the door. "I should have known from those damned golden eyes," they could hear him muttering while yet shaking the dampness from his fingers.

His fuming exit punctuated by a door-slamming thud, Tyrra issued a good riddance "Pah!"

Turning to her amused sergeant, Skyyra Jakivv expressed her contempt for Javatt by exclaiming aloud, "I always figured he wouldn't know how to pour piss from a quiver. But today Rooz Javatt demonstrated he doesn't know pee from passion' s call. Pah!"

After she stopped laughing, Tyrra thanked the Commandant for her timely intervention and proceeded to cleanse the puddled mess about her boots.

Jakivv nodded, "Aye." Then tongue in cheek she whispered, "You know, girly, you really ought to do something about that bladder problem!"

# CHAPTER XI

An angry sorrow swelled inside him. Without rest it rolled about Marz's chest bloating his diaphragm, painful with each contraction. It gagged every meal, tortured his sleep...becoming more pronounced in the black of night. Lying upon his mat, rain pattering on the roof overhead, he heard the echoes of Arabella reaching across the horizon of time. Nothing helped dispel the anguish. Deep breaths, forced burps, light food, exhaustive runs through the mud and drizzle; nothing purged his knot of grief. Specters of the massacre continued to torment his helpless mind. They ripped his soul like poisoned claws paralyzing his will to resist. Mylla's twisted corpse branded his memory. A persistent image not permitting him to recall the woman he had known: vivacious and beautiful, pure of nature yet passionate in her feeling for the young sergeant, attentive to his dreams, warm to the ardor he showered upon her. The smile, the eyes, the radiant smile and lilting laugh, all escaped him. Only her butchered cadaver, exaggerated in its ghastly pose, stayed with him. Her face caked with bloody mud, the hair matted in stringy clumps, the mangled neck driving him to horror. Blanching incisions had crisscrossed Mylla's jugular and wind pipe laying open a gruesome yawn. So deep had been her wounds that the head dangled, as if on a length of twine, when Marz had carried her to the mass grave. There he tenderly placed her among the others for whom she had cared, victims all, innocent beyond challenge. He cushioned the head, careful to obscure the ugliness marring her neck. Rain fell upon her pallid cheeks, trickling across the half open lips, cleansing away remnants of clotted earth.

Taratt's Chosen had fired virtually everything combustible at the asylum negating thoughts of a pyre. Even so the deluge would have doused any flame struggling to succeed. So the bolt was compelled to excavate a shallow pit doing their best to sluice off the seepage. At first they attempted to cover the bodies with a muddy gravel, most of which dissipated in the chilly downpour. So they layered them with a rock heap using chunks of collapsed masonry to fill in the bare spots. Perhaps it had been better this way, the piled stones and rubble forming a monument of sorts, albeit primitive. In drier times stone would not have been necessary. The rain dictated otherwise, and so an impromptu necropolis rose above their bones, to be added on over the years by well-wishers intent on preserving their memory. Marz wrapped her body inside a strip of tenting, temporarily protecting the bloodless, pale skin from the rocky blanket soon to pin her fast to the soggy ground. Eventually flesh and bone would vanish to dust as do all living things. He searched his person for something fitting, something he had touched to leave with her, something to escort her through the ages. To his dismay, nothing seemed appropriate. A piece of flint, a knife, a toggle button? Too impersonal all. Impulsively he cut a lock of Mylla's hair and separated it in two, then did the same with a clipping from his own head. He merged hers with his, leaving a pair of identical locks. He tied them into tight ringlets using blanket threads to do so. One he kissed before tucking it into Mylla's clenched hand. Hers for eternity. The other he also touched to his lips, and placed it in his pouch, the symbolism of his gesture unmistakable.

Zoog, the priest, had anointed the bodies with oil as was the custom of The Vag. Afterwards gee sang the death prayer loud and somber. Patiently the holy man passed among the corpses, granting each in death the respect which had eluded so many while alive. For the Children of Misfortune, the sacred rite confirmed that at last they were equal among Vaghi. Rain dribbled down Zoog's face, ger tears indistinguishable. Baritone lyrics carried above the windy downpour speeding the fallen toward Gala Rotaria's celestial realm. Many of the warriors wept openly, among them their sergeant unashamed in his lament. As the weary soldiers began the sodden trudge back to South Camp, a single thunderous crash blasted across the leaden sky perhaps attesting to the goddess' acceptance of her wronged souls.

"Rider approaching the gate!" The lookout's call passed down the parapet to the kilt manning the lower position. "Rider approaching the gate!" he repeated aloud. Sergeant Kavoyy raced up the stairs to join the sentinel. The rain had ceased that very morning, sun finally bursting through the weakening cloud cover. Slashing hooves tore muddy divots from the washed out road as the approaching courier encouraged his mount the last six hundred strides. Standing high in the stirrups he furiously waved his fist in wide circles, indicating the urgency of his dispatch.

"Lift the bar and open half the gate," shouted the sergeant cupping hand to mouth. "Quickly!" he prompted.

The detail below rapidly broke into action, perfect in its timing as the galloping rider bolted up the ramp and through the portal without his mount having to brake speed. Marz hurriedly descended, taking the stairs two at a time. With a rolling snort the sweat lathered beast was reined to a halt. It continued to prance in place, however, still energized by its master's earlier exhortations. Dismounting, the breathless courier asked for "Battle Officer Kavoyy."

"I am he," the sergeant said, not bothering to correct the man's mistake. "Is it news of the Kala?" he inquired. "Has the army engaged them?"

"As far as I know, there has been no action at the Chokepoint. But the army is drenched and worn down by sickness. Still they are prepared and anxious for battle. At least that's the rumor, sir." He flexed his fingers working out the stiffness from tightly clutching the reins over many medecs. "Nay, sir, these instructions carry no news of the Kala. I believe they are of a nature dealing with the Arabella rebellion." He unslung the leather pouch and removed the canister housing the dispatch. Handing it to Marz he stood close hoping to learn its specific details. By this time the bolt's full complement had rushed to the gate, they too eager to hear the message. As if to whet their curiosity, the rider smugly added, "The canister is marked by the seal of the great Lord himself. Such dispatches to bolt officers are rare indeed." A hush swept over the surrounding kilts, boggled that the Lord himself had sealed the dispatch.

If Marz was annoyed at the rider's comment, he didn't express it. Though it was true that the Lord all but never penned directions to soldiers of Marz's rank, the horseman had no business voicing his opinion. The fact that the messenger assumed Kavoyy was an officer probably stemmed from Marz's position as acting commander of South Camp, so it made sense that the man would address him in such manner. "Go walk the heat off your mount," Marz ordered. "Then, after you've seen to him, report to me for a return message... in case one is required." With that Marz climbed half the parapet steps and turned to face his warriors. "Men," he told them, "give me a few moments to read this in silence. If there is news that concerns you, I will share it. But for now I need to be alone." Ascending the final stairs he entered the parapet and dismissed the sentinel. Letting his fingers run across the imprint left by Lord Varaxx's personal seal, he closed his eyes wishing quietly inside that this would be the directive for which he had longed. Snapping the brittle red wax, he tore off the circular lid and withdrew a pair of scrolled parchments.

DISPATCH

TO:        BATTLE OFFICER MARZ KAVOYY
8th KORD/SOUTH CAMP

FROM:      GENERAL T. POVEZZ

ORIGIN:     ARMY HEADQUARTERS

DATE:      13 VERIVER 23/22

YOU ARE PROMOTED TO THE RANK OF BATTLE OFFICER EFFECTIVE THIS DATE.

SPECIAL ORDERS ACCOMPANY THIS DISPATCH. IT IS IMPERATIVE THAT YOU PERFORM YOUR DUTY WITHOUT HESITATION.

WEAR THE RED STRIPE WITH HONOR

CONGRATULATIONS AND GOOD HUNTING.

T. POVEZZ

GENERAL OF THE ARMY

*Battle officer, me? So the courier was accurate when he addressed me! But what's this about duty without hesitation? And good hunting? This can only mean one thing,* he supposed. The golden eyes re-read the dispatch taking note that Povezz's signature and seal both marked the parchment. Indeed it was unique for the number one kilt in the entire Vag army to elevate a sergeant to officer-hood in so hasty a manner. Such instances were rare for sure. Marz unfurled the second document confident that it contained the mission for which he yearned.

DECREE OF DECAPITATION
&
SPECIAL ORDERS

TO:        BATTLE OFFICER MARZ KAVOYY
(MARSHAL OF THE LORD)
8th KORD/SOUTH CAMP

FROM:      LANZ VARAXX, L.O.T.V.

174

ORIGIN:        THE CAPITAL

DATE:          13 VERIVER 23/22

BY MY ORDER, YOU, MARZ KAVOYY, ARE APPOINTED
MARSHAL OF THE LORD. YOU ARE INSTRUCTED TO PURSUE
THE RENEGADE HUUG TARATT AND GER FOLLOWERS
RESPONSIBLE FOR THE MASS MURDER COMMITTED
AT THE ARABELLA ASYLUM . ALL PARTIES DETERMINED
GUILTY BY YOUR JUDGMENT ARE TO BE EXECUTED
IMMEDIATELY. AS STIPULATED IN THE CODE OF LAWS,
HUUG TARATT'S MURDER OF NUNALES AND VIOLATION OF
THE GUGUBUBU BORDER DEMAND FORFEITURE OF GER
LIFE. TARATT IS ALSO GUILTY OF FOSTERING REBELLION
IN DIRECT DEFIANCE OF THE LORD. THEREFORE YOU ARE
COMMANDED TO SEVER TARATT'S HEAD AND BRING IT TO
ME.

AS MARSHAL OF THE LORD ALL RESOURCES OF THE WILD
COUNTRY ARE YOURS ON DEMAND. IN PURSUIT OF YOUR
ORDERS, YOU AND THOSE UNDER YOUR CONTROL ARE
AUTHORIZED TO ENTER THE GUGUBUBU AT WILL.

I AM LANZ VARAXX, LORD OF THE VAG.

I WILL NOT BE DEFIED.

WITNESSED THIS DAY BY TAZ POVEZZ,
GENERAL OF THE ARMY.

(Receipt of acknowledgment required.)

His warrior's heart stirred with excitement, but it was the realization that
circumstances were being shaped to fit his vision that energized Marz's soul.
What had been an amorphous window now crystallized into a perceptive
lens. Finally the opportunity to prove his worth, to stand apart, lay before
him. After years of obscure soldiering, notoriety stood suddenly in sight.
Surely the great goddess had orchestrated events to his advantage. He would
be her vindictive sword smiting the fiendish fanatics who had blasphemed
her goodness. Through her machinations Marz Kavoyy had been selected by
Lord Varaxx himself to destroy the butchers of Arabella, the very same who
had defied his worldly authority, who had dishonored The Vag. Aye, Marz

Kavoyy, Marshal of the Lord, ordained in the name of the Lord's justice, would destroy those who had shattered the peace, who had trampled the rule of law. Truly Gala Rotaria pulled his strings of fortune. It had been she who had maneuvered the army to the north, manipulated Rooz Javatt to leave Marz behind so that the Lord had but one choice to do his bidding...Marz Kavoyy! By the fingers, this would be the incident to propel him onward. Anointed by Gala Rotaria, groomed in the garden of Genu Zig, the man of the isthmus sensed a rapid path to destiny's gate.

As these things swirled his mind, Mylla abruptly entered, ghostly and distant, her face an empty death mask, hollow eyed and brittle. *And you, sweet Mylla,* he thought. *Perhaps you too have been a pawn in this whole drama, robbed of your existence as the pieces formed to drive my life. For this I apologize, though I had no hand in it. But I swear to you that Huug Taratt and ger brigands will answer to my steel. And with their demise I pray your spirit will find rest.*

The return message, in accordance with military procedure, was concise, without frills. First it confirmed receipt of both the Lord's and Povezz's dispatches. Second, the scroll informed of his intent to instruct Arabella's town administrator to have a militia group occupy South Camp as a safeguard against pilferage. And lastly Marz thanked the Lord for the faith he had shown in his freshly appointed Marshal. Confidently he ended it with assurances of a successful mission. He had flirted with abbreviating his title "M.O.T.L." (Marshal of the Lord), similar to Varaxx's habit, but thought better of it. No time to chance offending the Lord. For it would be a simple thing for the brandy sodden ruler to confuse imitation with mockery. And perceived impertinence, regardless of intent, did not sit well with Lanz Varaxx.

With every bound the dispatch courier grew smaller. Silently Marz watched horse and rider disappear, swallowed by the northern skyline. He used the time to gather his thoughts. Assembled kilts milled behind him, anxiousness filling each for it was obvious something was up. He turned slowly, not to dramatize the moment, but to carefully choose the words about to be delivered. Sitting approximately head high upon a parapet stair, he motioned his troops to huddle below him for he had determined the information soon to be dispersed would be best served in an informal gathering. With the flats of each bicep resting on his knees, he scanned the curious faces, a smile upon his own. "Well, boys," he guffawed. "Let's begin with the boring news! Through some miracle, the army has seen fit to promote me to the rank of battle officer." Before Marz could continue a great hoot rose among the kilts vigorously led by Monty Kelozz and several of the 'old timers.' His men truly admired their sergeant, having experienced him daily for the exceptional leader he was. The rise to battle officer, though slow in coming, formalized what they had known for some time. For Marz had inspired the bolt with a special spirit. He had them believing they were the finest unit in the Eighth Kord. Battlefield exercises saw them operating with a fluid precision the match of any, if not superior to all. So it was with great disappointment they had accepted Rooz. Javatt's decision to leave them behind. Raising his hands to quell the good natured hurrahs, Marz went on. "After all that racket, I'm terrified of telling you about the other miracle," he cajoled. Rolled eyes accompanied his banter.

"Tell us. Tell us," they howled, the grins lighting up faces that had been morose too long, the hideous task of dealing with the massacre's aftermath having burdened their vitality. "Tell us!" they clamored like children at story-time.

He stood fully, the wide shoulders squaring his physique. Silhouetted against the serene sky, Marz's pose implied information far more grave than a promotion was about to come. "The Lord Varaxx has rescued us from our despair, granting us a mission of the highest expectation. A mission I believe we have all languished for from the moment we witnessed the killing field at Arabella, the Children of Misfortune and other dear innocents slaughtered to the last. The Lord in his confidence for our readiness, has ordered our bolt. ..nay, CHARGED our bolt with avenging their murders. Our mission, my brothers, is to pursue Huug Taratt and ger demons, putting all to the sword! And Huug's head is the trophy we seek most. On a stick, in a bag, wrapped in fish net, swinging from a hook, how-so-ever we choose...to be delivered to the great Lord at the Capital." He paused allowing the impact to rattle their bellies. "And so, lads, we will be blooded after all! But it won't be Kala blood which licks our javelins. That would be too easy!" Marz spat hard and loud. "Pah!" Like a Capital orator he surveyed the mass of yellow eyes, a sea of thirsty agates drinking his every inflection. Meeting their orbs with his, he enjoined each pair to read carefully the words forming upon the strong lips. "Aye, our prey will be a more villainous lot. The death of one inferior Kala is a simple act of defense against an external foe. But the wild country scum we will hunt are traitorous enemies of The Vag seeking to gut our land, our families, the very breath of the Vag nation. And though they are a cowardly pack, Taratt's Chosen are more fitting of our wrath, a greater test for our blades than any Kala buck. For they possess weapons and the maniacal cunning of Huug Taratt. But ours is the upper hand because we are trained soldiers, skilled in our trade while they are disorganized rabble aggressive against the likes of docile children, but craven in the face of trained warriors." Again he rested, permitting the confidence of his words to seek their hearts. "So there has been purpose in our duty here at South Camp. When our fellows advanced to the Chokepoint we felt sorry for ourselves, angry that our service was to be shunned. But now we are the kilts of fate, positioned above every other bolt, poised to engage the vilest of enemies. The blood denied to us at the Chokepoint is but weak wine compared to that of Huug Taratt's swine. By the fingers, boys, we will be blooded!" The last sentence rasped like steel teeth on stone. "Are you with me?" he challenged, his jaw strong, a powerful fist pumping the air.

A thunderous response split the afternoon heat. Men whooped in unabashed reaction to their officer's spirited appeal. Marz Kavoyy had his answer.

"We leave at the dawn hour. Swords, shields, light packs. One javelin per man."

As he descended the stairs, another grand cheer erupted. If excitement could be smelled, the fragrance of enthusiasm swelling the campground would have rivaled a thousand bouquets. Sweet was the mood that prevailed long into the dark hours. Marz had infused the bolt with fire enough to conquer the universe.

That night after preparations had been finalized for the days ahead and others slept or tried to sleep, the man from the isthmus prayed. To Gala Rotaria he gave thanks for the chance to validate his worthiness. Goddess of the Vaghi, she had opened the portal to opportunity. Of that he was certain. As her anointed, he promised to do her honor, to answer the call felt so strongly years ago in the Hall of Protectors. They of the eyes of glass could rest comfortably in Marz's dedication to their calling. As he contemplated destiny's call, a numbing tingle enveloped his being, shivering the skin and spine, dizzying his brain, somewhat the same as had occurred in the great hall, but without quite the intensity. For him it signaled the spirit world's endorsement of the thoughts pouring from his mind, encouraging his will, steeling the resolve to overcome all obstructions standing between him and the throne of power. Shutting his eyes, he forced his inner self to travel to Mount Aryxx and the door of Genu Zig. To the old nunale he spoke in whispers, his sensory self reaching out to touch the wisdom which he knew radiated from the wizened sage like so many rays of sun. Instantly he was there absorbing Genu's spirit, the luminous glow lighting Marz's mind, warming his soul. "Genu, may the lessons of your tutelage be there for me when the time comes. Most likely I shall be matching wits with Taratt, and though ger mind is corrupt with evilness, it is shrewd and elusive. Stay inside me, Genu. Flood my intellect with knowledge, the kind that controls decisions in times of dire need."

If there was an invisible current connecting Marz and Genu Zig, it must have hummed its response at that very second. For the Marshal of the Lord came away with but a single thought. *Seek out thy genther, and gee will inspire the way.*

Though apparent from the start, it had required the distant inspiration of Genu Zig to suggest Marz's next step. His genther would be the key to tracking down Taratt. Earlier Zoog had told ger brother of living in Huug's stockade camp outside the Gugububu's northern rim. Perhaps the renegade priest had fled there with ger chalk faced killers, assuming they hadn't dispersed. No, Taratt's hold was too firm. It was doubtful gee would permit them to flee piecemeal. If the prophet had any chance to breathe new spirit into the aborted rebellion, the Chosen would be the instrument of Huug's resurgence. Taratt's base of power rested on their bully boy intimidation. The great flood had temporarily diminished Huug's popularity among those of the citizenry sympathetic to the prophet's cause. Over time they might re-enlist in the prophet's movement. The great Lord was right, his Marshal agreed. Cleave the head and the body of followers and potential supporters would wither. Before Huug could rejuvenate the easily misguided, Marz must destroy Taratt and the Chosen.

Having instructed the Arabella administrator to install a militia unit at South Camp, Marz connected with Zoog later that same day. At first the town's chief was reluctant to cooperate, but when presented with proof of the Marshal's unequivocal authority, he quickly fell in line, Marz' s piercing eyes promising dire punishment should he fail to comply...fully. With that behind him, the young officer and Zoog chatted in the latter's cabin regarding the likelihood of Taratt's whereabouts. His brood genther, anxious to assist, knew of several of Huug's haunts, volunteering to guide the bolt to all. Zoog's workspace was a dusty jumble of scrolls and papers of various proportion. It had been difficult to maintain orderly quarters with so much happening. Clothing lay about wherever gee had tossed them days earlier, too busy to wash out the grime.

"Mother should see this hog pen," Marz wryly commented, the trace of a smile curling his lips.

"She'll never know unless some blabbermouth lets it be known," the priest responded, ger own grin growing wider.

"Certainly I'd never be the one to squeal, but there could be a time when I might require a favor from you," he teased. "How could you possibly resist with such information dangling above your guilt ridden head."

"You're a dog, brother. To think my good standing with mother rests in your vile jaws. By the fingers, how could I have been so delinquent in my housekeeping," Zoog exaggerated. And together they embraced warmly their brood sibling bond strong as ever, their laughter loud as when they were teenagers.

In part, the cabin's disarray was a consequence of Zoog's diligence as he had been tirelessly seeking to discover the origins of their kind, confident gee was within an eggeth of cracking the mystery. Like a forensic investigator Zoog Kavoyy had amassed a great body of bits and scraps of circumstantial evidence pushing the scientist to several astounding hypotheses. But gee was still lacking the pivotal piece which would clinch ger speculations. Now in three volumes, the Translator had matured far beyond Huug's initial prototype. Word associations gleaned from the cavern wall and ancient scrolls had provided Zoog with rich insight to the past. However, that final fragment of hard proof, the linchpin to Vag origins, continued to evade gen. 'The people of the fifth field,' whatever the cryptic meaning, yet awaited interpretation.

Despite Zoog's rugged way of life relative to others of the gender, it was difficult for the nunale to maintain the quick gait of the bolt. Even over short hikes the priest's stout legs strained to keep abreast of Marz's warriors. To maintain a similar pace over long distance would be near impossible. So it was decided to requisition a pony and let Zoog ride forward of the formation usually a medec or two ahead but always in eye-shot. After several days on the march they passed through a series of small agricultural communities. At each the Marshal was sure to ask local officials of news regarding Taratt's cut-throat band. To his frustration the pattern was always the same. The administrators, fawning over Marz's Marshal supremacy, wanted desperately to see the Chosen dragged to justice, but alas they knew nothing of their whereabouts. In the wild country, where outlaws pushed the Lord's limits, silence had become a cultural way of life. However silent, Marz knew brutality had a way of loosening tongues. And as Marshal of the Lord, he was well within his powers to inflict pain in the pursuit of information. The problem, though, was how to determine who was legitimately ignorant of Taratt's hideout and who possessed real facts.

In the end it proved to be Zoog who uncovered the most promising lead. While Marz and his warriors were questioning locals, the priest sought out ger own. On the outskirts of a small hamlet known as Six Wells, Zoog called upon an elderly priest named Mag. Over cups of tangy herb tea the old nunale confided a strong revulsion for Taratt, terming the latter the Devil of Darkness and the Monster of Blasphemy among other equally critical epithets. For the holy man, the crime at Arabella damned Taratt to the deepest fire hole to which any nunale ever plunged. "Oh genther of my gender,"Mag wailed. "We nunales, gifted above all by the sweetness of Gala Rotaria, special by her design, have seen our kind dishonored by that evil masquerader. Pretending ger criminal acts to be the goddess' bidding, using her blessed name to commit the most treacherous of sins, Taratt has shamed us all!" Anguished pain cracked the high pitched voice.

"And to where do you suppose the villain has absconded?"Zoog probed, the inquiry sympathetic to Mag's complaint.

"I don't know to where gee has fled. But..."

"But what?" the younger nunale pressed.

"But I know where Taratt is <u>not</u>,"Mag smiled weakly.

"Really!" Zoog returned the smile, ger tone warm and reassuring as was ger true nature. "And where would that not be?" For the moment the scientist turned interrogator was content to play the negative word game.

"<u>Not</u> in the mountains," came the response.

"Why not?"

"Cattle," the old one shot back. "Cattle and oxen."

"Cattle and oxen! Beef on the hoof. Food for many," Zoog nodded following Mag's clue.

"Aye. Taratt's blackguards rounded up a slew of them before they disappeared heading east."

"And?" gee urged.

"Cattle can <u>not</u> climb the steep precipices of the mountainous hills. Only goats and perhaps sheep can negotiate such terrain." Mag winked and touched a finger to ger temple indicating the rationality of ger own deduction. "So they must remain on this side of the mountains."

"For certain!"Zoog blurted. "And cattle require pasture, or at least a parcel of decent grazing land."

Zoog was about to draw the next obvious conclusion when the old priest exclaimed, "And water, genther of my gender. And water!" The wrinkled face twinkled causing yet more wrinkles to form. Sparkling yellow eyes gleamed their satisfaction at having implied where to hunt the Chosen. A childlike smugness compelled Mag to cackle, "Logic is a wonderful thing. Is it not, my fellow priest?"

"Aye, genther of my gender," Zoog chuckled. "I am pop-eyed by the clarity of your reasoning."

"We all do our best,"Mag chimed, the grin bordering on the impish. "But some of us do it better than others. Of this I am more than definite."

The sun could be at its cruelest around mid-day, so the bolt rose early before the first sliver of light scratched the eastern sky. Far better to travel when the sun rested low. The hours immediately surrounding noon would see the men resting wherever shade could be found. Gullies yet flowed with water, the largesse of the great rainfall. Consequently cattle could be anywhere, not solely where wells and oases enjoyed a year round yield. Marz commandeered two scraggly ponies from a washed out farm, promising to pay the proprietor with barter credits when he returned. In a way the farmer was relieved because it was all he could do to scrimp a meager handful of vegetables from the mud without having to worry about the pair of old plugs. Mounting his two lightest kilts, Marshal Kavoyy ordered them to fan out ahead of the column, sweeping over land that realistically could ease the small herd's transport. Zoog had suspected all along that Taratt's choice of refuge would be the stockade camp where the two had first met. Assuming Huug's shanty community was still intact, having not succumbed to the destructive flood, the camp's wells could probably support the animals once the resurgent heat had evaporated the standing water. And the surrounding low profile hills should, at least initially, supply ample grazing, with the stockade penning the herd at night. But mostly, reasoned Zoog, Huug Taratt was a scientist, and nunales of the technical pursuit do not wish to be far from their laboratories. Aye, Taratt's gadgets and library would beckon the wolf back to the lair. If it took a nunale scientist to think like one, then Zoog Kavoyy's instinct said the stockade camp housed the murderers of Arabella. So having expressed ger hunch to brother Marz, the bolt proceeded pell-mell toward the stockade camp, the saddled priest leading the way.

Two and a half plodding days later they paused a couple of medecs short of their goal. As they had drawn nearer the camp, the evidence of a small herd became apparent, hoof prints and droppings marking the way. Something else was evident as well, cartwheel tracks! The oxen Mag had mentioned were no doubt being used to pull carts across the rugged wild country. On a flattened hill the Marshal settled his troops into a defensive position, occupying the western slope away from the prospect of inquiring eyes. Leaving a savvy soldier named Julz in charge with instructions for the men to maintain a discipline of silence, Marz ventured out to reconnoiter the stockade camp taking Monty and another kilt with him. Leaving shields and javelins behind, the three headed north by northeast planning to scout the camp from a relatively concealed angle, one which limited their own detection. Zoog with pinpoint memory had briefed them in detail to the camp's alternate routes of approach.

Motionless as the stunted trees around them, Marz and his companions squinted at the herd of roughly two dozen animals. Feeding on thin brush the skinny beasts moved slowly, always staying together, compact in their cluster. "No oxen," breathed the leader. "Only cattle." Extending his gaze beyond the livestock, he added, "And no activity within the camp." Stealthily they crept a hundred strides closer, squeezing through the herd without disturbing a single one. The picketed walls were now under their direct observation. Still no signs of stirring inside. The ramshackle collection of sticks which served as a gate lay open, an easy invitation for them to enter. Cautiously they held their position, prone on their bellies watching for any hint of human presence. After a half hour a woman, slender to the point of gauntness, the tendons of her neck stretched like tight thongs, lumbered out of the gate. She had lived probably no more than thirty eight years but her time had been harsh, the face appearing at least fifteen years older. A zigzagged smear of white blazed the bronzed forehead. As she walked she pinched off the final stubborn scraps from a cowhide which she now stretched to its fullest, fastening the comers to the stockade pickets, there to dry. They observed her for another half hour as she affixed four more hides to the fencing.

"Obviously they've slaughtered part of the herd, more than enough to fill their stomachs for several days," Monty offered.

"Aye," Marz responded, "but our report states there are about seventy among the Chosen. If they'd just butchered five animals you'd think there'd be some busyness about the grounds." He thought for a long moment then exclaimed, "By the fingers, they're gone! Hauled off the meat in ox carts I'll bet!"

"But to where?" asked Monty, his voice a low whisper.

"Let's ask her," the Marshal replied, directing a finger at the woman securing knots to the fresh skins.

The startled hag was uglier up close than at a distance. Gawky in posture with little grace to her carriage, the face looked somewhat equine. Large oversized teeth swelled her mouth, the appearance that of an angry mare. "What do you want?" she screeched, exposing a mouthful of bulbous gums rivaling the teeth for dominance. Monty held her arms, though she had given but token struggle, while the other kilt entered the gate making a quick inspection of the interior. Satisfied no one other than their prisoner was in residence, he reported back to his leader.

"Information," answered Marz sternly, his eyes cold in their inquisition. "Where are Huug Taratt and the others?"

"Where the likes of you will never find them," horse-face screamed, arrogant in her capture.

"Oh, we'll find them all right," Marz said calmly.

"Then you'd better hitch up your damned kilt and head for the Gugububu, sonny. That is, if you've got the nerve," she taunted. "If the sun doesn't boil your blood, then the Lord will split you in half for violating the Gugububu. His highness isn't one to want his dear soldier boys treading the hot sand, you know! Hee hee. Either way, you lose, you army scum, you!" She spat at his feet, the spittle landing upon Marz's boot.

Marz chose to ignore the insult, opting to trap her like the fat eels which ply the Big Lazy. "Even so, Taratt and the Chosen will burn like charcoal themselves," Marz provoked, hoping her retort would spill more information. "Every fool knows there is no water in the Gugububu. Their tongues will swell like loaves in an oven. It is suicide to enter the desert hell."

"Pah! That's what unbelievers like you are apt to assume. Once before the great prophet promised water from blood and gee delivered more rain than anyone expected. Did gee not? And now Huug Taratt pledges water from sand, enough water to satisfy the thirst of all the Chosen. And cool shelter too," she snickered, "in the middle of the flaming Gugububu."

"Even for the oxen?" Marz baited.

"Even the oxen!" she shrilled, haughty in her response.

"All of them?"

"Aye. Gone two hours ago pulling three wagons with enough to feed them until you drop dead in your search!" She was proud of herself for telling off this lackey of the high and mighty Lord. Unwitting in her defiance, horse-face had provided the Marshal with invaluable intelligence. Taratt's rag-tag renegades had crossed the rim into the Cauldron with draught animals, the prophet guaranteeing water plentiful enough for a long stay, and protection from the devilish heat.

To be sure Marz entered the compound and made for Huug's stone house, right where Zoog told him it would be. Inside the emptiness caused his steps to ring hollow, his boots echoing in the stillness. Empty. Completely empty! *Taratt's scientific gadgets, the library, everything missing. No doubt they're packed in a cart heading for the desert.* If proof was required that Taratt wouldn't be returning soon to the stockade camp, this was the strongest of evidence. Huug's departure, if not permanent, would be long in absence.

Back outside the gate, Marz and his warriors prepared to race back to Zoog and the bolt resting a few medecs away. As they turned to leave, Marz called out to horse face. "Why didn't the prophet take you along?"

"Isn't it obvious?" she shot back. "They'd be fighting over me like dogs in heat!" With that she primped her ragged hair, the enormous teeth flashing their self-perceived allure.

"It must be the chalk that makes them hallucinate," Monty supposed. "Remind me never to inhale the stuff!" Laughing as one, the three moved off at a quick trot. The enemy had a two hour head start. By the time they readied the bolt, another half hour would be lost.

It didn't take long for them to pick up the wheel tracks for Zoog's familiarity with the terrain told them that only one approach to the desert rim could accommodate carts. Even so the enemy was probably three hours beyond that point. And in the Gugububu things like tracks had ways of disappearing quickly. Standing on the desert fringe the two siblings conferred. "You've been absorbed in thought, Zoog. What does your instinct tell you?" Marz reached out touching his genther's shoulder.

Eyes closed Zoog seemed to be visualizing the ensuing landscape, the head weaving slowly as though moving through a maze of sorts. Within moments gee snapped out of it. "Based on what the hag has divulged of water and cool shelter, there can be only one refuge to where they flee, brother. A great cavern holding an ever full cistern large enough for their needs. I know because I have been there."

"In the Gugububu?" an astonished Marz inquired. "You've been there, genther?"

"Aye, Marz. Many times. A place hidden from vision even if one should stand atop it. I believe that Taratt and I are the only living Vaghi aware of its location. Though Huug genself took me there, gee believes I could never return on my own. However, unbeknown to Huug I have done it quite a few times. Aye, I'm sure that is where they have fled."

"Are you able to lead us there?" the Marshal asked already confident of his genther's reply.

"Surely. But look," Zoog said pointing to a bump in the shimmering distance. "The cavern is in that direction...more to the southeast. Yet the tracks run southwest. That is because the more direct path will not permit cart wheels to pass. So Taratt, who is an excellent navigator, must travel an alternate, more circuitous route. If the bolt takes the more direct trail, there is a good chance we'll be able to beat them to the cavern, even with their head start. This is a calculated gamble, brother, for if the Chosen arrive before we, they can hole up inside while we expire from dehydration. And believe me, brother of my brood, the Gugububu heat is void of mercy."

"How far must we go?" Marz asked. He studied the landscape, bewildered by an unsteady horizon, the product of excessive heat radiation.

"Perhaps eight medecs. With many hills and dips."

"Marz shut his eyes, squeezing hard to ensure their tightness. He wished no light to enter his supplication. *Genu Zig, guide me in this decision. For the lives of my warriors, my genther, my very destiny are at risk.* Though no spirit touched him, no tingle of response, Marz recognized the intuition which had guided him these many years. And so he told his genther to ride ahead of the bolt, leading the way until the pony dropped. Then turning to his kilts he swiftly announced their marching orders. "Drop your packs and drink heartily from your canteens, then leave them here. Take your scabbards and sling them across your backs so they won't interfere with your stride," he instructed. "In a few minutes we're going for a little jaunt in the Gugububu. But you're trained for it. A little heat. A little sweat," he laughed hoping to raise their confidence. "You've been hot and moist since birth!"

The men laughed, but it was of a nervous kind, more bravado than belief. Stories of the Gugububu were horrific, terrifying them since childhood. Going into combat was serious enough, but the great, unforgiving wasteland had the reputation for gobbling up trespassers with nary a surviving relic.

Sensing their uneasiness the Marshal called out. "We won't be penetrating too deeply, men. Only about eight medecs. Zoog Kavoyy, whom you have grown to know, has been there before and returned safely every time. Gee will guide us to the enemy and we shall perform our duty by annihilating them." As he spoke, Marz positioned his sword across the shoulder blades, adjusting the buckle for a snug fit. His warriors followed suit, for the moment eased of the Gugububu's fearsome reputation.

Having fortified their bodies with deep draughts, the stalwart kilts took up the shield and javelin. Jittery in their anxiousness to get on with it, resigned to following their leader's call, the bolt took off slowly. Building to a hasty gait, the unit ran with ease, Marz setting a rhythmic pace. There had never been any real reluctance on their part, only hesitation. Whatever leeriness existed was soon to vanish, the brotherhood of the bolt uniting their collective will. Crossing the first ripple of hot sand they ascended a long grade which dropped off slightly at the crest. They had set foot where very few had ever ventured. They had pierced the Gugububu.

After three medecs the sweat saturated every thread of his tunic, the leather kilt also heavy with perspiration. Marz's hair dripped its salty wetness down the forehead where it hung on the brow before releasing, trailing down his tanned cheeks. The air in his lungs was hotter than any he had ever breathed. Clutching the cumbersome wood-hide shield in his left hand, the javelin resting against the right shoulder, he fought to keep his eyes focused on the buttocks of Zoog's tired pony. Glancing back he saw the fatigue straining each kilt's face. Yet they pushed themselves onward, dutiful in their endeavor. He knew he must intercept Taratt's group before they reached the cavern. Hopefully, by cutting the hypotenuse, the bolt would be in position to block their flight. Somehow his warriors must find the moxie to maintain the momentum of the forced run. The sound of a hundred boots crunched dully in the blistering heat, lungs pained with exhaustion, calves suffering the first tinge of cramps. After a while the terrain became a tangle of rock slabs and distorted formations unlike any Marz had ever seen. "How could Zoog ever have remembered the way?" he whispered through burning lips. Like machines they drove on, the pace as torrid as the blazing sun. He was sweating less now. Perhaps the body's natural cooling system was running out of coolant. *Time to slow down. Spare the men, Marz,* he ordered himself. *Spare the men or there will be nothing left to battle the Chosen.* Raising his javelin high he slowed the pace to a rapid walk, the rocky labyrinth necessitating a single file through its narrow defiles. Dismounted, Zoog awaited them. The slender canyons prevented any appreciable line of sight so gee relied on markers of ger own making. Ger pony spent, the nunale would guide them afoot for the remainder of the hike. Gee estimated another two medecs to go and suggested they take a break before proceeding the final treacherous distance. Without being told, the warriors created shade by angling their shields against the high sun. Underneath they took turns swigging from a half dozen canteens that Zoog had slung over the saddle pommel. The water was very warm, in some cases hot, but the men drank greedily, grateful for whatever wetness coursed their mouths. Zoog's scrawny little horse, weary from the first day gee had acquired it, had stumbled to a fall, its wobbly legs no longer able to support itself, much less a rider. Fortunately the canteens had been removed prior to its collapse. Unfortunately for the pony no water would flow its way. They left it there to expire and prepared to renew the march.

Having regained their breath they moved out again, the nunale gamely trotting in the lead, ger brother ten steps behind. Zoog's eyes darted about picking out natural landmarks and those he had blazed with ger own hand on earlier trips. Delirious with heat a few kilts fell behind, legs unsteady, their javelins dragging in the sandy gravel. Still they persevered, desire barely able to overcome prostration. On they straggled behind their comrades, ever dutiful, ever courageous. Mercifully, when their was no pluck left in their gut, the grit gone from their veins, a teetering Zoog threw up a halting hand. "We are here," gee gasped. Men dizzy with heat fell to the scorching ground hardly able to raise their shields against the sun. A few true to the bond that ties soldier to soldier, walked back to assist those staggering to keep up.

Breathless, the Marshal lifted his kneeling genther. Together they ambled to the hill crest. Waves of hotness radiated from the edge, distorting the scape before their eyes. Across the blistering sweep a vista of desolation greeted them. Zoog pointed out a stone field where the cavern entrance sat, though Marz could not make it out. "And there, there is the only approach capable of accommodating carts. They must come from that direction if they are to come at all." Gee traced a fingertip through the air tracking the line.

"Aye, but could we be too late?" asked Marz. "Is it possible the Chosen have passed this spot and are already within the cavern? Perhaps the horse-faced one lied about the time. Maybe they left the camp four or five hours before she said." Concern etched his reddened face.

Still talking in slow pants, Zoog gulped, "I doubt animals as slow moving as oxen could make the roundabout journey even in six hours. Also I don't see any carts near the cavern and it would be impossible to fit them inside, so I must conclude they have yet to arrive."

"Then it is best that we wait here for a while," Marz concluded. "If we see no signs of the Chosen, we'll occupy the cavern ourselves. For now though this is our best vantage point. Ours is the high ground and they must pass beneath us exhausted from their long trek. The advantage lies with us.

Superior position, rested troops, crack warriors infinitely better trained, the best of weapons, and above all, the advantage of surprise!"

"Spoken like a general, brother,"Zoog admired. "The day will be yours."

"And with it the unholy head of Huug Taratt!"

At first it appeared as an uncertain scab in the western distance. Within ten minutes it grew larger to the point where Marz was confident it was no illusion. Using a hand to deflect the sun from his eyes, he squinted through the glare in an attempt to determine exactly how great were their numbers. "Seventy two," he counted. "And three pairs of oxen in the rear, each hauling a cart." Barrels told him two of the huge carts carried food and water for the trip. The other probably contained Taratt's precious belongings and various objects for the stay: bedrolls, utensils, tools and the like. The laboring oxen would no doubt be slaughtered once the men were securely settled for it would be impossible for them to survive the cruel Gugububu. Futilely Zoog attempted to identify Huug Taratt from afar. Inasmuch as all wore hoods or protective rags to stave off the sun, Huug's identity remained unknown. Because the prophet's physique was fairly non-nunine it too provided no help. One could only speculate that Huug must be up front for only gee knew the way, but even so, eight figures fanned the lead rank.

Marz was satisfied the Chosen were fatigued to the edge of exhaustion, their steps short and shuffling, heads bent to the ground. Sun had leeched their strength for at least five hours, maybe more. *One more advantage for our side,* Marz figured. Though hot beyond that any had ever experienced, the Marshal's troops were relatively well rested. On the hill's unexposed slope they poised ready for the call. Marz moved back to brief them. They would use a staggered attack formation of two ranks, each warrior in the rearmost rank standing directly behind the gap between the two men to his front. Should a front ranker go down, the soldier in the gap would step forward to maintain a unified line. With twenty five soldiers in each row Marz would have the advancing lead rank hurl its javelins at close range, then halt while the second rank stepped between the gaps and heaved their own. It was a tactic they had drilled many times on the practice fields of South Camp. Today, however, was no exercise. Before forming them, he supplied one final order. "The Lord Varaxx has instructed us to slay them all, just punishment for their murders at Arabella. Let our cry be Remember Arabella!

The disheveled train of Taratt's Chosen drew almost perfectly in line with Marz's hidden warriors when the Marshal marched them over the lip. Staggered in two dressed ranks, each man even with the warrior to his right, the soldiers raised the deadly javelins to throwing position. Shields held just below the chin, they had descended about fifteen strides before a single chalk face took sight. So horrified was he that no alarm was screamed, allowing the bolt to advance another seven paces, a distance between them now of no more than fifty strides. Perhaps the man's baked senses told him he must be looking at a mirage...for soldiers of the Vag never entered the Gugububu. Finally alerted, the Chosen were slow to react, and when they did it was without discipline. Less than half drew swords, shouting frantically at the others to form a defense. Many stood frozen in their panic, staring with unbelieving eyes at the Lord's troops moving upon them. A few backpedaled bumping into their stationary brethren. An enemy is at its most vulnerable when on the march, strung out and exposed. Worse, Taratt, their leader, was a nunale, without military training, lacking true command. Marz knew he had them like pigs in a butcher's pen.

Advancing on the left flank with his lead rank, Marz gave the order. "Ready javelins!" His powerful voice carried above the terrified yells escaping the prophet's thugs. Held close to the ear, parallel to the ground, the bronze tipped shafts awaited the command. When there were but twelve strides separating them, Marz Kavoyy, Marshal of The Vag, gave the order for which he had yearned upon viewing Mylla's brutalized corpse. "Throw!" In one motion the forward rank's javelins shot through the desert air, each soldier aiming at the closest belly. The impact blew the petrified assassins backwards like stalks of dry wheat, nothing to protect them. Not a single shield among the entire pack. Screams erupted from the wounded, javelins protruding from thighs and torsos. Precise in its maneuver the bolt's second rank stepped forward and at point blank range the order "Throw!" was repeated, Marz's voice again carrying above the din. One more time the slender missiles crashed through those who dared to hold their ground. What was left of the line buckled and fell. The few reeling survivors had no choice but to stand and await their fate. "Remember Arabella!" came the cry, and drawing their short swords the methodical kilts tore into the shattered Chosen. Pushing hard with their shields they performed to perfection the violent lessons of their profession. Thrust and rip. Thrust and rip. Over and over. Bowling through the enemy they swiftly dispatched those who had withstood the javelin attack. A few attempted to surrender but there would be no battlefield captives this day.

Breaking down into teams of two, the avenging kilts ran down the fleeing Chosen, silencing them forever.

With a mighty javelin toss Marz aimed for the widest part of his adversary's body, but the man twisted offering the narrowest target, and as a result took the point in his sword arm pinning the bicep to his rib cage. Unable to wield his weapon, the man, a scrawny redhead dropped to his knees squealing, "Mercy," just as the sword of Varo entered the soft flesh beneath the chin. Instantly it punctured the hard palate, the steel tip exploding into the brain. The force of the stroke lifted him off the desert floor like a bundle of rags, blood squirting upwards in a thin stream. Keeping his shield at the ready position Marz shook the sword point loose causing the head to dangle... as if from a length of twine. Stepping over the twitching gore he shouted "Remember Arabella," and proceeded to search for a deeply tanned nunale of wolfish visage, clean-shaven to the scalp.

Suddenly amid the screams of dying Chosen, a desert wind spinning with great force, swept upon the scene. And with it stinging sand filled the air, restricting vision, entering nostrils with its gritty residue, choking the breath of comrade and enemy alike. Combatants in the final throes of battle struggled to continue their grisly toil, the killing field having been transformed into a dusty cloud. It lasted but seven or eight minutes. In its aftermath the stunned victors stood motionless surveying the fallen, the latter layered in part with desert sand. Zoog had come down from the hill to assist the bolt's wounded, and was administering to a young kilt slashed across the upper arm when Marz approached gen. "Come genther. You must help me identify Huug Taratt from among the dead. For my duty is not complete."

Finishing to the wounded kilt's need, Zoog nodded and followed ger brother to the line of carnage where the Chosen had suffered the brunt of their fatalities. For close to a half hour they examined every still face, searching for the one whose head the great Lord had demanded. They too walked about those chopped down on the perimeter of the battlefield and among the drovers by their carts, studying each grotesque stare. No Taratt! Seventy one lifeless bodies they tallied. One missing. Somehow the renegade priest had slipped away, probably using the sand storm for cover.

"The cavern, Marz" the priestly Kavoyy called out. "Huug must have escaped there in all the confusion. Come. I will show you."

The macabre spectacle behind them, Zoog led ger brother through a winding morass of splintered rocks. "Here," gee puffed, the angry sun laboring the nunale's every move. To Marz's amazement Zoog's fingers pulled hard on a slab causing it to shift along its chiseled groove. A rush of cool air greeted their intrusion as they penetrated the slim corridor, Zoog in the front. The drop in temperature gave new vigor to bones gripped moments earlier by the Gugububu's stifling hold. Cautiously the priest moved, careful to peek around the corner. There was no telling what lay waiting in the darkened yawn. "Close it," whispered Zoog, and Marz, obedient to his genther's instruction, eased the stone back into place. If Taratt was here, they didn't want gen sneaking out while their attention was directed elsewhere. As their eyes adjusted to the chilly dimness, a flicker of weak light danced along the corridor wall. The illumination of man made flame became evident as they tip toed forward, the smell of burning oil filling the air. Entering the cavern's great hollow, Marz held his breath, awed by the sight. Two lamps sat at each end of a double stone altar, between them the supine figure of what the Marshal recognized to be the end of his hunt. "Huug Taratt?" he asked of Zoog.

"Aye," came the muffled return. "That is the one who has caused more pain by far than any other nunale in the history of time."

Turning ger head ever so slightly toward them, the haggard wolf attempted a weak smile. Spying Zoog, gee said, "So it was you who betrayed me. I should have known." There was no bitterness in Huug's voice, simply acceptance.

"There is no betrayal, Huug Taratt. For betrayal suggests there was once loyalty." Zoog spoke softly, not wishing to debate with the doomed priest soon to fall victim to ger brother's sword. "Only the bond of science connected us. Never were there common values or even friendship."

"Perhaps you are right," gee murmured, resigned to a terminal fate. "And your friend here, is he to claim the glory of confirming my death?"

Zoog stepped closer, an uncomfortable look upon him. "This warrior is my brood brother, designated Marshal of the Lord by Lanz Varaxx. His charge is to execute you."

"Ah ha ha!" The prophet's scornful laugh reverberated across the cavern's hollow keep. "Your brood brother is he? Well, Marshal Kavoyy, I have saved you the trouble. I, Huug Taratt, have taken it upon myself to die at my own hand. At my own choosing!" Lifting both arms for them to see it was evident Huug's wrists had been slashed, life's blood draining the open veins. "So you see, soldier of the Lord, I triumph in death. And in doing I have removed the executioner's burden from your conscience. You are but a witness to my suicide." Taratt looked away, pleased gee had robbed the Lord of a final vengeance. The prophet dropped ger arms so they hung below the altar speeding the flow of gravity. The trickle of blood ran down Huug's palms, tracing a crimson path to the finger tips where it splattered to the stone floor. An obsidian blade, the one Taratt had used to bring on death, lay but a short distance away.

"Nay, Huug Taratt," Marz's voice boomed, his eyes fired with wrath. He strode forward, his warrior boots fixed in the prophet's bloody puddle.

"You mean I am to live?" the wolf asked, not understanding the true nature of the Marshal's response.

"Nay, you beast of damnation. You will not cheat the ire of the Lord, nor of my own rancor, for I too lost someone precious to your fiendish insanity. Nor will you escape the Children of Misfortune crying out for retribution across the chasm of time. You see, Huug Taratt, I, Marz Kavoyy, Marshal of the Lord, have come for your ugly head!" A gleam unlike any Zoog had ever seen ignited ger brother's golden eyes. "And my orders say nothing of letting you die first before severing you at the neck."

Terror distorted the face of Huug Taratt, the wet red hands stroking ger throat...for the last time. "But it is not necessary," the prophet gasped. "It is not necessary! You can choose to let me die first." This time the plea came out sounding like a squeal, the horror having squeaked Taratt's voice.

Looking down into the terrified eyes which now were blinking uncontrollably, Marz's monotone declaration informed, "The only choice is whether to chop or slice." Unsheathing the sword of Varo, the man of the Isthmus held it high, the lamp flames dazzling the mirrored blade.

"No, no," cried the wolf struggling to lift genself.

"By the Order of Decapitation," Marz invoked in bold voice, "signed by Lord Varaxx, for defying his absolute authority, for entering the Gugububu, and for the murders at Arabella including multiple acts of nunicide, I, Marz Kavoyy, Marshal of the Lord, claim your head."

The prophet raised a futile hand attempting against all hope to ward off the killing blow. With a single powerful chop the honed meteorite steel, gift of the great goddess, sliced through three protesting fingers on its downward stroke. Cutting into the bone, it cleaved the body cleanly, a great torrent of blood gushing from Huug's torso. Indeed the blow was so mighty the edge clanged against the altar stone. The skull with eyes agape fell to the floor where it rolled several times before stopping nose up. "May you know no rest in the spirit world, your soul condemned to the fieriest of pits for eternity." Marz's curse echoed through the great cavern, the only eulogy Huug Taratt would ever exact.

At the point of beheading, that is where the sword cut through bone and muscle to strike the stone, the force had cracked the huge altar. In slow reaction to the impact, the slabs began to break apart, the weight of Huug's headless body exerting pressure upon them. With a muted thud, the twin stones collapsed sliding Taratt's corpse to the rock hewn floor. In their fracture, the altar stones which had been stacked one upon the other, separated exposing a discolored parchment. The latter had been protected by extra blank parchments on each side which now fell away. Zoog who had jumped back to avoid the crashing altar, moved forward to examine the strange leathery sheet which had been secreted between the stones probably for as long as the altar had stood. As gee knelt to retrieve it, Zoog noticed curious markings distinguishing it as a map. At once gee recognized it for what it was. A great joy sprang from the nunale' s heart, ger fingers trembling with nervous exhilaration.

For among the odd markings stood out the letters V AGER printed at the top of the ancient document, and below it on the map proper, its shortened version, V AG. The mystery of The Vag had been solved!

# CHAPTER XII

Together they ascended the wide stone steps entering the Lord's residence, side by side. Both wore the leather kilt, each bearing the red stripe. Along the corridor they marched past two saluting guards. The younger officer stood taller by a hand than the other. Freshly scrubbed and clean-shaven, he looked every bit his title, Marshal of the Lord. He had arrived at the Capital that very morning, pausing at the city barracks to wash off the dust and don fresh clothes. Under his left arm he carried a brown wicker basket, the lid tightly secured. For nine days the container had never left his presence. Even as he slept he kept it tethered to a wrist.

They were expected, the more senior Vag notifying the Lord in advance of the need for an audience. *By the fingers,* he growled inside, *I hope the man is sober!* General Povezz had been under a mountain of pressure lately. The Lord, who could swing from complacency to rashness within the course of a single sentence, was most unhappy with the Kala situation. Reports of hundreds of thousands of the blue devils swarming above the isthmus had sent the entire Vag army rushing to defend the Chokepoint. Only a handful of Kala had materialized, leading to accusations of 'over reaction.' And with his massed troops exposed to flood conditions the worst in memory, the Lord carried on like a spoiled brat, blaming everyone from cooks to high priest for their incompetence. "Alarmists," he termed those officers overseeing North Camp, especially the post commander, threatening him with the harshest of humiliations. It was all Povezz could do to maintain control of the army, to provide instructions of a rational nature in the face of the Lord's unreasonable communiques. And then that maniac Taratt resurfaced with a senseless uprising. Arabella had driven Lord Varaxx to ranting binges vowing to raze the wild country. And the brandy, always the brandy consumed in gluttonous quantities, forcing delusions on a mind already crowded with mad thoughts. Povezz's musings were suspended by a nunale scribe hurrying by. Seeing they were about to arrive at the salon door, he whispered to his companion, "You'd better let me enter first. There's no telling his mood." As the general readied his fist to knock, the door swung open, a beaming Lanz Varaxx there to greet them.

"Well, come in, lads," he chirped. "I've been as antsy as a bride. Come in. Come in."

"Good afternoon, Lord Varaxx," the senior officer said. "May I introduce your..."

"Yes, yes. My Marshal," he interrupted, "bearing me my trophy." His behavior was that of a birthday child, eager with expectation. Wringing his hands at the prospect of a longed-for gift, Lanz Varaxx, the largest Vag in the room, bounced with juvenile delight.

Not knowing exactly how to react, Marz offered a pleasant, "Good day, sir," bowing his head slightly, the basket making it impossible for him to salute.

"My Lord,"Povezz continued, "Marshal Kavoyy has provided you and the nation a valuable service in ridding The Vag of Taratt and ger rebels. And in keeping with your dictate, he has brought you the trophy of which you speak."

"Excellent, excellent," the charmed Varaxx bellowed. "I am delighted beyond words, Kavoyy. I must admit though, that when General Povezz suggested that you were the man for the job, I had my doubts. By the fingers," the Lord exclaimed. "He was downright adamant that I appoint you my Marshal, as though he had some sort of divine inspiration. Can you imagine that, a bloody sergeant my Marshal! But we fixed that, made you an officer." Then bowing to the general, he complimented, "Povezz, you were right as usual. Damn fine general you are. Damn fine!"

"Thank you, my Lord," he returned, a half smile upon his lips.

Varaxx clapped his meaty hands, anticipating the spectacle which he had directed weeks earlier. "So, I think it's time for the...how shall we call it, the unveiling?" laughed the big man. "What say you, Kavoyy?"

"Aye, sir,"Marz answered. "Shall we...unveil it on your table?"

"By all means," the gleeful Lord agreed.

Marz strode to the center table which doubled as the Lord's desk. With a sweep of his hand Varaxx cleared it of its clutter, sending scrolls and writing instruments clattering to the marble tile, indifferent to the mess he had caused. The desk was remembered as the same piece Marz had stood before years earlier as a teenaged courier. Placing the basket upon it, he unworked the toggles which held the lid fast. With a wiggle he worked off the cover at which time a sweet fragrance filled the air. "Aromatic leaves," explained

Marz. Dried leaves, a kind of potpourri surrounded the grisly prize, masking the rotten odor as well as cushioning it during the journey north. The young officer reached inside searching for something to grab. When he found it he pulled upward causing many leaves to spill out littering the desk surface. Holding a twined topknot, he slowly eased the netted head from its wicker casket.

"Ah," exhaled the enthralled Lord. "The eyes are yet open. All the better for you to view the words fanning upon my lips, Huug Taratt. I told you," he scolded, wagging a finger at the unseeing stare. "I will not be defied. And, indeed, it cost you dearly.!"

"Shall I remove the netting, my Lord?" the Marshal inquired.

"By all means, yes," answered Varaxx, never taking his attention off the head. For the moment the effect was hypnotic, the actual head of his antagonist resting before him. "And, general!"

"Yes, sir?"

"Remove that porcelain vase from the columnar stand and bring the stand here that we might have a proper pedestal for our friend's head. Yes, I think that would be fitting," he laughed, "Taratt desired to be elevated in the Lord's residence and today that aspiration is met!" The Lord was enjoying himself.

Povezz quickly did as ordered while Marz undid the netting. The infatuated Lord lifted Taratt's head, gripping it by the ears, and placed it on the pedestal, adjusting it for position twice before he was satisfied. "So Huug Taratt," he reprimanded. "You were foolish enough to push the limits of your Lord. Now look what your insolence has gained you. You have been relegated to souvenir status, nothing more."

"Is there anything else, my Lord?" Povezz asked. "Perhaps you wish to grant Battle Officer Kavoyy a boon?"

"How could I refuse anything on this magnificent day of triumph," Lanz Varaxx bubbled. Then pivoting toward Marz he said, "Name your wish!"

Caught off guard, Marz took a few moments to consider. *What would Genu Zig advise?* he thought. *Don't ask for the obvious. Ask for something that will build to the future.* Pushing his posture more erect, he answered, "My Lord Varaxx, I know that my title, Marshal of the Lord, is a temporary one to be rescinded now that my duty is performed, your enemy's head delivered, the Chosen slain to the last man. However, my wish is to permanently retain the title, Marshal of the Lord, to serve at your beckon!"

Varaxx nodded, not quite sure if this was meant to flatter him or to merely advance Kavoyy's stature. But he decided either way he liked it. "You could have asked for land, you know. Or a military promotion. Most would have," he pointed out, the broad smile displaying his approval. Turning to the general, he asked, "What do you think, general?"

The senior soldier grunted his consent. "I believe it is both the honorable and smart thing to do. Make him permanent Marshal of the Lord, the first to hold such a position, I believe. But he is to return to South Camp for the duration of his current service, about a year I suspect. There in the wild country he will be ready to serve at your call should it be required again. Then after Kavoyy's hitch is completed, I can transfer him closer to the Capital. A proper way to handle it, I would think."

"So be it,"Varaxx bellowed. "Have the paperwork readied for my seal with copies to the usual administrators. Also we'll instruct the court artisans to fashion a medallion of his title, his to wear with my blessing."

"Aye, my Lord,"Povezz acknowledged, at the same time signaling to Marz it was time to leave the room.

"Thank you, Lord Varaxx." The permanent Marshal saluted, and followed the general out the door. The Lord barely nodded, preoccupied with the head. As the two walked hurriedly down the corridor, they could hear the voice of Lanz Varaxx chastising Huug Taratt, taunting the blind eyes with reminders of "I told you so!" By tomorrow he would have the prophet's noggin mounted near the city gate, a gruesome lesson to all that the Lord of The Vag shall not be defied!"

Outside on the Concourse, General Povezz congratulated his subordinate on a job performed to perfection. "I shall see to it that the kilts of your bolt are honored for their valor as well as recognition for Zoog's invaluable service." The general glowed with satisfaction continuing his praise as they ambled to the military quarter. "Equally outstanding was your response to Varaxx's offer of a boon. Permanent Marshal of the Lord! By the fingers, Kavoyy, I would never have thought of it. It will provide you a lifetime of permanent prestige!"

"To be truthful the idea came to me at the moment the Lord proffered the offer. I had never considered it until that instant," Marz confessed.

The general punched a fist solidly into his open palm. "By the ten fingers," he burst out. "The old timer was as right as ever!"

"I'm lost,"Marz laughed. "Who is the old timer?"

"My grandmother's genther of course," the general teased.

An amused puzzlement lit Marz's face. "How would your grandmother's genther know of me?" he queried.

"Oh, because gee is the wisest of all Vaghi. You know the old timer as Genu Zig. Do you not?" he winked.

"Genu Zig is your great genu?" the young officer rasped, pleased by his own astonishment. "You knew about me from Genu?"

"Aye, lad. I've been aware of you from almost the beginning. Genu summoned me after you left Mount Aryxx. By the fingers, son, who do you think has been looking after you all these bloody years? Protecting you from the irrational barbs of Rooz Javatt! Aye, it was I. But I had to let you earn your journey, to establish your own prominence. And you've done it with the style of a lord." The general gripped Marz's forearm with a patriot' s fervor. "From the brickworks to your military training and beyond. I even maneuvered you to South Camp away from Javatt. Aye, Marz Kavoyy, I've been there for you! For you are the only hope that The Vag will be spared from a future lordship held by Rooz Javatt or some other jackass of the same ilk!"

Tears of sincerity glistened the golden eyes as Marz faced his newly discovered mentor. "I am in your debt, general. All those years I thought I was alone, you were watching over me." He placed his palm atop the general's hand which yet gripped his arm, rubbing it warmly, his gratitude expressed with every pat.

"Well, at least I was there some of the time!" Usually brusque, Povezz spoke now in tones of friendship. "I must leave you now. But know this. I am sending you, Battle Officer Kavoyy, to finish your term at South Camp for two reasons. First to keep you away from Varaxx. Though he honored you with the Marshal' s title, his generosity is often attached to invisible strings.

This way you will be away from his influence until after the boon is no longer fresh in his mind. Do you understand me?"

"Perfectly," Marz answered. "You wish me not to become his unavoidable puppet."

"Exactly," Taz Povezz confirmed. And pulling Marz close to him, he breathed, "And Varaxx plans to replace Commander Morann with Rooz Javatt at North Camp. A bad move, but at least you'll be free of him down south." He looked about to see if any passers-by were drawing near. Satisfied none were in earshot, he cautioned, "It is also best no one suspects you are my protégé, or that our relationship is anything but distant. If the Javatt believe you are being groomed for higher things, they are liable to act against us. Now be off. And not a word of this to anyone, not even your most trusted companion. Good fortune, Marshal of the Lord."

"Rooz darling," she rejoiced upon catching sight of the tall officer hurrying toward her. "You look exquisite!" Kaara Varaxx arched her back off the lounging sofa in anticipation of his rush to her side. He didn't disappoint her, rapidly coming to the cushioned divan, kissing both rouged cheeks. Kaara thrilled to his attentiveness. They had always doted on each other, the link between them as strong as mother and son, or at least she thought so. Regal in manner Kaara wore her dark hair up, a thin maroon diadem stretching across her pale forehead. The upswept tresses accentuated her slender neck, adding to the stateliness of her bearing. Dusty green in color, the gown hung in soft pleats, a silver and onyx broach holding it fast at one shoulder, the other exposed, her alabaster skin looking cool and supple. The years had been kind to Kaara. Her face showed little sign of aging, the area around the eyes yet free of creases. Hoops of gold surrounded each wrist extending up the forearm. Her long fingers, bejeweled with no less than eight rings, wiggled with enthusiasm as they caressed her handsome visitor's hands, nibbling his knuckles with a flurry of little kisses.

"Auntie, you look simply scrumptious," he gushed, playing the sycophant's role to the hilt. By any measure Rooz was an attractive man, the curious yolk eyes being the only physical quirk, though they didn't necessarily detract from his overall presentation. To say the eyes marred his splendid appearance would be overstating the issue. As commander of South Camp he was, at a relatively young age, well established in The Vag's military hierarchy. His rapid promotions obviously came as a result of his family relationship through Kaara to Lord Varaxx. As the first lady's favorite nephew, he enjoyed the benefits of the Lord's largesse. Barren of offspring, Rooz had become her surrogate son. She had fawned over him since the day his father Gaiz first brought the boy to the residence for visits. As Kaara's brood brother, Gaiz Javatt gained many advantages for young Rooz. Indeed the child often spent weeks at a time close to his aunt. With the cunning of their family reputation, the two brood siblings and their father had plotted Rooz's future ascendancy to the throne. Though now a soldier of high standing, she continually cooed in her nephew's presence, smothering him with complimentary pap. Lately, however, their roles had shifted somewhat. Obvious in her desire for his appreciation. Kaara pestered him whenever they got together, nagging Rooz to acknowledge auntie's continuous efforts on his behalf. Rooz had learned how to play to Kaara's emotional wants, supplying her ego with just enough recognition to keep her hungry for more.

"Is everything going well for Rooz? Has your auntie done enough?" she purred.

"You've been magnificent, dear Aunt Kaara." His yolks rolled lovingly, their insincerity hidden from her gullible eyes.

Rooz's two kords were being readied for the march from the isthmus back to South Camp when he had received the dispatch instructing him to report to Lord and Lady Varaxx at the Capital. Compliant to orders, he had traveled on horseback to the great residence hopefully expectant of the Lord's favor. Passing through the city gate Javatt saw a leathery skull impaled on a pole. Asking whose head decorated the portal, the officer of the guard informed him that its previous owner was the scoundrel priest Taratt. Javatt rode on, pleased that the impudent bastard had been executed. He was a bit miffed, however, that he himself had not been the one to oversee the prophet' s demise. Oh well, he couldn't be everywhere at once. Rooz never suspected though that Kavoyy had been the one to exact the Lord's revenge.

"Auntie, why did you and Uncle Lanz summon me to the Capital? Am I to receive some new charge?" His attitude was that of an innocent child, knowing full well she enjoyed him best this way.

Kaara giggled the laugh of one who has been up to a tad of mischief. "I'm afraid the Lord wasn't party to the dispatch. It was I alone who summoned you, using his seal to do so."

"But why?" Disturbed by her charade, his eyes took on a look of consternation.

"I was bored." Her lower lip protruded in a little pout, the kind she had rehearsed on many occasions before the reflecting glass. "Are you angry with your auntie?" Kaara's eyes fluttered in feigned contrition, admitting their little girl's naughtiness. "It's just that I haven't seen you in such a long time, Rooz darling. You know how I feel about you. Ours is a special bond. Do I not always persuade the Lord to elevate your status, to grant you favors? Am I a bad auntie for savoring your success?"

"No, not at all, sweet Aunt Kaara. But sometimes, as in this instance, you overstep your authority," he chided. "Forging the Lord's mark is an act which will tempt his anger."

"I didn't forge his mark. It is the legitimate seal of his office I borrowed." The lip continued to protrude.

"Alright, so it wasn't forgery." He was becoming somewhat exasperated. "Nevertheless, it was unauthorized."

She dismissed his protestation by not responding. Instead Kaara emitted a throaty laugh. "I just love it when you behave so professionally. You remind me so much of my brother. Aye, you're just like Gaiz. All fuddy duddy business! Why I recall once he..."

A sharp rap broke her recollection. On the far side of the door a servant's husky voice called out. "Lady Varaxx, are you there?"

"Yes, what is it?" she snapped, annoyed at the intrusion.

"Lord Varaxx commands your presence immediately. And that of your nephew, Rooz Javatt. Now!"


The great room looked as though a herd of Kala had rampaged within. Shattered furnishings littered the floor. The fluted marble stand which had once boasted Taratt's dome lay in two pieces, akin to the prophet genself. Anything capable of being lifted or ripped from the wall had in fact been tossed. Drapery, chairs, goblets, a flattened silver ewer, shards of vases and pottery, scrolls and food joined the upturned desk, now sporting three legs, on the Lord's floor. Lanz Varaxx was unhappy! News of his wife's summoning of Rooz Javatt had come at a most inopportune time for Kaara because her husband was drunk again, his mood ornery. The tantrum which displayed itself in destructive rage was by no means over. Reeling with a brandied meanness, he cursed Kaara, vowing to make her pay for her most recent transgression. Because this time she had usurped his power, an unforgivable act. Kaara Varaxx had defied the Lord!

They entered together, Rooz, a sheepish look upon his face. She however, behaved haughtily, perhaps attempting to demonstrate her independence to their nephew. Viewing the shambled salon, she observed aloud, "My, my. I see we've been busy!"

"Close the door, Rooz!" the Lord commanded. He sucked in a huge breath trying to regain his equilibrium. The drunkenness for the most part had left him, possibly dissipated by the exertion of his one man brawl. Wading through the jumbled mess, he kicked at a goblet, his heel barely making contact. Still it was enough to send it spinning.

Javatt shut the huge wooden door, testing it to make sure the lock was secure. Best it remained closed tight for he sensed the Lord would be addressing him in humbling terms. To accept his lambasting was one thing, but for the servants to overhear it would be an unbearable insult.

"So what is your problem, Lanz?" She persisted in her haughtiness, a woman long indifferent to his berations. Without doubt this would be another in a forgetful list of tirades. She realized the Lord had no real way to punish her. After all, Kaara's family had manipulated him to the throne. Varaxx was beholden to the Javatt, the true power brokers of The Vag, she reminded herself. Besides she knew too many of the Lord's secrets to be relegated to a lesser position, specifically, a divorce. The esteem afforded the first lady would not be easily surrendered by Kaara.

"In there," Varaxx directed in commanding voice. He pointed to a small sitting room off the salon. "Both of you." Reddened to a near purple hue, the puffy face looked as if ready to explode.

Oddly her feet were prancing, almost dance-like. As if to further grate her husband's discontent, Kaara hummed tunelessly.

A most serious Rooz followed her into the little room, bowing respectfully to the Lord as he stepped over the debris cluttering his path.

"Sit!" Lanz Varaxx barked.

Obedient to the command, Javatt immediately sat, but Kaara purposely took her time, pretending to decide which chair met her fancy. Finally she flopped upon the one closest to Rooz. Impertinent in every movement, in each expression upon her face, Kaara settled into a sprawling posture and stared at the ceiling. The language of her positioning was evident to both men. In effect she was communicating her boredom with Varaxx's power play.

Rooz observed the unfolding drama with keen attention. Was the Lord so weak as to accept this behavior, or had Kaara grossly miscalculated the Lord's wrath. The nephew felt he was in no danger himself After all,.he had responded correctly to what he had believed was the Lord's bona fide dispatch ordering him to the Capital. Even so, Rooz knew the Lord possessed the capacity to act irrationally. He must maintain a respectful demeanor, not get caught up in the first lady's scorn. Aye, he must be careful not to ruffle his uncle's feathers. Nothing must be permitted to jeopardize Javatt's future ascendancy. Nothing! Everything, everyone, was expendable toward the achievement of that singular goal.

Apparently Lanz Varaxx had recaptured his composure, temper's discoloration faint on his brow, the huffing dispelled. Calmly he positioned a chair to the front of the two. He had already calculated his little inquisition, the words pre-positioned in his mind. He let himself fall to the seat and rushing his hands through the mane, he eased out a smile. Aye, the Lord of The Vag was apparently at peace, the demon of furor purged from within. "So," he politely began. "What in the name of the sweet goddess possessed you to summon your nephew from his duty, using my seal to command his presence?"

Without removing her eyes from above, Kaara placed both hands behind her head, interlocking the fingers to form a nest of sorts. "I felt like it!" she answered, the tone dripping with impertinence.

Coolly the Lord nodded. "You felt like it, eh? Rooz is preparing to march two bloody kords from one end of The Vag to the other, and your capricious little whim compels him to race here...an unwitting dupe to your childish stupidity. Meanwhile supply wagons are being harnessed and loaded, then unharnessed and unloaded, rendezvous times rescheduled, troops standing and waiting, provisions recalled, the entire camp turned upside down because of your indifference."

"So what!" she shot back, not caring to grasp the severity of her conduct. She would show Rooz how the Lord's partner put him in his place.

"Hmmm!" Varaxx gave the impression that he was in thought, but he had already figured it all out. Resultantly there was little emotion in his response. "The curious thing about you, Kaara, is that you really never understood that I am the Lord of The Vag and you are..."

"The Lady of The Vag!" she interjected, cutting him off in mid sentence.

"No, no, no, you meddlesome, frigid bitch," he smiled, enjoying the repartee. "I am the Lord of The Vag and you are nothing! Nothing!" Turning his attention quickly to Rooz, he asked, "Is that not true, nephew?"

Rooz knew he was being tested. To him the Lord looked too much like a man prepared to spring the nastiest of traps. Fidgeting with a kilt strap, he responded, "Whatever you say, my uncle. For you are unquestionably Lord of The Vag."

"Exactly, Rooz. And it is your ardent desire that someday you yourself will be called Lord of The Vag. Is that not true also?"

"Aye, sir. That is my aspiration. To follow in your boot-steps." The younger man was beginning to sweat, the wetness forming in little beads on his forehead. *He's setting bait. I can feel it*, he thought. *Time to be wary.*

"So, Rooz Javatt," the Lord continued, "if I command you to obey even my most radical order, you are obligated to do it. Because as you said, I am your Lord and therefore cannot be defied. And also because you need my good favor to position you for the lordship. Without my patronage, you would sink like an iron fish before ever swimming to your coveted throne. Am I not correct again, nephew?" Lanz Varaxx thrilled inside, the game titillating him like no other he had ever experienced. Across from him Kaara watched with a fascination so intense it held her tongue in check.

"Aye, uncle. My loyalty to your lordship is unwavering."

"Yes, yes, I know that. But would you perform a duty for me regardless how distasteful...to guarantee your ascendancy? Let's say I dismissed that alarmist Morann, and gave you command of North Camp. The whole bloody command. The Ring of Kilts, First Line, all the troops, the most prized assignment in all The Vag. How would that suit you, Rooz Javatt? Your credentials would be infinitely above any candidate who might surface. The throne would be but an easy step from there once my tenure expires."

"Uncle, I would be honored. Speak your wish and I will deliver what it is you seek." Rooz had rushed in, committing himself totally. Anything for the throne.

Varaxx licked his lips. "Strangle your auntie, dear lad," the Lord commanded. "Strangle her now. Our secret alone. The throne for her wretched life!"

"But, but, she is brood sister to my father," Rooz protested. "And I am of her blood. Surely, you're not serious?"

The color blanched from Kaara's rouged cheeks. "Stop it, Lanz. You've taken this ridiculous game playing a leap to far. Can't you see you've upset Rooz. He thinks you might be serious. Stop testing him this instant!" No longer was the ceiling the object of her sight. She sat upright, her honey eyes challenging Varaxx's bizarre overture.

It was the Lord's turn to act smug, and he relished the mood. "Kaara, you naive fool, you've never really understood human nature, never been aware of what truly drives men in pursuit of power. It is a compulsion like no other. Rooz has no choice!"

She gasped, "No! He wouldn't! I've been like a second mother to him." A shock of terror caused her to tremble. Her sureness shattered, she emitted a pathetic whimper, a hand quickly covering her lips lest another escape.

"Silly woman, you are but an insect in his path," Varaxx contemptuously shouted. Then directing his order to Rooz, he hissed, "Place your thumbs on her throat, Rooz."

*She's right,* the nervous nephew determined. *Lanz is testing my obedience. He will never let me finish the act.* With that he rose swiftly and turning to his aunt, he encompassed her unflinching neck with his hands, putting the thumbs directly on the bob. "Sorry, auntie," he apologized. So horror-struck was Kaara that she gave no resistance, offering instead a pleading stare into his orange hued orbs. Rooz rested his thumbs, applying no pressure, awaiting Uncle Lanz's order to cease. *It is nothing more than a test,* he was certain. *The*

*Lord is now assured of my fidelity.. The throne is guaranteed me.* So positive of his instinct was he that he nodded comfortingly to Kaara. The Lord indeed had taught her a lesson she would not soon forget.

"You're going to have to squeeze harder than that if she is to die," Varaxx instructed. "Press your thumbs. Use your strength, lad."

*So it is to be!* Closing his eyes, Rooz jerked his hands tightly, the tips of his fingers clenching the nape just below the upswept hair, his thumbs pushing inward with great force collapsing the windpipe. A helpless Kaara clutched futilely at Rooz's wrists as she succumbed. Disbelief yet etched her eyes. Her darling Rooz had made his choice.

"Now don't release her until she's gone," the impassive Lord advised. "Maintain your pressure." It was as though he were directing a play. So dispassionate was his manner that the Lord appeared carefree in her murder. He had pulled it off without panic, in absolute control. And in the aftermath, no anguish would torment his soul. Like Kaara's was a death he welcomed.

Never opening his lids, Rooz continued squeezing the limp neck long after she had expired. Varaxx had gone into the salon to retrieve a drapery to wrap her corpse. Returning, he tapped Javatt's shoulder. "She's gone, lad. As dead as Huug Taratt." Rooz released his hold, allowing the body to slump to the floor. Dazed by the experience, he stood speechless, dumbstruck that he had actually gone through with it.

"You did well, Rooz," the Lord complimented as he tossed the drape over Kaara's lifeless form. "Command of North Camp is yours. Tomorrow I shall dismiss Morann and appoint you his successor. Life is simple!"

"Aye, sir," Rooz mumbled, the numbing starting to wear off. "You are most generous."

"True, but my generosity has been paid in advance." Varaxx proceeded to adjust the heavy cloth snug to Kaara's body. "Early in the morning I will announce she has died in her sleep or choked on a bone, or whatever I feel is appropriate. And tomorrow night she'll burn like a torch on a glorious funeral pyre...in keeping with her wishes of course. She always fancied spectacles." The Lord bent to uncover Kaara's head and examined the throat. "Hmmm," he reckoned, "I think a high necked gown would be most functional. You know, to hide any bruises. Lad, you gave her one heck of a bloody squeeze!"

"Aye, sir, a funeral pyre tomorrow night! I'll be there dutiful to my blood." Rooz let out a conspiratorial grin which his uncle returned. Within a minute of sweet auntie's death, he had come to simplistic terms with his act, rationalized it as a necessary expedience without the slightest of misgivings. Varaxx was correct, life is simple. The transformation caused the Lord to see him in a more admiring light.

"That's the spirit," the Lord encouraged. "Hold your head high. March out of here with some snap like Marz Kavoyy!"

"Kavoyy?" Rooz repeated. "What do you know of him?"

"Why he's my Marshal, the fellow that lopped off Huug Taratt's head!"

# CHAPTER XIII

Dag Goraxx had instructed the servants to light a lamp in every window so ger visitor could view the villa from a great distance. After yesterday's dreadfully tedious funeral, Dag especially looked forward to Zoog's return, the scientist priest having written ten days earlier that gee was en-route "bearing discovery of the most profound nature." When the young nunale arrived, it was with grand rejoicing that they embraced, Zoog good-naturedly commenting, "So many lamps! At four medecs afar I thought the whole bloody villa was afire before my very eyes!"

It prompted a great laugh from Goraxx. "Same old Kavoyy, I see. Years in the wild country haven't dented your irreverence in the tiniest!" Examining the boots and grimy tunic, Dag insisted ger house guest wash and change to a clean robe and sandals before dinner. Without hesitance, Zoog accepted ger patron's kind hospitality. The journey had been considerably absent of hygiene.

The pair dined for over an hour on roasted fowl stuffed with onions, mixed vegetables, spices and sweet nuts. A tender lettuce salad slicked with pungent olive oil accompanied the entrée. Dag was boastfully proud of the oil, squeezed from the fruit of the villa's orchards. Figs and melon followed, the farm steward having scrupulously salvaged enough from the heavy rains to maintain Goraxx' s larder. The older priest entertained Kavoyy with local gossip, placing particular emphasis on the untimely passing of Kaara Varaxx. Zoog reciprocated with several stories, including the grim tale of Arabella and subsequent desert engagement. In Capital circles, the younger nunale learned, the Battle of the Cauldron had become the latter's official historical title. Before Zoog could relate the odd relationship gee had crafted with Taratt and the narration of "discovery," the high priest insisted on doing it "properly" over brandied tea, "in celebration of Zoog Kavoyy's safe and successful return to the civilized portion of The Vag."

Though Dag projected an ebullient mood this evening, gee was very tired, having officiated at Kaara's service the previous night and into the early morning. Almost as trying had been the quick preparation leading to the ceremony. The Lord's call for a prompt funeral had frenzied the priestly entourage with so many details to mobilize on short notice. Everyone had been surprised at the suddenness of her death, the stroke having come in the presence of the Lord and her favored nephew, Rooz Javatt, quelling *any* suspicions of foul play. But looking at the Lord last night, Dag felt somewhat uneasy. Even Rooz appeared a bit quirky, nothing that one could place a finger upon; it was just a feeling that came over Dag. Kaara's wish for an immediate pyre with no preparation of her corpse, other than a specific gown, had been revealed only to the Lord. Even the first lady's 'girl friends' were mystified by her strange request. But which woman would be fool enough to doubt the great Lanz Varaxx? For nothing but grief would come to the challenger! Besides, there could be no evidence. The fire had seen to that.

Standing before the pyre, the bereaved husband had tossed the torch igniting the huge bonfire. In minutes a mountain of flame climbed into the night. With a resounding whoosh, the ashes of the first lady were carried to the sky, presumably floating her to the comfort of Gala Rotaria. Varaxx wore his droopiest face, somber in every manifestation. Those associated with the court knew theirs had been an arrangement marked by years of caustic estrangement. Though the residence was spacious enough to house them both with little personal contact, their few mutual attendances often ended ugly. Behind the doleful mask, the Lord crowed with Kaara's violent parting. Without question he could have strangled her himself. But a fiendish pleasure came in demonstrating to his wife that her sweet, darling nephew would murder her without compunction. How Varaxx had enjoyed the drama as her pathetic eyes pleaded with Rooz Javatt's unyielding lids. Rooz had refused to open up, giving her no opportunity to penetrate what ragged conscience survived within. No beseechment in all the Capital could unlock his resolve. And so she had perished, victim to the Lord's malice, to her nephew's ambition, the basest of motives. Once again Varaxx had compromised an ally, adding Rooz to a lengthy list. The tally included, among others, his high priest whose rich baritone led mourners in the death chant while the fire charred the remnants of Kaara's mortal remains.

Sipping generous refills of the fortified tea, Zoog narrated a tale of investigation, culminating in ger extraordinary conclusion. Scholarly in every detail, it caused Goraxx to gasp in awed enlightenment. Supporting evidence buoyed each premise leading to the scientist's masterpiece of discovery. The mystery of The Vag had been solved to Dag's great satisfaction. In three days time a convocation would be convened at the Academy of Science. There Zoog Kavoyy, backed by the high priest of Gala Rotaria, would present the findings of ger prodigious undertaking. The question, *Who are we?* Would finally be satisfied to the content of the scientific hierarchy.

"Tonight," a rapt Dag acknowledged, "I will drift into the most wondrous sleep of my existence, transported back through the ages, touching the voices of origin. Tonight I am whole. Thank you, dear friend, for delivering the great answer."

Aftershocks of the long deluge rocked North Camp in delayed waves of dysentery, laying low the troops in great numbers. The crush of soldiers and limited sanitary conditions discouraged efforts to control the problem. Half the military units were pulled back several medecs to more southerly bivouacs in the hope that a reduced population would alleviate the recurring sickness. Diarrhea, fever, cramping, affected every warrior at one time or another. Nunine physicians schooled in the science of pharmacology did all in their power to remedy the symptoms. Still it was not enough. The Seventh and Eighth Kords scheduled to make the difficult hike back to the wild country had to be delayed, so vile was their ailment. Such was the situation Rooz Javatt inherited as he sped to his new command. It called for a leader of patience and logistical foresight, neither of which could be attributed to the Lord's impulsive nephew. Luckily the Kala had roamed beyond the surveillance of the camp's scouts, hopefully not to return in the near future.

In the Capital a genial Lanz Varaxx, basking in Kaara's riddance, decided the citizenry needed to feel as cheery as he. The collective impact of the flood, Kala threats on the frontier, the Arabellan massacre and Kaara's untimely passing had imposed an emotional malaise on the city's populace, if not the whole nation. Even the flaunted head of Taratt effected a dismal tone. A day of festival could be just the medicine to cure the prevailing mood, he determined. The Lord himself was in mourning which precluded any pomp saluting his personal glory. However, a parade and public celebration honoring the gallant kilts who defeated the chalked menace ought to perk up the crowd. Kavoyy' s bolt, probably the halest in The Vag, given its distance from the Chokepoint, would be on display for all to view. The people would see for themselves that the army was healthy and fit, shooing rumors circulating to the contrary. And Kavoyy, a strikingly handsome chap, would be singled out for commendation, a hero for all Vaghi to adulate. Thus removing minds from things pessimistic. Aye, nothing like a pageant with musicians and revelers to bolster morale. And wine, pouring freely from the Lord's cellar! Lanz Varaxx, master of the superficial, would orchestrate the return to normalcy.

Despite the limitations imposed by the bulbous figure, Zoog assumed the classical orator's stance in preparation for ger treatise. Straight of posture, chin up, the young scientist showed no sign of nervousness, offering nods of acknowledgment to scholars who had once instructed Zoog, as well as friends gee had known during ger student years. Dag Goraxx, already privy to the discovery, sat in the theater's front row accompanied by the dean of the Academy of Science. Also attending were many sages, having made the trip from Mount Aryxx. Among them, Genu Zig waited unperturbed, the first time any could ever recall having seen the revered savant outside Aryxx. Truly this was the most august group to be assembled at the academy in many generations. Word had spread quickly during Zoog's trip from the wild country. Priests, scientists, intellectuals eager to hear the brilliant Kavoyy anticipated revelations of Vaghi inceptions reaching back to the point of origin. The younger members speculated the magnitude of Zoog's disclosure would stimulate a complete re-evaluation of The Vag and its social institutions. Conservative by nature, the senior nunales tried to conceal their excitement, presenting a wait and see attitude. They would demand more than hypothesis. Evidence, not unsupported theory, would be critical to their acceptance.

On several tables to Zoog's rear were heaped a curious stack of papers bound between wooden plates, what Goraxx had learned was the Translator, four volumes in total, the first of which had been initiated by Taratt. Additionally three dozen or so scrolls numbered in sequence accompanied the stack. Many bore inscriptions meticulously copied from the cavern wall. And preserved between a pair of thin, wooden slabs rested the most ancient of relics, a map pointing to a time before the first Vag was known by that name.

"Genthers of my gender," gee called out, a most appropriate salutation inasmuch as every soul among the two hundred was nunine. "Under the generous and unswerving patronage of Dag Goraxx, high priest of Gala Rotaria, and with the blessing of the scientific community, I set out roughly three years ago to seek answers to the mystery which has confounded us since curiosity became the agent of knowledge. Specifically, it was the origin of our Vag existence I sought!" Zoog Kavoyy then proceeded to relate ger initial investigative queries and the procedures undertaken to guarantee scientific integrity. Though boring, gee felt it necessary to strengthen what was to follow.

The wild country had seemed a logical area to delve, gee told them, because the elder inhabitants, especially the aesthetes of that most inhospitable of environments, yet spoke in part with the old dialect. Their vocabulary and patterns were the least evolved of the Vag tongue. Therefore, gee reasoned, migratory Vaghi probably worked their way north from there, developing their own linguistic style over the centuries. The newer tongue, though more sophisticated, clearly had its roots in the archaic form, Zoog' s documents would clearly demonstrate. Kavoyy' s massive compendium, the Translator, with its countless word progressions would be available for all to examine. The scientist went on to tell them of primitive settlements, now nothing more than linear rubble but, nevertheless, more ancient than anything uncovered in the more lush reaches of the north. Indications were also there that the wild country once enjoyed a temperate climate, therefore more habitable, before the Gugububu's slow crawl encroached the perimeter, upsetting the land and its productiveness.

Zoog realized gee flirted with an associative guilt when the name of Huug Taratt was invoked, and the renegade priest's scientific belief of the wild country as the womb of origin. Careful with each word, Kavoyy was attentive to recognize only Huug's technical contribution, taking pains to castigate the wolf' s terrible exploits. By now everyone had been apprised of Zoog's part in the hunt for Taratt, and of ger brood brother's act of decapitation. It exonerated the young nunale from any notion of sympathy for Huug's deeds. For it was Zoog Kavoyy, the assembly recognized, whose chant lamented the dead at Arabella, who anointed the tortured corpses spiriting their souls to the goddess' fold. Aye, Zoog Kavoyy had conducted genself with honor of the noblest character.

Spinning the tale with a storyteller's rhythm, Zoog related several incidents including ger chance encounter with the 'emaciated one,' the old man who had identified the *Kwinarvy* site, at the time a meaningless appellation. Then after taking them through the Gugububu to the great cavern and its literate wall scratchings, Zoog paused to study the hushed aggregate. Awed in mass, the nunine audience hinged on Kavoyy's every word, drinking in each nuance. With a touch of showmanship, the scientist spoke of leaning on the slab altar, interpreting those phrases which after unknown millenia gee was able to understand. The original writers, historians of the earliest days, identified their kind as *Arvum Quint.* From this Zoog had been able to deduce that *Quint* was an abbreviation for the ordinal *Quintus* or *Fifth* coupled with the noun *Arvum* or *Field.* Zoog raised both arms to the gallery "We are the people of the Fifth Field!" he stated. In the ancient sense, *Arvum* was in actuality a cultivated field, one which yielded produce. But what did it mean? *People of the Fifth Field!* An odd identity for any people regardless of origin. However, that most ancient of settlements, *Kwinarvy,* supported that discovery...because *Kwinarvy* and *Fifth Field* are one and the same. *Kwin* is *Quin* respelled, and *Arvy* is but a corruption of *Arvum.* As I dug further into the various texts and walled messages, the old tongue was referred to as *lingua Latina,* it having been the speech of the first Vaghi. Remember these points, genthers," Zoog guided the avid gathering. "For I will return to them soon." Again the scientist hesitated, looking to the response upon their faces, making sure they recognized each guidepost of ger findings. Methodically gee took them through several word regressions permitting disclosure of the cavern's enigmatic scratchings. Diligently the nunale of the isthmus showed them the word mechanics of another age.

"My fellow scholars, we are all aware of the colorful myths which thrill many of us to this day. Since childhood we've heard yarns of the first Vaghi, sprouting full grown with farm animals and pets from a great seed or egg, stepping onto the land of Gala Rotaria. A nation hatched overnight, clothed, armed and tooled. An instant civilization! This is legend, is it not? Definitely not a component of our religious dogma. Most of us believe it to be wonderful fiction. The Vag literature is rich with such stories, the great seed being but one of many myths which have entertained us since our tender years. However, in the wild country's deeper recesses where isolated communities are untouched by modern thought, the story of the seed persists as fact, handed down from parent to offspring, generation after generation. For them it is accepted historical truth. We scientists and priests often scoff at these *yokels,* judging them to be uneducated, therefore, blind to rational explanation. But often where there is myth, my genthers, an underlying ember of credibility glows. So it was with enormous interest that I read *Semen Magn* from the very same cavern wall. To decipher *Semen* I only had to look to our current word *Zemen* which of course means *seed.* And *Magn* is a shortened spelling of *Magnus* or *great.* Thus the mystery started to come together. *We are the people of the Fifth Field transported here in a great seed!"* Zoog could hear their sighs filling the hall.

"Weeks later while pouring over the ancient manuscripts which had been gathering cave dust for countless time, I found a picture, a line drawing actually, looking somewhat like an elongated triangle but with an ovate point. *Siliqua Magna* it was titled. Today's word for *pod* we all know is *Zilkwa*. No doubt it grew from *siliqua*. Thus *Great Pod* became interchangeable for *Great Seed.* A most logical conclusion considering our image of a pod is pointier than that of the average seed, certainly in the analogous sense. So now I had the earliest diagram of the vessel of our conception, a huge pod capable of carrying our people through space. Interesting!"

Zoog momentarily turned ger back on the convocation to retrieve the map and removed the plate which served as a cover. Holding the parchment aloft with its supporting backplate, the scientist proclaimed it "the key which unlocks the portal to our beginnings. Behold," gee announced, "a chart more venerable than any in the land. Your eyes cannot read its jotting from a distance so I will describe them to you. And then later it will be available for your close scrutiny. It is a map, not very intricate in design. However, it instructs two *cohorts,* the old word for *kord,* of four hundred eighty men each, to assemble with their animals, tools and weapons to V AGER. Understand this, my genthers, at the time of the ancients some letters were both alphabetical and numerical." And so gee demonstrated. "I is one, V is five, X is ten, L is fifty, C is one hundred, D is five hundred, M is one thousand." Some in the audience were ahead of Zoog, already determining where they were being led. "In the midst of the map," gee continued, "is marked the point of embarkation, an abbreviation of the map's V AGER title. It is shown simply as V AG. *Ager* in lingua Latina is a synonym for *Field.* So the number and the letter when read literally, flow together as VAG!"

Gasps of wonderment exhaled through the spellbound crowd Some touched hands to lips, hushing exclamations which might interrupt the moment.

Kavoyy nodded in serious expression. "Aye, genthers, we are Vaghi, the People of the Fifth Field, selected for transportation across the starry breadth. Ostensibly we are descended from that specific group which departed from the V Ager, the Fifth Field, destined for Gala Rotaria. For indicated near the map's edge is an alternate location, perhaps for another group of travelers. Its identity is II AG., unquestionably people of the second field. So my fellow Vaghi, we are the children of spacial migration! Or at least half so. The other *half,* I will now explain."

The dean of the Academy of Science, at Dag Goraxx's encouragement, approached the map. Reverently gee touched the ragged edge as if to feel the soul of its maker. Squinting at the old symbols, gee contemplated the possibility that a people were able to leap across the spectrum of the universe. Odd that people with such powers would record their origin on so primitive a document. Perhaps Zoog would unravel this paradox as well. With barely an audible grunt, the aging dean returned to Dag's side and signaled the patient scientist to go on.

"As you will remember," Zoog's lecture proceeded, "I said two cohorts of men collected themselves at the Fifth Field. Yes, males only, exclusive of nunales and females. These men were hardened warriors of another age, disciplined by a military tradition not unlike that which our bothers perform in the service of The Vag. But who were these men the great seed force had propelled to Gala Rotaria? The manuscripts describe them as soldiers of the same *legio,* or legion, who had been rewarded for their loyal tenure with land on the extreme boundary of their native region. The men, legionaries, had been drawn from the tribes of that very same part of a great peninsula. Most of these tribes had partially fused becoming a single people. It was their soldier progeny which eventually entered the pod. The territory from which they came was known to them as *Ager Gallicus,* a land of mountains and rolling hills sweeping eastward to a blue, salt sea." Zoog's finger traced an imaginary line above ger head accentuating the terrain of Ager Gallicus.

"In the scriptures our progenitors often referred to their ancestral tribes as a way of identifying themselves. Using the lingua Latina I will call out these names to you for it has probably been thousands of years since their names were called aloud. And in doing, hopefully, I honor the roots of our ancestors." The passion on Zoog's face signaled to the nunine scholars that gee was linking with their paternal cradle, pushing ger spirit back in time. A new quiet prevailed, ears straining to ingest each uttered syllable. The tribal bloods which pulsed every vein within the academy hall, flowed with special energy as Zoog Kavoyy enunciated the old names. "I pray my tongue does them honor," gee announced, "that it does justice to the long wait. *Umbri,*" gee called out. "*Sabini* and *Piceni* who I believe were two related people. *Senones* of the *Galli* also referred to as *Celtae.* And apparently some time before the great trip, the tribes had absorbed *Graeci* from the Elbow or Ankon as they called it. It is still unclear to me what the Elbow's significance is. But possibly it was a strategic point of land jutting into the salt sea. And after arriving here on Gala Rotaria this daring corpus of men gave familiar names to what they found. As an aside I can tell you that the River Metaurus of the Ager Gallicus donated its name to our Metarz River."

Artful in the most significant dissertation of ger young life, Zoog could feel the admiration filling the theater. More than pride, a sense of gratification swelled the nunale's heart. An accomplishment fantasized during stable chores at Kavoyy Station was being realized with every disclosure. Modest of attitude, Zoog projected to all that scholarship, more than personal glory, dictated ger motivation. For the brilliant scientist, each discovery was a shared experience to be spread among the nunalehood, among every Vag who ever glanced the mirror and asked *why? From where?* And also, if one could behave more chauvinistically, in the familial mode, Zoog had brought esteem to the heretofore undistinguished house of Kavoyy and the sibs of ger brood. Aye, Tyrra and Marz would rejoice in their genther's stupendous accomplishment.

"But why would our fatherly ancestors depart the comforts of their homeland and voluntarily venture to such untamed ground as Gala Rotaria?" Zoog queried. "Or said another way, why would the forces of the grand cosmos lift them as one great body and convey the lot here? Was there a more profound purpose in mind?"

Questions such as these tantalized the enamored throng desirous to appreciate every aspect of Zoog's marvelous secrets. Even Genu Zig leaned forward. For the old savant this was a wondrous moment, as amazing as any gee had ever experienced. Inside Genu's heart and mind gee recognized the validity of Zoog's treatise. The nunale Kavoyy was brood genther to Genu's protégé. And like Marz, the genther was an exceptional gift to The Vag, sent by the great goddess to effect change and to enlighten. Zoog's credentials were celestially wrapped, Zig was certain. The Kavoyy represented a historical turning point in the evolution of their nation, of their people. No doubt, in some future capacity, the brood sister would excel also. *Now this,* Genu Zig mused, *was well worth the trip from Aryxx! I would have crawled here on my wrinkled belly to witness the words of Zoog Kavoyy.*

Easing into a delivery that was more conversational than oration, Zoog revisited a topic referred to earlier. "Before, when I informed you that only men were delivered in the great seed, I couldn't help but notice looks of puzzlement among you. For it requires both male and female to procreate. And that is precisely why our forebears traveled the cosmic track. In pursuit of women! Call it what you wish, sexual or romantic, but the passioned urges which drive our male brothers to behave like barnyard roosters, were as powerful back then as they are today. Being nunale, unencumbered by ecstasy, it is difficult for us to appreciate how such physical needs can smother reason. Regardless, it is constant in the masculine nature. Enticed by the goddess' universal force, the legionaries of Ager Gallicus were promised alluring mates of the *oculus aureus!*" Adjusting the ankle length robe, Zoog pushed at the sleeves, riding each cuff up the forearm. Times like this gee wished for tunic and bragghi. Though decidedly less nunine, gee had grown used to less flowing garments. The placid face showed signs of perspiration about the upper lip and pate. With so many bodies occupying the gallery, heat had built to an uncomfortable level. In the audience small hand fans appeared, breezing their owners with short rapid strokes. "You see, genthers, at the time the pod arrived, The Vag was occupied by the yellow eyed people we call Orri or Auri! Docile as lambs, the Orri were facing extinction. Kala feasted on their kind at will with virtually no resistance other than flight to hidden sanctuaries. So a deal was struck between man and the supreme being. Our forefathers would be transported to the land of the Orri within a swift vessel of great proportion, and upon arrival would drive the Kala off the land, pushing them beyond the isthmus. This, we are told, took many generations. And during that process our distant fathers took the Orri women for their own, slaughtering protesting males with few qualms. Unfortunately ours is a heritage of violence" gee observed. "The surviving Orri were relocated beyond the Barrier Mountains where they enjoy a peaceful existence to this day, mostly as shepherds. Appropriately, the first sheep were supplied them by Vaghi, perhaps out of guilt, maybe friendship. To this day our Orri neighbors enjoy the protection of Vaghi kords with hardly a tacit recognition of the role we play. Those taken women of whom I spoke became the mothers of the Vag race. As a result, every nunale in this room is a descendant of those first couplings. Aye, genthers, we and our sibs, verily every Vag who walks the land, are half Orri. Indeed our language is a mix of the lingua Latina and Orri, which is why, as the Barrier traders tell us, there are so many Orri words which are easily understood. Those common words were not necessarily learned earlier from us. Most likely they are indigenous to the Orri tongue which the first mothers integrated into the lingua Latina forming the language we call Vag." No shock paled the pond of faces, no outcry of disbelief, so Zoog went on. "Now I'm going to bring to light a few things which some of you might find distressing. But you shouldn't because most of us are scientists, and science is about truth. Apparently when two races of people, which have been isolated from each other by the great universal plane, are ultimately united, the resultant offspring take on the dominant characteristic of one parent or the other. These characteristics can be physiological or personality in nature. For instance, our warrior fathers possessed eyes of various color: brown, blue, gray...even green! Yes, it is true."

A few "Oooohs" rippled through the room. Animals were known to own peculiar eye colors, but not people! The notion of irises other than yellow stimulated their interest.

"The Orri eye characteristic overwhelmed that of the legionaries, and so every Vag offspring born to this day carries the yellow eye trait...in various shades. No other color prevails. So it is safe to say the maternal eye triumphed.

So it is also in childbearing. Boy-girl twins are the rule in The Vag as among the Orri. The journals tell us that in the homeland of the warrior fathers, twin births were the exception, whether of same or mixed gender. So again the Orri trait has prevailed. For within the wombs of Vaghi mothers twins are the normal process. Aye, in The Vag the brood is a given fact of conception. Except!" Zoog pointed a resolute finger upward, ger smile transferring itself to the audience. To a nunale they glimmered with anticipation. "Except for the specialness of our nunale kind, genthers! We nunales are included in approximately one out of every ninety pregnancies, so our broods are triplets in number. In the land of Ager Gallicus from whence the first father's came, and indeed the whole of their land mass, there was no nunine gender. So speak the ancient scriptures! And we know as well, that within the Orri race there are no nunales. Even among the Kala, and it is debatable whether they qualify as soulful people, there is no sexless gender. Therefore, we must conclude that we are a unique product of miscegenation, exclusively gifted to the Vaghi by the goddess of our prayers. Aye, we nunales are an extraordinary gender unmatched among other peoples." Zoog let it soak in. What gee wished to avoid was the feeling that somehow they were freaks, mutants spawned of a genetic accident. Calmness held fast, however, so the scientist continued. "Our first fathers provided physical characteristics of size and strength to the new race, along with attitudes of organization and aggressiveness, virtues lacking among the Orri. To our great fortune they also brought the most spectacular product of their earlier society, writing! A most priceless contribution for the written word enabled communication and the transfer of knowledge." Nods of agreement bobbed within the rows of benches.

"Orri females, as mentioned, advanced the *oculusflavus* or *aureus,* the yellow or golden eye, to the new breed. Additionally, the Orri dimension of brood birthing, ensured generational replacements for both parents. By the ancient writings, we are further informed, that when the miracle of the nunale first came, parents were confused, never having witnessed any such phenomenon before. But once the richness of the goddess' hybrid gift became apparent, they rejoiced. With powers mystic and academic, with disposition gentle and compassionate, the nunale *is* considered a boon to families lucky enough to be blessed. Since those initial nunine births millenia past, our kind has continually given rationality and harmony to the Vag race. But perhaps more than anything else, we have provided solutions through conceptual thought and logic. We are inventors and solvers ever dutiful to our Vag society. And that my dear genthers is what I have attempted to do this fine day, furnish a solution to the mystery of our root existence." Not knowing whether to bow or raise ger hands to the applauding crowd, Zoog permitted genself a toothy smile. Standing erect, hands hung to either side, the scientist of the isthmus savored the moment. Cheers accompanied a rhythmic hand-clapping as nunales of every age saluted their brilliant genther.

Genu Zig's slow, choppy claps signified gee too approved Kavoyy's treatise. For it confirmed some suspicions gee genself had entertained in part, though Genu never had proof nor came close to approximating Zoog's conclusions. Making eye contact with Zoog, the sage of Aryxx mouthed, "Thank you. Thank you." Genu Zig's recognition swelled the young scientist's heart with gratification, the like of which had never touched Zoog before. Dag Goraxx and the dean also conveyed their congratulations with ringing superlatives issued from the front row.

Sensing the praise was going too far, and uncomfortable in its path, Zoog Kavoyy called out, "Genthers. My deep thanks for your reception. Should you care to examine the Translator and ancient relics upon this stage, please feel free to do so, remembering they have survived the many centuries and are fragile. But before you do, are there any questions or curiosities you wish satisfied?"

Many were eager to request details of the astounding revelations. However, before a single voice could be heard, Dag Goraxx, primate of The Vag, rose. Immediately a respectful hush befell the assembly. "A splendid presentation,"Dag complimented. "I believe I speak for all of us, Zoog, when I say you have delivered an explanation of immense proportion. You have unlocked voices long mute across the spectrum of unmeasured time." The high priest used the opportunity to let every Vag know that gee had been privy to all that Zoog Kavoyy had revealed, raising mindfulness of Dag's importance in the protocol of information. Thus Goraxx reminded all that the hierarchal pecking order had been maintained. Evidently Dag felt both ego and office demanded such. "Several nights ago when we deliberated these matters, Zoog, you touched upon two aspects of our culture, the evolution of Gala Rotaria and the origins of words like 'Medec." I think the group would find them as interesting as I do." Goraxx half turned to the crowd while smoothing the perspired gown and sat down.

Zoog paced a few steps, collecting the words to be offered. Sweat had seeped through the garment's armpits. Years in the wild country had pretty much immunized gen to the discomfort of heat. Still it would be enjoyable to soak ger ankles in a cool tub, perhaps sipping a goblet of fruit nectar from the chilled cellar of Dag Goraxx:. Three nights of brandied tea had left ger throat bordering on the hoarse, not to mention the tiny ache which buzzed the head. Alcohol would be out of the question today. "Aye, high priest of our religion, I am pleased to tell of it," Zoog said. For a brief instant gee closed ger eyes, again searching for phrases well chosen to set the stage. "Genthers, we nunine bond are aware that time is relevant only to those who use it, who gauge activity. But in the vast cosmos where millenia flit like seconds, time is an unimportant dimension, for the forces of the universe remain constant. And constant is the power of the goddess we call Gala Rotaria. Known by many names from the beginning of what we refer to as time, she is the giver of dreams, the nourisher of life. Hers is the totality of all we are and see. As our first fathers streamed across the spacial heavens and saw from afar the swirling mass that is the completeness of our land, several called out, *'Gaea, Gaea Rotaria.'* For Gaea was the personification or goddess, of their departed world or Terra as they knew it. Those warriors descended from the Graeci of Ankon, the Elbow, are credited with first expressing *Gaea Rotaria,* Gaea being particularly associated with their ancient culture. And over the generations, 'Gala' rolled off Vaghi tongues with greater ease, I suppose. As a result, she has come down to us as Gala Rotaria. But regardless of how we pronounce her name, she is the same throughout the universe. Because she is constant! Ever respectful of the goddess, we acknowledge her as the *foundation of all that is.* Gala is Gaea and Gaea is Gala."

"Spoken with the inspiration of the sweet goddess herself!" Genu Zig, until now silent, energetically confirmed Zoog's interpretation. "Young priest, you have managed to weave science and religion into a beautiful tapestry without offending convictions of the soul. My compliments to your skill and sincerity."

Zoog bowed courteously to the savant of Aryxx. Their eyes contacted, and for a quick moment they delved though at a distance. A peaceful warmth entered Zoog Kavoyy. Prizes come in many kinds, however, to be recognized by one as wise as Genu Zig represented the ultimate reward.

Zoog lazily drifted off to another plane yet contemplating the nature of Gala Rotaria and Genu Zig's ensuing commendation, when Dag Goraxx broke the reverie. "Don't forget the medec story," Dag reminded.

"Ah yes," Zoog said as he blinked, "it is but a simple thing of which the high priest refers. I suspect it will be amusing to those who enjoy the mechanics of language, especially you scholars who thrive on the nuances of word origins. This particular example of the 'medec' is also germane to today's treatise inasmuch as it supports my earlier point of how numbers and alphabet can meld. In the old tongue, I told you before, M is one thousand, D is five hundred, and C is one hundred. Add them up and you get sixteen hundred, the exact number of strides in a medec. So M-et-D-et-C equals Medec, hence the source is uncovered. As I said, it is a simple thing!" And beaming broadly, Zoog held out ger arms to the charmed audience. Truly it had been a day of scholastic triumph unmatched in the history of The Vag.

# CHAPTER XIV

Memories of the parade yet echoed in Marz's head. The Lord had been most liberal in the honors extended his bolt. Medals of commendation attesting to each warrior's participation in the desert fight had been struck, the faces of which bore images of the sun in rayed splendor, a sword and the word 'Cauldron.' On the obverse a profiled relief of Lanz Varaxx and the battle date were inscribed, all in shiny bronze. Each kilt had also received a quantity of barter credits sufficient to purchase gifts for the folks back home with enough left over for several bouts at the post tavern. For the Marshal of the Lord, recognition of his title came in the form of a proclamation read aloud by Varaxx in the great square. An oversized badge inter-worked with silver and gold validated Marz's office, the energetic Lord himself pinning it upon the officer's chest. As the bolt passed in review before Varaxx and General Povezz's staff, a spirited citizenry cheered and whistled. Children skipped alongside the soldiers, young women tossed flower petals in sparkling showers of pink and white, and the band struck up and replayed every stirring march in its repertory. Truly it had been a spectacular afternoon. Warm sunshine bathed the warriors in beams of yellow light, the same gleaming their new medals with added luster. Singled out for his "exceptional leadership and victorious conclusion to a most difficult mission," Marz Kavoyy, Marshal of the Lord, was further declared Hero of The Vag.

Within the tight knot of dignitaries circling Varaxx, it was apparent the Lord had imbibed more breakfast brandy than was his customary dole. A man of excess in every respect, he snorted out exaggerated praise, referring to Marz as, "that supreme pillar of duty," and "a soldier deep in martial virtue." By reputation the Lord had a knack for overdoing things, especially when all eyes were upon him. This day had been no exception. Embarrassed by Varaxx's display of hyperbole, Marz glanced uneasily at Monty Kelozz and the other kilts standing at attention. Enjoying his glorious predicament, Monty's proud grin communicated the stead in which he held his comrade. Most were hoping the Lord's long-windedness would quickly play itself out, for the night ahead promised wine and lasses into the wee hours. Mercifully, after seventy nine minutes' tenure, Lanz Varaxx surrendered the podium to the high priest. To everyone's delight Goraxx's benediction was eloquent, the blessing short. Within minutes the wine spigots rained their rubied bounty, pastries, sausages and meat pies filling every free hand, and musicians played with unending vigor. Merriment continued long into darkness, the last, tenacious revelers eventually saluting the new day's sun. Lord Varaxx had hosted one hell of a party.

That next morning following the festivity, Marz Kavoyy's bolt received instructions to help haul fresh supplies to North Camp. With so many troops tied down up north, every available body was needed to maintain the food flow from the Lord's warehouses to the Ring of Kilts and nearby bivouacs. Rejoined with the Eighth Kord, they would make the long hike back to the wild country once the Eighth was fit.

Fingering his badge of office, Marz's thoughts eased back to yesterday's triumphant parade with its attendant well wishers showering adulation and hearty congratulations upon him and his mates. Coming off a resounding acclamation of ger treatise, Zoog also had been there to share the day with him. Afterwards the two toasted each other's accomplishments, setting before them a third goblet of wine for their brood sister guarding the frontier. With affectionate words of tribute they honored Tyrra before sipping from her cup, then poured the remainder to Gala Rotaria's soil. Aye, sacrifice, regardless how modest, would please the Goddess. The fact that two of her rising luminaries remembered to pay homage would help maintain their sib in the great mother' s grace. Twice a victim of the infectiousness plaguing the hood, the huntress of the eye could use all the assistance she could summon.

At the Capital for the gathering, Genu Zig had pridefully observed Marz's march down the concourse, noting to genself that the young officer's star was on the ascent. The pieces that would distinguish him above his peers were coalescing to form a dimension greater than the sum of its measurements. Afterwards the two had chatted warmly, but Genu cut it off, mindful that there should be no public hint of their association. The Javatt and their minions were everywhere. No need to stir their curiosity. This way, even to the casual ogler, Genu was simply extending a word of gratitude to the Hero of The Vag, as so many other well wishers had already done.

It had happened again, mused Marz, revisiting the strange sensations of years past. With a shudder his spine had fed an eerie vibration to his extremities, tingles enveloping even the nails of his fingers and toes. As the parade took him alongside the Hall of Protectors, tiny tremors had swelled him like so many needles pricking his innards. They of the eyes of glass were stirring. *You have shown the patience,* they hummed. *You have ridden the trail of experience. Be prepared! Opportunity is imminent!* The fingertips slid from the polished badge to his sword's pommel. Everything that had occurred did so for a reason, he knew. From the moment the great goddess had delivered her meteorite steel to Kavoyy Station in one ominous whoosh, the perfect blade overseen by Varo, his course had been set. From compelling voices in the Hall to Poona and Genu Zig at Aryxx, all had pointed the way. The dusty brickworks, the footrace with Rooz Javatt, sweet Mylla and Taratt's bloody head tethered to his avenging wrist, the journey of destiny was now ready to culminate in Gala Rotaria's final truth. Be prepared, Marz Kavoyy, for every eventuality. Your soles tread the circle of fortune's wheel. Guided by fate's pull, its spin shall bestow the prize of prizes upon only those who dare to play. Victory shuns the passive!

Kaara's murder was but a month in the past. For Lanz Varaxx no postmortem anguish tormented his conscience. If anything be was more at ease these days. The Kala menace bad evaporated, Taratt was but a dull memory, fields and orchards were recovering quicker than had been predicted, and the mending troops would soon be returning to their permanent bases. Indeed his cup ran full. To further a mood already steeped in self-content, the Lord's weight had dipped noticeably, evoking comments rich in flattery among the residential staff. Events great and minuscule had contributed to a greater appreciation of life as contradictory as that might sound in the face of his conspiracy with Rooz. Never an early riser, the last few weeks saw him briskly strolling the Capital streets shortly after dawn, inspecting buildings and various public facilities. Even the binges were under control. It was as though the great Lord had been reborn, delivered from the womb of civic virtue. Now in the waning part of his lordship, his attitude toward The Vag had become somewhat fatherly, viewing it more a patrimony than lordly realm. Conversations saw him talking about a "vision for all Vaghi," spouting things of which he had never before entertained. A man lacking progeny to legitimately call his own, the people of his nation were emerging as his 'children.'

Having relaxed for a half hour in his perfumed bath, a more slender Lanz Varaxx slid into a light, cotton robe and prepared to enter his sleeping quarters. Waiting naked under the covers a young housemaid, smooth and nubile, chewed on a mint sprig. Varaxx liked her lips sweet, the breath fresh. She was no more than fifteen. Months ago she had learned that her friendliness with the Lord excepted her from the drudge of everyday chores. So the friendship progressed. The girl had pleased the master many times, enjoying the Lord's generosity after each "adventure" as he called their activity. Her wardrobe had grown considerably, rewarding her attentiveness. Shrewdly he had recently given her a large jewelry box, the inference implicit. Baubles of the glittering kind would fill its emptiness as she heightened her 'adventurous' behavior. Tonight he would challenge her ability to earn the first of many gemmed gifts to come. He smiled, anticipating the pleasures moments away. Every day the flavor of life grew extra delicious for the Lord, its sweetness more luscious than the minty freshness upon his nymphet's tongue. And best of all, he titillated, the finest years loomed ahead.

Peeking out between folds of the fluffed coverlet, her lemony eyes sparkled an invitation meant to arouse Varaxx's expectation. Allowing the robe to drop from his shoulders, he took but a single step before sensing something wasn't right. What started as a ringing suddenly cracked through his brain in one furious bolt shattering all in its way. Speechless, he stood immobile, the pain searing, as though slivers of molten steel had streamed to the very center of his skull. Only the bulging eyes communicated something had gone awry. A second shock wave forced his chin to tremble involuntarily before he collapsed in a thud.

Void of emotion she stared for a while at the unflinching heap on the marble floor. Satisfied he was not about to rise, she sprang from the bed and touched the flabby chest, testing his reflexes, hoping to stir him to consciousness. No squeeze, no prod would ever stimulate him again. The Lord was dead, the massive stroke having lasted less than two seconds. Like a deflated wine skin his huge body, emptied of life, looked smallish. Death has a way of shrinking the mighty, reducing them to the puniest of mortals. Powerless as a blanched ewe, the corpse of one who would not be defied would never demand obedience, never terrify again.

Gathering his robe she rifled the pocket until she felt the metallic hoop. Removing the silver bracelet she placed it upon her wrist, admiring the polished blue stones in the soft lamplight. *It's very pretty,* she thought. Then slipping into her gown, she ran to the door and screamed for over a full minute.

Among the Vaghi it is believed that lightning signals the death of a Lord. The more explosive the bolts, the greater the Lord. In the case of Lanz Varaxx, the sky barely blinked.

# CHAPTER XV

Ever mindful of the Lord's disdain for alarmists, Rooz Javatt had made the decision to maintain a low level of reaction to "inflated reports of Kala activity." How Rooz could confuse overreaction with readiness troubled his staff. Yet he persisted in countermanding their efforts to beef up the defense of First Line with a strong complement of troops, preferring to keep them within or near the encampment. Consequently a token force held the Chokepoint's forwardmost position. Less than a half kord stood atop the wall, a skeleton of what should be keeping watch. His reasoning maintained that two hundred fit troops were better than five hundred unhealthy ones. True but impractical considering reports of Kala so prevalent.

In the wake of Skyyra Jakivv's chastisement of his conduct toward Tyrra, an animosity to the Ravenhood had fomented. History dictated locating the archers close to First Line, but Rooz had moved their camp to a poor site deep to the rear of the massive ring. Should an emergency arise, it would be difficult for the hood to reach their firing points before the initial enemy wave hit. Once again Javatt had allowed pettiness to override prudent judgment.

Unbeknown to the commander of North Camp, the only man Javatt sought to please had been dead for six hours, the dispatch courier bearing news of the event only now departing the Capital for Kavoyy Station. By law every Vag who had earned the leather skirt owned the right to assemble at the Ring of Kilts in thirty days time, there to elect the next leader.

Two days past, scouting parties reported having heard sounds reverberating north of the isthmus. If one could imagine thousands of chirps blended in an unending, cacophonous trill, that would be the sound which strained their ears. When Javatt learned of their accounts, he dismissed them outright, a skeptic's frown punctuating his derision. Several thousand Kala grazing afar were of puny concern. Javatt surmised the few who had been crazed enough to attack after the great rain, had been annihilated with a storm of arrows; most likely the filthy giant who escaped had learned his lesson, and would steer whatever herd existed away from The Vag. Even so, the moat, wall and troops mounting it, were ample defense especially when backed with his huge reserve force. No reason to pester Lord Varaxx and General Povezz with vague reports of chirping. For all the scouts knew, it could have been flocks of migratory birds, he scoffed. Javatt would demonstrate to his officers how calmness should prevail in the face of unsubstantiated guesswork. Aloof to the scouts, Rooz, borrowing a phrase from the Lord's script, ridiculed them as 'frightened alarmists.' And so he sapped their initiative. The officers of the kords once steady in their alertness during Commander Morann's tenure were now slack in vigilance. With their leader so blasé to Kala signs, it must be that no threat existed. Or so they reasoned.

Aye, with familiarity comes an erosion of one's alertness. Signals that once provoked keen precaution are presently ignored. Antennae which heightened to the most minuscule stimuli now lay flaccid. And therein lurks the most pressing danger. Rooz Javatt had engendered a mood of adequacy among his soldiers, diluting their wariness in the act. With daydreams of the Lord's throne parked under his kilt, Javatt twittered away the sharpness of his military command. For complacency is the environment upon which tactical surprise thrives. His enemy, unaware of this very advantage, loomed over the horizon. The Kala horde, larger than any that had ever ventured so near the isthmus, obediently pushed southward to the prods of their grinning chieftain. Kalahead, king of the Kala, had merged many herds into a confluence beyond the imagination of Rooz Javatt or any other Vag for that matter, A super-horde in excess of six hundred thousand would be funneling into the Gorge of Skulls in less than six hours. And in their ranks many of the bucks brandished sticks chewed to a point. Primitive though their weapons, however uncoordinated their thrusts, the sheer volume of Kala numbers made them more dangerous than those who had ever confronted the army of The Vag.

Sniffing the wind, the lead elements determined the presence of edibles off to their front. Among them, Kalahead sensed the aroma would unleash a blind charge into the gorge. By the time they reached the great earthen wall their impetus would be spent, energy consumed. Attempting to stave off its gathering momentum, he moved to the fore of the pressing horde. As they entered a narrow valley he slowed the pace figuring no one would dare pass him by. If one did, more would follow and Kalahead would lose control. Therefore, he must restrain their impulse to stampede at all cost.

Inevitably a sinewy buck rambled by him, ignoring the chieftain's gestures to remain to his rear. Either the buck's brain was too weak to comprehend the leader's motions or he simply chose to assert his independence, Kalahead was uncertain. But the head man recognized that rule belongs to the powerful. And to maintain command, might must be re-established in the presence of the lot. Swiftly he strode to the offender and hissed his discontent, demanding an act of subservience, a lowering of the eyes, a cowering recoil, anything which acknowledged remorse or even better, inferiority. Compounding his earlier mistake, the offender hissed back. Having been challenged, the chieftain lashed a hand across his face, the claw-like nails laying open the cheek. The buck shrieked both in pain and in wildness to Kalahead's attempt to tame him. In one rapid stab the huge Kala jabbed his spear stick into the buck's throat and withdrew it. In and out. As the writhing buck died before him, Kalahead searched the many eyes, seeking out other protesters to his dominance. None showed. As in The Vag, Kalahead had discovered the primary tenet of supremacy, 'I shall not be defied.'

Manning the forward wall, two companies of the Eighth Kord stretched into the boredom of another day. With an easy breeze upon their backs they wiped the morning dew still clinging to the stacks of javelins. In the towers sentinels scanned the northern hills, seeking indications out of the ordinary. Like a painted landscape nothing moved. Only shadows stirred by the rising sun varied the scene. Hugging the gorge floor a stubborn mist held fast restricting the vision of the Vaghi lookouts. Making his rounds, a dutiful Marz Kavoyy checked his kilts, ensuring each had received his breakfast bread. Bisecting the Chokepoint from west to east, straight as a spear, the huge moated wall of First Line had never been breached in its long history. Usually a full kord defended its heights when no threat was apparent. As a rule three more kords were held in reserve inside the ring. However, Rooz Javatt had relaxed normal procedure. The troops poised atop the bastion had been thinned to what many felt was an uncomfortable level. From five hundred kilts the wall force had been reduced two hundred, as if daring the ignorant enemy to storm the isthmus. With the camp overloaded with troops, perhaps Rooz was doing just that, hoping to lead the complete host of soldiers out of the Ring of Kilts to First Line's rescue. Aye, to vanquish the Kala in a glorious victory would seal the lordship for him with or without Varaxx's influence. Indeed, triumph over a Kala invasion would be the crowning halo in his quest for the throne.

All nine kords of the Vag army were clustered at North Camp including the Ravenhood, the latter sometimes referred to as the Ninth Kord. Additionally the three companies normally garrisoned at the Barrier Camp were also present. A total of 4,800 kilts, many still recovering from the obstinate dysentery which had ravaged the army, were under Rooz's control. Soon that number would be shrunk dramatically as the units returned to their posts at South Camp, Central Camp, Jarra and Barrier Camp. But for now Rooz held them under his pennant, his to deploy as he deemed appropriate.

Inspecting the wall's long sweep, Marz couldn't help but shake his head at how thin the troops were spread. True, the steepness and moat combined to form a formidable obstacle, but a sizable horde of Kala concentrated at one point possibly could overwhelm the dwindled defenders. *Perhaps my personal dislike for Rooz Javatt prejudices my assessment,* he reconsidered. *No,* Marz finally decided *The wall is undermanned!* A sense of unease bothered him. It had started last night when he awoke with a shudder. Something significant had happened or was about to happen. But he couldn't figure what it was all about, only that the feeling had remained with him throughout the morning' s dark hours and into the sunlight. Marz had no way of knowing about Varaxx's passing, hence, no idea that in thirty days a new Lord would assume the seat of power, would reign for twenty-four years. The feeling that surged his veins last night, that shocked the sleep from his drowsy bones, had been a message delivered by those spirit forces paving destiny's path. Though no whispers accompanied the experience, he recognized it for what it was. Circumstances were turning. Be prepared.

Previously bound to the Capital by the Lord's incompetence, General Povezz would finally have the freedom to see first hand how Rooz was running North Camp. Old friends in the officer corps had trickled information to him attesting to Javatt's reckless moves. Even Skyyra Jakivv, Commandant of the Ravenhood, the most taciturn of senior officers, had gotten word to him of Rooz's unsound behavior. Reluctant to venture from the Lord's side, fearful he would impulsively overturn orders or promote unworthy candidates, the general had stayed close to Varaxx. In the Lord's mind Povezz's constant attention was viewed as a respectful allegiance to the commander-in-chief. In reality nothing could have been farther from the truth. With Varaxx's sudden demise, General Povezz now was unchained, able to run his own game...at least for thirty days. Hopefully in that time he would be able to usurp Rooz Javatt and help steer the throne to one more worthy. "By the sweet fingers, if that yolk eyed fool becomes Lord, I will resign!" he had confided to Genu Zig.

"If the Javatt hold the power, you won't have to," had come the response. "Rooz will do it for you!" the old nunale chuckled. "Besides, in Marz Kavoyy the great mother has delivered us the fruit of her grand plan. But you must position the players in the Goddess' vast stratagem, to expedite the result both she and we desire. Of this I am certain, as certain that the morning light will appear on the eastern horizon. When the time is most propitious she will require us to do her bidding, Taz. For she only rewards those who act with conviction, who are diligent in their personal sacrifice. Otherwise she will let the seeds fall wherever the fickle winds of fortune choose."

Thinking back on that conversation, Taz Povezz, patriot of The Vag, ordered ponies saddled for him and his escort. He would leave within the hour for Kavoyy Station, and from there on foot to The Ring of Kilts and his army!

The first indication that something was askew came through the air. The breeze which had been at Marz's back suddenly stopped, neutralized by a shove of sorts in the air to his front. For a brief moment a stillness prevailed. The men around him pricked their ears, straining to determine what could be causing so strange a shift. Within seconds birds, some in flocks, others by the pair, flew down the gorge and over their heads. Almost immediately small animals, mostly rodents, could be seen darting in frenzied patterns across the plain. Confused by the moat and wall, they zigzagged furiously, fugitives seeking escape from whatever was driving them. It would not take long to discover the cause of their flight. The rumble of over a million callused feet pounding the bleached bones of Kala skeletons long dried of their marrow split the isthmus with a terrifying thunder. Down they came through the Gorge of Skulls crunching over the ossified layers, the weight of their numbers crumbling the boneyard to powder. Like a tide of chirping insects the great blue horde pushed forward, the stench of its ever exuding waste fouling the air all the way to the wide eyed kilts atop the wall. Sensing a splendid meal, the massive herd shrilled its expectation, the strident chirping exhorting its population to frantic hysteria. Out of control the herd's ravenous vanguard charged across the breadth of the open plateau bent on being the first to chew the flesh of human prey.

"Kala! Kala," the tower sentinel screamed. It seemed as if all two hundred troops holding the front line repeated the shout in unison. Raising the red signal pennant to the top of the pole, Marz's line officer hoped the camp commander could react quickly enough to hurry reinforcements to their aid. But how could he? The Kala rush would be upon them in minutes. True the brambled moat and wall would retard their advance, but only temporarily, Marz reckoned. Two hundred Vaghi spread thin across the perch could never hold so many at bay. Javelins were distributed, two dozen each to the man. Even if every bronze point struck home, they would only account for forty eight hundred dead, a cheap pittance. Amid hungry Kala intent on devouring sweet Vag meat such losses went unnoticed. Born void of emotion, things like sorrow and joy were unknown sentiments within the mindless mass. Suicidal in their driven frenzy, only blind instinct controlled the herd.

A thousand strides back at the ring, Rooz Javatt, cock of the walk, strutted along the central rampart, aware he was the focus of every eye. His purpose was to be seen, to savor the glamour of his presence. Pretending to inspect various aspects of the fortification, he glanced beyond the wall just as a red flutter unfurled in the distance. He had spotted the 'Under Attack' pennant rising above the First Line rampart at the same instant the lookouts sounded the alarm. "Kala! Kala attacking First Line," came the cry. The alarm bell followed, rousing the kilts with its ominous peal. Up ahead at First Line the clanging buoyed the small contingent. Help was on the way.

Reacting poorly, a stunned Javatt yelled to no one in particular. "Gather the troops!" Turning about he watched as soldiers bumped into one another attempting to form up in their respective units. With so many soldiers living inside the ring it was difficult to locate one's bolt, company or kord. Early on Rooz Javatt had not insisted on formation drills, so important especially with the recent unit rotations. The relocation of Vaghi kords should have demanded precise exercises quickening reaction time to the barest minimum. Preparation so key to success had evaporated during Javatt's brief stay. Instead of speeding the two kords first to be assembled on their way to the besieged First Line, Rooz yet stood upon the wall waiting for the entire army to be formed. No need to move piecemeal, he thought. The Kala were probably a rag-tag two or three thousand who had stupidly roamed south into the gorge. But he would use the event to magnify his own prowess. At full strength he, Rooz Javatt, would lead the army out of the ring across the moat ramp and rescue First Line. It should be a magnificent victory. And when history was written of Javatt's exploits, perhaps the eyes of glass would hinge on this very battle. Heroically, Rooz would march at the very front. For all to witness. Later he would commission a mural commemorating his courageous leadership. Such were the grandiose thoughts of Rooz Javatt. Unfortunately the delay in forming his parade would cost The Vag dearly.

Awaiting their orders, Skyyra Jakivv and the Ravenhood formed up quickly and moved to a position where Rooz could observe their readiness. Every warrior carried four quivers, two slung over the back, another pair carried in the crook of a single arm. The free arm saw its fist gripped about the longbow of Jarra, its lethality reconfirmed weeks earlier during the minor Kala incursion. Over five hundred black hooded archers stood silently, their anticipation taut as the strings of their bows. Behind them three hand-carts carrying arrows gleaned from the armory were prepared to roll wherever Javatt commanded. Petty to a maddening fault, he chose to ignore the most efficient killing machine in his arsenal. "You will remain here," he ordered. "Climb the wall and wait if you wish." And having rejected them, he promptly spun on his heel and hurried to the milling kords. No artillery of arrows would pierce the Kala crush attacking First Line this day.

Standing in the front rank, Sergeant Tyrra Kavoyy seethed, wishing the pee she had dripped on Javatt's fingers had been venom powerful enough to burn a trail to his heart. *Not only is Javatt a pompous rake, but an incompetent dolt unfit to command a one hole latrine.* At the same time her sympathies reached out to Jakivv, a lioness among Vaghi, humiliated to the core of her warrior's soul. Indeed the entire Kord of Jarra had been slapped, victim of one man's malignant vanity.

Deep among the kilted archers, Gaara, the talented archer bested by Tyrra at the great tournament, boiled at Rooz's insult. Called up during the Kala threat along with a number of other retired bow women, she had rejoined the hood. Gaara spat hard into the isthmus dirt. "Pah," she reacted, breaking the discipline so prided within the hood. Like the effect of echoes in a vault, there followed the sounds of bitter saliva purged from every ranker, accompanied by an equally audible,"Pah!" The angry hood had expressed its collective opinion.

Glaring at the lot, Skyyra and her officers showed their disapproval. Pointing her bow at the tough kilts, the commandant yanked the black cowl off her head exposing the ire flushing the weathered face. "You pack of mutinous bitches," she harangued. "How dare you! There is no excuse for insubordination. I don't care how unfairly treated you may feel. The next kilt who so much as squeaks will rue that decision for the remainder of her bloody days. By the fingers, am I understood?

"Yes, commandant," they hollered. Skyyra Jakivv had made her point.

Nostrils flared, lips stretched fiercely across bared fangs, the rabid herd galloped onto the plateau with a reckless hysteria. So long was their flow that the tail elements were still pouring into the gorge when the lead wave slammed against the cruel brambles. Thorns slashed and punctured the leathery skin, prompting horrific howls. So forceful was their momentum it plowed the leaders into the tangled branches snapping wood and bone alike. Indeed the impact caused a tremor to jog the wall. Buried beneath the stampeding soles, Kala dead quickly glutted the moat before the first javelin was hurled. Below the heights of First Line more Kala fell victim to their own kind than had perished weeks earlier under the Ravenhood' s bows. For the moment the wall and deep moat had blunted their drive, the blue bulge recoiling like a school of fish having blundered into a taut net. Renewing the assault the fuddled Kala were met with a spray of javelins. So thick were their numbers that missed targets were of no consequence, other Kala dying in their place. Bucks and females, adults and juveniles fell victim to Vaghi mounted atop the steep bastion. In less than five minutes the last javelin had been tossed. From here on the wall would be defended with swords and shields.

"What in the sweet name of Gala Rotaria is keeping the reserves?" shouted the line commander to Marz. "Javatt should have sent them on their way by now, but I have yet to see a single kilt coming. Those blue demons are scaling the wall like insects. And we're spread too damn thin to hold them off for long!"

Clawing their way up the close-to vertical precipice, the Kala saw themselves repeatedly pushed backwards by the grim warriors. Though they owned the advantage of the high ground Vaghi soldiers were hard pressed to cover their individual flanks. So diluted were the defenders that the beleaguered kilts had to race left and right repelling the enemy. As screeching heads appeared above the wall's edge they were stabbed or pushed with shields, tumbling them down upon their wild cousins. Thrusting the sword of Varo with recurring deadliness, Marz dispatched nine attackers in the initial assault. Off to his right a Kala buck slithered over the stone lip and snatched the ankle of a warrior boot. Pulling the soldier off balance, he allowed his own falling weight to carry them down. Together the two plummeted into the moat already choked with blue corpses. The doomed kilt's scream could be heard by most of the troops manning that section of the citadel. Within minutes he was tom to shreds and devoured in total, even his leather skirt and boots finding their way to Kala stomachs. There was nothing they could do but continue the killing for if they hesitated they too would suffer an identical fate.

The extreme left portion of First Line was being held by the other bolt of Marz's company. Using their shields with great effect, they bulled the off-balance Kala struggling to gain the rim. In most cases the superior strength of soldiers pushing from behind their shields proved to be a most efficient tactic. .Down the enemy pitched, knocking others of their kind off the wall face. From the edge of the moat to the fortress top, the defensive wall stood about eight strides tall or the height of four men. Utilizing their own dead as an incline, fresh waves soon were able to establish footholds almost equal to the heights. One soldier, the hand grip having broken free from his shield, fought furiously with sword and knife. With so many screaming blue bodies to his front, it was difficult to determine which carried spears and which did not. In an upward slash his sword splayed a buck attempting to spring from the ghastly pile onto the rim. A second, though, was successful, managing to sink his teeth into the man's wrist. The bite pierced a nerve, momentarily causing this hand to numb, his sword clattering atop the stone precipice. Ripping his flint knife into the enemy's chest, he snatched the Kala and in one motion lifted the body above his head. As he was about to toss the lifeless form upon others scrambling up the incline, the greatest leap in Kala warfare was witnessed by the surrounding combatants. Off to the soldier's flank, a female, somewhat smallish even by Kala standards, rammed a skinny stick into the soldier with all her strength. The splintered point penetrated midway up the thorax, entering between two ribs. It went in about four digits deep. With a gasp the stricken kilt heaved his load just as the air went out of him, the perforated lung collapsing. He fell to a sitting position before slumping onto his back, the shock paralyzing his larynx. No scream would part his lips, though he tried. Yanking free the spear she instinctively plunged it into his chest until the shaft snapped. Staring at the stub yet between her fingers, she wasn't quite sure what she had done or precisely how she had done it. Nevertheless, the first Vag ever to die from a Kala spear lay at her feet. The triumph of weaponry gave her a curious satisfaction without having to actually think about it. Tossing the stick aside, she dove upon her victim's throat and proceeded to gnaw the warm flesh. Though short-lived, It was the most succulent snack of her brief existence. Within seconds a bronze blade smote the back of her neck almost severing the head.

From his vantage point on a small knoll, Kalahead observed the turmoil. Like a massive theater the assault played out before him, shrieks of the dying ripping the isthmus air. With every surge it appeared that his Kala were gaining the advantage. He sensed that once the great wall was surmounted, unlimited food would be available, lush vegetation and warm-blooded creatures, theirs for the taking. Curiously the killing sticks which rained from the sky during the earlier incursion weren't bothering them this day. Strange, the beings defending the heights possessed greater size than his people. Attached to their hands shiny objects gave them the power to slay many. Maybe they grew from the bodies like antlers. Hmmm. Ever grinning, Kalahead cocked his shaggy head, a new sound prickling his ears. Cheering. He had heard that noise once before after the killing sticks had destroyed the little, splinter herd he had steered through the gorge many suns past. Cheering. What did it mean? Though he tried, his undeveloped brain couldn't understand things so complex.

Heartened by the sight of Rooz Javatt astride a gray-white pony leading the army down the ring's moat ramp, the forward troops fought with renewed strength. Relishing his self specter, Rooz had deployed the soldiers in drill formation, his mount prancing on cue as if the whole thing was a ceremonial parade. Looking down from her perch, Skyyra Jakivv shook her head in disgust. *The army should be making haste, double timing to their comrades' aid,* she thought. *Does Javatt not now understand the severity of the scouting reports? Save the parade for after battle, you fool!*

Stacked in ever growing heaps, the ramp of Kala dead was approaching a level almost equal to the heights. "We can only hold the line but a few more minutes!" the line officer shouted. "We'll be forced to evacuate if Javatt's not here quickly." Glancing over his shoulder he spotted the distant parade. "By the fingers! Why are they dawdling? Don't they realize what's going on here?"

The left flank cracked first, unable to resist the mounting pressure. Blue figures were atop the wall rolling up the line. Pushing soldiers backwards along the walk, the undersized Kala continued to perish in droves. Dreadful though the prospect, Marz recognized the exhausted Vaghi would not be able to dispatch them fast enough. In attrition warfare the side with the fewest numbers is most vulnerable to losing the day. Seeing their plight, Marz rushed to bolster the sagging warriors, the sword of Varo singing its gory tune. His fury temporarily stymied the Kala surge. Finding himself side by side with Monty Kelozz, the two along with a half dozen other Vaghi stalwarts, tore into the howling enemy, time and again thrusting their metal into the naked abdomens, spilling blood so freely their boots slid along the wet rampart. Maintaining low thrust angles they prevented crawling Kala from sneaking underneath their shields. "Push high, thrust low!" shouted

Battle Officer Kavoyy rallying his weary bolt. Regardless their effort, the wall was being overrun. Bit by bit the Vaghi were being collapsed into a pocket near First Line's center. Like a bulging horseshoe, the open end preserved their only avenue of escape out the back ramp. Marz was appalled to assess their losses. Over fifty soldiers were missing, one quarter of the defenders digesting in Kala stomachs. The remaining warriors faced a similar fate unless the fresh reserves could overpower the enemy and retake the fortress. It was then that Marz heard the clatter of hooves on the back ramp. Riding a few hundred strides ahead of the army, Rooz Javatt had seen Kala on the wall but until he himself was within the horseshoe, he had no appreciation of the invaders' strength. Standing high in the stirrups, he was able to view the teeming blue bodies extending as far as his yolked eyes could observe, clear back to the Gorge of Skulls. Accurately he determined his reinforcements were too late. The first good judgment he had made that day. Already Kala were descending the wall's rear, soon to swarm the plain. Dismounting he called out to the line officer reporting to his side. "First Line is done," Rooz pronounced. "I'm going to tum the army around and race back to the ring. You are relieved of your orders. Get your kilts out of here and join us there!"

"Yes, sir," the haggard line officer answered. He wondered if his troops had enough stamina left to sprint the thousand strides to outrun the pursuing Kala.

Spotting Marz, Javatt shouted, "You, Kavoyy, remain here with fifty men and protect the ramp so your comrades can escape. Defend it to the death if you must!"

A disbelieving Marz glared angrily at the commander. Javatt had botched the defense from the start. Now he was dooming them, sacrificing their lives to cover his dereliction. "Aye, sir," he spit. If he was to die, he would at least let his antagonist know the contempt he felt.

Returning to the fray, Kavoyy and the line officer began pulling kilts from the horseshoe, instructing them to flee while those remaining closed ranks. When there were but fifty holding the narrow bridgehead, the line officer, a good soldier, shook Marz's hand. "It is wrong that you must remain, Kavoyy. Once we are clear, take your boys and run like the wind. The luck of Gala Rotaria be with you." Certain he was the last to depart, the grizzled line officer bolted toward the great ring and safety.

At the same time the select defenders were preparing to pull back, Rooz Javatt attempted to remount his skittish pony. Upset by the commotion, it reared as he snatched the reins, hooves treading the air, its frightened whinny rising above the battle din. Unable to gain control, Rooz turned and raced down the ramp. The horse be damned! He would use his sprinter's gait to carry him back. As he ran toward the army almost upon him, Javatt signaled the lead officers to reverse their course and hightail it to the Ring of Kilts. Seeing Rooz's distress, the soldiers acted in similar fashion. Suddenly a disorganized rabble, Javatt's kords were sent scuttling back to the protective walls of the ring. With its huge wings completing the isthmus' bisection, the great citadel was all that was left to save The Vag. Bordering on panic, the army of Rooz Javatt had been misled, mis-used and now demoralized by the bungler who would be Lord.

Holding First Line's back ramp, Marz Kavoyy understood his tenacious little band would be encircled in less than a minute. The retreating force was by now mid-way to the ring, time for him and his mates to escape. Dropping his shield he stripped off his tunic and held it over the eyes of Rooz's pony. Blind to the action, the animal lost its nervousness. Marz led it to the fore, and spying Monty told him to quickly instruct the others to flee once the animal was among the Kala. Seeing the opening, Marz dropped the tunic and with his knife stabbed the terrified creature in the rump. It bolted into the Kala, flashing hooves breaking up their tight cluster. Kicking hard the pony crushed a few Kala ribs before stumbling to a knee. The sheer size of the four legged meal distracted their attention away from the Vag rear guard. Predictably they all attempted to get in on the kill. Some were already chewing upon its flanks before it had been dragged to the ramp floor. That Rooz was not yet in the saddle was but the single regret flashing through Battle Officer Kavoyy's mind.

The ploy had worked. Seizing the opportunity, Marz and his kilts charged off the planking and onto the hard dirt. At full gallop they slashed their way through a group of Kala just beginning to close the circle. Fatigued from the ordeal, the legs of many were void of vigor. The combat had sapped their last reserves of energy. Even with the adrenaline rushing inside and the prospect of being chomped to pieces motivating their flight, a few could only manage to trot. Riding their backs like crazed jockeys, the Kala clawed at the staggering prey, ripping off their ears with savage glee. Among them Monty Kelozz fell, the weight of his rider too much to bear. Down he went in a rolling tumble of isthmus dust. In seconds others of the blue skin were attacking him, their ravenous screeches the last sounds he would ever hear.

On the ring's cap Tyrra viewed with horror Monty's peril. Helpless she turned away not wishing to watch the soldier from the Barrier gobbled by vicious fangs. She had recognized him and Marz, her archer's vision able to distinguish their features from long off. Tyrra's golden eyes, the very same Monty had praised during the grain harvest years ago, now ran wet with tears. The only romance her heart had ever known lay but a damp spot where a minute earlier had breathed a noble kilt. Without doubt the incompetence of Rooz Javatt had stolen his life. Had it only been Javatt who had fallen under Kala claws her eyes would have been as dry as Gugububu sand. Alas, it was not to be. The goddess in her infinite justice someday would call Javatt to answer. Perhaps she and her sibs would be the instruments of her wrath. To be the arm of Gala Rotaria's retribution would suit Tyrra fine. But for now the Kala flood had to be stemmed, The Vag preserved.

"Ready arrows!" The voice of Capitana Ryya Ferann ordered the bow women to action. Ferann, now deputy commandant of the hood, was everyone's best bet to succeed Jakivv. Once Mistress of Recruits, the lanky Ferann's steel was every bit as firm as her superior. Raising her bow, Tyrra elevated it to the appointed distance. Finally within range, the Kala hounds attempting to chase down the last straggling Vaghi warriors would feel the sting of Jarra. "On command. Fire!" The simultaneous snap of over five hundred strings delivered a great whir as the deadly missiles shot into the sky. Falling upon the unsuspecting targets, the diminutive Kala were sent sprawling. Protruding arrows puzzled the wounded. Even the untouched were perplexed. Nothing in their range of experience had prepared them. Swords and javelins, technology unfathomable to their pea brains, had muddled their instincts, confusing them to awe. The killing rain presently in their midst was a phenomenon even more baffling. What to do? For a few minutes they halted, standing stupefied in the lethal shower, dying without evasive reflex. Just dying. Finally spurred by the next wave, the survivors once again picked up the charge. The ramp leading into the Ring of Kilts having been withdrawn, they dashed upon the moat, disappearing into the brambled tangle as their kin indifferently stomped them to compaction, themselves to soon receive the same death but at a loftier level. Among stratified cadavers there is no hierarchy of status, only layer upon layer. In the mounting graveyard beneath the citadel, generations of Kala stacked themselves like so many bricks in a wall. Such is the way of the Kala.

As the army of The Vag tried to reestablish its defense, General Taz Povezz traversed the Lizard's Tongue and gazed with disbelief at the panorama below. The plain between First Line and the Ring of Kilts was swarming with Kala. And beyond that hundreds of thousands more were making their way across the plateau. The chaotic scene within the ring indicated the soldiers were void of organization. His position allowed Povezz to view the situation with a sense of detachment. Almost every kilt was crowded atop the wall, making it near impossible to mount an effective defense. Jammed tightly they got in each other's way while attempting to hurl javelins into the onslaught. Apparently the units had become intermingled for the kord standard bearers, on the heels of their commanding officers, were racing to and fro seeking locations to set their poles. From their firing perches the Ravenhood systematically shot volley after volley. Firm in their mastery, the archers ravaged the horde, accounting for many lives in that initial assault. Relentless in their suicidal rush, though, the Kala kept pushing forward, the moat quickly stuffed. Those who escaped the hail of arrows fell to the javelin throwers. Watching the oversized diorama unfold, Povezz assessed immediately what must be done. The troops had to be rotated, perhaps four kords defending the wall while four rested inside the ring. As the fighting units became fatigued the fresh ones would replace them. It was the simplest of plans, but apparently one that had escaped Rooz Javatt in his panic. *But how could First Line have capitulated?* he asked himself *With so many troops at Javatt's disposal, the narrow First Line should have repelled the Kala. Surely the scouts must have reported so huge an enemy presence. What had gone wrong?*

Darkness provided the respite needed to reorganize the jumbled army. The Kala had broken off the siege to pile. Creatures of sunlight, the rhythm of their biology dictated inactivity during the night hours. Comfortable in pulsing heaps, they did what they'd done since their beginnings, sleep and fornicate. Dawn would see them assailing on a broad front with the same abandon exerted the first day.

Povezz, after learning of Rooz's stupidity, used the time to install a proper defense. Rather than dismiss Javatt outright, he simply asserted the general's dominant role, rendering Rooz his subordinate. To sack Javatt while the battle was still in progress might confuse lesser officers. No, Povezz would assume overall command, instructing Javatt precisely what actions to take. Rooz in turn would continue to interface with the kord commanders, passing on the general's orders. By now everyone had learned of the Lord's death. There was no telling how the rankers would react to the news. For most of the young kilts, Lanz Varaxx had been the only ruler they had ever known. And if Povezz dismissed Javatt, whom the kilts didn't necessarily hold accountable for the debacle, it might erode morale already shaken by the retreat from First Line.

The following morning the thirsty Kala stirred from thousands of throbbing piles and licked the dew off backs and limbs. As was customary, the outer layers stood still permitting others to lap the wetness. However slaked their dryness, the empty stomachs yet hungered. Treading in tight circles, they worked up a momentum before charging toward the only direction capable of providing breakfast.

On the wall the First, Second, Seventh, Eighth and Ninth Kords braced for the attack. The Ninth, or Ravenhood, methodically restrung the longbows of Jarra and reached for their dwindling quivers. When there were no arrows left, the archers would stand ready to fight hand to hand if it came to that. For now, though, they would cascade a killing fury on the Kala swarm. Callused fingertips toughened from countless hours on the practice range were beginning to peel. During the evening some had used pickling brine to maintain the tough layer.

As the day progressed, the enemy fell in immeasurable amounts. Inevitably the last arrows were loosened, the final javelin driven into a blue chest. Povezz had details sent down the isthmus in pursuit of stones. Hauled up to the wall top they were hurled at Kala attempting to claw their way up the earthen rampart. Easy targets, fractured skulls joined many causes of enemy death. And so the killing heaps grew higher. Fittingly a blood red sun sank into the horizon putting hostilities on hold. It was time to pile. The morrow would see them renewed yet once more.

Kalahead, having satiated his lust with a half dozen partners, slithered out of the snoring pile. In the moonlight he observed the huge bastion that was the ring. Several hundred thousand of his kind littered the scape. Indeed a sweep of corpses ran inclined against the wall. For two days his Kala had been attacking on the broadest possible front without having come close to conquering the heights. But the death sticks had ceased. Only a few stones fell upon them. That meant the horde could get very close to the wall before being cut down. Hmmm. Forcing himself to think, he twisted his head from side to side. It was so difficult to concentrate. The head twisting seemed to help stimulate original thought. Instead of assaulting the entire breadth of the fortress, maybe it would be better to push all their might against the short portion of one side only. This way a ramp of Kala corpses would grow fast, forming a graded causeway into the heights. Hmmm. And the wall people would not be able to use all their numbers to fight the Kala. There wouldn't be enough room for all of them to maneuver against his attackers. Besides, the enemy would have to retain their people along the entire wall in case the Kala decided to strike another part. Hmmm. He must make the inside of his head show him how to mobilize his resources, how to push them against the western wall. This thinking was difficult stuff, but he would stay at it.

By first light, Kalahead had tossed together a tower of corpses in line where the great ring joined the western wing and about two hundred strides to its front. Once he had bullied the awakened herd into position, he would climb to its peak and using his spear like a baton, would direct the Kala flow. Slapping the stick at the leaders, he herded them toward where he felt he could best manage the assault. Having intimidated them to the precise spot, Kalahead cut loose with a terrifying screech unleashing a frenzied stampede. Then scrambling up the corpse tower be waved the spear toward the direction he wished the herd to follow. On they came obedient to his supremacy. Shrieking at a pitch shrill enough to turn the thickest blood to water, they ran over yesterday's victims and catapulted their expendable bodies against the wall. By mid-morning a slope of dead Kala extended at an angle able to carry their trailing kin into the Vaghi swords. At last they were on equal footing. Now the horde's overwhelming bodies could smother the defenders, could stomp them into the fortress' bowels. Aye, once they breached the walls, Kala would engulf all with a bestial fury.

Aware of their plight, the Vaghi warriors chopped them down by the thousands. Unfortunately the tumbled dead broadened the macabre causeway, enabling the invaders to widen the conduit that was the ramp. With arms held rigid, the Kala spear sticks were run directly into the shields, the impact causing soldiers to stumble. Those who fell, if not rescued by their mates, were torn to shreds. Wading into the melee Marz Kavoyy led a counter push to split the Kala charge up the middle forcing them off the sides of the ramp. Though a bold tactic, its success was but temporary. Within minutes the rift was closed.

The prospect of arrows disappeared, Kalahead arrogantly built another tower within one hundred strides of the wall. Atop it he exhorted the oncoming horde to channel its flow up the causeway, intent on inundating the Vaghi like an unstoppable blue river. Submissive to his leadership, they went where the baton pointed, the naked deluge threatening to overwhelm the heights. As kilts saw their own ripped and chewed, fresh reserves stepped forward to meet the rush. Kalahead again moved to a closer mound, this time but fifty strides before the wall. Undeniably his exhortations were accepted as commands. His leadership, albeit primitive, had shifted the course of battle.

Watching the action, Skyyra Jakivv and Ryya Ferann wished for more arrows. With the fall of First Line, twenty thousand housed in the arsenal had been lost. It agonized Ryya to think what twenty thousand arrows could wreak upon the Kala foe, and she said so.

"Just one," responded Jakivv. "Just one!"

"What do you mean, just one?" asked Ferann.

The First Arrow slammed the quirt of her rank into an open palm. "If we could kill that grinning son of Kala bitch, the attack would fall to pieces. One arrow is all it would take."

Capitana Ryya Ferann thought back to the initial assault, recalling that a single arrow had slipped from the shooters' perch and fallen over the lip. At the time, she had watched it slide down the incline to where it came to rest on a protruding boulder, the latter uncovered by the great rain. Leaving Jakivv she hurried along the rampart to a point directly above where the arrow had fallen. Peering over the edge she spotted the shaft yet laying horizontally on the huge stone about four strides down. Spying Gaara, she of the silver arrowhead, Ferann sent her to fetch one of the ropes that had been used to hoist rocks up the back wall. Minutes later Gaara returned with the rope and six sisters of the hood to lower one volunteer over the side.

"Once I've recovered the arrow, I'll place it between my teeth. When I shout 'Pull,' yank me up quickly." Fearless, Ferann would make the retrieval herself.

"Aye, Capitana," a respectful Gaara answered. "But be cautious of that pile of dead. A few might have enough life left to cause trouble."

Nodding to her warriors, Ferann knotted the rope about her waist and signaled them to take up the slack. Slipping over the rim she eased her way down the face until her hand was even with the arrow. Snatching it, she put the shaft in her mouth and through clenched jaw yelled, "Pull!" The band of kilts responded on command, heaving hard on the coarse rope. Their load shot upward less than half a stride before halting with an abrupt jerk. As Ferann had re-gripped the rope, she had allowed a loop to form, not a very large one, but enough to wrap itself around the jutting boulder. In order to free her, they would have to slacken the line so she could un-snare the tangle. "Drop me down a few strides," she called. As they did a sharp pain shot through her thigh and then her buttock. A Kala buck bleeding from a gashed head had risen from the heaped bodies to clamp his teeth on the fleshy inside of Ryya's thigh. Biting through the bragghi, his claws digging deep into the derrière, he ripped out a mouthful. Like bait on a hook, she was helpless to fight back. Seemingly out of nowhere three more Kala appeared to join the slaughter.

Alert to the crisis, Gaara slid down the rope and with her broad shoulders bowled over two of the bucks. Unsteady on her feet, the piled corpses rubbery under her boots, Gaara managed to plunge her dagger into a blue chest. The second recovered to jab his dull spear into her mouth before she wrestled him to the pile. As he snapped and slashed at her, she worked the sleek blade between his ribs and twisted, killing him instantly. Jumping to her feet, the sturdy warrior dispatched the other two with remarkable quickness. They had been so preoccupied chewing on the dangling Ferann that they had paid little attention as the dagger tip found its way to their spines. Un-snaring the loop, Gaara clutched the rope and screamed, "Pull!" Up they shot to the rim. Waiting hands muscled them over the stone lip and safety. But it was too late for Ferann. Her throat had been ripped open, the jugular torn wide, its red flow complete. Clenched between the perfect white teeth, the last arrow in the Ring of Kilts awaited an archer skilled enough to shoot it through the heart of Kalahead.

Having witnessed Ferann's and Gaara's heroic action, Skyyra Jakivv removed the shaft and spoke to Gaara. "Grab your bow and come with me. You've got a shot to make!"

Through swollen lips she winced, "Nay, commandant." And holding up her right index finger, she showed off its ugly wound. In the scuffle the fingertip responsible for pulling the bowstring had been bitten down to the bone. It would be quite a while before Gaara would be a proper sharpshooter again.

Too involved in the task at hand to mourn the sacrifice of her deputy, Skyyra Jakivv shouted to the little knot of warriors. "Find Sergeant Tyrra Kavoyy and have her report to me at once! And tell her to bring her bow!"

Waving his spear stick in wide circles the Kala chief continued to spirit his horde onto the causeway. He had stacked another dozen bodies on the bizarre tower allowing every living eye to see him. Even those now coming over First Line's crest could spot him easily. Atop the summit he appeared to be enjoying the spectacle. Realizing the enemy no longer commanded the rain of killing sticks, his fixed grin became more taunting to those defending the wall. It was as if he were mocking them. 'Here I am. Strike me if you can!' Unspent Kala moving onto the plain immediately responded to his direction, crooning chirps acknowledging their compliance. Kalahead's newfound ability to control the actions of so many exhilarated him. He had fallen victim to the intoxication of power, the fevered eyes dancing with excitement. Jumping up and down on the un-protesting bodies of his own dead, he harangued the assaulting herd with wild shrieks. Before the sun rested, he would dine on the sweet meat of the wall people. Of this he was certain.

"Kill that son of a Kala bitch. Shoot this arrow which has been paid for dearly. Shoot it straight into his ugly heart. It is your shot to make, Tyrra." The words of Skyyra Jakivv lit a flame that reached to her very soul. "You are Jarra's finest archer, proven on the tournament field. Slay Kalahead and the Kala will scatter like dust!"

"Aye, commandant. I will make the shot!" Cradling the arrow, Tyrra could feel the dented impression left by Ryya Ferann's teeth. Indeed it had been paid for dearly. Closing her eyes she sought the spirit of her dead mentor. *Your sacrifice will not be in vain,* Tyrra Kavoyy promised. *By the fingers, it will not!*

As Tyrra proceeded to inspect the tightness of her bowstring, she glimpsed Gaara from the comer of her eye. Tough as a leather kilt, the husky archer offered the most basic of advice, hoping to release whatever nervousness Kavoyy might feel. "Keep your elbow up, girly," laughed Gaara through torn lips, her fractured teeth painfully sensitive to the touch of her tongue.

"Aye, girly," Tyrra answered with a half smile, determination firing her golden eyes. "It's the only way I know." And finding a vantage spot to her liking, where the footing was solid, the angle ideal, she settled into a comfortable position. Spread-legged, she set her heels where there'd be no slippage, and nocked the precious arrow. Looking out at her grinning target, Tyrra expertly gauged the distance and checked for wind. There was none. Good. Inhaling through her nose she closed her eyes and deep within beseeched Gala Rotaria to guide her arrow true. For this shot, among all she had ever taken, was the most crucial. Perhaps the fate of the entire Vag civilization hung on its accuracy, rode on the feathered fletching. The tingle which followed her prayer began in the tendons which connect the rear of the heels to the calf muscles. Like a spark climbing her legs, it surged through her thighs, almost sexual in its sensation. And then it stirred inside the chest, an inner vibration filling her soul. She knew then the force was there. The goddess would pilot her arrow to Kalahead's breastbone. So it was with great confidence Tyrra Kavoyy measured the shot.

Aiming at the broadest part of his body, she let fly the deadly missile in one smooth motion. A twinge of anguish touched her as Kalahead stooped over the very instant she released the string. The shot would be wasted, she gasped. But in his sudden movement the bushy head dropped to where his chest had been. In a blur the shaft streaked into his eye with such force it penetrated through the tiny brain, the arrowhead erupting from the skull's rear where it stopped. For a long moment the uncrowned Kala king stood motionless, the arrow seeming to impale him to the air. Teetering front to rear, he finally tumbled over but remained atop the tower, a ghastly monument to the most decisive shot ever made. Cheering exploded from every kilt manning the great wall. Sisters of the hood embraced Tyrra, her back enduring hundreds of slaps. Everyone wished to touch her. To be able to say, "I was there when Tyrra Kavoyy made the greatest shot ever made. Verily, I witnessed her arrow enter the eye of Kalahead!" It would be a recollection cherished among all others, a tale to be retold whenever warriors reunited.

Under the joyful crush, Tyrra raised her bow to the sky in salute to the goddess of her destiny, and emitted a triumphant scream. Following her lead the enthusiastic throng acted likewise, the noise drowning out the distant chirps. It was only then that it came to her. That starry night on Mount Aryxx, Poona had predicted her to be "Huntress of the eye. Twice!" And so it had come to pass, the slender arrow projecting from Kalahead's shattered eye testament to the exactness of Poona's premonition. Yet it became a bittersweet moment as Monty's image crossed her thoughts. *This shot was for you too, Monty. Wherever you are, carry the glory in your soul.*

A delighted Skyyra draped an arm about Tyrra's neck and squeezed hard, interrupting the sentiments playing within her. With a hearty laugh the usually stem commandant teased, "I thought you were going to aim for that bastard's heart!"

"I did," admitted the huntress of the eye wearing a sheepish smile.

"Well, girly, I won't tell anyone if you won't!"

With Kalahead dead, the intensity of the attack waned. Instead of continuing to direct the assault over the causeway, they futilely spread out along the broad front. In the evening the Kala piled as usual. And a little after sunrise, while they were milling, a few started drifting north. More followed. And soon the entire horde was pushing up the isthmus, climbing over First Line and disappearing through the Gorge of Skulls. Over two thirds of their number had been slain. More than four hundred thousand perished in less time than it would take to drag their carcasses into the gorge, there to rot over the winter. Come spring only the skeletons of their self destruction would remind the Vaghi scouts of all that happened. And so the great Kala war had ended. Perhaps the madness was their way of thinning out the herd, of insuring enough food would be available to nourish the survivors in their harsh existence.

A possibility which begs to be considered revolves around spirituality and the Kala. Specifically, does each and every Kala body possess a soul? Certainly they are humanoid, some form of people. Assuming the brain and the mind are one in the same, do the Kala own enough thought to be conscious of an inner self, to ask 'Why am I here?' Do full moons provide the slightest spiritual inspiration or are they objects of illumination, there to solely facilitate midnight piling?

Watching the last, slow moving Kala tramp out of the plain, a pensive Tyrra Kavoyy asked the commandant, "What do we do now?"

Eyes staring above the cloudy skyline, Jakivv's voice cracked in its answer. "We mourn our dead comrade and return her ashes to Jarra. And in our keep comes that head with the arrow yet intact. To remind us and the sisters who follow of the greatest shot ever made."

That night at Ryya Ferann's pyre, a half dozen fire arrows retrieved from Kala bodies, were fired into the blackened sky. Yellow streaks flashed the darkness, lighting her way to the eternity of souls.

# CHAPTER XVI

As the north wind moved through the Chokepoint, the stink of putrid flesh yet fouled the air. It had taken over two weeks to drag the Kala dead into the gorge. There they rotted to shrunken decay, carrion bounty visited freely by the very rodents and birds which Kala mouths would have eaten had they the opportunity. Maggots and other insects also thrived. With so many to choose from, little competition existed for the remains.

Upon learning of the Lord's death, Rooz Javatt effected a campaign intent on ingratiating himself to the same troops his incompetence had jeopardized. Their votes represented a key block in the upcoming election. Twenty days had elapsed since Varaxx's passing. Rooz would use the next ten spending generously of his family's resources. His father, Gaiz, ever the puppeteer, had sent quantities of sausage to augment the kords' tired menu, along with wine from the Javatt vineyards. To be certain, announcements of Rooz's "boon to the kilts" accompanied each delivery. Masking the true purpose for his gifts, Rooz claimed they were a "commander's reward to the splendid soldiers who had vanquished the Kala horde, in celebration of their heroic effort."

Promoting his own image, the son of Gaiz Javatt busily mended his reputation, rewriting the role played in the Kala War. From Rooz's viewpoint, had it not been for his lightning quick decision to abandon First Line and reposition the army at the ring, The Vag would have been lost. Only his decision to make a gallant stand at the Ring of Kilts had stemmed the enemy. He had forced the Kala to blunt themselves at First Line thus sapping their momentum and losing countless thousands on the field. The cession of First Line, he contended, had been a central component of his winning strategy. Among the officer corps, most scoffed at the assertion; however, for the rankers dining regularly on Javatt sausage and red wine, it seemed a logical claim. Though Rooz had not yet formally proclaimed his candidacy for the lordship, everyone felt it would be his to pursue. Over many centuries the Javatt lineage had seated a number of Lords upon the throne. There seemed to be a consensus that the Javatt, a family of great influence, were born to lead. Besides, no other candidates had surfaced, suggesting it would be Rooz's by default.

Meanwhile, ever pulling strings at the Capital, Gaiz encouraged all those veteran kilts long retired, who were beholden to the Javatt," to make the trek up the isthmus, to divide in favor of his brilliant lad. Nothing like older heads to influence the young. But it was the assistance of the high priest he demanded most. Years past Lanz Varaxx had compromised Daag Goraxx, had extracted ger oath to invoke the contrived support of Gala Rotaria. Goraxx would claim to having received a vision from the goddess identifying her anointed favorite. Supposedly it would be a most cryptic recognition. Daag's vision called for one bearing "a mark of the sky" to rule The Vag. For Rooz Javatt possessed such a birthmark, a flaming sun positioned high on the left rib cage, visible only when the arm was lifted. The mark would be the clincher in case another seeker of the throne stepped forward. It was only because Varaxx owed his lordship to the Javatt that he had promised to engineer Rooz's ascendancy, to corrupt the high priest in Rooz's favor. And thus Gaiz Javatt had visited Daag every day since the Lord's fatal stroke, reminding gen of the agreement. Gaiz Javatt, infinitely more cunning than his son, believed the Javatt were destined to lead. In the politics of the divide, Gaiz felt all manipulations were valid, any trick, any subterfuge proper to gain the seat of power. Of all the precepts he had impressed upon his son, *the justification of any act in quest of the throne* was the one he had spoken loudest.

By the morning of the thirtieth day, a multitude of Vaghi filled the ring. All had donned the leather kilt with the exception of one. Daag Goraxx, primate of The Vag, wore the robe of ger priestly office. Though exempt from voting, gee would officiate over the proceedings, in the end declaring a winner and administering the oath. Daag's sanctification of the duly elected leader would mean Gala Rotaria herself blessed the choice of the kilted electorate.

Perhaps sixteen thousand had shown up including the eight kords on active duty. Of the total only two hundred or so were females. Presumably the Ravenhood was back at Jarra, either caring not too participate or too busy tending to matters of the hood. Most of the men felt the archers were a strange breed of women, difficult to figure out. Kept to themselves, they did. But a critical component of the Vag army...as evidenced by the one who vanquished Kalahead with a single arrow through the eye. By now the story had circulated throughout The Vag, the shot's distance growing longer in each retelling.

In total it would be a small group which would elect the next Lord. Though tens of thousands more were eligible to divide in favor of one or the other, the long journey to the ring for but a twenty minute ceremony discouraged many, didn't warrant their attendance. Apathetic to the vote, farms and family dictated they remain behind. Others were of a different persuasion, placing the election above all. Vaghi too old to make the distant hike, too frail to attempt the mountainous climb, depended on sons and kin to carry them over the difficult stretches. Indeed the pasture at Kavoyy Station held the ponies of travelers from as far south as the wild country, and east to the Barrier Mountains. Pride in the kilt, having earned the precious vote, drove them to the ring even though the result was probably foregone. For many close to their fortieth year it would be the first time they would divide, and possibly the last. Carrying their food in timeworn knapsacks, the kilted pilgrims had plodded through hot sun and drizzle determined to exercise the privilege earned at Muraverdus years ago. Upon their arrival, all smelled first hand the devastation the army had wrought on the Kala horde. A few even ventured into the gorge to see what their noses had told them. The sight awed their eyes, confirmed to them that the new Lord had better be a man strong enough to secure the nation's defense.

Two evenings prior to the election, Rooz Javatt made the rounds visiting units of the army. Claiming to have been approached by kilts both active and retired, who beseeched him to seek the throne, he was now announcing his candidacy. Obedient to their call, Rooz Javatt had formally entered his name for election to the Lord's throne. For the public good he was stepping forward to lead The Vag. As he put it, "I have been drafted." Which inevitably was followed humbly by the line, "I know I can depend on your vote." Beaming with false sincerity, the yolked eyes belied the contempt he felt for the institution he sought. Confident he would win what appeared to be a one horse race, he yet asked those around the campfires if there were rumors of anyone else planning to stand for office. "Nay," always came the reply. So on the eve of election, he went to sleep certain the division would go his way. That night he dreamed the dream of achievement realized, satisfied tomorrow would crown a life's ambition.

Lying upon his back Marz studied the starlit sky as though to catch a signal reinforcing the destiny he believed was his to capture. Genu Zig sitting cross legged under the same canopy no doubt knew the significance of tomorrow. Surely gee must be thinking the identical thoughts of Marz Kavoyy. The man of the isthmus meditated so profoundly a trance came to grip his mind. Magically it bonded with that of the nunale sage many medecs away. Through the mists of space and minds their images entwined. *Have you prepared?* he sensed Genu asking.

*Aye, Genu Zig. I have prepared as best I know. You yourself have filled me with the knowledge of readiness.* Though his lips moved not, the answer emanated like a wave across water, crossing the gulf that is space.

*Have you learned from experience?*

*I believe so,* Marz returned. *So much has happened since you took me into your keep on Mount Aryxx. Truly there have been moments when my life hung in the portal of death. But through the grace of the goddess I have survived. And in that time I have witnessed the two eternal forces which have tugged mankind since the first soul bearer inhaled the sweetness of life. Aye, Genu, good and evil have danced before me. I now recognize them regardless how disguised their faces.*

*Good, good,* gee whispered. *So now the golden moment rises before you, Kavoyy of the isthmus. Tomorrow be honest in your pursuit. But once it is in your grasp, speak with the muscles of your soul. Seize the opportunity using the fortitude of your inner spirit. And remember, Marz, that though you are in the goddess' favor, nothing is given to the reticent. She smiles only on those who act boldly, who act with the convictions of a robust spirit.*

*Aye, Genu. Tomorrow I will act the greatest role of my life,* Marz affirmed. And having declared himself, the vapor that united their spirits dissipated, releasing them back to the custody of bodily dominion. As his eyes opened, a thin streak slashed through the heavens, a shooting star perchance telling him the goddess had approved their conversation. *Tomorrow.*

As the many thousands collected in the ring, a somewhat polarized mood prevailed. On one hand festive kilts renewed old friendships, calling out to each other at the discovery of mates long unseen. News swapped, experiences revisited, for them the assembly took on the emotions of camaraderie, the vote almost secondary. Rooz circulated among the throng, appearing ever confident, cheerful in his salutations to people he knew not. For some of the more patriotic Vaghi, though. there sparked an undercurrent of distrust concerning the Javatt. Rumors of Rooz's botched command had fueled their discontent. But what was the alternative? No Vag had risen to challenge for the throne. With a reputation for vindictiveness, the Javatt would surely find a way to punish the loser and his supporters once Rooz had gained absolute power. Resigned to yet another warped reign, those in desire of fresh leadership were certain The Vag would suffer cruel years under the lordship of Rooz Javatt.

While the electorate readied to divide, Marz Kavoyy entered the officers' wash area and rinsed face and hands in preparation for his moment. From his kit he withdrew a sleek obsidian blade and dragged it across his cheeks and chin cleansing away two days' stubble. Then he did something very strange. Removing his bragghi he worked the razored edge beneath his kilt and stroked the skin just below the abdomen. Luckily no one was present to question his action, not a single eye there to observe the odd behavior. Stuffing the bragghi and blade inside the kit, he strode briskly into the open air and made his way toward the wooden stand erected for the election.

Under the watchful eye of Gaiz Javatt, Daag Goraxx deliberately mounted the stand with measured steps. Purposely slow in ger actions, Daag wanted to give the chattering crowd time to take notice, time to settle down. In perhaps thirty minutes Rooz would take the oath, The Vag his to rule. The high priest wasn't particularly enamored of the Javatt or the deceitful role gee would play in Rooz's election. But what was gee to do? Daag had maintained ger primacy and its sumptuous lifestyle, villa inclusive, by agreeing to the Lord's perverse plot. Goraxx's submission, albeit under duress, had disturbed the holy man's soul, pangs of guilt sickening Daag's conscience. The moment gee had dreaded was finally here. Over the years Daag had been able to heave it from ger mind under the pretext that time and events would somehow erase the day that was today. *With or without my compliance,* gee rationalized, *Rooz will assume the throne. Therefore, my involvement is of little consequence. So let us get it over and done with.*

With arms held to the isthmus sky, Daag Goraxx hushed the buzzing multitude. Motioning all to kneel, the high priest invoked the name of Gala Rotaria and chanted the benediction in strong voice. Located where the ring's acoustics were clearest, the rich baritone incantation confirmed to each kilt that they were honor bound to seek divine guidance in the division to come. And to remind all that the Lord was an instrument of the goddess as were all Vaghi. In concluding the oblation, Goraxx gave thanks for the recent great victory and to ask her acceptance of the brave souls whose sacrifice had denied the Kala beast.

Returning to their feet, the electorate appeared more sober in attitude. Goraxx's words had instilled a feeling that the vote was a thing to be deliberated. That the spirit was to be consulted in tandem with the brain. Of course all this would be academic if but one candidate stood for office. As Daag was about to call for candidates to make their names known, the cadenced slap of hands on leather could be heard, its thwack resonating from outside the ring. Jogging in precise step, the Ravenhood of Jarra, the beat of the slap announcing its presence, entered the south portal. Over eight hundred cowled archers had made the trek, sisters from kords past rejoining the hood for the great vote. Viewing their kind with pride, women already in attendance sprinted to swell their ranks. Halting her warriors, the figure of Skyyra Jakivv saluted the high priest, a playful smirk upon her lips.

Not knowing how best to welcome the warriors of Jarra, Daag groped for appropriate words. "Well, well, Commandant Jakivv. Your last minute arrival is a wonderful surprise. I think most of us had given up on your coming," gee smiled.

Tossing her head back, she let the hood drop to the square shoulders. The glint of mischief lighting her handsome face, she laughed in booming voice, "You didn't think we'd let these bastards vote without us, did you?"

A huge roar went up from the throng. Who else could call them a bunch of bastards and have them enjoy it? Fists on hips her smile teased them, her personality overwhelming even the sourest of prudes. Uncomfortable with Jakivv's presence, Rooz pretended to be enthralled with the hood's sudden showing. He didn't like Jakivv nor did he care for surprises. Hers would be the second dismissal he would command, the first being that overbearing 'alarmist,' Povezz.

After the group had resettled, Goraxx continued with the business at hand. Calling for all candidates to mount the platform and state their case for the lordship, the priest went through the motions of scanning the crowd. Inside gee was certain but a single man would come forth. Sure enough he walked a path through the parting Vaghi and climbed the steps. Resplendent in red tunic and polished black leather, the effect of the latter almost liquid in the high sun, his yolk eyes triumphant, he proclaimed his right to serve. "I, Rooz Javatt, declare myself the most fitting of candidates to be Lord of The Vag!" Twisting his body ever slowly so all could view their next ruler, he accepted the cheers of his countrymen.

Seeing no others of similar intent, Goraxx called out. "Are there any who also feel worthy to seek the position of Lord?"

Pushing his way to the fore, the clean-shaven battle officer was about to shout his candidacy. Long of stride his legs were without quiver, the chin resolute. This was the moment of which he had imagined since boyhood. As the words were about to leave his lips, a gruff voice pierced the stillness. "I, Tad Povezz, General of the Army, hereby resign my command. As of this moment I am civilian Povezz with no ability to influence or intimidate the warriors who have served me so well. And as civilian, my first act is to nominate a warrior of proven leadership, of heroic bravery, and most of all of purest motive. I nominate Marz Kavoyy!"

A fair amount knew of Marz from Cauldron notoriety. Some had even attended the Capital parade and subsequent commission to permanent Marshal of the Lord. However, the name escaped most of the rural Vaghi. But the warriors of the kords knew of him, recognized him for his defense of First Line's back ramp, holding the Kala at bay. An irate Rooz Javatt was more than aware of Kavoyy. With eyes dilated wide as the yolks to which the troops had likened them, he watched the nominee spring up the stairs two at a time. "If you will have me, I, Marz Kavoyy, declare myself candidate for Lord of The Vag!" His golden irises twinkling their special brilliance, strong jaw squaring his handsome face, Marz' s modest smile reached out to the crowd. Cheers equal to those which greeted Javatt echoed the ring. Loudest of voice were those of the hood. To a woman they despised Javatt. And the fact that Marz was brood brother to the Huntress of the Eye tilted whatever doubt might have lingered.

Standing side by side, the aspirants tried not to look at each other, determining instead to present a more lordly image to the electors soon to divide. Though a bit shaken, Rooz knew the 'sign of the sky,' would trump whatever credentials Marz possessed. The upstart Kavoyy would have no answer, no way to combat the mark hugging Rooz's skin. In the political arena where the sly trample the naïve like grapes, Rooz Javatt planned to stomp his foe to the juice of obscurity. Years of manipulating had established his covert sunburst as proof of his worthiness. It was doubtful rubes like the Kavoyy could sow the seeds of victory so far in advance as the Javatt had. And when the gullible fools divided in Rooz's favor, the harvest that is the lordship would be his for a virtual lifetime.

Goraxx looked to Gaiz standing in the front row. As their eyes met, the elder Javatt barely moved his head laterally. His subtle signal instructed the priest not to invoke the goddess' sign just yet. So Daag proceeded with the customary request for the candidates to declare their credentials, giving each two minutes to state his case.

Eager to get on with the vote, and knowing he had the sunburst as a final irresistible persuasion, Rooz's speech sounded a bit dull. Rather than talking of a vision for The Vag or even his own bogus achievements, he chose to tell them how the late Lord Varaxx had endorsed him as his preferred heir, going so far as to term Javatt's rapid promotions as 'evidence.' Many gray heads among the kilts, though loyal to the throne, felt Varaxx to be a bungling alcoholic; thereby giving little significance to Rooz's claim. Most of his speech emphasized the Javatt, of the familial heritage which destined him for the throne. In his arrogance Rooz stated it was in his blood to lead, the gift of his lineage to rule The Vag. Who else could tackle so prodigious a task? Who else could make the decisions which would determine the future of their children and grandchildren? "Certainly not an unseasoned lowborn who five years earlier had been shoveling manure in an isthmus stable! Nay. It is the Javatt to whom you must turn. Rooz Javatt is the rational choice. Empty yourself of my challenger's petty notoriety and divide in favor of me, me who championed our nation over the Kala horde!" Supporters of the Javatt whooped and stomped their boots, calling Rooz's name aloud.

Their racket subsided, Marz Kavoyy stepped forward, stretching to the fullness of his height. He sucked in a chestful of warm air and searched the expanse of faces hoping to find someone he recognized. Surprising himself he was able to pick out a familiar pair. There, erect as an isthmus tree, stood his father. Gurz Kavoyy, who had imparted a parent's wisdom to the young Marz when first his journey began, beamed a quiet pride. His son was reaching where but a handful had dared in Gurz's lifetime. Win or lose, this moment would stir his heart until the goddess called him to her fold. And beside him, looking older than his years, but taller, Varo twinkled every bit as proud. Though not really Marz's uncle, he told those who cared to listen that the lad was his "nephew by choice!" Apparently Varo had stacked split kindling under his heels raising his height to that of Gurz. Spotting them, Marz gave out a reassuring grin as he prepared to speak his mind. Returning his recognition, they nodded their good wishes.

Knowing he had only two minutes to convince the mass of kilts, he mobilized his thoughts, ready to deliver the speech rehearsed in silence many times these past few days. As Genu Zig had reminded time and again, preparation is the master of oration. Remembering also to move his head and eyes, to seek out different areas of the audience, he would strive to give all the feeling that he, Marz Kavoyy, was speaking to individual Vaghi. For he recognized his was an appealing presence, a personality to which those of honest heart responded. Magnetic in his attraction, the warrior who would be Lord spoke with powerful conviction. "Brothers and sisters of the kilt," he began. "I stand before you fixed in my belief that I am the best man to lead The Vag while doubt leaks from my adversary's eyes like beaten eggs through a sieve." The reference was obvious. Spiteful though it might have been, Marz felt he at least owed it to Monty Kelozz to tweak Rooz's nose. Rolling through the kords, muffled laughter responded to Marz's dig. "Though I am younger, mine has been a life of earned honors, not of privilege and inherited distinction. Warriors who vote blindly for nothing more than a family name should question their motive. One could conclude he or she is lazy of mind who chooses the so-called familiar name without deliberation of thought. Our history is replete with Lords lacking in substance, shallow in their decisiveness...and we as a nation have suffered the consequence. Aye, with an absence of forethought, voting for nothing more than a family name could push us down the same path. Tempting as it is, or should I say simplistic as it is, to divide for the reputed name of Javatt, one should be especially cautious. For when a man's appeal hinges on his forefathers' name alone, it sometimes masks the fiber of his true worth. Remember, your vote is tallied usually once every twenty four years, so shouldn't you agonize over the weight of a candidate's value? Shouldn't one consult the depths of conscience? The Vag could either stagnate or flourish contingent on how you divide this noon. Regardless which side you choose to stand, do so with conviction." He paused to assess the impact of his words. They were very quiet. But what did it mean? Were they responding in unspoken thought...or was he putting them to sleep? Shifting his position a few steps compelling their eyes to follow his movement, he continued. "And know this! The lordship is not a ceremonial throne gifted to the offspring of the influential elite. It is a difficult job like that of a blacksmith, plowman, weaver and yes, a stable hand, but on a grander scale, demanding foresight beyond the immediate. Aye, decisions made today may very well influence generations of Vaghi yet to breathe life's sweet air. To lead the people one must be of the people! And that I am. Marz Kavoyy who stands before you, knows the aspirations and pain of ordinary Vaghi...people like you!" His hand with finger extended swept a wide semi-circle, pointing it seemed to every eye before him. "My adversary claims that by virtue of his rapid promotions it was Lord Varaxx's intent he succeed him to the throne. That is nonsense. Our law states that it is the kilts and only they who determine the next Lord. If it were not, I could stake a similar claim. For I, Marz Kavoyy, was ordained the permanent Marshal of the Lord by Lanz Varaxx only weeks prior to his demise. Could not this distinction be interpreted as his last endorsement for the throne? But I will not draw that conclusion as you should not. For it is not the way of The Vag. My loyalty to duty is statement of my worthiness. It was my blade which defeated the chalk faced Taratt and took ger head, as was my Lord's command. Again, twas I and my fellow kilts who held First Line's back ramp so our comrades might escape. My credentials are untainted, without suspicion. Is this true of Rooz Javatt? You decide!" Once more his sweeping finger emphasized the point. "I notice the holy Daag Goraxx indicating my time is short. So let me close by saying this. Moral worth, my brothers and sisters, solid judgment, responsibility and a reverence for the office to which I aspire is what Marz Kavoyy offers the citizenship of our beloved Vag. If you search your souls, if you consult the intellect with which the goddess has blessed all of you, I am confident you will divide in my favor."

A great hurrah erupted from the thronged electorate. No one had ever spoken to them with such honesty before. He had appealed to their intellect and in so doing had placed personal value on each person's vote, encouraged every kilt to act with independence. But had his words cracked the mistaken belief that authority emerges intuitively from wombs nourished by the sperm of Javatt? Had he established a charisma of his own, credible enough for they of the kilt to say, "There stands a Vag of intrinsic honor, one who talks to the goddess and she to him. There stands the Lord?"

With a pronounced nod, Gaiz informed the high priest the moment was nigh. Time to invoke the validity of Gala Rotaria. No Vag could dare resist her imprint. To do so would be heresy. Kavoyy had waged a compelling skirmish, Gaiz conceded. But the battle had already been won via seeds planted years ago. The Javatt had made their covenant with Lanz Varaxx who in turn had compromised the primate. Today, conveniently, that same high priest would administer the divide. Aye, Daag Goraxx was a key in the Javatt pocket. With one twist of the key the sunburst would be unlocked, freed for all to examine, throwing open the throne-room door. Preparation had been the watchword of Gaiz Javatt's life. And presently his care to detail would see his son elevated to the pinnacle of Vag supremacy.

Quieting the kilted assemblage with palms held outward, Daag Goraxx readied to perform the act that had disturbed the priest's conscience since the instant it was conceived. Daag had bargained ger soul, allowed it to be corrupted, placing in peril the eternal grace of the hereafter. Like a conniving merchant, Javatt with Varaxx's aid had squeezed out the commodity of a future harvest in trade for favors discharged long ago: retention of Daag's primacy, its attendant prestige, the villa. All had been paid to Goraxx in advance... exchanged for a single lie. The high priest now would perjure genself before the goddess' children, a betrayal so vile it would torment Daag's spirit 'til the last breath slipped from ger devious lips. "Until now I have remained silent," Goraxx's rich voice reached out, "allowing the political discussion to run its course. And so it has gone, two fine candidates vying nobly for the great throne, each speaking eloquently on his own behalf. Indeed I have been stimulated by the sincerity of their arguments. However, as one who does not vote, one who is neutral in the result of your preference, I am duty bound to inject a note of divine guidance. When Lord Varaxx died, I prayed that Gala Rotaria shine her everlasting goodness on the greatness of his soul." Though Daag's own words revulsed gen, gee maintained a course aimed at filching the Lord's throne for Rooz Javatt. For the high priest too had been persuaded by Marz Kavoyy's oration, and knowing the brilliance of his genther Zoog, was convinced The Vag would enjoy superior and compassionate leadership from Marz. Still gee persisted. "And having prayed to her, I made offerings that a wise and strong leader would emerge to sit the seat of power. To my great awe, a vision crystallized in the depths of my bosom. Gala Rotaria, her gentle breath wanning my inner self-like morning sun through the windows of my heart, spoke these words. 'The new Lord is already marked. A sign of the sky marks his body where few can view. There it shines unseen until it is bared. And last night under her starry heavens, on the eve of the divide, again she made her message known. One marked by the sign of the sky.'"

Gasps of wonder rippled the kilted mass. Marked by a sign of the sky. What did it mean? The smugness of victory charging him, Rooz stole a glance at the bewildered Kavoyy. Oh this was a splendid turn, the confident Javatt cackled inside. And in the first row, Gaiz, pleased by Goraxx' s magnificent playacting, sensed the delicious sweetness of triumph tantalizing him.

Daag Goraxx, eyes yet fixed on the audience, gestured a hand at the candidates, while advancing the question all wished answered. "And so I ask Rooz Javatt and Marz Kavoyy to confirm the goddess' message. Are either of you marked by a sign of the sky, one that unequivocally identifies you as the choice of Gala Rotaria?"

Feigning amazement by his own realization that he possessed the goddess' sign, Rooz, mouth agape, stuttered, "I, I believe I am blessed with such a mark. But I never never understood until now what it meant."

Goraxx played the perfect foil, sternly demanding, "Well, we must see it, Rooz Javatt! It is not enough to simply claim ownership. Much rides on its authenticity."

Rooz unbuckled his waist belt and let it fall to the stage, the heavy sword banging against the plank floor. Removing his tunic, he tossed the garment toward Marz's feet. Then stretching his arm skyward, he displayed a strawberry birthmark, an almost perfect circle, a half dozen flaming tongues extending from its edge. "It is a bursting sun," shouted Javatt. "Unmistakable in its form!" It was a scene to glow father, son and all the Javatt with their minions in attendance. Descending the stand, Rooz romped about the entire gathering, pausing periodically for inspection among the doubting. With both arms held aloft he twisted his torso in an effected dance. When he approached the Ravenhood, he took particular pleasure in flaunting it. "Perhaps you wish to touch the mark sanctified by Gala Rotaria herself, Commandant?" he asked of Skyyra Jakivv. "Maybe you would like to test its genuineness? Go ahead, for you will never get another chance!"

She said nothing, her slow nod tacit acceptance of Rooz's proof. Tyrra and the entire kord of archers remained silent, quiet concession, bitter in their craw. For how could one reject the goddess' impression blazed upon the skin of Rooz Javatt? To do so would ignore her very essence.

Rooz chose to savor the adulation, traipsing about the applauding kilts with an arrogant gait, content that every eye had examined first hand the glorious sunburst sanctified by the great mother. Then returning to the stage, he basked in the limelight before signaling Goraxx to continue.

*He overdoes it,* thought Gaiz. *Get on with the divide, my pompous ass of a son, before the goddess finds a way to douse your solar sham.*

Daag Goraxx attempted to quiet the enthusiasm threatening to disrupt an orderly divide. Arms outstretched, gee begged the convocation's quietness.

After much stir the noise subsided allowing the priest to commence the proceedings. Once again in charge, Daag commented aloud, "Well, I guess Rooz Javatt has met the test." And with both hands held to the sky gee announced, "It is time to divide!"

Before the last word spilled from Goraxx's mouth, Marz Kavoyy, certitude lighting his face, the lustrous golden eyes alive, stepped forward to take control of his destiny. A gloating Rooz, in expectation of Kavoyy's surrender, folded his arms and assumed a posture of haughty confidence. Looking to the high priest and then the crowd, Marz asked, "Will you not afford me the same opportunity as my adversary? Rooz has shown you a blurred birthmark, claiming it a bursting sun. At best it is but a distorted ball of garbage! And I reject it as a true sign of the sky!"

Rumbles of concern could be heard as the convocation reacted to Marz's bold challenge. To deny the sunburst denied perhaps the will of Gala Rotaria.

Responding to Marz' s insulting denunciation, Rooz shot back, "In the absence of his own mark, he refutes the authenticity of what is clearly the goddess' intent. It is the backbite of one drowning in inadequacy. Gala Rotaria has spoken through the vision of the high priest. Now let us get on with the divide, unless, of course, Kavoyy is marked with a truer sign."

Marz smiled. Like a rodent in pursuit of cheese, Rooz had rushed to the bait. "Why I thought you would never give me the opportunity to demonstrate my own mark, unmistakable in its form, as true a sign as ever there was."

"By the fingers, Kavoyy!"Rooz roared. "What in the name of the great goddess are you talking about?" Exasperation colored the flushed Javatt, his patience ruffled by the calm opponent.

Unbuckling the kilt, Marz shouted to all. "Behold a star so perfect of point, so symmetrical its shape, it cannot be confused with anything else. It is a permanent sign of the sky, never to leave me!" As the leather skirt slipped to the wooden flooring, it was obvious no bragghi covered his loins. Simultaneously Daag and Rooz gasped with surprise. There, exposed by Marz's shaved pubic hair, was a perfect five pointed star. Tattooed by Genu Zig during the young Marz's education on the slopes of Mount Aryxx, it proclaimed its stellar identity to every gawking eye. When Genu, the mentor, had said to him *we must shave your pubic hairs,* Marz had been confused to what the old nunale meant. But as the sage pricked the clean surface of

Marz's white skin using needle and black ink, gee explained the purpose. The time might come when it would be necessary to trump the Javatt at their own subterfuge. Aye, as Genu had often stressed, preparation is the mother of success! Void of modesty, Marz Kavoyy now moved among the audience permitting all to see the perfectly pointed star, undeniably the mark of Goraxx' s vision. Making his way to citizen Povezz, he showed off the pubic star with deliberate showmanship. Povezz, Marz knew, had risked his future in support of his challenge. The ex-general winked his approval before shaking his balding head in admiration of Marz's coup. Gurz and Varo whooped it up like little boys unable to restrain their delight. And when Marz trotted to the cheering Ravenhood, the residue of bashfulness having left him, he exhibited the mark with gleeful pride. Skyyra Jakivv, overjoyed at the turn of events, pumped the quirt in vigorous acceptance of the sign's trueness. Moving through the ranks, each warrior was given opportunity to view it. "It is a beautifully perfect star!" a warrior was heard to exclaim.

"Aye," replied a toothless Gaara. "And the tattoo is a pretty thing too!" A gush of raucous laughter erupted from the surrounding archers. Only Tyrra blushed at her brood brother's nakedness. When he arrived to her front he touched his sib's forehead, and she his. Bonded forever, as is the custom of the brood, his triumph was hers. As the Huntress of the Eye had fired an arrow into the pupil of Kalahead, so had he felt the same exhilaration.

Indeed every kord cheered Marz Kavoyy as he passed their files. So stricken was Rooz, he never attempted to counter Marz's extraordinary stroke of upmanship. The sight of the star had crumbled what little resourcefulness he possessed.

The division was a rout! Only a few hundred, those with unyielding allegiance to the Javatt, split in Rooz's favor. Having regained his kilt, it was a more dignified Marz who stood before the multitude and recited the oath taken by Lords of The Vag since the first leader raised his hand millenia past. With thoughts of nation and family, of Genu Zig and Varo darting within his mind, the words echoed through the Ring of Kilts. "Know this. l, Marz Kavoyy, am the Lord of The Vag. In me all power rests henceforth for twenty four years. I am the head of state in the absolute, holding all executive, administrative, military, judicial and spiritual power. I do acknowledge the Code of Laws and vow to obey it. I also remind all citizens that to be Lord of The Vag is to be undefied." Kneeling before the high priest, Marz invited Daag Goraxx to bestow the blessing of Gala Rotaria upon him. With the primate's hand resting upon his forehead, the chant of inauguration confirmed Marz's installation. Tomorrow he would ride to the Capital and formally sit the throne. Marz Kavoyy, anointed of Gala Rotaria, hero of the Cauldron, taker of Taratt's head, Marshal of the Lord, defender of First Line's back ramp, the same man who had outrun Rooz Javatt outside Muraverdus' walls, and today thwarted the very same's treacherous deceit in the Ring of Kilts, had ascended to The Vag's seat of power.

As Marz left the platform planning to circulate amid the kilts who had rebuked the Javatt in his favor, Gaiz Javatt moved to his fore. Patriarch of the Javatt, he had something to say. Peering into the Lord's eyes, Gaiz searched for the inner man. Satisfied with what he read, he knelt before him. "My Lord," he said. "You are the best man. Though I used every trick in my grasp to place my son on the throne, your skillfulness fouled our every ploy. Minutes ago I was your enemy for that is the nature of politics. Now that you are the kilts' choice by honest division, I am your servant. But I respectfully beseech you to also be aware that I am a patriot. And so I pledge the loyalty and resources of my family to you…Lord of The Vag."

Marz reached out and assisted Gaiz Javatt to his feet, and was about to acknowledge the senior Javatt's comments when Rooz, who had observed his father's humility, interrupted. Face red, spittle glistening his mouth, an embittered Rooz assailed his father's offer. "How can you grovel at his boots after he's stolen the lordship from my hold. You, who told me since childhood, it was mine to take. You who said no matter the price, it was the only thing worth hunting. Seduce those of low character, you insisted. Buy them with empty promises. People are worthless pawns to be sacrificed like game pieces!"Rooz cried, the anguish distorting his face. "Even life itself was worth destroying if it would guarantee the throne, you suggested. Well I learned my lessons well, father dear. I strangled your sweet brood sister with these very fingers," the distraught son blurted. "Throttled the life from her, ignoring her pleading eyes throughout the act. I did it willingly did I to enlist Varaxx's support. Aye, my father, it was Rooz Javatt who murdered his aunt at Varaxx's evil encouragement!" The same hysteria fueling Rooz's tirade overpowered all efforts to restrain him. Confession, perhaps, would purge his torment. Friends of the Javatt attempted to pull him from Gaiz's sight, but he would not move, preferring to enjoy the horror twisting his father's visage.

"You strangled Kaara! You ungrateful beast! You have violated the bond of the Javatt. Murdered my brood sister did you? May the goddess cause a fire to consume your bowels 'til the sun is but a black spot!" And turning to Marz, a pained Gaiz begged, "Lord Kavoyy, I implore you execute this admitted murderer for his despicable deed. His life is yours to extinguish."

Mesmerized by the unfolding drama, the encircling throng had crowded close enough to hear Rooz's and Gaiz's ugly exchange. They shook their heads in disbelief. To think that Rooz and the scheming Javatt were that close to holding the throne for twenty four years confirmed the astuteness of their division. Aye, it was a sobering moment.

In response to Gaiz Javatt's request for his son's execution, Marz answered, "Nay! My first act as Lord will not involve the spilling of blood. Future generations might be mistaken in their interpretation, assuming it was retribution against a political enemy." And turning to the object of Gaiz's ire, he declared, "Rooz Javatt, the evil murder of Kaara Varaxx, freely admitted before your Lord, your father, and the electorate of kilts, is punishable by death. However, instead of forfeiting your life, I return it to you. But in doing, I banish you from The Vag forever. You will be given a canteen, one blanket, and allowed to keep a bronze sword. In thirty minutes you will be escorted to the Gorge of Skulls and pointed north. Never to return to The Vag again, your proscription is permanent...under penalty of death!"

Gaiz, hoarse with despair muttered, "You are wise in your first judgment, my Lord."

Numb to his sentence, little expression showed on the younger Javatt. The days he had left would be spent scratching for food and avoiding Kala. Resigned to his fate, he would not beg his enemy for clemency.

And so the ascendancy of the Kavoyy was complete. The prime brood of Gurz and Shaara had sought destinies identified at Mount Aryxx by the mystical force which steers few beings to greatness. Indeed they of the golden eyes had captured the glory of their promise. Zoog had solved the mystery of origin, uniting science and spirituality in perfect harmony. Vaghi, People of the Fifth Field, at last owned a portal to their past. For Tyrra, heroine among warriors, the prophecy of Huntress of the Eye twice met fulfillment. The skull of Kalahead, with arrow yet intact, would remain at Jarra until the last archer passed on. And to Marz Kavoyy went the prize which but one may hold for twenty four years. Lord of The Vag. He will not be defied!

# GLOSSARY

## GENDER REFERENCE

| Male | Female | Nunale |
|---|---|---|
| Man | Woman | Nunale |
| Masculine | Feminine | Nunine |
| Boy | Girl | Nu |
| Son | Daughter | Nuun |
| Brother | Sister | Genther |
| Uncle | Aunt | Genu |
| Nephew | Niece | Yogen |
| He | She | Gee |
| Him | Her | Gen |
| His | Her | Ger |

## MONTHS

| 1 | Pola |
|---|---|
| 2 | Cryys |
| 3 | Ventus |
| 4 | Fyum (also called Month of Rivers) |
| 5 | VeriVer |
| 6 | Month of Two Moons |
| 7 | Month of Eyes |
| 8 | Month of Mothers |
| 9 | Month of the Yellow Sky |
| 10 | Seccus |
| 11 | Olz |
| 12 | Gala Rotariana |

## KAVOYY FAMILY

Father: Gurz
Mother: Shaara
Prime Brood (Brother/Sister/Genther): Marz, Tyrra, Zoog
Second Brood (Brother/Sister) : Borz, Zaara


GALA ROTARIA: Goddess and mother of the planet which bears her name.

GALA ROTARIANA: The twelfth month of the year. The fourth week of Gala Rotariana is a holiday, a time of feasting and gift giving.


THE TEN FINGERS OF GALA ROTARIA: The ten basic elements to which everything belongs. They are linked in pairs.

| 1 | Water |
|---|---|
| 2 | Land |
| 3 | Air (includes wind, clouds and smell) |
| 4 | Sound (includes thunder and music) |
| 5 | Life |
| 6 | Light |
| 7 | Death |
| 8 | Darkness |
| 9 | Fire (includes lightning and volcanoes) |
| 10 | Iron (so rare, it is a gift of the Goddess) |

Note: Vaghi oaths and ejaculations often invoke the above, i.e. "By the ten fingers," or simply "the fingers." There are many variations.


THE THUMBS OF GALA ROTARIA: Among the ten fingers are the "thumbs" which are <u>water</u> and <u>land</u>. They can work in tandem or oppose each other.

| DISTANCE/<br>UNITS OF MEASURE: | Digit = About 1 inch<br>Stride = About 1 yard. Slightly less than 1 meter<br>Medec = About 1 mile<br>36 Digits = 1 stride<br>1600 Strides = 1 medec |
| --- | --- |
| THE VAG:<br>(rhymes with fog) | A land and nation on the planet Gala Rotaria. Always with the article "The." |
| VAG: | A citizen of The Vag. Vag is a singular noun. Also an adjective used to modify singular nouns and other adjectives. |
| VAGHI:<br>(rhymes with foggy) | Citizens of The Vag. Vaghi is a plural noun. Also an adjective used to modify plural nouns and other adjectives. |
| LORD OF THE VAG: | Absolute ruler of The Vag. He is an elected tyrant serving a single term of 24 years. |
| DIVISION: | An election. Simply stated the electors stand to one side or the other signifying their preference for a candidate. The side with the most electors wins. In the Vag, only warriors of the kilt are allowed to divide. |
| GUGUBUBU: | The great desert at the southern extreme of The Vag. It is a place of intense heat, so dangerous that, by law, Vaghi are prohibited from entering. |
| KALA: | Sub-primitive humanoids who roam in herds north of The Vag. |
| ORRI: | Docile people inhabiting a huge peninsula adjacent to The Vag. Their land is separated from The Vag by a mountain chain. The Orri language enjoys a few similarities to that of The Vag. No real central government exists. At best it is a loose confederation of clans. |

| | |
|---|---|
| MOUNT ARYXX: | The highest point in The Vag. Though not a holy place it is revered as a symbol of The Vag nation and people. |
| RING OF MURAVERDUS: | Enormous earthen citadel outside of the Capital. It is believed to be the initial settlement predating the actual city. In the present it is used for various religious rites and festivals. Each male and female Vag in the year of his/her 17th birthday is required to assemble at Muraverdus prior to training. Outside of the Ring is a military encampment called Central Camp. |
| RING OF KILTS: | A similar earthen citadel but much better fortified. It houses North Camp, the northern most military post and point in the Vag. The Ring with its wings extending to the sea on two sides bisects the isthmus, its purpose to prevent invasion. Part of the complex is a defensive wall just above the ring known as First Line. The Ring of Kilts is the site of division for the election of the Lord. New warriors swear their oaths of allegiance at the Ring. |
| THE WILD COUNTRY: | A sweltering region of scrub vegetation and parched gullies adjacent to the Gugububu. Vaghi who inhabit the Wild Country are considered to be an unruly lot. Often undesirables and those who live on the fringe of the law find their way here. The South Camp military post is located nearby. |

ARABELLA :

A small farm town near the wild country. Arabella is also a synonym for the hospice close by which houses the Children of Misfortune.

CHILDREN OF MISFORTUNE:

Though not exclusively children, they are Vaghi either born deformed or with mental defects. They are. cared for at an asylum near Arabella.

LONGBOW OF JARRA:

Primary weapon of the Ravenhood of Jarra. 1.75 strides (63 digits) in length. Constructed of a single piece of springy yew wood, it could accurately propel an arrow 300 strides. A skilled archer could get off 7 to 9 arrows per minute. Arrows were fashioned from cedar, pine, spruce and fir; each 28 digits long.

METARZ:

Principal river and water thoroughfare of The Vag, flowing north to south. Because of the slowness of its current it is known as the Big Lazy.

AGE:

The great planet Gala Rotaria lies farther from its sun than earth does its own. As a consequence Gala Rotaria's annual revolution is roughly 15% longer in duration. Using a formula of one Gala Rotarian year equating to 1.15 Earth years, a 16 year old person on Gala Rotaria is the equivalent of 18-1/2 years on Earth. (See comparative chart)

| G.R. | E | |
|---|---|---|
| 1 yr. | 1 yr. | 55 days |
| 10 yrs. | 11 yrs. | 190 days |
| 15 yrs. | 17 yrs. | 102 days |
| 16 yrs. | 18 yrs. | 157 days |
| 17 yrs. | 19 yrs. | 212 days |
| 20 yrs. | 23 yrs. | 15 days |

## MILITARY UNIT STRENGTH:

10 Warriors/Kilts = 1 Stick
5 Sticks = 1 Bolt *(50 Warriors)*
2 Bolts = 1 Company (100 Warriors)
5 Companies = 1 Kord (500 Warriors)

## MILITARY RANKS:

| Officers | Command | Contemporary Comparison |
|---|---|---|
| General | Army | General of the Army |
| Commander | Camp | Brigadier General |
| Senior Capitanus/a | Kord | Colonel |
| Capitanus/a | Company | Captain |
| Battle Officer | Bolt | Lieutenant |

Note: The Senior Capitana of the Ravenhood is also titled "Commandant"

| Non Officers | |
|---|---|
| Senior Sergeant | Sergeant Major |
| Sergeant | First Sergeant |
| Minor Sergeant | Platoon Sergeant |
| Kilt | Private |

## TROOP DEPLOYMENT:

North Camp    (Chokepoint/Ring of Kilts/First Line/Isthmus) 4 Kords

Central Camp    (Ring of Muraverdus/Capital) 2 Kords plus Cavalry Company or "Wing" *

South Camp    ("Desert Camp"/Wild Country/Gugububu) 2 Kords

Barrier Camp    (Orri Peninsula Gateway) 3 Companies

Jarra    ("The Fortress"/Ravenhood) 1 Kord **

* 2 recruit kords are also trained at Central Camp
** 1 recruit company is also trained at Jarra

# About the Author

Leonard A. "Len" Ferraguzzi, author, adman, entrepreneur, soldier, runner, historian, was reared primarily in Yonkers, NY, with a lot of growing up in Connecticut.

Following a stint in the US Army, he attended NYU, earning a Bachelor of Arts in History.

Along with his wife, Olga, he settled in Redding, CT, where they raised their family. Len currently lives in Florida.

Len Ferraguzzi's previously published work includes *Valiant the Few* (2016, Suncoast Digital Press, Inc.), a World War II novel.